GIANT THIEF

"A fast-paced, witty and original fantasy, reminiscent of Scott Lynch and Fritz Leiber."

ADRIAN TCHAIKOVSKY, author of the *Shadows of the Apt* series

"Fast-paced, quick-witted, engaging; as apt a description of Easie Damasco, reluctant hero, as of the novel itself."

JULIET E McKENNA, author of the *Tales of Einarinn* series

DAVID TALLERMAN

Giant Thief

**From the Tales of
Easie Damasco**

**ANGRY
ROBOT**

ANGRY ROBOT
A member of the Osprey Group

Midland House, West Way
Botley, Oxford
OX2 0PH
UK

www.angryrobotbooks.com
Saltlick's city

An Angry Robot paperback original 2012

ISBN 978-0-85766-211-8
eBook ISBN 978-0-85766-212-5

Printed in the United States of America

9 8 7 6 5 4 3 2 1

For Peg.

CHAPTER ONE

The sun was going down by the time they decided to hang me.

In fairness, they hadn't rushed the decision. They'd been debating it for almost an hour since my capture and initial beating. One of the three was in favour of handing me over to an officer from amongst the regulars. The second had been determined to slit my throat, and was so set in his opinion that I'd hoped he might make a start with his companions. On that basis, I'd decided to lend him my encouragement. "He's right, you know. It's quick, but painful, and less messy than you might expect."

All that had earned me was a particularly vicious kick to the forehead, so I'd settled for the occasional nod or mumble of assent instead.

I'd often been told that sooner or later I'd steal the wrong thing from the wrong person and end up with my neck in a noose. While I'd occasionally suspected there was some truth to the theory, I'd made a point of trying not to think about it. Hanging struck me as a needlessly drawn out and unpleasant way to go, so I'd comforted myself with the knowledge that – law enforcement in the Castoval being what it is – I'd never need to worry unless I got careless or exceptionally stupid.

That day, unfortunately, I'd been both.

The debate went on, and I followed it as best I could, while surreptitiously dodging their clouts and trying to work my hands free. Despite their posturing, I felt sure they had recently been fishermen, likely down from the coast above Aspira Nero. They wore no colours, and no armour except for leather bracers and skullcaps. Their amber skin was weathered and leathery from sea spray; their speech was thick, and as rough as their manners. I was heartily bored of their company by the time they reached a consensus, not to mention tired of the irregular blows.

One – the tallest, his face glossy and flushed behind a straggle of beard – turned to me and said, "You hear that? We're going to string you up." He was the one who'd been arguing for it all along.

"I heard. I still think you'd be better off with throat slitting. It's much more straightforward, and I'd be less likely to foul myself. Still, it's your time to waste, I suppose."

"That it is," he agreed, darting a warning glance at his companion, who was toying sulkily with a bone-handled dagger.

If they'd decided my sentence beyond question, I could see no harm in telling what I thought of him. "I suppose it would be too much to expect any finesse from someone so oafish and malodorous, and whose mother in all likelihood–"

I'd planned much more, but my concentration was broken by another whack to the head, this one hard enough to knock me down. For an instant, everything went black. The next I knew, my lips tasted of blood, and though the blood was mingled with dirt, I could tell I was no longer on the ground. There was something rough and warm between my legs and something else tight around my throat. The warm thing identified itself by whinnying irritably. The other I recognised without any assistance.

I considered not opening my eyes. It didn't seem likely to be fruitful. Then it occurred to me that I didn't want to die in darkness. But the view was disappointing. Everything was as I'd left it: the road still stretched to our left, still busy with traffic meandering toward the encampment ahead; the fishermen's cart still sat upon the grass; the old beech tree was where it had been all afternoon. My view of it was a little different, though, now that I was suspended from one of its branches. The moon was clearer in the sky, the sun almost gone. I judged that only a few minutes had passed since they'd settled my fate.

"He's awake," observed the shortest, the one with the obsession for throat slitting.

"I am," I said, the words garbled a little by the noose around my throat. "So can we get on, please? There's a nip in the air, I fear it's going to be a cold night."

I'd like to think this sounded courageous. More likely, the impression was of fear-maddened babbling.

"He's right," the tallest agreed, "who wants to stand around in the cold? Let's get it over with." He turned his attention to me. "What's your name again?"

"Damasco," I told him, for the third time. "Easie Damasco. Remember it when my seven brothers come to avenge me in the night."

"Damasco," he said, "do you have any last words? Be civil and perhaps we'll pull on your legs for you."

"I'll simply remind you of my complete innocence. You may not see it, but your gods will, mark my words. Justice will be served in this life or another."

"Ha! Goodbye, Damasco."

There were other things I wanted to say, and they seemed tremendously important. Just then, however, he motioned with one hand to someone behind me. I heard the swish of a lash, the horse complained, and suddenly there was nothing between me and the ground except air.

I tried to reach for the noose, forgetting that my hands were tied behind my back. One shoulder cracked unpleasantly, and I gave up the attempt. For the first time, I began to panic. I thrashed my legs, as if this might somehow bridge the gap between feet and ground. I tried to scream, and heard a sound like water burbling, which was strangled off immediately. The pain in my throat was astonishing. It seemed to surge outward, filling my extremities, draining them of strength. Still, I struggled. I knew on some deep level that if I once stopped moving I'd be dead. But my energy was fading by the moment.

"What do you think you're doing?"

Something went "thud" above me. An instant later, incomprehensibly, I was falling hard into tall grass. I landed feet first, and tumbled backward. Gritting my teeth, I struggled to my feet. I was surprised to find that I'd closed my eyes at some point and opened them again, looking to where I thought the voice had come from.

There were a dozen riders, all similarly dressed, but he stood out like a hawk amongst sparrows. There was little physically to distinguish him: his horse stood a hand or two taller, his cloak and armour were evidently expensive, though devoid of decoration. His skin was noticeably darker than my own olive brown, his hair and thin beard bound into coils with whorls of wire, his features sharply angled. Though the effect was striking, the characteristics were typical of many a northerner. What told me this was the warlord Moaradrid of Shoan was something altogether more subtle. It was in his bearing, in the way his black eyes darted over us, in the intensity of his smallest gestures. He exuded authority, even at rest.

Other than that, his only mark of rank was the deference paid by his bodyguards. One still had his bow hoisted. I followed the angle and saw where his arrow had sliced my noose free at the bough. The three fishermen had fallen to their knees, with their brows scraping the roadside. I thought it prudent to follow their example.

"Do we waste men?" asked Moaradrid.

Every syllable had weight. The composite effect was like a rockslide.

"Your majesty, sir..."

"Do we waste capable men?"

"No lord, but we caught him stealing from the baggage train–"

"Then he has use of hands and feet."

"Yes sir, only–"

"You," he said to me, "do you want to be hanged?"

"Truthfully, I find the prospect unappealing," I replied.

My throat still felt constricted, and the words stung like salt in a cut.

"Would you prefer to serve in my army?"

"That, lord, was precisely why I was here, before these ruffians misguidedly apprehended me, and–"

"Take him to a volunteer brigade," said Moaradrid, speaking again to the self-declared leader of the fishermen.

He turned away, drove his heels into his mount's flank, and started up the road. His bodyguard fell in around him.

I watched him go without interference from my newfound companions, who seemed to be still in a state of shock. I couldn't help but admire his posture, the simple elegance of his dress, and the way his free hand rested on the pommel of his scimitar.

What most impressed me, though, was the size of the coin-bag just visible at his waist.

• • • •

"Back there... you were about to say something about my mother."

"I was?"

"You were."

"I'm surprised by that. I'm not generally the sort to comment on someone's parentage. It would take unusual provocation to make me to sink that low."

Costas – the self-appointed leader – snorted and turned away. He had been trying to pick a fight for the last five minutes, and while I wasn't averse in theory, I was hardly in a suitable state. I'd been exhausted and half starved when they caught me. They wouldn't have done so otherwise, and for that matter, I wouldn't have lowered myself to pilfering from a baggage train. The subsequent beating and hanging hadn't done much to improve my condition.

Costas was certainly tall, but he was lanky, and under normal circumstances, I reckoned I could have handled him. The short one, Armando, was more of a danger, and the middle one, who'd hardly spoken, remained an unknown quantity. In any case, it was three against one, so I'd thought it wise to try to play nice. Costas hadn't been making it easy, and I was glad he'd finally lost interest.

I was sat with Costas and the quiet one in the back of the cart, perched on crates that reeked of cabbage and dried fish past its prime. The road was poor and the cart's suspension was long gone, if it had ever had any, but it was marginally better than walking.

"So what's this volunteer brigade then?" It seemed a more neutral topic of conversation. All three ignored me at first, so I added, "Better work than being a sword for hire, I imagine?"

Armando sniggered from the driver's board.

"You'll see."

"It can't be that bad."

"Can't it?"

This was getting me nowhere, and I thought I knew the answer anyway. It was likely one of the reasons Moaradrid was down here in the Castoval, rather than up in the far north where he belonged. The plains beyond Pasaeda were a miserable place, neglected by the king because there was nothing there worth having. They were home to countless tribes, most nomadic, and traditionally they spent their time fighting between each other over women and horses, not necessarily in that order.

Moaradrid had changed all that. In so doing, he had united a third of the tribes together within the space of a year. His initiative was simple: where others had been content to take a new wife and a good stallion from a defeated enemy, Moaradrid took their warlord's head and all of their fighting men.

Making one last bid for a safe subject, I began, "I imagine there are plenty of opportunities here for a resourceful and hard-working sort like myself."

"Maybe, if you survive the night." That was Costas.

"Of course," I agreed cheerfully.

"Which you won't. You don't get it, do you? You'll be lucky if they give you a weapon. The volunteers' job is to line up and throw themselves at the enemy until they're all dead or you are. If you're still useful after that then maybe they'll let you into the regulars. But odds are you'll be dead or worse."

Though I was intrigued by the question of what might be worse than being dead, I didn't want to give him the satisfaction of asking. There was one question, however, that was burning in my mind. Until a couple of weeks ago, Moaradrid's campaign had been amusing tavern gossip. Then he'd changed direction. It made a certain sense; eventually he was going to come into contention with the king, however oblivious the old fool was, and it would take more than a horde of unruly plainsmen to profit from that encounter. What had me curious was what had happened next. Most of Moaradrid's force had camped here on the plain near Aspira Nero, while the warlord himself and a small retinue had journeyed on. They had avoided the hastily gathered southern defenders, and hardly a drop of blood had been shed on either side. Now here he was again. I'd watched them passing for a while before I'd decided to chance my hand with the baggage cart. Amongst the fighting men had been a succession of large covered wagons, their contents invisible.

What was Moaradrid up to?

Even if these three knew, which I doubted, I'd missed my chance to ask. We'd been trundling steadily toward the main camp for about an hour. The last daylight was gone, and the bulbous moon hung low in an overcast sky. I'd identified the camp by a few angular silhouettes near the river that must be tents, some widely spaced fires burning higher up the slope on our right, and by the stink, which had been building for the last few minutes. I couldn't make out any details, but that rank conference of scents gave me a fair idea of how many bodies were waiting for us ahead.

I knew this region. It was at a point where the Casto Mara swung close to the eastern foothills, near the mouth of the valley. The only nearby town was Aspira Nero, which marked the boundary of the Castoval and the court-controlled Midlands, and was generally considered neutral territory. Here there were only small farms, with olive plantations higher up the slopes and rice grown on the riverbank. It would have been good land except for reliable yearly floods that turned it into a swamp. I wondered where all the locals had gone. Perhaps they were dead. Perhaps I'd been meeting them soon as fellow volunteers.

At the edge of the camp – an arbitrary distinction given how unruly it was – we were stopped by a guard, a plainsman with his hair slung in a single braid over one shoulder.

"Where are you headed?" he asked without interest.

"These men," I said quickly, "are mercenaries of the cheaper sort. I am a volunteer, come to serve Moaradrid with my youthful vigour and courage."

"But not with your sword?" he asked, looking at my empty belt.

"It was stolen by bandits," I told him sadly. "I killed nearly a dozen, then thought it prudent to leave unarmed but intact. I'm sure someone will be good enough to loan me a new one."

"I don't doubt it."

He waved over a colleague, who was lounging nearby against a post.

"Take him to the disposables," he ordered, pointing at me.

The soldier grunted, and motioned for me to climb down. The officer said something to Armando as I did so, and the moment my heels struck the ground the cart lurched forward.

"Good luck, volunteer," called Costas. He spat after me, missing by an arm's length.

"May your aim be as precise when your life depends on it," I shouted back.

My escort glared at me, and fingered the handle of his sword where it hung from his cloth belt. The sash was a reddish-purple, like a fresh bruise: the colour of Moaradrid. That meant he was a regular. I decided it might be better not to annoy him further.

"Shall we go?" I suggested.

He grunted again, and set off into the camp. I fell in behind.

Moaradrid's campsite was, frankly, a shambles. I got the impression that the vast majority of his troops had spent the last few nights in the open, with only the officers and veterans housed in the tents and commandeered farm buildings down by the water's edge. The fact that they hadn't bothered to make more permanent arrangements suggested they didn't intend to stay much longer. That in turn meant a battle was probably imminent. I knew our army was located nearby to the north. Now that Moaradrid was back from his mysterious journey, it seemed inevitable that the long-brewing conflict would come to a head.

Of course, it wasn't really "our" army – or at least, not mine. I was now the enemy, strictly speaking. It was a depressing thought, on many levels.

To cheer myself, I drew from the folds of my cloak the stash of food I'd taken from the cart: a hunk of bread, a quarter of wilted cabbage, and some foul-smelling fish. The bread seemed least unappetising, so I tore a lump and chewed ruminatively. I broke it in half when my escort stopped to glare at me and offered him the remainder.

"Stolen?" he asked.

"Not from here," I said, fairly truthfully. In fact, I'd acquired it just before the officer stopped us at the camp border.

"I'll have some fish as well then," he told me, so I halved that too.

After he'd eaten his share and kept it down, I followed his example. It was surprisingly good – though since I was starving, my own boots would have probably tasted delectable right then. The soldier finished his bread as well, then took a swig from a water skin and handed it to me. It turned out to contain wine. Though objectively I knew it was vinegary and heavily diluted, it too seemed delicious. I grinned at him gratefully, but he only grabbed the skin back and kept walking.

We'd been heading upwards all the while. I couldn't tell much beyond that. While the moon was almost full, it was cloudy, with a storm brewing over the eastern hills. The only real light was from camp-fires, and there weren't many of those, maybe due to the scarcity of wood this close to the river but perhaps also because Moaradrid didn't want to betray his numbers. My escort seemed to know where he was going, which implied that there was some order to the gaggles of men and bright spots of firelight. That didn't help me much. If I was going to escape before the battle, as I was determined I would, I'd need a better idea of where I was.

We came to a halt. There was a pitifully small fire, close to a stunted olive tree and what appeared to be a large upright rock like an obelisk. There were fig-ures around the fire, though I couldn't judge how many. I could only count the innermost few and those were evidently a favoured minority. My escort glanced around. His night vision was better than mine, because he focused on one black shape no dif-ferent from any other and called, "Lugos, how are your numbers?"

A stocky man loomed out of the darkness. "I've lost two to sickness, and one in a knife fight." His voice was coarse yet high-pitched, and the flickering or-ange glow upon only half his face served to emphasise his ugliness. "Why, have you brought me a new body?"

"I have if you want him. He's skinny and a thief. That hardly matters for what you want, eh?"

The man named Lugos turned to me. "Not at all," he said. "Skinny thieves die just as well as other men."

"My name is Easie Damasco," I said, "and stealing once to fend off starvation doesn't make me a thief."

"Who cares? Sure, I'll take him off your hands," he said, and my escort nodded and turned back the way we'd come. Then, to me, he continued, "Damasco is it? There's a few rules you'll need to know. Do what I tell you. Don't argue. When it comes to it, don't run away. And don't mess with Leon and Saltlick."

"I think I can remember all that. Who are Leon and Saltlick?"

"Here, I'll introduce you, and you'll know who to keep away from."

He led me around the campfire. One or two men cried out as we trampled blindly on their extremities, then shut up quickly when they recognised Lugos. We stopped near to the large rock I'd noticed before. There was a lean figure sat at its base, and he looked up as we drew close. He seemed surprisingly young to have been singled out for whatever special authority he had.

"This is Leon," Lugos said, and Leon waved a skinny hand at me. "And that," he went on, pointing to the black mass the boy was resting against, "is Saltlick."

"What? Behind that rock?"

Leon chuckled, and Lugos barked out a laugh. I wondered what could be so funny – until the rock moved. The clouds flurried away from the moon for an instant, and I saw a monstrous hand, each finger as long as my head. I leaped backward, and Lugos gripped my arm and held it tight.

"Careful," he said. "Or Saltlick might just decide you're food."

CHAPTER TWO

The night wore on. I tried hard not to think about what was coming when it ended.

A pack of cards materialised from somewhere, and one of my shadowy companions suggested a few rounds of Lost Chicken. In an hour, I managed to turn my quarter of cabbage into a hunk of unidentifiable meat, a few coppers, two more loaves of bread, and a small, cheaply crafted knife. Normally I'd have found such success cheering, but my thoughts kept getting in the way, however much I tried to avoid them.

I'd reached the conclusion that escape was possible but unlikely. Moaradrid wasn't an idiot. Realising that most of his troops would rather be somewhere else, he had sentries patrolling all around the camp borders. I'd heard them whistling to each other in bad imitation of various night birds. There would be plenty of guards within the encampment as well. The risk of fleeing, in my state of borderline exhaustion, far exceeded the hope of success. I was stuck there.

I would likely get my first taste of war before the sun came up.

And that wasn't even the worst of it.

I had no doubt, after what I'd seen, that I'd be on the winning side. I would normally have taken some consolation from that, but just then it was difficult to do so. While I had no love of its authorities, who insisted on putting my name on "wanted" lists and generally trying to catch and jail me, the Castoval was my home and I was fond of it. I didn't want to see it crushed under the heel of a tyrant. I didn't want to see it overrun by monsters.

Yet that was apparently to be its fate. Moaradrid had found himself a weapon that the Castovalians couldn't defend against.

Later, when the sky had lightened to a drab charcoal grey, Lugos stoked the fire and heated some soup, which was doled out in dirty wooden bowls. In a rare act of charity, or more likely defeatism, I shared my bread and meat amongst my closest companions. I received a little weary gratitude in return. Most of them spoke with such wild accents or thick dialects that they might as well have been talking another language for all I understood. We were a group of strangers gathered from the length and breadth of the land, and all we had in common was our future, which was likely to be short. No wonder the atmosphere was grim.

The soup – mostly water and rice, with a few chunks of turnip and scraps of goat meat floating on the surface – was warming, at least, and my appetite made it seem better than it was. That, together with my acquisitions from cards, left me feeling full for the first time in longer than I could remember. I wouldn't die hungry, at any rate.

We'd barely finished eating when Lugos, now dressed in a hauberk and tattered leather helmet, stepped up close to the fire and shouted, "Listen up, fifth volunteers."

I assumed that was us.

"We'll be going into battle soon. It won't be fun, but if you do your best you might just survive. Don't try to run. There'll be archers on hand and they'll make sure you don't get far. Most importantly, keep away from the giant. He answers to three people only: Moaradrid, Leon, and myself. Anyone else he's likely to step on. That's all. Fight like the bastards you are."

It wasn't the most motivating speech I'd ever heard. It did, however, make me wonder again about the hulking thing they called Saltlick. We Castovalians knew in theory that the giants existed, somewhere high in the southern mountains, but they'd always minded their own business and we'd been more than happy to leave them to it. The arrangement had stood for generations – we didn't bother them, they didn't bother us – until their existence had become little more than legend. What could have drawn them down into the Castoval? What threat or promise could Moaradrid have used to bind them to his cause?

The sun was just below the horizon. The sky was a miserable wash of grey, rising from a sickly shade touched with yellow just above the hills, through deep storm cloud hues, to almost black far above us. The light was at that tricky stage it reaches just before dawn, but I could see the giant clearly. He stood back from the rest of us, in a wide clearing amidst the forest of bodies. Lugos's orders seemed superfluous since no one was going anywhere near him. He was as tall as two big men and about as broad. He looked only slightly less like a rock than he had by moonlight.

Lugos had no illusions that we were anything other than what we were: a bunch of potential escapees. He didn't try to make us behave like professional soldiers, or any kind of soldiers for that matter. He had a couple of henchmen drawn from the regulars, both of whom carried bows and wore short swords. A few of us were armed too, with wooden cudgels and staves. If we'd been less dispirited, an insurrection might not have been out of the question. I would cheerfully have jabbed my new knife into Lugos's throat given the chance. What would it have achieved, though? In the midst of Moaradrid's camp, and with that giant towering over us, we wouldn't get far.

So we followed his orders, such as they were. Lugos bullied us into two straggling lines and, after a brief discussion with another officer who'd ridden up from the main force, set us off at a fast trot, angling slightly uphill and northward.

It was still dark below, and I couldn't tell much about the disposition of the two armies. Banners stood out as stains of colour in the defender's camp, but Moaradrid apparently disdained such frivolity, marking his divisions by some other means. He'd kept his army all together on the eastern bank, whereas the Castovalians had a small force on the western side of the Casto Mara, with their back line around the bridge. It was the only thing of any strategic value nearby, unless your strategy involved rice and olives. Their force, made up of militias from the towns, were mostly on horseback, and fast enough that if the fight went against them they could fall back and demolish the bridge behind them. It was a sound plan as far as I could judge, one that played to their strengths and the terrain.

They still didn't stand a chance.

As for us, our function was becoming clear. When we came to a halt, I could see two more platoons of bedraggled volunteers on our right. Lugos had us line up four layers deep, and the giant lumbered in behind us, Leon knelt clinging to a platform that rested over its shoulders. The other platoons assumed a similar arrangement; between us, we covered a good length of the hillside. We were a cordon, there to stop the defenders fleeing into the hills. It didn't matter if we were competent or not, or even if we fought back. While they were tangled up with trampling over us they would be cut down from behind.

Something had begun to happen in the valley. Horns blasted the air. A steady drumming started, which rose and rose until I realised it was actually the pound of feet, backed with a bass rhythm of hoof beats. A fine rain began at that same moment, and the sun finally breached over the horizon, deathly pale and shrunken by its blanket of cloud.

The lines of battle met with a crash that echoed between the hills and seemed outrageously loud even from our vantage point. Clashes of metal on metal joined the turmoil. The two dark masses swelled and churned against each other, until it was impossible to tell them apart, or to say if one was doing better than the other.

Moaradrid knew his business. What better time could he have chosen to unleash his new troops than at dawn, when they would be nothing but monstrous shapes plummeting out of the gloom? Had he planned for the rain as well? It was tearing from the sky, which had sunk back into nighttime blackness, with only odd shafts of light pricking through.

I don't know how long it went on for. Time didn't mean much right then. At some point, though, it became apparent that the defenders were losing ground. I imagined, with my lack of military knowledge, that they might just be feinting, backing off from one point only to swing round on another. Maybe to some extent I was right. Still, in general it seemed they were being forced back, and more and more as the morning wore on.

I was sure that Moaradrid must have more giants in reserve. I'd seen at least four dozen of the mysterious covered wagons go past before they'd caught me. Each of the three volunteer brigades had one giant as backup, and that was all I'd seen of them. We were too far away for the defenders to be aware of their existence, so Moaradrid's element of surprise remained intact. What was he waiting for?

There were signs that the defenders were falling back in earnest. They were drawing in their flanks around the bridge, although no one had made a move to cross as yet. Moaradrid's troops took the opportunity to spread out around them, manoeuvring northward and onto the higher ground beneath us. If the Castovalians would only flee towards the west, I'd be safe. The Castoval would probably be lost, but that didn't seem very important by then. Let them just escape over that bridge and it would all be over.

Below the bridge, beyond the fighting, something drew my gaze. The water was churning white, as if rocks had plunged up through the surface and the river was battering against them.

No. Not rocks. It was the giants.

The river was shallower there but men still couldn't have hoped to cross, not even on horseback. The giants could, though. Their heads were bobbing dots haloed with foam, moving with painful slowness. I hoped they'd be swept away. Surely, nothing could be strong enough to push through that rain-swollen torrent. Even as I thought it, a pair of shoulders bore out of the flow, grew a torso and arms, and thighs thick as tree trunks.

The defenders, caught up in their retreat, already focused on attacks from three sides, remained oblivious. Even as the last giant broke free and dragged itself ashore, even as they lumbered towards the Castovalians holding the west bank, no one looked their way. It was only when the rearmost riders started over the bridge and saw huge shapes striding inexorably down on them that the panic began. The handful of men holding the far bank routed instantly. The main force, unaware of what was taking place across the river, were still trying to withdraw. The giants marched nearer. Those already on the bridge found themselves pressed from both sides. The bridge itself began to weaken under the strain. Timbers splintered into the waves beneath.

The Castovalians were already in chaos by the time the giants reached them. I glanced away, my eyes stinging. When I looked back, one giant had a horse raised over its head, the rider still dangling from the stirrups. As I watched, both horse and rider were hurled back into the fray. I thought I could make out the animal's scream against the clamour of background noise.

Moaradrid's main force, meanwhile, was still hammering against their front. The defenders had collapsed into a clumsy wedge, with the horsemen – worse than useless in such close confines – pressed towards the centre. The bridge sagged at its middle, and then split like wet paper, plunging a last few bodies beneath the waves. That slowed the giants, at least. They lined up on the west bank, as if unsure what to do next.

The Castovalian cavalry, what few of them remained, chose that moment to try to break free. They charged in a single mass against their opponents. The ranks bulged, and held. The Castovalians wheeled back, and drove forward once more, clustered even more tightly. This time Moaradrid's lines buckled.

The riders surged through, aiming directly uphill.

That meant they were heading straight towards the middle of the three volunteer platoons, which brought a ragged cheer from my own.

Then, at the last minute, having drawn that middle platoon a little way down the slope, they swung in our direction. They were incredibly fast. They'd succeeded in creating a diagonal gap in our lines, and they pushed hard for that slim chance of an opening. There were perhaps two hundred of them, nothing compared with how many must have ridden out in the night. I recognised insignia from five different towns. In the forefront, two horsemen were picking the way: the leader small and slight, wearing a close helm over dark hair that streamed behind, the other large to the point of fatness and somehow familiar-seeming.

I'd no time to wonder why. They'd be on us in seconds. I decided I'd stay close to Lugos. Either he was a good officer who'd try to protect his men or, a thousand times more likely, he was a rodent who'd sacrifice every one of us to keep his own skin whole. Whichever the case, it seemed sensible to be near him. I edged forward a row, and darted to my left.

Lugos picked that moment to turn part way around and shout back, "Hold your ground, you sons of whores!"

An instant later, we were failing to do precisely that.

Many of the riders were wielding outstretched short bows. As the head of their group dashed for the diminishing gap, the tail fanned out and slowed, and those archers unleashed a volley in our direction. If it was clumsy, it was no less devastating, since no one was prepared to stand and be shot at. Those that didn't go down under the fire panicked and broke in all directions. I stood like an idiot, watching black shafts plummet through the air towards me. It was a few moments before I even realised I hadn't been shot.

At least I was still close to Lugos. I saw that he was pointing and screaming something. There was an arrow embedded in his shoulder, with the tip just visible above his shoulder blade, though he seemed not to have noticed. He wasn't pointing at me but past me, towards the back of our beleaguered platoon. I followed his finger.

There was the giant, Saltlick. He waited motionless, with arrows raining around him and a couple stuck in him, one jutting from his chest and another above his knee. He was faring better than young Leon, who hung limp below the giant's waist, yet another arrow broken off in his neck.

"You," Lugos screeched, "get up there! Make that bastard monster do something useful!"

Well, I wasn't about to do that, though I didn't mind the idea of having my own giant. "How do I make it obey me?"

Lugos looked like he wanted to kill me for my stupidity. Instead, he caught my arm and broke into a run.

Our shattered platoon had dissolved into a sheep pen with a dozen wolves at one end. The Castovalians knew why we were there, and that every moment's delay would cost them dearly. So they were herding us. A few had hung back to keep the way open while the remainder drove on for the hill-top. The stragglers continued to plunge through us like a sword through butter, spreading waves of bodies to either side. One rider swung so close that I could clearly make out the tang of his horse's sweat and hear its laboured breathing.

Lugos followed its passage with his eyes and happened to notice his shoulder, with the fletching protruding there.

"Shit," he said quietly.

This time, I gripped his arm – the one that wasn't leaking blood, sadly – and led him. "The giant," I reminded him.

When he looked up his eyes were glassy. "There's an arrow in my arm," he said resentfully.

"We all have our problems," I replied, and kept dragging.

The giant still hadn't moved by the time we reached him. Both sides were avoiding him now. The last few horsemen were almost past us and my erstwhile colleagues, despite fleeing every which way, had somehow managed to leave this one area clear. I saw him properly then for the first time. Apart from a cloth skirt around his waist, he wore nothing except a leather harness strapped around his shoulders and chest. It supported a sort of wooden platform, like a horizontal stocks, that fitted round his neck. Poor Leon dangled from a tether attached to one corner, his last expression one of total bafflement.

"Hello again, Saltlick," I called.

The giant ignored me.

"How do I make him listen?" I asked Lugos.

His concentration had drifted back to the wound in his shoulder. I shook him gently.

"Lugos, we need the giant. To protect ourselves."

He looked at me.

"To protect you, sir," I corrected.

"The giant?"

"That giant." I pointed.

"Oh." He looked up. "Saltlick. *Saltlick*. Listen to me, you pig's arse."

Saltlick's gaze drifted towards us. I couldn't read any expression on those vast, impassive features.

"It's me, Lugos. Lugos, who was appointed over you by Moaradrid himself. This man here..." He paused, and hissed, "What's your name?" Then, "This man, Easie Damasco, is your new rider, do you hear? You'll do whatever he tells you, until you hear otherwise from Moaradrid or me."

Saltlick nodded slowly.

"Good," Lugos said, "that's good."

He crumpled backwards.

I assumed he'd just fainted, since his wound didn't look mortal. My first urge was to kick him, but glancing downhill, I saw Moaradrid's main force drifting up the slope. If I were going to make good my new-found advantage, I'd have to do it quickly. I gave Lugos's prone body a rueful glance and turned back to examining the giant. There was no obvious way up his front that didn't involve climbing Leon's corpse, so I darted round to inspect the back. The harness there included a net that hung as far as the hem of the cloth skirt. That still left a gap nearly as high as I was. I began to wonder seriously about my plan. What if the giant wasn't as passive as he seemed? What if he took badly to me climbing his back? One swat would turn me to paste.

Moaradrid's troops were getting nearer. Saltlick was my best hope for escape, and even for revenge. That suddenly seemed a real and pressing concern, for – standing there amidst broken bodies, some of whom I'd been playing cards with a few hours ago – I felt an uncharacteristic anger building. Who was Moaradrid to behave like this, to drag me into his wretched plans? Suddenly I was almost shaking with fury.

I leaped up, caught the lowest cord of the netting, and scrabbled with my feet against Saltlick's thigh. He didn't flinch. I put all my strength into hurling one arm up for a higher hold, brought the other in behind and, bunching my body, managed to get a foothold. It was relatively easy from there. Not once did the giant try to help or resist me.

I clambered to the platform. The webbing continued across its width, and there was a pole jutting from the outer edge, both presumably intended for the rider to hang onto. Suddenly aware of how high up I was, I did just that. For a few moments I could only kneel there, hanging on for dear life.

Then somebody called out nearby, and I knew somehow it was directed at me. When I dared to look up, I saw that a large force was still pursuing the Castovalian escapees – pretty hopelessly, I thought, since they were out of sight now – and that a small detachment of horsemen had broken off towards us. Their leader was pointing and shouting in my direction. There wasn't much left of my platoon. Those still standing had spread over quite a distance, and were wandering aimlessly. Odds were that the new arrivals were on their way to restore order before anyone got any funny ideas.

It was a little late for that.

"Saltlick, can you hear me?"

No answer.

"Saltlick, are you listening?"

"Listen."

I'd never heard his voice before. It was astonishingly deep. The syllables rubbed together like millstones grinding.

"Good. Saltlick, how would you feel about getting out of here? Going home? No more fighting, no more being told what to do?"

He took a while to respond, and I wondered if he'd failed to understand again. For all I knew he liked being there, and would turn me in right then, or just crush my skull for disloyalty.

"No more fight?"

"Not if I can help it. Would you like that?"

"No more fight," he agreed.

I grinned, and slapped him firmly on the shoulder.

"Then, Saltlick, it's about time we got out of here."

CHAPTER THREE

I'd made enemies of two armies in the space of less than a day.

The survivors from the Castovalian force wouldn't look kindly on my serving against them, however much I might point out that I'd been coerced and done nothing by way of actual fighting. At least the odds of my ever being recognised were slim. Moaradrid's party were a more immediate concern. With the battle over it wouldn't take them long to do a head count and notice one of their giants was missing. I had a decent start, but that wouldn't help much. Fast riders could run us down in no time. All in all, it was a bad fix I'd got myself into.

I was about to make it far worse.

I'd taken a gamble, and directed Saltlick back towards our campsite of the night before – or more precisely, towards where the handful of tents still stood. I reasoned that, while it would lengthen our route if they came after us, there was a chance our pursuers would think we were on some official business and leave us alone.

Sure enough, the horsemen who'd been tailing us turned back before we'd gone very far. I heaved a sigh of relief and called for Saltlick to stop.

We were on the edge of the camp proper, some way downhill from where we'd spent the night. There were two dozen tents of various sizes, accompanied by carts, wagons and the oxen that drew them, grey ghosts of campfires, and countless piles of refuse. The ground had been churned into mud, by feet and hooves last night and by the rain this morning, which had eased now to a fine drizzle. It looked more than anything as if the river had flooded and subsided in the space of a few hours. I was pleased to note that there weren't many people around. Those who hadn't been involved in the fighting, craftsmen, menials and the like, had gone to gawp at the battlefield or were busy looting from the dead. There were few guards. Presumably, Moaradrid didn't want able bodies idle in his camp while a battle was raging. Most of what was worth stealing was out there anyway, in the shape of weapons and armour.

It was sound logic. I couldn't help wondering, though, if anyone would go to fight wearing a burden-somely heavy coin bag. Further, I'd spied one tent larger and much grander than the others, guarded by two soldiers who wore the narrow-bladed scimitars favoured by plainsmen. I didn't doubt they knew how to use them. Both looked as if they could chop me into offal without thought or effort. They were likely from Moaradrid's personal guard, which meant that this was Moaradrid's tent.

I had no rational justification for what I was planning. It was insanity, and I knew it. My only excuse was that I was still seething at the indignities I'd suffered, at the lives Moaradrid had so casually thrown away and the fact that one of them had nearly been mine. If I'd spent that life in trouble of one sort or another, it had always been trouble personal to me. To have it endangered by someone who didn't even know the name Damasco seemed somehow infinitely worse. I felt an overpowering need to scratch that name into Moaradrid's memory.

If I couldn't do that, I could at least ruin his day. Anyway, that glimpse of his coin purse had made a real impression.

Still, I wasn't suicidal.

"There's something I want to do, Saltlick," I said, "down in that tent. I'm going to talk to the guards, and hopefully they'll give me what I ask for, but maybe they won't, and maybe they'll try and hurt me instead. If that happens can I count on you to back me up?"

I was still perched precariously on his shoulder, hanging for dear life from the pole and netting. All I could see of his face consisted of one cauliflower ear, a cheek like an upturned dinner bowl, and hints of eye and mouth. It was difficult trying to talk to him, and disconcerting. I had no way to judge what effect my words were having, if any. When he didn't answer, I assumed he'd failed to follow my meaning.

"If they attack me, will you fight them?"

"No more fight."

I was impressed by how much meaning he crammed into those three syllables.

"I know that's what I said, and I meant it. I'm not asking you to charge in right now and pummel them senseless. I just want to know whether you'll help me if it comes to it, which I'm hopeful and even confident it won't."

More silence. Either he didn't understand or was sulking. Stealing a giant was already starting to seem like an act of bewildering stupidity, and I resolved to lose him in favour of a horse at the first opportunity. It would likely be faster, certainly less traceable, and the conversation might even be better.

In the meantime, a change of tactics was in order.

"First things first, get those arrows out of you. They're unsightly."

Saltlick plucked out the two arrows he'd received during the fighting, as I would have a thorn that was causing some mild discomfort. He didn't even flinch. The only sign he felt any resentment at being shot was the way he crunched the shafts into splinters before dropping them.

"That's better. Now, go over to that tent," I said, pointing. "Go along with what I say, and try to look uncomfortable."

Saltlick lumbered the last distance to the bruise-red pavilion, and came to a halt in front of the two guards. They looked up enquiringly, yet without any obvious surprise that a giant stood in front of them. That was promising as far as my plan was concerned.

"Business?" asked the one on the right.

"Urgent, and by direct order of Moaradrid."

He didn't answer, only continued to scowl at me steadily.

"He's sent me for the medicine."

Still no answer. It was obviously going to be a day for one-sided conversations.

"This one's sick, and maybe some of the others too. Moaradrid's sent us for the bottle of medicine he keeps. He said it was crucial it be brought to him immediately."

"What's the day word?" interrupted the other guard.

A number of words immediately went through my head. I doubted any of them were the one he was after. "Moaradrid never said anything about that. Look, as much as I'd like to pass my morning exchanging niceties with you, I have my orders, and I'd rather not be beheaded for disobeying them if it's all the same."

"No day word, no entry." That was the first guard again.

Here was my opportunity to abandon the whole foolish endeavour and flee while our absence was still unnoticed. I've never been good at walking away from a challenge though, especially one with the possibility of coin at the end of it. "It occurs to me that I don't even need to go inside," I said. "One of you can go in my place. It's a bottle, about so high, it will likely say medicine or have a picture of a giant on it or some such. Probably glass or perhaps clay. If you could bring it to me then I'll be on my way."

Neither of them moved so much as an eyelash.

"Damn it," I cried, "this poor creature has an enflamed gastric distension, and while we're standing here talking it's only going to get worse."

In a flash of inspiration, I slipped my knife from where I'd been keeping it in my boot, and nicked Saltlick's shoulder. He grunted irritably.

"Do you really want to be responsible for that? Do you want to be the one cleaning up the mess when it finally bursts?"

I thought I saw the slightest hint of concern pass across their faces.

"What does it look like again?" asked the leftmost.

"A bottle. Of medicine."

He nodded, and ducked inside the tent flap. A minute passed, and another. Clattering sounds echoed out to us. The flap twitched, finally, and he stepped out. He held up a rounded flask of grey pot.

"Oh dear," I said, and sighed with theatrical exasperation. "Kneel, Saltlick."

He obeyed, and I climbed down the netting on his back, trying hard to look as though it wasn't the first time I'd done it. I strode to the guard, snatched the flask from him, and waved it in his face. He actually flinched.

"Do you know what this is?"

"Medicine?"

"No. Not medicine."

I pulled out the stopper, and sniffed. From the rank, peppery odour, it might actually have been some herbal remedy. I took a long swig – or rather, feigned one, an old trick I'd perfected from hustling at cards. Still, a little slipped down my throat. It tasted

worse than it smelled, and I hoped it wasn't poison-
ous. When I was sure I wouldn't throw up, I grinned,
and said, "Medicine for a man's soul, perhaps, but not
much good for his body. We'd best return this for
when Moaradrid wants to celebrate his victory."

I moved towards the entrance of the tent.

An iron grasp on my shoulder held me back. It was
the guard who'd brought the bottle out. I stood very
still. From the strength in his fingers, I suspected my
arm might snap if I didn't.

"Look," I said, as calmly as I could manage, "why
don't you come with me? You can stand sentry just
as well inside as out, can't you? Only, I have to find
this medicine or we're going to be up to our necks in
– well, let's just say we'll all be happier if it doesn't
come to that."

I craned my head to see his face, and tried to judge
what was going through his mind. It was about as
helpful as watching a tree to see whether it was growing. Eventually, however, he turned to his companion
and said, "One minute."

His grip on my shoulder turned into a shove; I tumbled into the tent. It was very dark inside, and what
little light came through the flap was cut off when the
guard stepped in behind me. A lamp hung from a
bracket inside the smoke hole, an elegant construction
of black iron patterned with stars and diamonds of
coloured glass, but it was extinguished, as was the
hearth beneath it. My escort paced past me, tore the
flask I was still carrying from my fingers, and returned
it to its place on a low set of shelves to our right. Beside

the shelves was a large collapsible table, with maps, charts, and other papers spread over its surface. The only sign of luxury was a few patterned rugs tossed over the dirt floor, seemingly at random. Most of the remaining space was taken up with the bed, a low wooden frame draped with furs.

Looking past, I saw the metal-bound chest beside it. My heart clenched.

"Did you look in there?" I asked, pointing.

"It's locked."

Well, of course.

"I'm sure Moaradrid would have mentioned that. It's probably just stiff."

I walked over to it and kneeled down. It was large and decorative, made of some reddish wood and ornamented with a flowing geometric pattern along the metal bindings. All that really interested me, though, was the lock. It looked like a standard five-pin tumbler, and not a very sophisticated one at that, for all its artistic embellishment. I kept my body between it and my escort and drew my picks.

"Are you sure there's nothing on that table?" I called.

"I've looked."

"Well look again, can't you? Perhaps if you lit that lamp we could both see better."

Sliding in a pick, I sought for the back pin. When I was sure I'd found it, I followed up with the tension wrench. The back pin and the fourth broke easily, and I started to feel confident.

"What are you doing?"

"I think it's caught on something. Give me a moment…"

The third was trickier. I kept misjudging, and losing it. At last it broke, with a definite click. I moved straight to the second, and an instant later, that went too.

There were footsteps on the carpeted floor. He was coming towards me.

The front pin was another difficult one, or my nerves were getting in the way. My fingers were greasy with sweat.

"Get away from there…"

My tension wrench turned as the cylinder popped. In one motion, I palmed my picks, swung the lid up, and reached in with my free hand. "Ah, there we are. There's nothing in here, though, only clothes. I'm sure he said…"

My fingers closed on rough leather. I snatched my hand back and let the lid drop.

"No, nothing," I said, slipping the bag inside my cloak and into the hidden pocket I had sewn there. "How about you?"

"Stand up," he said, "and get away from that."

"Fine. I told you, there's nothing here but clothes. Have you found it?"

His hands were clearly empty. Instead of answering, he glared as if he'd like to strangle me.

I pointed past him. "What's that?"

It was the pot flask he'd originally brought out, sat on the shelf where he'd left it. I marched over before he could stop me, and called, "This might be what we're after."

"That," he said, anger dripping from every word, "is the one I gave you."

"Is it? Are you sure?"

I pulled the stopper, sniffed, and tried not to gag at the familiar odour.

"Really? Now that I think about it, it does smell something like medicine. Could it be…?"

I turned back to him, an idiotic smile plastered across my face.

"Wait, there's writing on the bottom: 'For inflammations, distensions, and eruptions'. This must be it."

I didn't like the way his fingers were twitching around the hilt of his sword.

I went on quickly, "You've been a huge help. I'll make sure to mention that to Moaradrid and skim lightly over how obstructive you were earlier."

I bounded to the flap and ducked under it before he could decide that chopping my head off might be worth the subsequent aggravation.

"Look, Saltlick," I cried, "we found the medicine. Your agonies will be over in just a minute."

I heard the tent flap rustle as my watchdog came out behind me. I darted towards Saltlick, who was where I'd left him, thankfully, still kneeling on his colossal haunches.

With his bulk between the guards and me, I made a noisy show of emptying the contents of the flask into the mud, calling, "Just a dash, old friend, this has to go round your companions as well."

I pocketed the bottle, leaped up, and hauled myself back to my perch upon his shoulder. I was gratified to find that both guards had resumed their posts and were glaring back at me. As long as they weren't trying to kill me, that was just fine.

"Gentlemen," I shouted, "your help has been indispensable." To Saltlick I added, "Hurry, back up the hill."

He did as instructed, and moments later we'd reached a point where other tents obscured the view between Moaradrid's pavilion and us. I let out a shuddering breath, and realised how terrified I'd been, how close I'd come to gambling my life away. It was worth it. Revenge and wealth both in one, and all for five minutes work! No one would take Easie Damasco lightly ever again, not now that I'd proven myself the greatest thief in all the lands.

I knew our departure was long overdue. But I could feel the moneybag bulging against my stomach, and what difference could a few seconds more make? A glance around told me that neither the main force nor Moaradrid's guards were on our heels.

I reached in and drew it out. It was satisfyingly weighty in my hand. I loosened the drawstring, pried wide the opening, gazed inside.

I nearly choked.

CHAPTER FOUR

I avoided looking in the pouch for the next few hours. Nothing was worth the way it made my heart palpitate.

It would have been difficult, in any case. Saltlick pounded along the road for mile after mile, seemingly immune to fatigue or distraction, and I hung on for dear life, bemoaning the sore spots multiplying across my body and trying not to think about what was inside Moaradrid's moneybag.

We passed alongside rice paddies at first, endless expanses of green rising out of mottled water. Farmers sloshed amongst their crops, old men with their wizened chests bare and women with sodden dresses scrunched around their thighs. Their skin was tanned to leather and regardless of sex they wore wide-brimmed hats, leaving every face disguised by shadow. They hardly looked up at our passing, showing the traditional peasant aptitude for ignoring things that were none of their business.

The rice fields began to peter out towards noon.

We'd travelled mostly across the flat until then, with the road always within sight of the Casto Mara, flowing bloated and sluggish on our right. As we drew closer to the region called the Hunch, that wide offshoot of hillside that splits the whole eastern portion of the Castoval in two, the river began to drop out of sight. It would only be for a moment at first, when it was obscured by a turn; but the periods soon became longer, as our path took us further inland or the waters disappeared into a stretch of gully.

I was glad to reach the Hunch. A man riding by on a giant was the kind of thing the locals would pick up on, however much they feigned disinterest, and there hadn't been a speck of cover amongst the paddies. While the lower slopes of the Hunch weren't much better, there were dips and rises on the top that would hide us. The more the day wore on, the more I was convinced we were in need of hiding.

The camp had been out of sight all morning thanks to a low mound just beyond its southernmost boundary. It came back into view as we started up the fringe of the Hunch, flecks of black and occasional colour in the far distance shifting like an ant nest. About a third of the way between the camp and us, a column was threading along the white surface of the road. I estimated a hundred men on horseback. It seemed incredible that they would be after us. The obvious and sensible course would have been to send an officer and at most a dozen fast riders. Saltlick and his brethren might have been formidable in the confines of the battle, but out in the open we'd be helpless to archers. One well-placed shot – through my head, say – would settle any fight. To commit any more men than that made no sense. They'd travel more slowly, and if they kept together they'd be easier to evade.

Perhaps that column was heading south for some other purpose, then. Yet that didn't make much sense either. It was too many men for an envoy, and far too few to stand a chance against any decent-sized town, even one that had committed most of their defenders to the morning's battle.

Still, those troops were there for some reason, they were heading our way, and they weren't taking their time. The sooner we got higher up the Hunch and gained some decent cover the better.

There was, however, another more immediate consideration – and that was the severely bruised state of my arse. I'd taken to sitting backwards, with one leg slung down Saltlick's back and the other stretched behind his neck, my right arm bent behind to hold the pole, my left tangled in the netting, and my torso twisted round so I could see ahead. It had practical benefits, that I hadn't fallen off being the most obvious, but it was far from comfortable. I ached through every inch of my body, my fingers and toes throbbed with the pain of hanging on. My backside, though, had suffered worst. I'd convinced myself through mile after mile that it couldn't get any worse. My rump had been pounded into mince and that was that. For mile after mile, I'd been proved wrong.

Finally, I called through gritted teeth, "Stop, Saltlick! Stop while there's still a chance I'll walk again someday."

We were perhaps a third of the way up the Hunch, and the road was gently inclining. The fields of the lowlands had given way to small rock outcroppings, ragged bushes, and the occasional wiry tree jutting out from the red earth. The sun was at its apex and viciously hot, having burned away most of the morning's cloud over the last few hours. I was drenched in sweat, and Saltlick reeked, something like a horse but worse.

I cursed myself for not acquiring some supplies during our escape; a couple of skins of water, perhaps even some food. It wouldn't have been difficult. Saltlick could probably have dragged a whole cart without much loss of pace.

I eased myself down onto a ledge of rock beside the road, whimpering as my bruises made contact. I glanced at the column, which was now about half way between the camp and the beginning of the Hunch. It was still a fair distance, but I swore they'd closed the gap slightly over the last hour. It would have to be a short break.

"Have a rest, Saltlick," I said. "We've a long way to go yet."

The giant grunted, marched over to one of the small trees, and snapped off a branch. He stripped the leaves with one ham-sized fist and crammed them into his mouth.

"Hey, don't eat that!"

He looked at me quizzically.

"That won't make you sick? Eating leaves?"

"Good," he said, through a half-chewed mouthful.

"Well all right, you enjoy it then," I said, a little peevishly. Saltlick wasn't about to starve, even if I was. At least I didn't have to worry about finding giant-sized portions of food. I still intended to ditch him once I was certain we were in the clear, but in the meantime, I couldn't have him dropping dead beneath me.

Water would still be an issue. Even if he had the stomach of an ox, he was bound to need watering like any creature. That meant finding a village, assuming we couldn't divert back towards the river.

I didn't want to think about that right then, though. My mouth was drier than the rock I sat on and it was only getting hotter. I slipped the pouch out of its pocket instead. I hefted it in my hand, enjoying its weight. I took to toying with the drawstring, easing it apart by fractions, watching for glints from inside. Then, bored with tormenting myself, I opened it all the way and gazed again at its contents. A sigh parted my lips. I thought for a moment I might actually cry.

The pouch contained three things: a few onyx coins and a half-dozen coppers, enough money to buy a good horse or a week's hard drinking; a rock, dull brown striped with red, the size and shape of a flattened goose egg; and the biggest ruby I had ever seen.

The reason I wanted to cry was that it was the most beautiful thing I'd ever laid eyes on and I knew I couldn't keep it. The most valuable haul of my life, worth more than all the others put together, and it was practically worthless. No fence in the Castoval would give me a hundredth of its value, especially if they had the faintest inkling where I'd acquired it. It was too valuable to risk keeping on my person for long. Common sense demanded I get rid of it, and the sooner the better.

Just thinking about it made my heart want to break.

I drew the pouch shut, replaced it, and turned my attention back to Saltlick, who was still absorbed in feeding from the now almost naked tree. My initial estimate of his height – the same as two tall men – had been about right. His proportions were basically human, though his arms were longer, and they and his legs were stockier. He was splendidly ugly: his head was very round, with a wide rectangular jaw, large oval eyes, and an almost comically small nose. His skin was pale, faintly grey, and he was mostly hairless, with only a few feathery tufts sprouting from the dome of his skull. There was something appealing in his expression that I hadn't really noticed before, a certain good-natured idiocy. I wondered again what Moaradrid could possibly have done to convince such formidable yet docile creatures to fight his battles for him. It was hard to imagine anything that could be used to manipulate a whole mob of giants.

"Saltlick," I said, "how are you feeling?"

He gave an exaggerated nod. "Good."

"You think you can run some more?"

"Run all day." An entire tree's worth of leaves clearly constituted a decent lunch for a giant.

"Well, I'm starting to consider surrendering for a cup of water. We should get going."

• • • •

I mainly occupied myself through the long afternoon by searching for a more comfortable position on Saltlick's broad shoulder. I tried kneeling, squatting, sitting forward with my legs dangling over his chest, and even – briefly and almost disastrously – standing. Nothing met with any success. I still hurt more with each jogged step.

In between bouts of wriggling, I tried to divert myself in more productive ways. I noted how the scenery of the Hunch became more rocky and wild as we travelled nearer the summit. I listened for any sound of nearby water, though if there was any it was drowned by Saltlick's drumming feet. Primarily, my attention was absorbed by the distant figures creeping along the road behind us.

I lost sight of them when they reached the base of the Hunch. I was certain by then that they were gaining on us. I'd been able at the last to make out details I was sure had been invisible before. Even if they weren't concerned with us, that was bound to change if they'd seen us or heard any hint of a giant wandering loose through the countryside. What if I ditched Saltlick, and put as much distance between him and me as possible? The plan had some appeal, until I envisaged myself trying to evade a hundred armed horsemen alone and on foot. No, until I found an alternate mode of transport the giant was my safest bet. The fact that he was also a beacon for my enemies was something I'd just have to accept.

We broke the brow of the Hunch before sunset. It was highest there on its north side, and I could see most of the plateau stretched before me. It was a drab expanse of browned grass, more scrub trees and wilting bushes, broken by long scars of exposed white rock, with occasionally a cactus standing sentinel over some patch of stony earth. To the east, it sloped to higher ground, and eventually to the mountains. The view ahead continued at a slight decline for a few miles, before the abrupt drop of the south slope back toward the floor of the Castoval.

Southeast, in the distance, I could just make out Muena Palaiya. I hadn't given much thought to a goal, but Muena Palaiya, the nearest large town, was a definite possibility. I had friends there. Well, one anyway, and though I was dubious about how much help I could expect from him, it was an option at least. Those seemed to be getting scarcer as the day wore on.

Anyway, we wouldn't be reaching Muena Palaiya that night. Nearer, there were any number of small villages dotted about, their cream-coloured walls glowing amber in the early evening sun, standing out brightly against the parched landscape. I couldn't expect any charity there. Past indiscretions would earn me a beating on sight in one or two of them. But nor could I go on much longer without food and water.

"Saltlick, do you see that village?" I pointed out the nearest.

He angled his neck to follow my finger and grunted in accord.

"Head towards it. There should be a fork coming up on the left."

Sure enough, barely a mile had passed before the road split. The way we'd been on continued along the western brink of the Hunch, offering a view of the Casto Mara tumbling below. The other branch curved inward, towards the mountains. Saltlick followed my instructions. We trekked for a while through wild scenery of jagged rocks and short, knotty trees. The sun was a crimson mound spilling behind the horizon. As the last light began to fade, we turned a corner between short cliffs of flaking orange mud and found ourselves on the edge of the village.

It was a miserable, dilapidated place. A dozen straw-roofed shacks of whitewashed stone were gathered around a small square. Most had wattle shelters for stores and animals tacked onto their sides, each looking as if it would collapse in a strong breeze. The square had been paved once, but the slabs were broken and irregular now, and a few had been pillaged to shore up holes in the buildings.

I didn't much care. The place had one thing going for it, and that made up for all its failings combined: an uncovered well sat in the centre of the dusty plaza.

There was a bench outside one of the larger houses. An elderly man in off-white trousers and shirt sat on it, a wide-brimmed hat pulled low over his face, a pipe clenched in his teeth. He squinted at us with tiny black eyes from amidst a haze of bluish smoke.

"My name is Easie Damasco, and this is my companion Saltlick," I called. "Good evening."

"Could be." His voice was faint and wheezy, his tone noncommittal. If the arrival of a giant in his village alarmed him, he was hiding it well.

"It is, for both of us. You can provide us with supper, while we have sufficient coin to pay you for it. Our first priority is refreshment from your well. I'll follow that with whatever food you can spare, while some dried grass or hay would be adequate for my companion, so long as the quantity is ample."

Half a dozen doors crept open as I spoke, revealing faces peeking out. All of them were either very old or very young; the rest of the populace probably passed their evenings in some nearby village advantaged with a tavern. The children peered in astonishment at Saltlick, and whispered and giggled to each other. Their decrepit guardians stared suspiciously at me. There was a long hush when I finished. Finally, one of the villagers stepped out. He looked inordinately ancient. Though he was bald except for a few grey wisps, his lip was distinguished by grand moustaches hanging below his collar, died black and waxed to a luxurious sheen.

"Welcome to the village of Reb Panza. Sadly, your stay must be a brief one. We are hopelessly poor, and not equipped for generosity."

A murmur of agreement rose from the doorways.

I whispered in Saltlick's ear. He squatted, and I swung to the ground, and then regretted the acrobatics when all of my bruises complained at once. I started towards the moustachioed patriarch, trying not to limp too noticeably.

"Perhaps you misunderstood? I have more than sufficient funds to pay."

"Yet these days – when we hear talk of war to the north, which tomorrow may be war on our doorsteps – what is worth more, coin or food?"

"A nonsensical question. Name a price, and we'll have a basis for discussion." My stomach was rumbling ferociously. My mouth was dry as a picked bone. I was in no mood for haggling or sophistry. Unfortunately, for me, both were popular local pastimes. "Tell me what you'd consider a reasonable price for two loaves of bread and some meat or fish, water, and a cartload of grass. We can start with that and consider sundries later."

The patriarch stood thinking about this for a particularly long time, with his chin nestled on one fist and the other hand stroking his moustaches. While I didn't dare hurry him, I could have gladly throttled him for the delay. I glanced anxiously over my shoulder. There was nothing to see but Saltlick, who had sat down with the children gathered around him. One had bravely clambered up his leg to perch on his knee. I sighed, and turned back.

Thankfully, the patriarch picked that moment to complete his rumination. "Perhaps, just perhaps, we may be able to accommodate you."

"Excellent news."

"You must understand that we are starving ourselves, and also, that our well is nearly dry. Who knows what will happen when it's exhausted? Here on the Hunch even hay isn't easy to come by."

"You have my sympathies."

"Thank you. Taking all of these factors into account, we can't help but sell our goods at unusual prices. That said, a sum of three onyxes doesn't seem unreasonable."

I confess my mouth gaped a little. The patriarch's house was barely worth three onyxes. Even as a starting offer, it was outrageous, and it would leave me with only five coins. Nevertheless, I didn't have time to barter – or for that matter, intend to pay if I could help it. "Done!" I exclaimed.

This time it was his jaw that dropped.

The bargaining concluded, I was escorted to the well and gratefully guzzled cup after cup, until I was afraid that water would dribble from my ears. I called Saltlick over and he came with an escort of laughing children clutching his legs and jumping to grab at his loincloth. They watched in awe while he downed three brimming buckets full, then wiped his hand across his lips and burped happily. After that, he was led to a lean-to filled with dried grass, and I was directed to the old pipe-smoker's bench. He moved aside grudgingly to share it with me.

The sweet smoke smelled faintly of lavender, and made me drowsy. By the time my food was brought out, I was starting to nod. The aroma of warm, fresh bread roused me instantly. I looked up to see an old woman hobbling from a nearby doorway, a wooden platter clasped in hands so arthritic that I was terrified she'd drop it. She succeeded with steady determination and moments later the platter was perched beside me. As well as the bread, there was a pot of greasy rice mixed with olives and scraps of meat, and a small hunk of goat's cheese.

I'd planned to save half for the next day, but hunger took over and I ate in a stupor, stuffing food into my mouth and hardly tasting it, oblivious to everything. I had only a third of a loaf left by the time reality reasserted itself. Ruefully, I dropped it into one of the pockets inside my cloak. If I wasn't full, at least I no longer felt like my stomach was trying to devour the rest of my organs.

I stood, stepped out into the square, glanced to the north – and froze. On the high edge of the Hunch, half-visible between trees, a pinprick line of fires burned. They could only be torches. Our pursuers had made up a huge distance. Something about those steady, bobbing flames made cold sweat bead across my whole body.

"Saltlick," I called, forcing my voice down to a steady pitch, "it's time we were moving on."

Saltlick, having made considerable inroads into the grass, now sat beside the shelter, the gaggle of children still clambering noisily around and over him. He could have snapped any one of them in half with the wave of a hand, yet they were perfectly unafraid and trusting. I realised how much my perceptions had been coloured by seeing the giants fight that morning. I remembered the one holding a horse and its stricken rider in the air, about to cast them to the ground, and shuddered. They hadn't seemed so placid then.

Saltlick looked up. When I barked his name again,

he stood and lumbered over. I tried to motion north-ward with my head, but I couldn't tell whether he understood.

Before I could say anything, the patriarch darted over, with a surprising turn of speed. "So, both satis-fied? It's a shame to leave so soon, and in the dark, with mountain lions, bandits, and worse abroad. We could provide lodgings at reasonable rates, and per-haps a barn for your friend."

"A gracious offer. Sadly we have far to go, and time is precious."

"Well then. The price is three onyxes, agreed fair and square."

I wondered how quickly I could get onto Saltlick's shoulder, and if he would leave when I ordered him to. Perhaps he would even take the villagers' side over mine. None of them was in any shape to pose much resistance, but there was something unsavoury in the idea of trampling our way through a barricade of old people and children. I pulled out Moaradrid's purse and opened the drawstring with a resigned sigh.

Looking inside, a thought occurred to me. "You've been very generous, not to say hospitable. The rice and cheese were an unexpected bonus, and your youngsters have made my companion welcome. In short, I wonder if three onyxes is ample payment."

The patriarch's eyes flickered between greed and suspicion. "That's true, our kindliness is famous here-abouts. Still, a deal is a deal, and rarely improved by last minute alterations."

I drew forth the ruby and laid it in his palm.

"I'd intended this to be a gift for my paramour. The more I think about it, however, the more I realise she's proven herself unfaithful and inattentive on far too many occasions. It's worth a thousand times the agreed sum. Nonetheless, I'd like you to have it."

I backed towards Saltlick and eyed the netting. I could see the line of torches behind the patriarch, partly hidden by a rise but definitely closer. I had a vague hope that he'd bring the gem to their attention, either by boasting or by trying to sell it, and that finding it might convince them to abandon their pursuit. But if we waited much longer, I'd be giving it to them in person.

The patriarch gawped at the glittering thing in his hand. The others had gathered around to stare with him. Only the children were unimpressed. He found his voice eventually. "Pretty though it is, this won't buy us grain."

"It's worth all the grain on the Hunch."

He continued more certainly, "Trinkets are all well and good for rich folks. For peasants, ready currency is the only useful sort."

I pointed past him. "If you can't appreciate it for its aesthetic value, I'm sure those gentlemen will take it off your hands."

He seemed uncertain, now, even nervous. "Are those riders?"

"Yes indeed. Maybe *they'll* require lodgings."

I grasped the netting and made to swing up, but he stopped me with a glare. Seeing no option, I drew out an onyx and tossed it towards him.

"Here, for your more pressing needs, though I feel less inclined now to speak well of Reb Panza's hospitality."

I clambered to Saltlick's shoulder while he was scrabbling in the dust.

"I can't say it's been a pleasure doing business. Still, I wish you a good night."

I pointed Saltlick towards the road, and we were gone before the patriarch could raise any further objections.

The road took us quickly higher, so that the trees and foliage thinned out and the boulders grew more rugged and pronounced. It swept up in long curves, doubling back on itself time and again. Its convolutions gave me a good view of the way we'd passed – and of the line of torches approaching in our wake.

I'd taken pains to impress our urgency on Saltlick, though I doubted he wanted to be recaptured any more than I did. He had redoubled his pace, so that it took all my strength to stay on his shoulder, and all my willpower not to throw up. I wasn't about to complain. I suspected now that the riders had deliberately idled through the day, taking a gamble that we would either exhaust ourselves or try to go to ground. Whatever the reason, it was clear they'd only begun to stretch themselves after nightfall. They'd covered a remarkable distance during the hour we'd wasted in Reb Panza. Even now, with Saltlick jogging at what seemed an outrageous speed, they were still gaining.

After a few minutes, the lights bunched together. That seemed odd, until I realised they'd reached the village. There was no illumination except for the torches, a performance of shimmering yellow dots on a black stage. Some spread out to form a wide circular border while the remainder drifted into the centre.

When, five minutes later, they were still in that pattern, I began hesitantly to relax. "Slow down a little," I told Saltlick, "I think they've stopped."

He did as ordered, and I continued to watch. It was dull entertainment. The dots in the centre bobbed and weaved, with inscrutable purpose. The outer circle held firm without so much as a tremor. After another five minutes, I decided that the chase was over for the time being. Either they'd recovered the ruby and were satisfied or they'd decided to camp for the night, confident in their ability to run us down in the morning. I faced forward, breathed a sigh of relief, and wondered if we might be safe to find a campsite of our own.

Steadily, though, a sense of unease crept back over me. I couldn't explain it at first. There was nothing to hear, no rumble of hooves. I decided it was something in the quality of the light. The sky seemed inexplicably brighter behind than ahead, as though the sun were rising early and in the wrong direction. We'd come to a region of large boulders, however, my view was obstructed on both sides, and I couldn't make out why.

Eventually, another turn brought us out near a ledge, with nothing beyond it but a steep decline. Then I understood.

There were the torches, not far behind us, fallen back into their original formation.

Now they weren't the only things burning.

Reb Panza was, as well.

CHAPTER FIVE

I was no stranger to being chased. I'd fled from my share of angry shopkeepers and incensed guards, not to mention the odd mob. But those occasions had been a breeze compared to the hurricane I found myself in that night.

It was late when the hunt began in earnest, the moon near its apex. It was hard at first to separate the weaving torches from the conflagration of Reb Panza. It was hard to see anything much. The wind was from the north, and it wasn't long before a great cloud of stinking smoke had enshrouded us and the area all around. My eyes smarted and wept – though in truth, that was caused by more than just the smoke. I had a sick feeling rooted in my stomach, half numb horror and half disbelief. Why had they destroyed Reb Panza? It made no sense. Had the people been in it when it burned, those giggling children and their ancient guardians, the patriarch with his preposterous moustaches? And there was another question, even more urgent-seeming, which my mind kept returning to despite my efforts.

Had it been my fault?

Saltlick laboured on beneath me, feet pounding the dusty road, breath escaping in violent gasps. I'd lost track of how long he'd been running. I couldn't imagine what was going through his mind, or what pressures were tearing at his body. Behind us, that chain of fires commanded the near horizon. All I could see were flames weaving in the foggy darkness; but my imagination was eager to complete the scene. I saw a hundred riders, arrows notched, scimitars bared, grim determination on their faces. I saw their leader urging them on, screaming threats of grotesque punishment and promises of outrageous reward to the man whose blade first drank our blood. I saw my death encroaching, inescapably.

The wind rose, the smoke began to break up. The air still stank of charred grass, and at first retained a hazy thickness, lending an unreality to everything. Then a light rain began, and it was as though we'd been travelling within a chamber of grimy glass that was suddenly washed clean. The stars seemed very bright, the trees and rocks glistened. The bobbing torches behind us stood out like pinheads on a black velvet cushion.

That sight brought me back to the moment. I told myself that the men pursuing us must be insane, that they'd set fire to Reb Panza for no other reason than a love of destruction. It need only be the work of one madman, in fact, and the rest were simply following orders. There was no reason to think it had anything to do with me. Moaradrid's army probably burned

villages every day. The best I could do would be to
escape and carry word of their atrocity.

The issue settled, I tried to get my bearings. I wasn't
sure how long had passed since we'd left the village. It
might have been an hour or four. We didn't seem
much nearer to the distant lights of Muena Palaiya. The
town would have to be our destination now, if we
could possibly make it so far. We were travelling southeast towards it, though the road continued to twist
back and forth, never running straight for long.

Thanks to that serpentine course, a strange rela-
tionship began to form between our pursuers and us
as the night wore on. They would draw very close,
but be below us. Boulders, scrub bushes and loose
shale littered the steep slopes between steps of the
road. Their horses stood no hope of cutting the distance that way. Archers attempted shots, and some
flew close enough that I heard them whistle by. I was
convinced one of those shafts would plunge through
my body, or wreak some catastrophic injury on
Saltlick.

Yet it was probably at those times we were safest.
Occasionally a glimmer of orange would be extinguished, as a rider tested the incline and went
tumbling into the dirt.

At other times, they relied on their advantage of
speed. There could be no doubt they had one. Even
with Saltlick travelling at his fastest, they still gained
steadily.

How long could the horses keep it up for? They'd
been galloping for hours, and their brief break at Reb

Panza hadn't been enough to rest them properly. We had a slim advantage there. But then horses were built for speed and stamina, and giants probably weren't.

By the time I got my answer, dawn was smudging the horizon like a drunken whore's rouge. Saltlick had slowed to a jog, and was weaving between the verges of the road. His pace had been slackening for the last two hours, and I'd been helpless to do anything except hang on and mutter occasional words of encouragement. The riders, forced by the expediency of not running their mounts to death, were slowing too. Even the archers had lost some of their fervour. The chase would have seemed comical to an observer: a bend in the road would bring us within sight of each other, a few arrows would be fired half-heartedly, only to clatter into the dirt behind us, and another turn would separate us once more.

Nevertheless, nothing in the situation made me hopeful. Saltlick would grind to a halt eventually, and I'd have to continue, alone and on foot. My pursuers were sure to be faster, were vastly more numerous, and probably weren't half crippled with bruises. I didn't stand a chance.

Then, as we turned yet another corner, an alternative suggested itself. A large estate stood directly ahead, back from the road, a two-storey villa surrounded by corrals and outhouses. It was one of the many prosperous farms that clustered around Muena Palaiya. A line of lemon trees stood between it and the road and behind I could see fields of corn, with orchards mounting the hillside beyond. Either its owners were already in the fields or they were still lazing in bed while their labourers did the work, because it was past dawn and no lights shone.

I noticed other details. A hay barn extended from the right of the house, and abutting that were two fenced areas. The first, nearest the house, contained a herd of somnolent cattle. A pair of stallions stood in the second, taking an early breakfast on strands of grass that had slipped between the slats.

"Saltlick, head towards that barn," I said.

He slowed a little, and tried to angle his head to look at me. Finding it impossible, he mumbled something instead.

"What?"

This time he said it more clearly: "Run."

His voice was hoarse, and as painstaking as a dying man's last gasp. I realised how utterly exhausted he must be. He hadn't lost his knack of communicating much with a minimum of syllables, though.

"It's all right," I said. "They won't catch us. I have a plan."

Saltlick didn't seem very sure, but he took the turn-off between the lemon trees. He loped through the low-walled courtyard fronting the villa and came to a halt outside the barn. I clambered down the netting without waiting for him to kneel and dropped the last distance to the dirt, gasping as the impact jolted tortured muscles.

"You see the hay, Saltlick? You have to bury yourself in it, as quickly as you can. Then stay quiet, whatever happens."

"Hide?" he asked doubtfully.

"Yes, hide. Stay hidden as long as possible. They'll chase me. They won't be looking for you. The moment they've gone past, you head up into the hills. I'll come back and find you, as soon as I can."

I've always been an excellent liar. Still, something caught in my throat as I spoke those last words. To regain the initiative I shouted, "Hurry, Saltlick! Do it now, or we're both dead!"

I'd estimated we had about a minute's lead. Most of that was already gone. Our pursuers would turn the last corner at any moment. So though there were other things I might have said, I neglected them in favour of turning and sprinting from the barn. I momentarily forgot the battered state of my body and vaulted the first fence, ran through the first paddock – drawing lows of alarm from the cattle – and clambered over the second fence.

The stallions turned from their meal and eyed me distrustfully. I slowed to a jog, hoping that would seem less threatening. Even so, they backed away skittishly when I came close, and shared a neigh of distrust. I had no time for niceties. I kept moving forward. The worst possibility was that one of them would panic and kick my head off, and I wouldn't be any deader than if Moaradrid's troops found me.

Luckily, they were well broken. They merely continued to neigh anxiously and retreat. I didn't have time for that either. I darted forward and swung up onto the back of the nearest before he had time to react, then clasped my arms around his neck and dug in with my knees as he tried to shake me off. It was a brief, half-hearted effort. The horse really had been broken, probably with more than a little cruelty. Though he was clearly on the verge of panic, he quickly accepted that he had no say in his own destiny.

I urged him towards the corral's gate with a sharp tap of my heels. I could hear the rumble of hooves in the near distance. When I looked, the lemon trees obscured my view. I reached for the looped rope that served as a latch, pulled it free, and gave the gate a push. It swung outward on well-oiled hinges. My mount seemed calmer, as though comforted by the familiar circumstances. I urged him through the gap, glanced over my shoulder – and my heart lurched up into my mouth.

I could see past the line of trees now, along the road, all the way to the corner, where twenty or more riders were tumbling into view, amidst a whirling sea of dust. I knew they saw me too. For an instant, it was as though the distance between us was non-existent. They were near enough that I could make out details of armour and weapons, even the expressions on their faces.

They looked pleased to see me, on the whole.

The moment we were clear of the gate I rapped hard on my mount's flanks, and shouted something indistinct in his ear. He surged forward, bewildered and terrified, narrowly avoided a tree, and then swerved when he struck the road, almost hurling me loose. An arrow thunked into the ground between his front hooves. Another ricocheted from the road ahead. Suddenly they were everywhere, lightning of wood and metal spitting up dirt in every direction. Something tore across my shoulder; it felt as though someone had carved the meat with a hot knife. I screamed, and my horse reacted with another terrified burst of speed. I didn't dare look at my wound. I lay as flat as I could, my face mashed into his mane, blind to everything but a small, blurred patch of road ahead. I had no idea what kind of lead we had. In my mind's eye, they were right upon us. At any moment, I'd be so riddled with arrows that passers-by would mistake me for some deformed, leafless bush.

The seconds passed. I remained alive. In fact, the cascade seemed to be slackening. Moments continued to stumble by, and with each, the rain of arrows lessened, from tempest to shower to drizzle. Finally, their clatter vanished altogether, to be replaced by distant shouts and curses.

I dared a glance over my injured shoulder.

I'd forgotten how the speed of our chase had been slackening for hours. It all came flooding back with the joyous sight of a horde of riders massed behind me, each trying to drive his horse to something faster than a trot. They had no hope of catching us. An expert archer on peak form would have had difficulty hitting us across that rapidly expanding distance. No one seemed inclined to humiliate himself by trying.

"Fools for ever crossing Easie Damasco!" I shouted at the top of my lungs.

Not only did that make my wound hurt more, it shocked my steed into another panic. Once again, I barely resisted being thrown. I realised I was better off concentrating on my course and on staying in one piece.

I couldn't help noticing one last detail, though, before I turned back. A detachment was peeling off from the main column, in the direction of the barn.

My wound didn't seem severe. That isn't to say it didn't hurt astonishingly, or that I was any less appalled to have received it.

The cut on my shoulder was really just a scratch, the arrow having grazed the flesh and carried on, but it was bleeding profusely and looked worse than it was. I could still move the arm, though it was already starting to stiffen.

I took a calculated risk on the lead I'd regained and drew my horse up by the side of the road. I climbed down, trying to favour my hurt shoulder. Pain still jarred through me when my feet struck the ground, from that and my countless bruises. I cried out, and a flight of crows erupted, cawing madly, from the roadside foliage. My horse winced, but thankfully didn't try to bolt. He seemed to have exhausted his supply of fright, and become indifferent to the whole business.

I cut a strip from the hem of my cloak and used it to make a tourniquet around my shoulder. It was next to impossible to tie the knot, or once tied to tighten it, and what I ended up with was little more than an embarrassing accessory. I could hear the rattle of hooves again by then, closer than I'd like, so I swung back onto the horse and drove him to a canter. Feeling suddenly sorry for him, I tried to be gentler, and even whispered some encouraging words in his ear. Perhaps my concern was misdirected, but I didn't feel like wondering what had happened to Saltlick.

It wasn't long before we'd outdistanced our pursuers once more. To my relief, I saw that we'd also come almost to Muena Palaiya. Though it was a while since I'd been there I remembered the area well. The road, having run roughly southeast for the last few miles, was forced aside by a cliff of grey-white stone and baked red mud, the western rim of the mountains. It continued in the shadow of the rock face, while the land sloped steadily down on our right. A line of stubby trees cut off my view, which otherwise would have been spectacular in the pale dawn light.

Not that I felt much like sightseeing. Muena Palaiya meant the end of my acquaintance with the horse, which I was starting to grow attached to and – perhaps through slight delirium – had nicknamed "Lucky". There are few more serious crimes than horse-thievery in the Castoval; a man can steal another's wife or rob his gold and still hope for leniency from the law, but if he's caught on a horse that isn't his he may as well lock himself up and throw away the key. It wouldn't pay for me to try to ride into Muena Palaiya.

I waited until the way broadened out. I knew it would split beyond the next bend, with one fork continuing along the cliff to the gates of Muena Palaiya, and the other dipping lower to skirt the town on its west edge. An open, grassy area marked by the occasional tree lay before the gates, where travellers who couldn't afford the local hospitality were prone to camp. It offered little in the way of concealment, and I'd be visible approaching from the gates. I didn't want to have to answer any questions or risk meeting old acquaintances, most of whom would be likely to arrest me. I didn't want anyone to be able to identify me to Moaradrid's troops, either, or to confirm my presence in the town. Fortunately, I knew another way inside. If it was more difficult, it would be infinitely more discreet.

I dismounted just before the turn, with a grunt of discomfort, and patted the dejected horse hard on his rump. "Be off, Lucky!" I slurred. "Go, live your life. You're free!"

He stared at me with red-flecked eyes, then wandered to the far roadside and began cropping grass.

I realised I was feeling distinctly unwell. No doubt it was the combination of hard riding, scant food and water, blood loss and the general stresses of the night. My brow was sticky, my mouth was dry, and even short steps made my head swim. I tried to remind myself that it would feel far worse if Moaradrid's thugs hacked it off.

Parched bushes of washed-out olive green and a few small trees lined the side of the road meeting the cliff, offering plenty of cover. As I pushed through them I realised I could hear hoof beats again, and that the sound was becoming so familiar it hardly shocked me anymore. I forced myself to hurry. Once I'd passed the bend, I could see the north wall of Muena Palaiya as speckles of ivory through gaps in the foliage. I carried on, scrambling sometimes on hands and knees, though it was particularly painful to do so.

It was slow progress, and I suffered countless scratches, along with tears and briars in my cloak. The rumble of hooves behind me became steadily louder and then stopped, presumably as they inspected the area around my abandoned mount. A few minutes later, it began again with renewed vigour.

I'd skirted most of the way round the open area by then. I could clearly see the reinforced wooden gates, still closed at that hour, and could just discern the figure of a guard on the rampart above. He was looking down and pointing, not in my direction thankfully.

I'd also reached the point I was looking for, and decided to take a moment's break. It was a mistake. The instant I stopped crawling I sagged to the ground, overwhelmed by fatigue.

At least I had a good view from where I lay. Through a gap, I could see out onto the grassy plain before the gates, where riders were massing. There might have been fifty already, with more arriving in a constant stream. Would they attack Muena Palaiya? Even with the garrison undermanned, they'd be hard-pressed. Those walls were sturdy and easily defended.

Either way, I was in too much of a corner to consider changing my plans. Maybe they imagined I was already inside, but it was just as likely they'd decide to make a search of the area. I hauled myself to my feet and squeezed through the gap in the rocks behind me. It was alarmingly narrow at first. On the other side it opened out a little into a sort of slim crevasse. Familiarity guided my exhausted steps, for I'd been this way more than once before. It had been known then, in certain circles at least, as the side door to Muena Palaiya.

The path – if path it could be called – crawled up and around the cliff face, which was less sheer at that point, a tumble of huge stones and jutting rock formations. At best the route was a narrow seam of loose dirt between boulders. At worst it meant sliding down perilous slopes of shingle or clambering over trees that jutted from the cliff face. I was in no shape for the endeavour. I soon noticed that I was leaving a snail-trail of scarlet over the white stone; my shoulder was bleeding again. I imagined myself tumbling over the cliff edge in a faint, and then bewildered townsfolk gathering round my broken body. The journey seemed to go on forever.

What made the route so difficult, however, made it secure. There were only a few points where I was visible from the town below. When I eventually reached Back Way Rock, I was confident I'd made it there unseen.

I lay flat on my face. I felt dizzier, and very muddled. Where was I? What exactly was I supposed to be doing? I decided I'd ask Saltlick, who I could hear behind me, chewing a mouthful of foliage. Memories jarred back into place. I recognised the sough of wind through leaves for what it was. The feverishness receded a little.

I dragged myself to the edge of the crag, and looked over cautiously. The eastern wall of Muena Palaiya was built around and partly into the cliff face, and the advantage of Back Way Rock was that it projected a little way out over the parapet, beside a particularly gentle and uneven decline. It was possible to climb down from there and, with more exertion, back up. It was a well-kept secret amongst those of us who liked to come and go without interference. At least it had been the last time I was in Muena Palaiya; the guards might keep a permanent watch on it these days for all I knew.

There was no one to be seen nearby, or anywhere on the eastern stretch of wall. A glance to my right told me why. What must have been the entire remaining garrison were gathered in a row on the northern wall around the gate, their helmets and cheerful blue cloaks bright in the early sunlight, staring down at some spectacle below. I could hear raised voices too, now that I listened. Was Moaradrid's force attacking? Their weapons weren't drawn, but perhaps that was only a matter of time. I decided to make my move, while they were otherwise occupied and I was fairly lucid. I pulled myself over to the side, looked down, and regretted it. The wall seemed unfeasibly far below.

Perhaps they'd shrunk it? Or raised the rock?

No, that was the fever talking, just as the distorted distance existed only in my fuddled brain. Focusing, I could see the first "step", a narrow outcropping worn by countless boots. I gritted my teeth, swung over, and managed to land a foot there whilst gripping the edge of the overhang. I looked for the second step once I was steady, and found that too.

Vertigo tugged at my brain. Sweat seemed to flow from my palms, making them slide wetly on their holds.

I couldn't remember where the third step was. I didn't dare look. I crouched, and lowered an exploratory foot. It found nothing but sheer, unbroken surface. I tried to pull it back, only to find that somehow I'd twisted around, my body angled away from the cliff.

I made to swing back, and my right hand slipped loose. I clawed frantically. My left foot slid free.

Scrabbling helplessly, I fell.

CHAPTER SIX

I landed hard.

A part of my mind reported with grim satisfaction that I was dead. That was it, every bone in my body was shattered, probably a few organs had burst too. It had been a tolerable life, on the whole, but it was over now. You can't win them all.

Another part pointed out that it still hurt. It still hurt a lot. I hadn't even fallen that far, nor had I landed on my head. In short, there was no reason I should be dead.

Does there have to be reason, the first part wondered.

Yes, replied the second.

Really?

Absolutely.

Well then perhaps we're not.

I opened my eyes and groaned. Death might have been preferable, overall. I hurt in places I'd never known I had.

The reality was that I lay across the parapet, limbs spread-eagled like dropped firewood, one foot and a hand dangling over the edge. I reclaimed them quickly, sat up, and propped myself against the cliff. Seeing that the guards were still focused on the north wall, I managed a sigh of relief. I didn't even seem to have acquired any new injuries. A quick survey told me that everything was in at least a semblance of working order.

I clambered to my feet and tried to get my bearings. Muena Palaiya was built on a slope; it was barely noticeable when you were within the town, but there on the highest edge the decline was obvious. Most of the houses, like the walls, were built of stone and many even had paved roofs. They tumbled down in a series of irregular whitewashed steps, following the contours of the hillside. Narrow alleys intersected everywhere, passing under countless arches and – where the buildings stretched to two storeys – even under floors. There was only one thing wide enough to be called a road, and that was Dancer's Way, which ran diagonally from the northern entrance to the other gate in the south-west corner. Below me, just stirring into morning activity, was the Artisans' Quarter. It was a warren even by the town's own standards, a region of cramped passages, odd smells, and countless disparate trades.

Though it wasn't where I wanted to be, it offered more privacy than the wall did. It was still quite dark, as the sun struggled to get out from behind the mountains. That wouldn't last for long, and nor could I rely on the guards staying clustered by the gates. I scurried to a point where the gap between wall and neighbouring roof was narrow enough to jump, and did so, landing clumsily amidst a tangle of netting and what appeared to be crab and lobster cages. I rolled over, half buried myself amidst the clutter, and lay still, enjoying the brief security.

I'd liked many things about Muena Palaiya. The wine was good, the pickings were easy, the girls amongst the prettiest around. What had endeared it to me most, though, had always been its rooftops. Nowhere were there roofs so untidy, so laden with assorted rubbish, or so closely packed together as in Muena Palaiya. Sadly, the populace had decided in recent years to elect a new mayor, a woman no less, and whether or not they'd meant the election seriously that was how she'd taken the job. I had no idea how the greater mass of citizens had fared under Mayor Estrada's regime, but I'd quickly found that her unreasonable focus on law and order sapped most of the fun from living in Muena Palaiya. I'd left three years ago, and hadn't been back since.

It was comforting to find the rooftops, the great Thieves' Highway, just as I'd left them. Perhaps it was too comforting. Lying propped against coils of rope and bundles of netting, shielded by the salt-stained cages, I was as snug as any lord in his silk-covered bed. I knew, deep in my fatigued brain, that if I fell asleep I'd likely wake in a cell. It didn't seem a very immediate concern.

There was a chill in the early morning air, which made me dig deeper into my nest and wrestle with my cloak. What finally made me stir, however, were the noises: preliminary sounds from the artisans, the clunk of hammers and squeal of saws, then once those had settled into their rhythm a hubbub of voices, which rose slowly or perhaps drifted nearer. It was coming from the direction of the north gate. I cursed and sat up.

The pain had eased to a general soreness. My shoulder wasn't bleeding anymore, though there were dark stains were I'd been lying and in smudges on my cloak. My head had cleared; the dizziness and nausea had passed. I still felt anxious, however. Had I slept? If I had, it hadn't been for more than a few minutes, for the light had hardly changed.

I shifted to a crouch, and crept through the wreckage of fishing equipment, more conscious of the aquatic reek rising off it, briefly puzzled by its presence such a way from the coast. Only a narrow gap kept the next building separate. I hopped over to land amidst roughly tied bundles of furs and tanned skins.

The voices seemed closer now. I decided it was something in the accents that had disturbed me. I couldn't place exactly what, though, or make out words.

I kept moving through a series of shallow leaps and one longer jump that I barely managed, which jolted my sore muscles and nearly made me cry out. I picked my way between barrels stinking of cheap wine, bales of cloth, smoked fish, baskets of olives, slabs of chalk, and squares of fresh-cut slate.

The voices grew louder.

I was beginning to feel oddly exuberant. I remembered the joy I'd taken from navigating those roofs, sometimes picking my way to a chosen target, sometimes fleeing after a job, but often travelling that way simply because it was most fun. My aches and pains seemed to bother me less. Old instincts guided my feet, reviving a deftness I'd almost forgotten.

I was out of breath when I stopped, though, and limping. I'd reached a wide roof covered with sacks of gravel, strips of unbeaten metal, and a few tall amphorae that smelled of oil. Memory, along with a change in the sounds from below, told me I'd reached Dancer's Way. I slipped to my knees and crawled to the low raised wall around the edge, found a spot between two crudely patterned jars and peeked down to the road below. If Dancer's Way was wide by Muena Palaiya's standards, it was also perpetually cluttered by traffic of people and animals, endless brightly covered stalls along its borders, the overflowing wares of shopkeepers, and an ever-present underclass of beggars, entertainers and ne'er-do-wells. Even at this early hour, it was far from quiet.

Of course that had as much to do with the party moving slowly up the street on horseback, stopping every so often for one of their number to converse with a street trader or passer-by. Three guards trailed behind them on foot, looking uneasy and keeping their hands close to their sword hilts. It was obvious they were supervising the mounted men, who in turn were questioning those they met, when they weren't bawling out a description to everyone within earshot. While the order of that description varied, the content remained the same: "Tall, skinny, dark haired, unshaven, wearing a green cloak over grey

trousers and black leather boots. Goes by the name
of Easie Damasco." Moreover, it always finished the
same way: "Twenty onyxes to the man, woman or
child who directs us to him."

It was bad enough to discover that the hunt had
followed me straight into Muena Palaiya, apparently
with the consent of the local guard. What was worse,
far worse, was that I knew the man riding at their
head. I recognised the austere elegance of his clothing, the stern, sharp features, and the intensity that
accompanied even his simplest movements.

Only one feature differed from when I'd last seen
him. He was missing his moneybag.

Nevertheless, there could be no doubt it was
Moaradrid, here in person, hounding me for a jewel
I'd given away, a giant I'd abandoned, a worthless
rock and a handful of coin. I decided then, with absolute certainty, that he was insane. I'd crossed him,
and now he would run me to the ends of the land –
not because he cared for his lost belongings, not even
as an example, simply because it was my misfortune
to have crossed a madman.

One of the riders glanced upward.

I ducked.

My heart pounded my ribs; my breath struggled
against clenched teeth. No shout came, no drum of
feet on the stairs joining roof to street. Still, I clearly
couldn't stay where I was. Was the rest of Moaradrid's
force scouring Muena Palaiya, street by street, a living
net constricting even as I sat there? Even if they
weren't, every citizen within the walls would soon

be looking out for the valuable commodity that was my face.

I scampered back in the direction of the cliff face, leapt in an awkward crouch over one alleyway and then another. I changed direction once I'd gained some distance from Dancer's Way, turning southward towards the Red Quarter.

Though the Red Quarter was as old as Muena Palaiya, its current name derived from one of Mayor Estrada's innovations. She'd insisted that any seller of illicit substances or services should hang a red flag or banner, or in some other fashion bear the colour on their premises. If she'd meant it as censorship, it had backfired. The local dens of iniquity had taken the notion enthusiastically to heart. It was where I'd lived, and where I'd enjoyed most of my time. Assuming Castilio Mounteban still owned the Red-Eyed Dog, it was also the one place I could hope to find sanctuary.

Halfway there I was pleased to discover some sacks of moth-eaten clothing left out in a corner. A quick search produced a faded purple cloak. It was too thin for sleeping in, the lining and hem were torn, but it had a hood, so I took it and left my own muddy, blood-spattered garment in its place. There weren't any boots, sadly, or trousers in remotely my size. A little further on, though, I found an open basket of figs left to dry in the sun. I took a large handful, and – although I was more thirsty than hungry – made a hurried breakfast.

With something in my stomach and a disguise of sorts, I felt better. New problems soon arose, however.

The Thieves' Highway became more difficult beyond the edge of the Artisans' Quarter.

First, there was a narrow slum of cheaply constructed houses, and my progress was slowed by avoiding badly made straw roofs that wouldn't hold my weight.

The Red Quarter, with its eccentrically fashioned buildings of two and more storeys, proved to be even worse. I managed to jump onto the balcony that ran around the first floor of the Crimson Gown and clambered over, trying not to tangle myself in the burgundy drapes suspended from the overhanging roof above.

I darted round the first corner and nearly ran into a woman, somewhat past the prime of youth, dressed in a robe that barely covered lurid undergarments. She was leaning on the rail, smoking a long-stemmed pipe. She turned to stare at me from beneath a mass of henna darkened hair, through eyes sharp with kohl and haggard from lack of sleep.

Feigning drunkenness, I stammered, "You're a very beautiful lady. I think I love you."

"You can love me after breakfast," she said, her voice gravelly from the smoke. "Come back in an hour."

"Every minute will seem like a day," I told her, and staggered back the way I'd come.

It was obviously going to be more trouble staying off the streets than it was worth. I pulled my hood up, wrapped the new cloak tight around me, and followed a flight of stairs down to the passage below.

The Red Quarter offered a degree of safety in itself. The ways were narrow, barely reaching the dimensions of alleys, and no one was eager to make eye contact. Few were out at that early hour. Those who were had either been drinking all night and reeled by or lay curled against walls groaning, or else were about to make an early start, in which case they stared ahead as if embarked on some tragic duty. I saw no sign of Moaradrid's troops, though I could hear them bellowing nearby. Presumably, they were still trawling Dancer's Way.

I hurried past endless establishments, each seedier than the last, and tried hard not to do anything else that might draw attention. Most of the drinking dens were too squalid to bear as much as a nameplate. They sported a splash of red paint above dark passage entrances, or a painted wooden board. A few businesses were more extravagant. Window boxes and hanging baskets decorated the Scarlet Lady, flowers overflowing in every conceivable shade of red. The Misbegotten Cherry was painted from top to bottom in an alarming ruby shade. Many signs brought back drink-fuddled memories of my time in Muena Palaiya.

I kept walking. Fond as my recollections were, I knew that half of those living there would turn me in for a tenth of the offered reward – and the other half would do it just for entertainment.

Just as I was beginning to doubt my sense of direction, I came out into a small plaza I recognised. A miserable orange tree grew in the centre, and waved yellowing leaves in half-hearted greeting. The Red-Eyed Dog stood beyond, easily identified by the painted design above the door of a rabid hound glaring outwards. Beneath, a passage led steeply downward; the Dog lay entirely underground, which suited its character perfectly. It had been the most degenerate, perilous dive in Muena Palaiya when I'd left, and I'd no reason to imagine it had improved with age.

There was a sentry on the door, a wide, dark northerner I faintly recognised. When I tried to pass, an arm of solid muscle thudded to block my path, showering plaster dust from the doorway.

"I'm here to see Mounteban," I said. "Tell him an old friend is looking for him."

"Mounteban's got nothing but old friends," said the sentry philosophically.

"Not like this one."

"And some of his old friends," he continued, "got names."

"Again. Not this one." I decided to gamble, and lowered the hood a little. "But he'll know my face. Perhaps you could draw him a picture?"

I thought he was going to hit me. He was evidently thinking about it. Instead, he said, "Wait here. You cross this line," and he scuffed a heel across the threshold, "I break all your fingers, one by one."

"I use my fingers a lot," I told him, "I guess I'll just have to wait."

He was gone so long, however, that I began to think about trying to sneak in, threats be damned. I could hear Moaradrid's men calling nearby, and I doubted they'd have the restraint to stop with my fingers. The minutes dragged by. The voices seemed

very close. Just as I'd decided to chance it, a face
loomed out of the murk: "Mounteban said he'll see
you," muttered the sentry, obviously not pleased by
his own news.

"Of course he did," I agreed, and pushed past.

Narrow stairs led into darkness. I took them carefully. Half way down my eyes began to water, partly
from the grimy smoke but as much from the smell of
hard liquor and old vomit. It was just possible to
imagine that, in better times, the Dog had been something more than a filthy drinking joint. The lanterns
were glass-panelled and ornate, reminding me of the
one I'd seen in Moaradrid's tent. Tapestries hung
from the bare stone walls, enough of the designs still
visible through the patina of soot and dirt to suggest
that they'd once been brightly colourful. The carved
benches around the outside were upholstered, even
if the cushions were grey and shapeless now. Even
the bar, beneath its countless scratches and dints, was
of solid wood, some nearly black timber I didn't
recognise.

"Over here."

The call came from the farthest corner. I weaved
between bar and tables, eager to avoid stepping on
any of the patrons. Anyone drinking in a place like
the Dog at this time of the morning was unquestion-
ably best avoided. At the back of the room, lit by a
meagre hearth, was a table in slightly better repair
than the others. A huge man sat behind it, dressed in
a faded, once-gaudy poncho. He drew smoke from a
water pipe perched on the table, and exhaled in long,

rough breaths. He took the tube from his mouth when I reached him, with one meaty hand. The other he held up, with the middle finger pointed downwards. "Sit."

It wasn't a request. I sat.

He leaned closer, scrutinising me with his one good eye. I'd heard he'd lost the other in a childhood tussle, in the years before he'd come south to the Castoval, though that wasn't the story he told. He looked older than I remembered. Some of the muscle that made up his bulk had run to fat – though not so much that you'd want to get on his bad side. He ran a hand through his beard, as wild and bushy as his hair, and said, "It's really you."

"It is, Mounteban. In the flesh. What's left of it, at any rate."

"I wondered if you'd come. Your name is on every lip in town, you know. It seems you've lost none of your ability to upset people."

"It's my fearsome wit and good looks. How can a man protect against jealousy?"

"Indeed." Mounteban leaned closer, and I followed his example. "I'd say it's good to see you, but it really isn't."

Suddenly I felt very sobered and sorry for myself. "I had nowhere to go. This isn't like anything before. I really think he'll hunt me to the end of the world. They shot me in the shoulder. I've hardly eaten in days."

Mounteban nodded sombrely. "Well I won't turn you in. I don't know what I can do to help you, though. Things will get bad around Muena Palaiya very quickly if they don't find you." His eyes roved behind me and fastened on something. He stood abruptly. "Wait here," he said, starting towards the entrance.

I looked after him and saw that a figure had entered, and now stood waiting in the deep shadows around the doorway. They were short, and wore a darkly shaded cloak much like my own, with a low hem and the hood drawn up. It seemed I wasn't the only one in the Dog who wanted to keep a low profile. They stood talking in whispers for what seemed an inordinately long time, but was probably only a couple of minutes. Then Mounteban unlocked a small door beside the bar and ushered the new arrival through. He turned back towards me. I looked away quickly, though I knew he'd seen me watching.

It was another minute before he sat opposite me again. When he did so, it was with a platter of bread, cheese and dried tomatoes in one hand and a cup of wine in the other. "One of my agents," he said, by way of explanation.

That surprised me. By the time I first met Castilio Mounteban he'd gone relatively straight, having put a lucrative and notorious career in thievery behind him to concentrate on running his bar, and occasionally fencing goods or dealing in questionably legal favours on the side. I'd never known him to have anything as prestigious-sounding as agents. For the first time since I'd arrived, I wondered what I might have blundered into. Mounteban and I had always got on tolerably well, but we'd hardly been the best of friends. He owed me nothing. Completing the thought, I said, almost automatically, "I have money."

"That's good," he replied, shoving the plate and glass towards me. "No one enjoys penury. We can worry about such things later."

I nodded. Perhaps that was what he'd been waiting to hear – though the truth was that my handful of onyxes wouldn't get me far. I made a start on the bread, and then drained the wine in one long gulp.

"You had a giant with you," said Mounteban.

I started. He hadn't been joking. He really did have agents.

"He was poor company and smelled like an unwashed horse. We parted ways."

"Do you know what happened to him?"

It seemed an odd question. But I was in Mounteban's bar, eating his food and begging his protection, so I thought I'd better play along. "I left him in a haystack, beside a farm just outside of town. It seemed best for both of us."

"Really?"

"Well, for me anyway. What's this about, Mounteban?"

"Nothing we can talk about here and now. Suffice to say you're only one detail of a bigger picture."

"Not to me."

Mounteban laughed, without much humour. "Same old…" He caught himself. "We need to get you out of here. Before someone remembers you used to know me and passes that information to Moaradrid."

He stood and started once more towards the entrance. I followed. When we reached the side door through which his mysterious agent had left, he stopped to unlock it again, pushed it open, and motioned inside. I felt suddenly nervous. Nevertheless, I stepped through as instructed.

The room beyond was evidently a store, with crates and casks piled against the walls on two sides, and cluttered shelves on a third. A lantern hung from the ceiling, giving out more smoke than light. It was just sufficient for me to make out the cloaked figure stood in the farthest and darkest corner.

I heard the door slam heavily behind me.

I was wondering whether it would be more polite to greet them or to pretend I hadn't seen them – when something crashed into the back of my neck, driving me onto hands and knees.

"Hey!"

I tried to roll over, to protect myself with my arms. Fingers gripped my hair from behind, pulling my head back.

"There's no need for…"

I never finished the sentiment. The second blow sent my plummeting into cold darkness.

CHAPTER SEVEN

Thud.

I opened my eyes, and looked out through a crimson web of pain.

Thud.

Darkness, split by flickering yellow; I tried to turn my head, regretted it.

Thud.

I was lying on some kind of litter. My feet were tied to the higher end where, if I strained, I could just make out a bulky silhouette supporting it. Perhaps they'd tied me carelessly and my head had been banging for a while, or maybe I'd slipped down as we travelled. Either way, I saw no point to suffering in silence. I groaned as loudly as I could manage. The noise came back at me alarmingly in a wave of muffled echoes. We jarred to a halt, and my head bounced off the ground once more.

"He's awake." The voice was muted, though curiously piercing. I presumed it belonged to the cloaked stranger.

"It seems so." That was Mounteban, sounding less than pleased.

"Can you knock him out again?"

"I could."

"You won't?"

"I will if you think I should. It's risky. You can only hit a man on the head so many times before parts start to rattle."

"Will he make trouble? We could blindfold him."

"No trouble," I gurgled.

I'd have liked to say more, but the throbbing between my ears, the angle I was at, and a cruel dryness in my throat all conspired against it.

My feet were lowered to the ground. Steps came towards me, echoing off some hard surface, stone flags or bare rock.

"We know everything," said Mounteban, from just outside my line of sight. "You don't want to make this more difficult than it needs to be."

I wondered what it would be like to know everything. It sounded a lot of work, and I didn't envy this mysterious "we". "I don't want things to be difficult," I agreed. "Only, my head hurts."

More steps, of a lighter tread. A face loomed over mine, but only a third of it was visible beneath the folds of the hood and that third was sunk in shadow.

"He's bleeding a little. His head's been knocking on the ground." I noticed again how sharply pitched his voice was. He seemed short and slight enough to be an unusually tall child, though it was hard to judge details from the loose-hanging cloak.

"It has," I agreed. "Repeatedly."

"We could turn him the right way up."

"You could."

"Shut up, Damasco!" Mounteban sounded more exasperated than angry. "Listen, you can't make things any worse."

I wasn't sure how to take that. On the surface, it seemed promising; I'd rarely come across a situation I couldn't aggravate. Yet an edge to his voice suggested I might do better not to try this time.

The cloaked stranger said, "Raise his legs."

A moment later my feet lurched into the air, and I found myself gazing up at Mounteban's florid, cyclopean face. He gave me one glance, of irritated disdain, then turned his good eye and patch resolutely towards the ceiling. His companion busied himself in passing a length of rope beneath and around my shoulders and knotting it tight, so that now I was bound securely at both ends.

"Let's get moving."

All this while, my head had been slowly clearing. While Mounteban laboured to lower one end of my litter and haul up the other, I pondered the fact that he seemed – despite his fearsome reputation, his standing in the criminal community, his enigmatic talk of "agents" – to be following orders. This was interesting, and might be useful. I'd never known Castilio Mounteban to follow anyone, for any reason. Was I in the presence of some fearsome criminal mastermind, some new lord of the Muena Palaiyan underworld?

My head and shoulders pitched upward, and were dragged through a half circle. Then we were moving again, and all I could see was a press of shadows merging into deeper darkness, with the only light the shuddering glow of our mysterious leader's lantern from behind me.

I thought I'd worked out where we were, at least. I had an idea, anyway, though if I were right it wouldn't do me much good. Back in the day, I'd occasionally had cause to visit the ant's nest of tunnels behind Muena Palaiya. Some were remnants of the old mines, some natural passages formed by waters that had once hurtled through the blackness. A few were claimed to be the handiwork of some ancient race who'd made burrows amidst the rock. None of that had really mattered, because for as long as anyone remembered the warrens had been the refuge of smugglers, fences and other unlawful sorts, who had adapted the excavations for their own ends. It had been another of Muena Palaiya's fine secrets for those of us in the trade. I'd only ever seen the edges of it; rumour had it that the full extent reached throughout the mountains, penetrating as far as the coast and in every direction.

So if I was right I was utterly lost, with no hope of doing anything about it, even if I could somehow work myself free and escape.

It seemed easiest to pass out again.

When I awoke, my head was still pounding. I was convinced at first that I was still on the litter, and still moving. I realised after a while that I'd just got used to the sensation. In fact, I was lying on a pallet in what appeared to be a small cave. It was just about high enough that I could have stood, had I wanted to. Ten steps would have taken me along its length, and half that would have sufficed for its width. The abrupt angles of the stone suggested it had been cut out, though it was possible the work of men had just modified an existing space. It certainly didn't seem to have been designed with any useful function in mind. The proportions were generous for a cell, stingy for anything else.

Light came from a single candle perched in a nook to my left. A door opposite, constructed of tightly sealed planks, blocked the exit. If there'd been anyone around, I'd have pointed out what an unnecessary precaution it was. I'd have been far too scared of getting lost to try and escape, and in any case, I was glad of the rest. The pallet was dirty and probably riddled with lice, but it was comfortable. Someone had even bandaged my shoulder with fresh linen and an unexpected degree of care. I was even more surprised, when I eased myself onto my elbows, to discover some bread and a jug of water.

I sat up properly, gulped down half the water, tore a lump of bread, and chewed thoughtfully. It was hard, but not stale. On an impulse, I began to search through my pockets. Of my limited possessions, my knife was gone. My purse, astonishingly, was where I'd left it. The strange stone I'd taken from Moaradrid was missing; however, my handful of coins remained.

Most bizarrely, my picks were untouched. The door had no keyhole and would undoubtedly be barred on the other side. Still, it showed an unusual degree of honesty in my captors. That was the last thing I'd have expected from Mounteban, who even after he'd gone straight had been more basically dishonest than many hardened criminals I'd known.

Captivity didn't seem so bad, all things considered. After the last couple of days – being forced into battle, spending excruciating hours upon a hygiene-impaired giant while barbarians tried to skewer me, and falling off a cliff – it was quite pleasant. I didn't have to worry about Moaradrid while I was in there, or anything much else.

I determined not only to make the best of it, but to prolong it if I could. Sat there chewing, watching the flickering patterns of amber and black shadow, I decided that all I really wanted for the foreseeable future was a little oil for my bread, some good cheese, and wine instead of water. Maybe such luxuries could be negotiated for, though it was hard to think what I could offer someone who'd already claimed to know everything.

Time passed. I had no way to judge how long. I drifted in and out of sleep, sometimes sat with my back against the wall, sometimes lying on the pallet, which smelled pleasantly of straw. I finished the bread, though I tried to ration my water. It occurred to me abruptly that they'd left me there to die, and the thought was so appalling that I nearly panicked. But that made no sense. Why drag me an interminable distance beneath the earth, only to leave my body rotting in a cave without so much as a word of explanation?

Still, after that I began to find the experience less pleasurable. Other troublesome theories limped around my aching brain. Perhaps I was being ransomed to Moaradrid, or held on behalf of one of the many enemies I'd accumulated during my time in Muena Palaiya. If neither explanation really accounted for my circumstances, that didn't stop me worrying.

I was actually relieved to hear the echoing approach of feet outside. I listened eagerly. There were two people, one tread heavier than the other – presumably Mounteban and his mysterious accomplice. I was a little surprised when the louder step halted some way before the door, while the other continued on to stop directly outside. A high, muffled voice said something I couldn't make out.

Mounteban replied, "All the same. You should be careful."

The response was similarly inaudible.

"Perhaps. But he's a petty thief, at best."

A clatter, of first one wooden beam and then another being lifted out of the way, obscured the next exchange. All I heard was Mounteban conclude with, "…wait here then."

The door creaked inward. The hole was so low that even the cloaked stranger had to hunch to pass through. He was still carrying a lantern in one hand. Its ruddy glow did little except lengthen and soften the shadows.

"I don't like the phrase 'petty thief'," I said. "It makes me sound short."

"At least you acknowledge you're a thief."

"From time to time I've done things that might, to a cynical observer, be considered thieving."

"And what would you call them?"

"My livelihood."

The cloaked figure laughed, a strangely pleasant sound amid such dreary surroundings. "Well perhaps you're something more than a petty thief, then. We'll see."

He reached up to draw back his hood. I saw narrow features cast into sharp relief by the lamplight, a soft mouth, large, dark eyes, and a mane of even darker hair flowing past shoulder length.

I stared, not quite able to close my mouth. Finally I said, perhaps unnecessarily, "You're a woman."

"See? You're already showing insightfulness beyond your calling."

"And I recognise you. You were in the battle, yesterday morning," I said, momentarily forgetting how I'd planned to keep my own presence there a secret. The image came back to me with sudden clarity: the rider at the vanguard of the escaping Castovalian force, black hair streaming past their shoulders. I realised, with astonishment, that the man beside her then had been Castilio Mounteban. "Now that I think, I've seen you before that too."

"Marina Estrada," she said with a small bow.

It all clicked into place.

"You're the mayor. The mayor of Muena Palaiya."

"And you are Easie Damasco, one-time resident of my noble town, who since then has made a nuisance of himself throughout most of the Castoval at one time or another. You managed most recently to fall in with the invader Moaradrid, and to fight against your own kinsmen."

My mouth felt suddenly dry. I'd given nothing away that she hadn't already known. Mounteban's claim of omniscience began to seem a lot more plausible. "I was coerced."

"That seems likely. You certainly left in a hurry, and with more than one thing that wasn't yours. Since then Moaradrid has shown an eager interest in your whereabouts."

She took a step closer. When she spoke again, her voice was so hard and sharp that I could understand how I'd mistaken it for a man's. "For all that, you're only a small part of a very big picture."

"Mounteban said the same. To me I'm a large part of a picture only slightly bigger than I am."

She laughed again. This time it was a harsh, humourless sound. She set the lantern in the centre of the floor and sat opposite me, just beside the door. "There's more at stake than you realise, and there has been from the start. Who knows what your blundering has cost the Castoval?"

"Whatever it is, I'll pay." Not wanting to be overly hasty, I added, "It may take a little while."

"The question we have to ask, though, is 'Was it blundering? Or was it cleverness?' You can see how we'd wonder. 'Here's a man who's met Moaradrid himself, who's spent time in his camp and carries his coin, and now, conveniently, comes running into our very arms.' Don't you think we'd be suspicious?"

I didn't like where this was heading. "I don't know about any 'we'. I couldn't run any further, so I came to Muena Palaiya. I asked Mounteban for help because I couldn't think of anyone else."

"That may be true."

She looked away, and paused to run long fingers through her hair. I noticed how tangled and unkempt it was, and then how it matched her whole appearance. The cloak was made for travel, and dirty and torn; smears of dirt ran down one side of her face, beneath a livid bruise only partly hidden by her fringe. There were grey bags beneath her eyes, and lines creasing their corners.

The interrogation seemed to have ceased for the moment. Marina Estrada sat staring at nothing, struggling with a particularly stubborn knot. I took the opportunity to wonder what was going on, what it was they imagined I'd done. It was absurd to think I could be in league with Moaradrid, or that he would have gone to so much trouble for an ex-criminal bar owner and a provincial mayor. What were the two of them doing together anyway? The partnership seemed more than unlikely. Perhaps Estrada's enthusiastic stance against crime had been nothing more than a screen for her own corrupt dealings. Maybe she and Mounteban were lovers, united by their paranoid distrust and enthusiasm for kidnapping.

"Amongst other things, you absconded with a

giant." Her voice had resumed its normal, faintly tuneful tone. "Then you abandoned him."

The question took me by surprise. "In a way, he abandoned me."

"That's not true, is it?"

"Well… 'abandoned' is a strong word. It was an amicable parting of the ways, with the hope that we might meet again one day. There were other factors, you understand. I never think clearly under the threat of imminent death."

"You abandoned the giant and stole a horse. You soon managed to discard that too. After that, we lost track of you for a while. You were next seen making a clumsy break-in from the mountainside; lucky for you the guard had orders to leave you alone. You made your way to see Castilio, as we'd hoped you might. Now here we are."

"And here is where again?"

"You don't need to know that. In fact, until we're sure we can trust you, you don't need to know anything. We've given you the benefit of the doubt so far, for one reason only: you can be useful to us. Even then, there are those who think we should just hang you on the off chance."

"Mayor Estrada, you're right. I could be useful. Under the right conditions, I could be extremely useful. With that in mind, what do you think the chances are of some more bread, this time with a little oil, and perhaps a cup of wine?"

Estrada stood and picked up her lantern. "Come on, Damasco," she said, "I've something to show you."

I sighed and hauled myself to my feet, only to nearly topple over again when I realised how numb my legs had become. Estrada offered me an arm to steady myself. I accepted it, and leaned against her until I was sure I had my balance. Her behaviour seemed overly generous toward a suspected enemy, a potential assassin even. I wondered how genuine her suspicions were, and how much was just a precaution born of circumstance.

Whatever the case, she was quick enough to pull away once I'd found my feet. She led the way and I staggered after, with a fond glance back at my cosy cell. A sinking sensation in my bowels told me it would be a long time before I knew such peace and comfort again.

Mounteban was waiting outside, and glowered at me. "Didn't I tell you he'd deny it?"

"Perhaps because he's innocent."

"Perhaps."

We were in a low passage propped and beamed with blackened timbers, likely an old mineshaft. Estrada led off to the left, holding her lamp in front, and I followed, conscious of how Mounteban moved in close behind me. We soon came to a crossroads, and turned left again into a lower, narrower tunnel, which proceeded to wind back and forth for a considerable distance. We came eventually to what at first glance seemed a dead end, until Estrada stepped onto a ladder that disappeared into a hole above. When I hesitated, Mounteban growled, "Hurry up, Damasco."

The ladder was sturdier than it looked. That wasn't saying much. With all three of us on it, it bucked and swayed with every slight motion. The climb took an unreasonably long time, and Estrada's silhouetted figure blocked the light from her lamp, leaving me in thick darkness. By the time I clambered out, my nerves ached to match my body.

We'd arrived in yet another tunnel, this one apparently natural and faintly lit by patches of phosphorescent blue mould at intervals along the ceiling. Estrada closed and padlocked a hatch over the drop, and then led on, until the tunnel opened out again. We'd come to another junction, this one large enough to be considered a cavern. I was alarmed when a shape glided out of the shadows, until our lamplight revealed it as an elderly man in patched leather armour. He saluted Estrada and asked, "How goes it, Captain?"

"As well as can be expected," she replied. "Any word?"

"Nothing new."

She nodded, and the man slipped back into the gloom.

Captain? I remembered hearing something once about a mayor being expected to lead their townsfolk in a time of war. Surely that wouldn't apply to a woman, though? I'd always assumed Estrada's appointment had been meant as a joke, and it had never occurred to me that others might see it differently. Yet I could think of no other explanation for her presence on the battlefield.

Estrada had moved to the cavern's far wall, where a low opening led onward. She turned back and said to Mounteban, "You can wait here." When he looked as though he'd debate the point she added, "No arguments. You can eavesdrop again if you like."

She crouched to hands and knees and disappeared into the entrance. Mounteban waved me on when I didn't follow, and I could feel the elderly guard's eyes on the back of my neck. I dropped to all fours and crawled after Estrada.

That short journey was worse than climbing the ladder had been. I couldn't lift my head without scraping it on bare rock, and the surface beneath my hands was just as uneven. Both were cold and moist, and once again I was travelling in near blackness. I was immensely relieved to see Estrada's shape ahead fringed with grey. The grey grew paler and paler, until suddenly she moved aside and dazzling moonlight filled my view. I clambered gratefully out into it, and if it hadn't been for Estrada's grasp on my elbow, would have stepped right off the cliff.

For that was where we'd come out: dizzyingly high upon the cliffside, perched on a slender outcrop, looking down over the eastern Castoval. I could make out the contours of Muena Palaiya directly below, illuminated by occasional glimmers of lamp or torchlight. Grander fires burned in the triangle of ground before the north gate, seething puddles of yellow spread between the silhouettes of tents.

Estrada, following my gaze, pointed down towards the encampment. "That's where Moaradrid's holding your friend."

"My friend?"

"The giant you travelled with."

"Oh. I wouldn't have chosen that particular word."

Her glance was disapproving. "No?"

"Anyway, I'm sure he'll be all right. He'll explain, in his monosyllabic way, that it was entirely my fault, and they'll likely take him back to his real friends."

"Even if that were to happen," she said, "It wouldn't fit with our plans."

"These mysterious plans again. Tell me, why exactly have we come all this way, when I could be asleep in that nice, warm cave?"

Estrada looked at me as if I was deliberately missing the obvious. "You can't very well rescue the giant from inside a prison cell, can you?"

CHAPTER EIGHT

I squinted at the makeshift encampment.

It was a bright, clear night and, if I concentrated, I found I could pick out the abrupt triangles of tents, the crooked shadows of olive trees, and even the figures of patrolling guards when they passed before a campfire or across a patch of moonlit ground.

None of that told me where they were holding Saltlick. I couldn't imagine they'd waste a tent on him, or allow him near a fire. He would be out in the open, and most probably tied to something. I personally doubted he possessed the guile to try to escape again, but Moaradrid wasn't to know the details of his last elopement, and – despite my earlier claim – I didn't really believe Saltlick would blame me. Apart from anything else, it would involve the kind of multiple-word answers he seemed to detest so much.

I noticed an irregular patch of darkness that wasn't a tent and, although it had protrusions that must be branches, wasn't quite the right shape to be a tree. There was something distinctly odd about its smudged silhouette. I stared at it, trying to tease its dimensions from the surrounding darkness – so that when it moved I nearly jumped out of my skin.

I pointed. "That's him, isn't it, by that big tree?"

Estrada nodded.

"That's right in the middle of the camp. It's hopeless. I count at least a dozen men on patrol, and there are bound to be sentries as well. Moaradrid must know he's vulnerable out there. He'll be expecting an attack."

"Yes. He sent back for reinforcements yesterday. Half his army will be here by tomorrow evening."

"It's impossible."

"You talk as if you have a choice." There was a new quality in her voice, inflexible and cold. "I don't like it, but there it is. We want the giant out of there and you have as good a chance of rescuing him as anyone. If they don't kill you, if you don't decide you like it better with them than with us, then perhaps we can trust you."

Every hint of softness was gone from her face. I realised then, really understood for the first time, how she'd been allowed to run a town and even to lead men into battle. In that moment, I found her no less frightening than Moaradrid.

Much to my own surprise, fear made me brave – or at least pragmatic. "I could get to him, perhaps, maybe even untie him. But the two of us sneaking out together? Possibly you haven't noticed, but Saltlick isn't exactly built for subterfuge."

Her features relaxed into the barest hint of a smile.

"Oh, don't worry about that, Damasco. We'll be ready when the time comes."

If that cryptic reply was supposed to comfort me then it failed miserably. Either way, it was clear that pleasantry or even discussion was off the menu for the remainder of the night. I was actually a little glad. The more I prevaricated, the more I'd consider what I was about to do. If I really had no choice, it was probably best I think about it as little as possible.

Still, there remained certain practical considerations. "So how do I get down there? Is flight amongst the miracles you're expecting from me?"

Estrada, by way of answer, motioned to her right. A thick wooden beam jutted from the rock wall near the passage mouth, extending out into space. A line of rope lay on the outcrop close to the overhanging end, and fed up through a simple pulley mechanism to a coil near the cliff. It was probably another relic from the mining days, or from the smugglers. Either group would have been glad of a way to move goods rapidly up and down the cliff face.

Of course, no sane person would have considered people amongst those goods. "You're joking."

"Do you have a better suggestion? No? Then start tying that rope around your waist."

I shrugged and did as instructed, reminding myself that a quick death on the ground below would be preferable to a slow, elaborate one at the hands of Moaradrid. I didn't hurry though, and by the time I'd finished, a dozen sturdy knots bulged around my waist. Estrada took up the main length, curved it round her body, drew it tight and braced. "I've got you. You can step off now."

I'd understood in theory that this moment was coming. Now that it was a reality, I still found myself staring at her as though she were speaking some incomprehensible language known only to the congenitally mad.

"Damasco, step off! I can take your weight, believe me."

Rationally, I knew this was probably true. The pulley would do most of the work, and in any case, here was a woman who could wield a sword in battle, which was more than I could honestly say about myself. It takes a lot of trust to put your life in someone's hands, however, regardless of what sense tells you.

I shifted closer to the edge, looked down. Darkness masked the base of the precipice, with nothing visible except vague shapes that must be bushes. I could see the cliff face clearly, though, and the sight of it sheering away beneath me made my guts melt.

I glanced back at Estrada. She was glaring impatiently. When she saw my expression, her own relaxed a little. "You'll be all right," she told me. "If you've proved anything over the last two days it's that you're a survivor."

I couldn't help but laugh – a slightly hysterical bark that came out too loud.

"I never looked at it that way," I said, and stepped out into nothingness.

For a hideous moment, I fell. Then the cord jerked taught.

Estrada called from above, "Look for the package!"

I had no idea what she meant, and didn't much care, because my downward momentum had turned into rapid spinning that swung me dangerously close to the mountainside. I was starting to get used to that when I began to drop again – in abrupt steps at first as Estrada got used to my weight, and then in a steady slide. Meanwhile, the spinning continued, stone and sky rotating round my head with nauseating speed. My sense of space buckled. I seemed to be plunging in every direction at once.

I was just beginning to right myself when I struck the ground, with a yelp more of shock than pain. It took me a minute to establish that I was lying on my back, with my limbs dangling and my head mostly in a bush. The rope was still taut, leaving my waist suspended above the grass. It only occurred to me then that I had no way to cut myself free, and that no slack meant no hope of loosening the knots. Estrada might realise eventually, or grow bored. In the meantime, my extremities were starting to go numb.

I began to panic, and stared into the blue-limned gloom, hoping for a jagged rock, a sharp stick, or anything I could use to try to rescue myself. I discovered instead the package that Estrada had warned me about. If I hadn't been confused and dangling, I'd have seen it immediately. It was large enough, and wrapped in vividly coloured cloth.

It took some manoeuvring to get hold of it and more to open it, but I was glad of the effort when the first thing to fall out was a long curved knife. It proved wickedly sharp. A couple of strokes were enough to free me, and left me panting flat on my back in the damp grass.

I struggled upright and inspected the package's other contents. The outer wrapping turned out to be a cloak. It was coloured Moaradrid's bruise red, though so dirty and faded that it wasn't obvious at first. Inside was a jacket of studded leather, with a ragged tear in the seam. It could only be meant as a disguise. The ill-kept armour wouldn't be out of place in Moaradrid's ragtag army, and the knife had probably been looted from a Northerner's corpse.

Was this Estrada's plan? I wander into Moaradrid's camp dressed not unlike one of his men, wave hello to the guards, cut Saltlick loose and march back out, with no one any the wiser? I'd come up with worse in my time, but only with the excuse of copious amounts of alcohol. It had audacity on its side, and the fact that the guards were expecting a full-blown attack, not a lone and woefully ill-prepared thief. That was about it.

On the other hand, I didn't have any better ideas. With a little improvisation, it might prove marginally less suicidal than simply throwing myself from the cliff would have been.

I spent a few minutes in preparation. The cloak was warmer than the one I'd acquired the day before, at least. I wore it open, to display the battered armour and the dagger stuck into my belt. I looked as much like a northern soldier when I'd finished as Costas and his idiot fishermen had done. I hoped that would be enough.

It took me a while to pick my way through the bushes and trees in the dark. When I broke out on the other side, I made sure to make myself as visible as possible. There was a shallow slope to the road, and I was half way down it when the challenge came: "Stop there!"

I did as instructed.

"Who are you?"

"Damn it, who are *you*? A man goes to relieve himself out of anyone's way, and not only does he find strange garments hung in trees, he can't come back into camp without an uproar."

A figure stepped from the blackness around the nearest tree. I could only make out the barest outline, at first. Then his sword became visible as moonlight caught the flat.

"Strange garments?"

"This cloak," I said, holding out my old one, "was hung from a branch. Not only that, someone has cut a mark into the back." This was true; I'd carved a ragged cross there before I set out. "It's suspicious, if you ask me."

He came closer. The sword point dipped. "Let me see."

I held it out. "What do you think it means? Some signal?"

Needing both hands to take it from me, he tucked his sword into his belt.

"It's filthy. Torn too. It probably belonged to some vagabond." He sounded uncertain.

A gruff voice called from deeper within the camp: "Shut up, dog-lovers. Get back to your bloody posts!"

My interrogator, looking suddenly nervous, called into the darkness, "Sorry, Captain." To me he said, "Get on. Stay inside the boundaries. Next time it might be an arrow not a challenge." He handed me back the bedraggled cloak.

"Watch out," I told him. "It's fishy, I tell you."

I strode past with all the bluff confidence I could muster, and he drifted back towards the inky environs of his tree. I was terrified that the mysterious captain would come out to question me. He hadn't sounded the type to be so easily fooled.

No one appeared. Nothing moved. There were only the tents, in a loose circle, and between them camp-fires with prone bodies scattered nearby. Apart from the occasional snore or grunt, it was deathly quiet. Rain had fallen while I'd been in the caves, and the air smelled fresh, with only the slightest intermingled odour of unwashed fighting men and cooked meat.

It was too good to be true. I felt sure I was being watched. All my thief's instincts sang out together. Nevertheless, I kept walking, and aimed for the centre of camp. If they came for me, I'd run – that way they were more likely to shoot me and less likely to take me alive. Moaradrid had chased me for two days. He wouldn't let me off with a spell in the volunteer brigades this time.

After a while, I thought I could make out Saltlick, still hunched beneath the tree as I'd seen him from the cliff. He was apart from the main region of the camp, perhaps due to that distinctive smell I'd often noted. Still, there were the store tents and corrals further out, and a perimeter of guards, not to mention more than ample moonlight for archers to pick us off at their leisure. The plan didn't seem any less preposterous close up.

On the positive side, there were no guards near Saltlick himself. I realised as I drew closer that it would have been a waste of manpower. He was securely bound, with his arms tied behind the tree and countless coils securing his waist, torso and neck to its trunk. He could move his head and perhaps twitch his fingers, nothing more. It might take me the rest of the night to cut him free.

I approached him from the front. It was too late for subterfuge now. No one came running. Either I really wasn't being watched or my disguise had actually worked. I learned early in my thieving career that once you get into somewhere and don't look dramatically out of place, nine guards in ten will assume you're supposed to be there. Even my interest in Saltlick wouldn't be suspicious in itself. Not all of Moaradrid's men would have seen a giant close up; passers-by had probably been stopping to gawp at him all night.

What worried me more was how Saltlick barely glanced up as I approached. Gruesome theories sprang to mind. Perhaps they'd burned his eyes out, or beaten him into a stupor? As I got close, I could see that I wasn't far from the truth. None of the wounds were deep or mutilating, but that was only because the intent had been pain rather than long-term damage. There were cuts beyond number,

bruises clustered on his arms and legs, even a few
raw-looking burns. A half-hearted effort had been
made to clean the worst of them but none were
bandaged, and some of the nastier gashes were still
leaking sluggishly.

"Saltlick."

I could have cried, seeing him like that. It was a
horrible sight – not just the physical damage, but his
utter helplessness.

"Saltlick, I'm here to rescue you."

Except perhaps for the twitch of an ear, there was
no response. Surely they wouldn't have deafened
him? Or cut his tongue out? Only an idiotic interrogator would make his victim unable to hear or
answer questions.

"Saltlick, old friend?"

It wasn't my imagination. There was definitely some
acknowledgement in the fractional tilting of his head.

"Old pal?"

"Go away."

The words began as a deep rumble and ended in a
whisper, like a landslide in reverse.

"Saltlick?"

"Leave alone."

I couldn't believe it. Here I was, risking my life, and
this was the thanks I received? All right, maybe I'd
contributed to his current predicament, but shouldn't
freeing him from slavery in the first place have guar-
anteed his eternal gratitude?

"I said I'm rescuing you, you pig-ugly monster!"
That came out louder than I would have liked.

Saltlick was going to cry out, I could sense it. With him sat down, I could just reach his head. I clamped both hands around his mouth.

"Don't!" I hissed. "I'll help you. We can even go find your family if you like. But if you call him back now then everything's lost."

I could feel the tension in Saltlick's muscles. After a moment, it eased, by the barest fraction. I hesitated, and then took my hands away.

"Go now," he said.

"Fine. Just let me…"

Saltlick flexed his wrists. The ropes snapped all together, and fell away in loops. He moved to stand. There was a creaking sound, and then the few remaining cords holding his torso split too.

"Oh. Right."

He stepped back. His face glistened and his chest was heaving. The exertion had reopened half a dozen cuts, and fresh blood mingled with a patina of sweat. "Must. Must go."

"That's more like it. Let me climb up and…"

Only then did it occur to me that they'd stripped the harness from his shoulders before they bound him. "Oh *shit*." No one would ever accuse me of bravery, but that night I was making a virtue of pragmatism. "Saltlick," I said, pointing back the way I'd come, "we're going that way, and you're going to have to run as fast as you can."

Saltlick's eyes followed my finger, and then came to rest on me. His fingers twitched. I realised he was sizing up whether he could carry me.

Well, there was no way I was about to die crammed beneath a giant's armpit. "Don't you dare! Run, keep running, and don't stop for anything."

When he still didn't move, I did instead, lurching off at my fastest sprint. A moment later and Saltlick fell in behind. I cursed through gritted teeth. Whatever chance we'd had of a quiet exit disappeared the moment those massive feet began hammering the ground. It sounded like cattle were stampeding in my wake. I knew he could have overtaken me in a single bound, but he hung back. All I could hear was the slap of his bare heels in the grass.

It was probably all anyone in the camp could hear.

My fears were confirmed by a muffled cry from our left, where the tents were clustered. Another followed it, more urgent. I could make out the rhythm of other feet now, drawing closer. Lights blossomed, close enough to show the faces of their bearers. In an instant, the camp filled with streaks of orange and flickering shadows.

Three figures appeared ahead, as if from nowhere. One was on horseback, a bow in his hands, an arrow nocked. One held a drawn scimitar, and the third carried their torch. They looked as worried as people about to confront a creature twice their size should be, but they weren't about to move. The archer sighted. He'd know as well as I did that a well placed shot would put Saltlick down long before he got close enough to fight back.

He squeaked, dropped his bow, and tumbled over. The torchbearer was forced to leap aside to avoid

him. The horse shied, catching the last man with a
flailing hoof, and he staggered backwards, blood
streaming from his ruined nose. By then we were on
them. The one still on his feet made a vague gesture
with his torch, until Saltlick swatted it away and
shoved him after it. As we plummeted past, I noticed
the arrow sticking from the archer's torso.

Before I could wonder how it had got there, the
shouting started. It was coming from our left: one or
two voices at first, then a high-pitched scream that
seemed to open the floodgates. Suddenly Moaradrid's
campsite was in an uproar. I couldn't begin to guess
what was happening. I wasn't about to wait and
find out.

A clatter of hooves started ahead, thundering rapidly nearer. It sounded like at least half a dozen
horsemen, more than enough to cut off our escape. I
was beginning to realise that the chaos on the edge
of camp must have something to do with Estrada. We
were close enough to the cliffs that a handful of good
archers could wreak substantial damage, at least until
their opponents realised and extinguished the torches
that were making them such easy targets. It was a
bold move.

It wasn't going to save us.

I ducked, in a hopeless bid to stay alive a little
longer. The riders plunged past in a deluge of noise,
so near I could feel the heat from their mounts'
flanks. I heard the animals complain as they wheeled
behind us, muffled shouts, and then hooves churning
wet ground as they urged forward. An instant later,

we were flanked on both sides, running in a corridor of equine bodies. I bent low and kept going, dizzied by the scream of my exhausted muscles, knowing it was useless.

An arm thrust towards me. I ducked, stumbled, and rolled headlong into the grass, yelping with pain. Saltlick swerved to avoid me and skidded to a halt, carving long ruts in the earth. Too exhausted to fight back, too exhausted to beg, I stared up at my murderer-to-be.

He looked surprisingly familiar.

"Damn you, Damasco," shouted Mounteban, leaning half out of his saddle to reach for me, "do you want to be rescued or not?"

CHAPTER NINE

I discovered later that there were a mere dozen archers perched on the cliff-side. However, they were all of them fine marksmen, and with their sturdy Castovalian bows and excellent vantage point, twelve men could wreak havoc. A hundred archers and a cavalry charge might have decimated Moaradrid's undersized army and ended the war in one fell swoop, but Estrada didn't have those resources to play with. Even chancing her few good bowmen was a terrible gamble.

It was a bold move, a desperate trade-off between future gain and immediate disaster. It had purchased Mounteban and his men as much as a minute in which to penetrate the camp, find us, and get out again.

It was nowhere near enough, of course.

"*This* is the plan? The mayor is a donkey-bred idiot, and you're worse for following her!"

Mounteban didn't bother to respond. He was focused on charging the last distance to the campsite border, and probably wondering how he was going to negotiate the small but well-armed force gathered to cut off our escape. It may also have been that my terrified grip around his waist made it hard to speak.

I wasn't about to let that stop me. "You're insane! We're all going to die. We could have cartwheeled out with more chance of success!"

I had more to say but suddenly no time to say it. A rider to our left went down in an incomprehensible blur of hooves and showering dirt. The beast's scream seemed to go on longer than it had any right to. I looked away, in time to see the man on my right jerk into thin air, as though suspended by ghostly hands, while his mount pitched from under him. He was spread-eagled on the ground before I saw the fletching jutted from his chest.

The squad of troops ahead was three deep now, painted in inhuman colours by the shivering torch-light. Not one of them looked like they planned to get out of our way. We might have been able to ride down the scimitar-wielding front row; but behind I could make out the cruel glint of spears.

Something passed us, a blur of movement against the sky. The other riders sheered away, barely in time. A rhythm like war drums drowned out our horses' thrashing hooves. I'd only just registered that the shadowy colossus was Saltlick when he struck the first line like a boulder rolled into a haystack.

Most of Moaradrid's men had the sense to dive out of the way. Those that didn't he batted aside. One sailed past us, his strangled cry echoing behind him, blood streaming from his forehead. A spear-bearer was brave and stupid enough to prod his weapon toward the giant. Saltlick caught it without breaking his stride, plucked up man and spear together and hurled them effortlessly over one shoulder. He broke through the last rank without pause and plunged on, indifferent and terrible as an avalanche.

Those Northerners still conscious and relatively whole were just beginning to reform when we struck in Saltlick's wake. One made a half-hearted swipe at us, and received Mounteban's boot in his face for thanks.

As we hurtled clear, I fought down a whoop of joy at the sheer outrageousness of our escape. That was until I glanced over my shoulder, in time to witness the remainder of our band meet the remnant of the defenders. Shocked and disordered though they were, they'd had an instant to recover. It was all they needed. The front rider was torn down by a forest of spears, which sprung up as if from nowhere. The other two reined in to avoid his staggering mount and lost – in quick succession – their momentum, their saddles, and their lives.

The exultation turned bitter in my throat.

If Mounteban knew what had occurred, he didn't let it show. He veered to the left, leaning low over his mount's neck, placing the bushes and short slope that bordered the road on our right. Saltlick, who'd come to a halt there, fell in behind. Mounteban threw us into another sharp turn, this time up the incline. Our horse nearly stumbled, then caught its footing and burst through the tree line.

I couldn't see what had guided Mounteban to this

particular spot, but there was a faint trail visible through the undergrowth. There was just space enough for us to pass at a canter. Saltlick pounded along behind us. As branches lashed into my face, I wished Mounteban had had the foresight to make him go first.

Almost immediately, I became aware of a light ahead. I couldn't identify its source until we came out right upon it. A crevice split the cliff face, men with torches guarding it to either side. They looked more surprised than pleased to recognise Mounteban. They'd likely had as much faith in our chances of survival as I had.

"The others?" one called.

"The same way we'll all be if you don't get inside," snapped Mounteban.

As my eyes began to adjust, I saw how great stones had been piled to both sides of the entrance, amidst mounds of broken foliage. The passage had obviously been sealed and hidden, and only recently cleared. When we dismounted and ducked into its mouth, I noticed ropes leading from the beams supporting the roof.

Further in were the two disgruntled mules to which they were attached. Mounteban's companions were trying to drive them forward, with hard slaps to the rump and a stream of curses. One chose to understand and strained forward, shifting its prop a hand's length inward. The other dug in its hooves, baring yellow teeth in a stubborn grin. The first heehawed appreciatively and followed its example.

Shouts and heavy footfalls growing louder behind told me we hadn't evaded our pursuers. An arrow thunking into the rightmost beam confirmed it.

Saltlick stood hunched inside the entrance, staring straight ahead. I called his name, expecting him to ignore me. Instead, he looked down. I hadn't appreciated quite how badly hurt he was until then. A fresh gash ran down his cheek to his shoulder, bleeding freely, and other cuts nearly as bad covered his torso and arms. He'd given worse than he'd received, though; the knuckles of each hand were wet with blood. I pointed to the beam beside him, the rope hanging slack from it. He seemed not to understand at first. His eyes travelled to the mules and hung there.

Another arrow hurtled from the darkness, embedding itself with a wet thud in his shoulder. He didn't appear to notice.

"Saltlick," I pleaded.

He shook his head, as though waking from a particularly unpleasant dream. He looked at me, and back at the beam. Then he reached with one huge hand and shoved it aside, as lightly as if it were a bundle of twigs. The roof moaned, and sank visibly. Dirt showered down, followed by pebbles and then rocks as big as melons. A couple struck Saltlick, leaving scarlet welts in their wake. He didn't flinch, let alone try to move.

The recalcitrant mule, panicked by the noise and dust, reconsidered its position. It drove forward, hauling the second, already weakened strut along with it. The wood split with a crack like thunder, and the ceiling dipped further.

I caught hold of Saltlick's free hand and hauled. He gazed at me, or perhaps through me. I realised I couldn't possibly move him if he didn't want to be moved. Then abruptly he strode forward, dragging me with him. It was just in time. An instant later, the cave mouth was gone.

I stood blind and choking, amidst dust so thick that it almost hid our frail torchlight. The earth grumbled and trembled around me, even after the last falling rock had rolled to a halt.

Someone nearby heaved a sigh of relief, and a voice said, "Come on. We're not home yet."

I recognised it as Mounteban's, though it sounded strange in the soupy air. The torch glow, still indistinct and a murky orange, contracted and darkened. I heard feet and hooves nearby, receding with the dimming light.

"Wait!" I called, and for my trouble got a lungful of dust that set me choking again.

I was still clutching Saltlick's fingers. They were unpleasantly sticky, his own blood mingled with that of Moaradrid's men. I didn't let go. In that filthy gloom, even the company of a gore-stained, sulking giant was better than being alone.

"Let's get after them," I muttered, striving not to suck down more dust.

I tugged at his hand. I might as well have tried to shift one of Mounteban's obstreperous mules by pulling its ears.

"I know you're hurt, but staying here won't help."

"Did bad."

Saltlick, as usual, spoke as if the words cost him the kind of effort usually associated with climbing mountains or swimming oceans.

"All right, I shouldn't have left you. But I came back, didn't I? I could just as easily have made a run for it."

"*Saltlick* did bad."

I stared, aghast – a waste of a good expression, since our torches were nearly out of sight. "Are you insane? You saved our lives."

"Bad. Not hurt. Not kill."

"You were defending yourself! And me, and that fat crook Mounteban. Can't you even do that?"

It struck me that there was a real risk of ending my life debating morality with a giant in a pitch-black mine shaft while my air slowly ran out. My mother had often told me I'd talk myself to death one day, and I wasn't about to prove her right.

Still, even that motivation possibly didn't excuse the ploy I fell back on. "Saltlick, if you don't come with me then who'll stop Moaradrid going after your family?"

He was moving almost before I finished the sentence. Running, I could just about keep up with his strides. It was a nerve-shattering business, with the constant risk of tripping and the passage creaking as if at any moment the rest might collapse. The space quickly narrowed, until Saltlick was jogging along crouched almost double, nearly blocking the scant light ahead. I could have reached from wall to wall by stretching my arms.

When it opened out again, I stepped into light so bright that I had to shade my eyes. I realised after a moment that it was only the torches. We'd caught up with Mounteban, his companions and the rebellious mules. They stood waiting in a small chamber, though after the confines of the passage it seemed vast. A contraption like a high-sided cart rested on a plinth in the centre, chains running in clusters from its beamed roof up into the dark. I decided it must be some sort of lifting platform.

Mounteban called, "Please, don't hurry. We only lost five of our best men saving your worthless hides."

It didn't seem politic to point out that I'd only needed saving because he and Estrada had sent me into the jaws of death. I stepped onboard, and Saltlick followed. Mounteban pulled on a cord and a bell clattered far above, the echoes reverberating frantically back down to us. We lurched upward, with a groan of timbers. The platform had been built to move ore or contraband, perhaps even men and mules, but full-grown giants were a new challenge, one it obviously didn't relish. Our progress was painfully slow. With nothing to see but damp, mottled rock and my gloomy companions, I considered giving up to the weariness creeping through my body and mind. It seemed an age since those hours of peace and quiet in my little cell. I thought of it longingly, and my eyelids drooped.

I was jolted out of half-sleep by the whole carriage rattling, end to end. We'd arrived in another, larger cavern. I couldn't tell if it was natural or man-made, but it was huge, with half a dozen exits leading off in every direction. The ceiling rose high above us, and then dipped off sharply towards the edges, like the roof of a pavilion. The cave was being used principally as a storage area, crates and barrels piled against the walls filling most of the space not taken up with the lifting platform and its mechanism. Light came from torches in plinths spaced around the walls. A couple of dozen men had turned to watch our arrival, all of them arrested in the midst of some chore: polishing weapons, oiling armour, or packing rucksacks and saddlebags from the sacks and boxes.

Marina Estrada stood with folded arms at the entrance of the lifting platform. "You made it," she said.

She sounded both glad and weary. If she'd been bedraggled when I'd last seen her, she now looked as if a strong breeze would break her in half. It had clearly been a trying night.

I wasn't about to make it any easier. "We made it, all right, no thanks to your hare-brained…"

Mounteban shoved me aside, hard enough that I nearly ended up in the dirt. The look of disgust he cast in my direction would have rotted wood. "I lost them all, Marina. I hope your scheme was worth that. I hope *he* was worth it."

He stormed past and disappeared into a passageway, followed by two-dozen sets of astonished eyes.

Estrada let out a sigh more like a shudder and said, so softly that she couldn't have meant for anyone to hear, "But you *did* make it."

She turned to me. "Nothing's ever worth the sacrifices." She shook her head. "Castilio understands that… or he will when he's had time to calm himself. You did well, Easie Damasco."

"I had no choice."

"If there's one thing I've learned over these last few days, it's that there are always choices, even when every one's terrible." She looked towards Saltlick. "Master Saltlick, isn't it? I'm honoured to have you here, and saddened by what you've had to endure."

Saltlick held her gaze for an instant, and then hung his head. There was something so dignified in her manner, just for that moment, that I couldn't tear my eyes away. Then the exhaustion took over her again, like a wave devouring an elegant pattern drawn in sand. Once more, all I could see was a woman in urgent need of a good night's sleep.

I could tell from her expression that there was scant hope of that. She turned to the motley crew lounging about the cave and called, "These tunnels will be in Moaradrid's hands by dawn. Everyone muster outside in ten minutes. Pass the word."

It was remarkable how they snapped to attention, as though lightning had darted the length and breadth of the chamber. In a few seconds, it was empty.

Estrada turned back to Saltlick and me and said, "You can't rest just yet, I'm sorry. What I told them is true; this refuge is lost to us. I've a proposition for you both, but I think you should hear what I have to say to the others first."

"Based purely on your record so far, the answer will probably be no."

"Perhaps. I can't force you this time. All I ask is that you'll listen."

"Well, I'm a little dizzy from blood loss and starvation. I'll do my best."

I thought Estrada smiled, though it was hardly more than a flicker. "There's food in those crates. We can't take it all with us, so help yourselves." She pointed to one of the cavern's numerous exits. "Just head that way in ten minutes time, and see if what I say makes sense."

I was too mesmerised by the thought of food to be sarcastic. I nodded instead. Estrada paced away, not in the direction she'd indicated but towards where Mounteban had gone.

I began to inspect the crates, glad that their arguments and politics were none of my concern. There was food, sure enough, and in abundance: bread, cheese, fruits and vegetables, goat meat, mutton, even a couple of live chickens dozing fitfully in a cage. There were butts of water and urns of wine, as well as a few bottles of some sour-smelling liquor.

Estrada was right, it couldn't possibly all be removed. It had evidently been gathered in a hurry, with little forethought. Most of the fresh goods wouldn't last another day. I settled for some of the less stale bread, a strong cheese that had stayed good within its husk of wax, and a few strips of dried meat. Such basic fare seemed to have become the staple of my diet lately, and it was pointless trying to fight it. There was a wooden cup beside one of the water butts; I filled and refilled it with wine, washing down every few mouthfuls of food, until I started to feel light-headed.

The entire meal had lasted perhaps two minutes. The average ravenous dog dines with more delicacy than I did then.

Once I felt I had my immediate physical requirements taken care of, I turned my attention to Saltlick. He hadn't moved since Estrada had spoken to him. "Will you stop moping! So you slapped about a couple of people who were trying to kill you. You'll get over it. We can go and rescue your family and everything will be fine."

Saltlick looked up. "Rescue?"

"Why not? But you need to keep your strength up. There's some dried grass piled in that corner, why don't you tuck in?"

Saltlick nodded profoundly, and followed my advice. His steps were almost sprightly as he crossed the cavern, and I wondered what had happened to change his mood so drastically. Whatever it was, I was pleased to see him plunge into his meal with gusto. He'd lost enough blood to fell an ox, and was still leaking from a couple of his more formidable wounds. He'd be no good to anyone if he dropped dead from exhaustion. If our fates were entwined, as it increasingly seemed they were, I wanted him as healthy and as much in one piece as possible.

While he ate, I took a minute to hunt out some new clothes. I discarded the ragged leather armour, which had already begun to chafe, and traded it for a plain hempen shirt I found in a sack of similar garments. After some thought, I traded the cloak in too, for a heavier one of indistinct grey. That done, I set to cramming as much of the remaining food about my person as I could, including a strapped wine skin that I slung over one shoulder. Estrada hadn't set any conditions on her generosity, so neither would I.

All the while, handfuls of Estrada's ragtag troop appeared from passage entrances and wandered past, in the direction she'd indicated. The parade was over by the time I'd finished, and Saltlick had turned to guzzling from an upturned water butt.

"Come on," I said, "It looks as though the after-dinner entertainment is about to begin."

The tunnel was short and ended in a wash of amber light, which resolved into a mixture of torches set on tripods and the first pale glimmers of dawn. A wide open area lay beyond, stretching on into an overhang that jutted from the mountainside. It was a stop upon the north-south mountain road. The trail was visible, snaking away in both directions, and this entrance – like the one far below – had evidently been hidden and only recently reopened.

Estrada stood on a small stage of crates near the southern end of the clearing, with her back to the mist-sodden void of the Castoval. Perhaps two hundred men were arrayed before her in clumsy ranks. They wore a haphazard variety of armour and carried an equally diverse range of weapons, from swords and bows to more eccentric choices. One had a blacksmith's hammer hoisted over his shoulder; another leaned on what was clearly a pitchfork.

I estimated that two thirds of them were professional militiamen or guardsmen of some degree. Of the
remainder, some were barely old enough to be away
from their mothers, and others looked too decrepit to
remember who their mothers were. Presumably
these were irregulars and volunteers who'd been
caught up in the retreat or recruited from Muena
Palaiya. One other enclave stood out, a tough-look-
ing mob with no hint of military discipline, who I
figured for cronies of Mounteban's. Mounteban himself was near the front, staring up at Estrada with an
expression I couldn't read.

Saltlick and I fell in on one flank, just in time.

"Friends," Estrada said, "I'm not here to comfort you."

That didn't strike me as a very promising beginning.

"I'm not here to tell you we're winning. I'm not
here to tell you we're safe. We were defeated two days
ago, in what may prove to be the decisive battle for
the freedom of the Castoval. Moaradrid will soon find
his way here, to our place of retreat. Therefore, we
must abandon this as well.

"I don't want to offer you hope. It's dangerous to
hope when we may all be dead soon, and our loved
ones enslaved by a monster who despises everything
we value. Because understand, if we can't find a way
to drive out Moaradrid that's what will happen. He
and his barbarians won't go away. They won't leave
us alone. There'll be no good end to this – unless we
make it for ourselves."

This was met with a vague murmur of agreement.
As popular as the sentiment undoubtedly was, it was

hard to take seriously when you looked around at the "we" in question.

At least Estrada had anticipated this. "We're too few now. We'd be outclassed and outnumbered, even against a fragment of Moaradrid's strength. So we run, without shame. We separate. We hide, if need be. If a final battle must come – as it must – we will choose the time. We'll choose the soil it's fought on. Because it's *our* soil, in *our* land.

"Until then, you have two missions. You must stay alive, and you must find others who'll fight for their home. We will go to every town and every village in the Castoval. We'll ask everyone we meet if they want to stay free, and what they'll risk for it. And they *will* join us. Because Castovalians have never worn a yoke, never called any man master, and they won't begin to now!"

A weary cheer arose this time.

I wanted to join in, but the noise stuck in my throat. I'd never been one for crowds, or noble causes for that matter. This one seemed more doomed than most. Could an army of well-intentioned peasants succeed where the combined garrisons of every town in the Castoval had failed? It seemed less than likely.

Estrada and Mounteban had been right about one thing. I'd only seen the war from my own small point of view. I certainly hadn't given much thought to what would happen if Moaradrid triumphed. The reality was like ice water splashed in my face. One phrase from Estrada's speech had lodged like a splinter in my mind: *there will be no good end*. That seemed undeniably true, for me at least.

I stood deep in thought as the assembly dissolved around me. I was vaguely conscious that Mounteban and Estrada were separating their shabby force into small bands, appointing leaders, setting destinations and meeting places. How many would simply go home? Was oppression by a foreign warlord truly worse than leaving your family to go hungry while you threw your life away in a hopeless battle?

I lost track of time. At one point, an old man dressed in a grubby, bloodstained poncho offered to clean and sew my wounds. I looked at him, confused, and then pointed to Saltlick. "It's him you want."

"You've been bleeding," he pointed out.

"He's been bleeding more."

The surgeon did as instructed, and I sank back into my fugue.

It was Estrada who eventually roused me. I realised that she was standing in front of me, that she was talking, and that she'd been doing both for some time. I tried to focus on what she was saying, and found it beyond me.

"I'm sorry," I said, "I haven't been paying the slightest attention."

She stopped, and looked at me with vague concern. "Are you ill?"

"I don't know. Possibly."

"You aren't badly hurt."

I thought about it. "No, I suppose not." Speaking to someone was helping to dispel the gloom that had fallen over me. Now I just felt phenomenally tired. "What were you saying?"

"I was asking for your help."

"Ah. You said you were going to do that."

Estrada nodded. "And you told me you'd probably say no."

"I did. So are you going to tell me what you have in store for us?"

"Not here. The fewer who know, the better. All I can say is that it will be over in a week, one way or another, and that I don't think any of it will work without you."

"I suppose it will be incredibly dangerous? Life-or-death scrapes, chases, people firing arrows at me, that sort of thing?"

She sighed. "Like I said, I can't force you. Even if I could, frankly I'm too tired to try."

I gazed at her. Marina Estrada, one-time mayor of a backwater town, now the last surviving general of the Castoval. A worn out woman overdue a wash and some clean clothes, trying desperately to do the right thing while knowing how doomed it almost certainly was. I remembered the night I'd spent in Moaradrid's camp before the battle, the fear I'd seen in every eye, the hopelessness of men about to hurl themselves over the brink into darkness. I thought, finally, about what I'd overheard Moaradrid say only a few hours ago. It hadn't really penetrated at the time – how he planned to march on the capital, to overthrow the royal court.

Would he stop there? Even if he did, what would be left behind?

I forced myself to grin, though I'd never felt less like it in my life. "Why not," I said. "It's not as if I have anything better planned."

CHAPTER TEN

My newfound conviction might have lasted all morning if someone had found a way to keep me awake. Sleep deprivation will do strange things to you, and if inexplicable bravery isn't recognised amongst them then it should be.

Estrada wasn't to know my commitment was purely symptomatic, of course. There was a glint in her eye, as though she'd won some personal victory, as she told me, "We can't leave for a while yet. We need to pack what supplies we can and make sure everyone understands their part. Despite what I said, it will take Moaradrid a while to find a way through those caves without the lifting platforms. You two should try to catch some sleep."

That last sentence might as well have been some magical incantation. I just managed to get out, "That's a fine idea," before my chin was lolling on my chest, blackness deep and heavy as an ocean swelling over me.

I woke to a vague memory of oblivion so fathomless it seemed criminal to abandon it. I felt refreshed, even though I could tell from the angle of the shadows that no more than a couple of hours had passed. I'd slept standing up, just as Estrada had left me. Saltlick still slumbered, curled with his back against the cliff wall and snoring cacophonously.

I could see the preparations were drawing to a conclusion. A dozen carts had appeared from somewhere, and were dangerously overloaded with barrels and crates. Perhaps forty of the men, including Mounteban and his ruffians, were on horseback, with the others gathered on foot, smoking pipes or talking in low voices. A smaller minority, Estrada amongst them, were coordinating with loud cries and – when a box tipped or a cord snapped – even louder reprobation.

What had I got myself into? There was something utterly desperate about the scene. Even if they made it off the mountainside, that caravan of the weak and wounded stood about as much chance against Moaradrid as a horsefly against a stallion. In a certain light, it might have seemed heroic. Beneath a leaden sky, in the early hours of a rain-spattered morning, it looked pitiful and hopeless.

Any thought of noble self-sacrifice vanished in that instant, like a glass of wine poured into a mill pool. Moaradrid would win. He'd *already won*. Did I really want to ally myself with this last pathetic cyst of rebellion, which would undoubtedly be lanced at any minute? The only sensible move was to place as much distance between them and myself as I possibly could. Even Saltlick seemed a lightning rod for trouble. There was no doubt things were about to get bleaker for the Castoval, no doubt that under Moaradrid its days of carefree independence were over. Nevertheless, there would always be a corner where someone like me could pursue his occupations.

There would always be another rock to hide under.

Before I could wonder where that last thought had come from, Estrada – who'd been busying herself at the head of the caravan – happened to notice me. "Are you awake, Damasco?" she called. "Come on, you can ride up here."

That was the last thing I wanted to hear. My burgeoning plan would have put me at the tail of the wagon train, where I could slip off without drawing too much attention. The road we were on led north and south, threading most of the eastern range. Northward it would eventually cut into the mountains, arriving beyond the pass at the port of Goya Mica. The southerly path would split in a few miles, with one route leading to the larger coastal town of Goya Pinenta, the other declining sharply to come out some distance behind Muena Palaiya. Presumably, that was the direction in which we were headed. I could find my way onto a boat from either port, though, and that opened a world of possibilities. I might even leave the Castoval altogether. What was it to me, after all?

Estrada was clearly growing impatient. I tugged at Saltlick's arm, and called, "Wake up you brute, we're leaving!"

His great head drifted from his breast, one watery eye blinked open, and he yawned. "Ghhrnrr?"

"I said, get up. Look, the mayor's waiting for us."

Saltlick unfolded his limbs with a sigh that rolled and echoed around the rocks. He too looked better for a rest. The old man had done a good job of bandaging his many cuts and scrapes, and none of them were showing fresh blood. His skin had lost some of its pallor, and his movements were less pained than they'd been a few hours ago.

I led him towards the front cart, where Estrada had turned her attention to retying loose ropes. Hearing our approach, she turned and smiled. "Saltlick," she said, "you look better. We haven't any seat big enough for you, I'm afraid. Can you walk alongside?"

Although she only got a nod in return, I could tell Saltlick enjoyed the way she spoke to him and that he liked her for it. He came to a halt and lapsed into his usual pose of relaxation: legs apart, feet splayed, eyes exploring some indeterminate spot ahead. I got the impression he could have stood like that for days if the need arose. Personally, I liked the idea of riding on a cart. After horseback, giantback and my own sore feet, it seemed the height of luxury. I swung up and settled myself upon the seat with a deep groan of satisfaction. If I was stuck with Estrada and her foolhardy would-be rebels for the time being, I might as well make the most of it.

Estrada gazed over the length of the caravan behind us and, finding everything to her satisfaction, called back, "Let's march!"

It soon became apparent that "march" was a gross exaggeration for what was actually taking place. Two hundred drunks trying to find their way home through a swamp would have produced a similar spectacle. The old and wounded were quickly outpaced by the young and hearty, creating a concertina effect of surges and long waits. The cart drivers, struggling with the idiosyncrasies of the mountain trail, constantly threatened to overturn their vehicles or squash errant feet. Most of the horses were clearly unused to crowds and seemed determined to get in everyone's way.

For the first couple of hours, no one talked except to curse or shout. All efforts were devoted to keeping the parade moving at a reasonable pace, without causing or incurring injury.

For my part, I was happy to alternate brief, blissful naps and – when the jolting became too much – entertaining myself with watching the shambolic march behind us. I sipped from my wine flask, nibbled a piece of goat's cheese, and in general found that my spirits were steadily lifting. It was the closest I'd been to relaxation since my short imprisonment. I wasn't about to spoil it by worrying about the uncertain future.

Estrada, on the other hand, seemed to be edging towards a nervous breakdown. I could tell she didn't have much experience in handling a cart, or understand the temperament of beasts of burden. It wasn't long before the two horses, who were bloody-minded enough to be cousins of the mules I'd met earlier, were being regaled with some distinctly unladylike language. In between outbursts, she sat with gritted teeth, staring fixedly at the road as if she expected it to disappear at any moment.

After a particularly vehement outburst, I said, "Let me take over."

"I can manage."

"You're barely conscious. If you keep on the way you're going, we'll be down long before anyone else – and in more pieces."

From the look she gave me, I thought she was about to wrap the reins around my throat.

"Fine, I shouldn't impugn your driving skills. You're doing quite well for a woman who hasn't slept in who knows how long, and probably hasn't eaten in days either. Trust me, though, you can only keep that up for so long. I'd rather not be sitting beside you when you collapse."

"You're welcome to walk." Then she sighed, and in a fractionally gentler tone, continued, "All right. Just for an hour, then wake me and we'll call a halt. There are plenty of people behind us in worse shape than me."

She shifted to the far side and handed over the reins. I barely had time to catch them before her head was lolling, a trickle of saliva working its way from her lower lip to the tune of rattling snores.

At first, I didn't have much more luck with the intransigent horses than she'd had. I realised after a while that, left to their own devices, they'd trot along quite happily. I only needed to intervene every ten minutes or so, when they decided I'd forgotten about them and they could get away with grinding to a halt.

The way through the pass to Goya Pinenta would be relatively busy at this time of year, but Goya Mica in the north had declined as a fishing port, and this stretch of road had fallen into disrepair as a result. Still, it was safe enough if you were careful. Steep sections were rare, and a lip of rock on our right separated us from the void beyond.

The day was becoming pleasant; the watery sunlight was surprisingly warm, but a sharp breeze kept the temperature comfortable even as noon drew nearer. With little to do except try to make myself comfortable on the jolting seat, I amused myself by listening to whatever snatches of conversation I could catch. The general tone was cheerful, with swapping of jokes and snatches of song. Everyone's mood seemed to be improving. Everyone's, that is, except Mounteban's: whenever the hubbub got too loud he'd shout, "That's right, make certain to enjoy yourselves," or "It's not as though we're fleeing for our very lives!"

He had a point. Without his interjections, the procession would have made even more feeble progress. Still, it was irritating, and spoiled the mood. I was glad when Estrada started awake, gazed around blurrily, and then crouched in her seat and cried, "Everyone halt! Let's take thirty minutes rest."

Stopping was more disastrous than starting, with horses running into the backs of carts and carts veering too close to the edge or threatening to disgorge their contents into the road. It was a good five minutes before everyone was settled and calm. Estrada got down and began arranging the distribution of food, checking on the wounded, making sure that cargo was secured and generally playing mother hen to her bedraggled brood. She did everything rapidly and ably, yet without appearing to hurry or neglecting anyone. It was hard to imagine a more militant approach keeping them together as well as her quiet but firm ministrations.

I had to remind myself she was likely shepherding them to their doom.

Since he was too bashful to ask, I spent a minute finding out where Saltlick could get some straw and a quantity of water capable of slaking his thirst. Then I settled down to my own lunch, which I was careful to take from the caravan's supplies rather than my personal stash. However things turned out, they probably wouldn't need them for much longer.

Sitting there chewing on some unidentifiable dried meat, I felt oddly detached, like a visitor in some strange city where the customs and even the language were different. Estrada had been right last night, despite my protestations. I *was* a petty thief. I had no place amongst men such as these. Heroics and grand gestures were all well and good for those with something to gain, but I'd be just as unwelcome whoever ended up in charge. Estrada might need me now. Would she be so glad of my presence when I resumed my trade in her freshly liberated Castoval?

We'd been stopped no more than a quarter of an hour when Mounteban rode to the middle of the train and called, "Everyone up! Try and remember our survival depends on haste."

A rumble of protest arose from the entire column, particularly towards the back where those least capable of hurrying had congregated. A few stumbled to their feet. Many others didn't. Seeing that, Mounteban's face reddened.

Estrada, pacing rapidly towards him from where she'd been helping the old surgeon fix bandages, said, "A little longer won't hurt, Castilio."

"Every moment we waste brings us closer to being slaughtered like pigs."

"The sick and injured are exhausted. Some haven't eaten. If we keep on like this we won't need Moaradrid to finish us." Her voice was hard, and rising.

Mounteban looked as if he was about to tell her what she could do with her sick and wounded. Instead, he made a choking sound, as though forcing down the half-formed words, and muttered, "It's on your head, Marina."

"Do you think I don't know that?"

Estrada let the break extend for another ten minutes before she returned to the cart and shouted, "March on."

This time there were no complaints. Everyone managed to get started without accident, as though to express their silent support. I wondered if Estrada and Mounteban might have worked it all out before hand, a sly take on the old "good guard, bad guard" routine. But unless she was an extraordinarily fine and committed actress, the black cloud over Estrada's expression made that unlikely.

As the afternoon wore on, matching clouds formed to join it in the sky above. The heat became humid and oppressive, the breeze died altogether, and it was obvious another storm was on the way. That prospect, given our already precarious circumstances, did more to hurry the pace than anything Mounteban could have done or said.

I found myself becoming increasingly bored, my good humour evaporating in the clammy air. Estrada was uncommunicative, and Saltlick plodded along with his head down, as interesting and companionable as the stone behind him.

Once again, I felt the sense of having blundered into unsuitable company. This time it occurred to me that, of everyone there, it was Mounteban I had most in common with. It wasn't so long ago that we'd been… well, not friends, but acquaintances, and compatriots in the odd venture. I couldn't see much justification for his recent behaviour towards me, except a desire to show off how damned honest and sanctimonious he'd become.

Thinking about that, spurred on by the uncomfortable silence and the sultry air pressing down on me, I grew more and more irritable. Finally, I hopped down from the seat. I nearly blundered into Saltlick, cursed him loudly and meandered back through the throng of sweaty, stumbling bodies. When I reached Mounteban, where he rode amidst his gang of ruffians, I fell into step beside him. "How goes it, Mounteban?"

"Piss off, Damasco."

"That's no way to talk to an old friend."

"I'll bear that in mind if I meet one."

I resisted a powerful urge to drag him from his mount and kick him in the teeth. Given that he was surrounded by bodyguards, and given that every one of them looked as though they could kill me in a dozen interesting ways without stretching their imaginations, it was probably for the best. "What's your problem with me, Mounteban? All right, we were never friends, but I didn't realise we'd become enemies."

"You belong in my past. I'd sooner you'd stayed there."

"Oh, of course. Because you're the big hero now. I heard you'd put your lifetime of misdeeds behind you, only I never quite believed it."

"And what do you think now?"

"I think, 'once a thief, always a thief'. But perhaps that's just me." Weariness was getting the better of my irascibility. I added, less than honestly, "Look, I didn't come back here to argue. We'll be parting soon, and I thought we might do it on better terms than we've managed so far."

Mounteban spat into the dirt. His tone was only a touch less aggressive as he replied, "Probably you can't understand a man wanting to put his past behind him."

"My past is nothing to write home about. I'd be the first to admit I'd be better off without it."

While this was probably true, my saying it had more to do with a sudden realisation. I was actually curious about Mounteban. What could have happened to make him hook up with this doomed bunch? In his heyday, he'd have been more likely to slaughter them for gold fillings.

"But you," I went on, "it takes courage to step out from the shadow of your own notoriety."

I was pleased with that, even if I wasn't entirely sure what it meant.

Mounteban also seemed caught between suspicion and accepting it as an honest compliment. His voice low, he said, "Marina approached me some weeks ago now, when Moaradrid's invasion wasn't much more than tavern gossip. She saw it coming though. She said she was talking to figures of standing in the community, whatever their trade – because a threat to the Castoval was a threat to all of us."

"She was very astute. From what I heard, Moaradrid had marched the length of the Castoval before most of the town leaders noticed anything was amiss."

"She *was* astute. It took me a while to see it though. Fortunately, she was insistent as well. Still, most of those she talked to are probably cowering beneath their tables in Muena Palaiya right now."

"You did a brave thing joining up with her, Mounteban," I said. I offered him my hand.

"Well, perhaps you're not entirely a coward yourself, Damasco." He didn't sound convinced, but he shook anyway.

As I hurried back towards my place at the head of the column, I congratulated myself on a job well done. Mounteban's enmity had been making life difficult, and if I'd done anything to rid myself of it then that was worth a little false praise. Having him on

side could only make life easier until I found a means
to slip away. I'd also gleaned some valuable insights
into what had occurred over the last few days. Perhaps best of all, I'd confirmed a suspicion I'd been
harbouring for some time.

Castilio Mounteban was helplessly in love with his
good lady mayor.

I hopped back up to the driver's board and grinned
at Estrada, who responded with a scowl of baffled irritation. I felt like a child with a secret, and had an
appropriately infantile urge to drop hints. Estrada's
expression soured my brief pleasure.

In fairness, she had a right to be on edge: heavy
drops were beginning to fall, and the clouds above
had congealed into a single ominous mass. The road
might not be too bad when it was dry; if it became
slippery then casualties would be all but unavoidable.

I breathed a sigh of relief as we edged around the
next corner, and heard Estrada do the same. Close
ahead was the point where our road met the east-
west pass. I could see the gap in the mountainside
where the trail to Goya Pinenta began. Both ways
joined at a wide intersection, and beyond that, the
main road twisted back on itself, continuing beneath
us to the floor of the Castoval. The road would be in
better repair after the junction, even fenced in places.
We should be relatively safe there, storm or no storm.

Given the pace at which we were crawling along, it
still took us a while to reach the junction. There was
some traffic there, as I'd predicted, mostly irate fish
merchants from the coast hurrying to get their produce

into Muena Palaiya while it was still fresh. Our pace slackened even further as we struggled to join the flow. No one was very pleased to see two hundred bedraggled armed men descending upon them. Some cursed us; others, assuming we were bandits, tried to appease us with offerings from their reeking cargo. Estrada asked me to take the reins again and passed a few minutes on foot, trying to retain order while propitiating our new travelling companions.

I found myself in the uncharacteristic position of leader. It crossed my mind to lash the horses and try to make my escape, but if I hadn't driven straight over the edge then Mounteban would have caught up with me in no time. I concentrated instead on setting a steady pace as we drew closer to the horseshoe bend that led into the last long decline. It was disconcertingly tight. The volume of swearing behind me increased tenfold as I crept into the turn.

Once the curve began to level out I could see the floor of the Castoval spread before me. Muena Palaiya lay ahead, chalk-white roofs tumbling leisurely down the slope, looking too small to be a town at this distance despite its high walls. The hillside descended gradually towards us on the town's south side, cut into terraces of vineyards and small farms. Beyond the road that hugged its western edge the decline dipped more steeply to the woodland below and on toward the Casto Mara, which flowed grey and frothy in the pounding rain.

I looked up and to the right. The road we'd taken was partially visible, a darker vein hanging tenaciously from the mountainside. Stood out on that vein, some distance behind, a file of miniscule black forms stole towards us. I couldn't make out details. I didn't need to. I was about to cry out when some urge made me look back down the other leg of the highway, towards Muena Palaiya. The shout strangled off in my throat. A matching procession was creeping along the road that threaded down to meet our own.

Estrada picked that moment to clamber up beside me. She looked at me bemusedly – the cart had ground almost to a standstill – and followed my line of sight.

"They've found us!"

The way those three words galvanised her tiny army was something to behold. It was hard to believe they were the same men who'd been singing, joking and tripping over each other's feet a few minutes before. The fish-merchants seemed even more alarmed by the transformation, as the rabble around them struck up a marching pace, as riders and carters stopped to scoop up those slowed down by injuries.

The cloud-piled sky chose that moment to shatter, with a cruel gash of lightning and a rumble that shook the earth beneath our feet. A liquid wall fell with the abruptness of a stage curtain. Immediately, the world was reduced to nothing but the road scudding by beneath us and rain so drenching that we might have been standing in a river.

Estrada lashed our horses, and they surged into motion. It was impossible to see ahead. Moaradrid's two approaching forces were utterly veiled from view, as was the tail of our own column. Though it was nowhere near evening it seemed like the most starless night, except when lightning lit the world blue-white.

When the thunder was silent, all I could hear was the rattle of the cart, the horses, and Saltlick pounding the road beside us. Though we couldn't have been travelling that quickly, I was convinced we'd hurtle over the edge at any moment. I gripped my seat and stared into the blackness, flinching at every slight turn and every flash or rumble.

It seemed miraculous that we reached the valley floor in one piece. It was stranger still to look back and see our party congealing out of the rain behind us, a battalion of sodden ghosts. Everyone had made it in one piece, as far as I could tell. It wasn't long before they'd surrounded us on every side, blocking the crossroads that joined the mountain road with Muena Palaiya and the rest of the Castoval. Mounteban loomed beside us, shaking water from his beard with fierce jerks of the head.

"Moaradrid's brigands are close," he roared.

"I know. It's now or never."

"They're not ready. It won't work."

"We have no choice."

Mounteban just nodded.

Estrada stood on the driver's board, rain-lashed, silhouetted against the pitchy sky. At the top of her lungs she called, "If we wait, they'll take us. So we separate. You have your instructions. We'll meet again four days hence at the designated place – or the Castoval is lost. Every man is on his own now. Good luck!"

The cheer that met her words seemed oddly wild amidst the storm. The crowd fell apart immediately, as though cleaved by some outside force. Estrada dropped back into her seat and drove the horses forward. Mounteban, his riders, and the greater part of the throng fell in around us.

Distant, hardly distinguishable from the drumming rain, I heard the pound of hooves.

Moaradrid's forces were closing – and here we were, as helpless as we'd ever been.

CHAPTER ELEVEN

Had there been anyone on that storm-lashed road to see us go by, we'd have made a strange and alarming spectacle.

First would have thundered past a convoy of riders and overloaded carts, all travelling far too fast for the drenched road, gear rattling, maybe a loosened barrel tumbling free. If lightning had chanced to flicker, they'd have seen the strain stamped on every face. They'd surely have gaped at the monster near the rear, struggling to keep pace, oblivious to the rain exploding from its back and head.

Then the last rider would have hurtled by. The noise – of clattering wheels, hooves, straining wood – would have faded.

Soon after, no more than a minute, the other horsemen would have appeared; looming out of the tempest, no attempt made to disguise weapons slung on backs and drumming against thighs. They'd have been travelling perilously fast too, and urging their mounts to even greater efforts – though without success. They'd have passed more quickly, like a moon-shadow. Not one would have so much as looked aside.

Moaradrid's men had been riding hard all day, and their horses were far from fresh. They simply weren't fast enough to overtake us. If they'd been closer at the start then it would have gone differently. But we'd lost more than half our following over the first two hours, as men peeled away at every junction, the wounded and old limping off towards farmhouses and hamlets. By the time they'd closed the gap, there was no one left on foot, and we were moving as fast as they were. All they could hope for was to wear us down.

And that was how it went for the longest time. They came closer, we pulled away, on and on through the dark and cold and endless rain.

Mounteban claimed that the force from Muena Palaiya had come after us and the rest had followed those who'd fled southward. No one apart from him found it important. In fact, Estrada would barely speak to him. Straight after the separation at the crossroads, they'd loudly fallen out. She'd asked why he was with us and not the other party as planned, and he'd grunted some excuse about choosing the wrong direction in the rain.

"Don't lie to me."

"Fine. I came to protect you."

"What makes you think I need protecting?"

"The fact that if you die, everything's lost."

"And them? What about them?"

That was the last she said to him, except for the occasional terse command. If not for that, even the decision to flee might have been open to question. Mounteban told her – soon after their argument, and possibly just to draw her out – that our pursuers were only a scouting party, no more than thirty men. If he was right, it meant we'd just about outnumber them in a fight.

"Of course most of our archers went the other way, so they'd have us there… but an ambush, perhaps…"

"We keep running," Estrada replied. And that was the end of that.

Those were the last words anyone spoke for hours. There was nothing to discuss. There was only the chase: its muted sounds, glimpses of shadowed forms behind us, and the ceaseless, hammering fear. They were gaining or we were, and each man could judge only for himself with a hundred half-snatched glances. With least to do, I kept a lookout more than anyone. I strained until my neck ached and my eyes burned. I couldn't see horses or men behind, only a single dark blot. I watched it grow larger, grow smaller – there was nothing else in the world.

Then suddenly it was gone. I didn't believe it. It seemed far more likely that the fault was with my vision. I strained until tiny lights seemed to pop and dance in the blackness. Still there was nothing, only empty road trailing into the rain-soaked night.

Someone called, "They've given up."

I kept staring. It was a trick, a trap. At any moment, that blot would reappear, maybe far closer.

Then we struck an incline that brought us higher than the road behind. At the same time, a little blurred moonlight fell in ribbons through the clouds. There they were. They'd fallen far behind; there could be no doubt of it.

Mounteban sent one of his bodyguards to investigate. He was a small, intensely quiet man that I'd barely noticed until then. There was something about him that made me want to avert my gaze – and now that I couldn't help but look, a quality to his movements that made the hairs on my neck stand up. He soon returned, and whispered to Mounteban, who related that their tracks made an about-turn and disappeared the way we'd come.

"It's far from good news," he added. "We've won a few hours' peace, that's all. The only reason they'd let us go is to report our position to Moaradrid, and to gather more men."

There followed a hasty meeting, to decide whether we'd chance making camp or try to continue. It was obvious from a glance around what the answer had to be. Everyone looked fit to drop, and a few were already nodding in their saddles. Estrada's decision, however, was to carry on until the next crossroads. There we'd separate our numbers again, and keep going for an hour more to give everyone time to spread out. That way, if an attack came in the night then at least some might escape.

I couldn't fault her logic. Still, the rest of the journey was torture. Everyone's nerves were frayed past tolerance by the day's events. We were soaked to the skin, so that the noise of teeth chattering seemed to drown out even the clack of hooves. I was one of the better off, having slept and eaten at least. Yet even I wanted nothing more than to tumble into the dirt, where a cartwheel running over my head might put an end to my misery. Estrada's face was a mask, white as bone. I couldn't imagine what was keeping her going.

When we eventually reached the crossroads, a gallows stood waiting for us, outlined skeletally against the sky. Though it probably hadn't been used in years, it reminded me of that noose around my neck outside Moaradrid's camp, of kicking frantically to find purchase on thin air. The men seemed wraithlike as they slunk away, lit by the barest sliver of a moon. Their horses and cartwheels, which had made such a racket before, were muffled almost to silence now.

It crossed my mind that they hadn't survived the battle after all – that I'd been travelling in the company of phantoms too stubborn to accept their fate. Even if it weren't literally true, it summed up Estrada's resistance as well as anything. Sitting perfectly still beside me, her hair fluttering from gaunt features, she could easily have been some ghostly harridan risen to gather us up.

Another thought made me shudder: had I really been rescued from that hanging tree? Or was this all some absurd final torment?

I felt saner once we'd put the crossroads behind us, though the close-packed woodland to either side, with its abrupt nocturnal noises, was hardly more comforting. With nothing to see except huddled trees I found it difficult to keep track of whether I was asleep or awake. If we jolted through a particularly deep rut I'd start as though waking from a nightmare, only to discover everything exactly as I remembered it.

I didn't even notice when we finally did stop, until Estrada said, "This should be far enough."

Her voice was barely a croak. I doubted she could have gone further, whether it was enough or not.

There was a clearing to our left, down a shallow verge. We managed to lead the horses there, though they protested bitterly. The wagon, drawn level against the tree line, would be well hidden until sunrise. We unshackled the cart and led the horses beneath the canopy, where they set wearily to munching the short grass.

There was no possibility of lighting a fire. There were no dry clothes to replace our wet ones. There'd have been no point, anyway, for though the rain had stopped the ground was saturated. All Estrada could offer were a few threadbare blankets. No one had the energy to eat – no one except Saltlick, who immediately began stripping fistfuls of leaves. I lay shivering for a long time, drifting in and out of fitful sleep that was punctuated by his steady chomp-chomp, close yet distant-seeming, like the grind of a colossal sea on granite shoals.

I woke, with a terrible thudding in my head, to darkness. There was no noise, not even the shriek of night birds or click of crickets. As my eyes began to adjust, I thought I could make out the palest glimmer of dawn beyond the wooded canopy. Every muscle in my body ached, and my nose was dribbling with cold.

The only thing in my line of sight was Saltlick's back. Someone had thrown the awning from the cart over him, though it only covered as far as his stomach. There was nothing in the scene that made me want to stay conscious. I scrunched my eyes shut, in the vague hope of finding sleep once more.

Something tapped my shoulder – exactly the sensation, I realised, which had woken me in the first place. I rolled over, and found myself staring into Mounteban's dirt-streaked features. His one good eye narrowed. He placed a warning finger to his lips.

I sat carefully, partly to avoid making noise and partly to ease my thudding head. There was just enough light for me to see that everyone but myself and Saltlick were already awake, and crouched together in the centre of the clearing. No, not everyone. The silent man who'd made me so uneasy yesterday was absent.

Once he was sure of my attention, Mounteban pointed towards the road. I could see Estrada in the corner of my vision, attempting to wake Saltlick with minimal success.

I mouthed to Mounteban, "what?" and then, "soldiers?"

He nodded.

His scout materialised at that moment from behind the bole of a nearby birch, hardly two paces from us. He gestured towards the road as Mounteban had, and then swept his hand westward.

"Gone?" Mounteban whispered, and the silent man dipped his head.

Estrada, having succeeded in rousing Saltlick, crept towards us. "There'll be more. We can't use the highways."

"I can guide you cross-country," said Mounteban. There was a hint of triumph in his voice.

"There's no time."

"We're about a day from the river. We might be able to find a boat."

"Then what?"

"Then… I don't know, perhaps we could ask its owner if they'd consider selling. What did you think I meant? If you find my past so unsavoury, Marina, perhaps you shouldn't have recruited me in the first place." Mounteban's voice rose, until by the end he was almost shouting. He glared around red-faced, caught between shame and anger. The silence seemed tangible as he and Estrada glared across the clearing at each other.

For once, it was she who backed down. "You're right," she said. "We should get going."

We spent the next few minutes unloading supplies from the cart and distributing them amongst packs and the saddlebags of the two horses. It was cellar-like in the gloom beneath the trees, the trunks resembling columns and the foliage a dripping ceiling that creaked with subterranean stresses. A mouldy odour rising from the damp peat floor only worsened the effect. As we flitted from one arch to another, glancing furtively towards the road, the tension seemed to rise like stagnant water, until it felt as though one snapped twig would bring catastrophe upon us.

Things improved once we got moving. We ate on the march, and if the food was barely edible then the effort of eating was at least a distraction. Light was breaking in the east by the time I'd choked down my last mouthful, and walking had gone some way to warming me and drying my clothes.

We made an odd parade. Saltlick hung at the back, where he trudged along stolidly, focusing all his effort into moving with a minimum of noise. Estrada, who'd begun at the front with Mounteban, fell back after an hour to join him.

I did my best to maintain an equal distance between them and Mounteban's ruffians, the only remainder of our original entourage. I'd been trying to ignore them, but I couldn't help paying furtive attention now that we were intimate associates.

It was partly that I'd belatedly recognised one of them: the bull-shaped character towards the back was the Northerner who'd been on the door at the Red-Eyed Dog. However, I'd also been giving some thought to the question of Mounteban's disconcerting scout. That might be his current trade, but it hadn't always been. He was too small, too lightly built, and his skin wasn't the leathered bronze it would be from a lifetime in the open.

I could think of only one other vocation that required his peculiar skill set, and it was one even career criminals got nervous around. Before Mounteban had supposedly gone straight, I'd occasionally heard his name linked – in the most privately whispered conversations only – with that of a man named Synza. He'd been discreetly referred to as Mounteban's problem-solver; but always with the implication that the absolute last thing you wanted was to find yourself the problem in question.

I had a horrible feeling Synza and I were now travelling companions.

Yesterday afternoon we'd left behind the terraces that joined the Hunch and Muena Palaiya to the valley floor. During the night, we'd penetrated the wooded region that continued to the riverbank, and which would eventually congeal into the forest of Paen Acha to the south. The whole region was pocked with farms and villages, even a couple of small towns, and tracks and roads laced it in every direction. For all that, it was scarcely populated, and it wasn't too hard to travel unnoticed, especially when most of our party had a proven record in that department.

Mounteban certainly knew the region well, no doubt from his days of shifting contraband between Muena Palaiya and the river. We followed a succession of paths for most of the morning, travelling through scrubby woodland or occasional meadows of high grass littered with bobbing thistles and bright splotches of wildflower. The sun was cool and watery, the sky still partly overcast. At least the rain held off, and the exertion of walking kept my temperature comfortable. There seemed little point in rationing my supplies, so I continued to eat as I walked, and sipped from one of my flasks.

It seemed we must have walked across half the valley by lunchtime, and I groaned when Mounteban called a halt to tell us, "We're a third of the way to the river."

My calves were aching fiercely by then, and the pain was beginning to creep up through my thighs and into my spine. I was pleased when he added, "Does anyone need to stop?"

Just as I was about to answer, Estrada said, "We're fine, Castilio".

I glared at her.

"Good. If we can keep this pace up into the night, we should have time to camp for a few hours. They'll have discovered the cart and horses by now. Even if they find our trail, though, they don't know the valley like I do."

I'd forgotten our abandoned cart. In fact, the whole notion of pursuit had receded to a vague wariness in the back of my mind, a sense that roads and inhabited areas were things best avoided. I suddenly felt less inclined to rest, for all my aches and pains.

As the sun rolled past the meridian and the afternoon wore on, there came other, more sinister reminders of Moaradrid's presence. First was a column of coal-black smoke rising up to our left, a few miles distant, though close enough that I could smell the pungency of burnt wood mixed with other less obvious odours. It might have been perfectly innocent. Certainly, Mounteban paid it little attention, except perhaps to hurry our pace a little. Yet I couldn't help thinking of the destruction of Reb Panza. Our pursuers wouldn't hesitate to burn a few villagers out of their homes if they imagined one of them might know where we were. Whatever the truth, the sight made me shiver.

If the second incident a couple of hours later was almost as ambiguous, it at least succeeded in getting Mounteban's attention. We were following a trail along the ridge of a hill, with a dense line of pines upon the crest and stunted aspens piercing the shale of the bank descending on our right, when a noise froze us all in place: the harsh staccato of dogs barking.

Mounteban took one brief glance over his shoulder, as though expecting to see hounds barrelling towards us. Then he cried, "Run!"

He was the first to take his own advice. The rest of us followed close behind. There was something insistent in the noise, as though the beasts were actually trying to draw our attention. I was surprised by how easily running came to my racked muscles – a minute before the idea would have seemed preposterous. Every bark seemed to quicken my feet a little more.

A minute later, and my panic was starting to subside. My sprint had turned into a clumsy stagger. Pain had returned with excruciating force, and every lungful of air seemed to have been drawn over hot coals. It was hopeless trying to work out whether the dogs were getting nearer. Though their frantic barking hadn't paused, it was the only sign of them we'd had.

I'd thought we were fleeing aimlessly, but I realised Mounteban had had an object in mind after all. A rocky indent split the bank, close ahead between the trees. When I reached the edge, I saw a wide stream gurgling through the gap, and meandering on down the hillside. Mounteban and his men were already wading, the clear water lapping as high as their knees. I plunged in, biting off a yelp at the cold.

Five minutes later, Mounteban signalled us to stop. He led us within the shade of a weeping willow, hanging dense enough to form a pavilion half way across the gully. It was cramped with us all in there, especially given Saltlick's considerable presence, but I was so glad to have stopped that I hardly cared.

Mounteban took a moment to recover his breath, and said, "I think we're safe."

"Are they after us?"

He shook his head. It wasn't clear whether he meant they weren't or that he didn't know. "We'll keep to the stream for a while, just in case. It would take a good tracker to stay on us."

Whatever the truth, we never saw any sign of the dogs, though we could hear them for an hour afterwards, their clamour growing fainter until it sounded like the stir of distant thunder. No one suggested going back for our two packhorses, abandoned on the brow of the hill with two thirds of our supplies. We went more furtively after that, as though we all suspected deep down that we'd been saved by luck more than judgement.

That caution probably saved our lives when we

had our first real run-in with Moaradrid's patrols. It was just after dusk, and we were pursuing a narrow trail through dense forest when Mounteban threw a hand up, our prearranged signal. We all ducked into the brush. Fortunately, the rhododendrons rising to either side were bulky and overgrown enough to hide even Saltlick. The briefest inspection would have identified bare toes amongst the roots, and the tip of a giant elbow jutting out. Moaradrid's men didn't make one; nor did they try to disguise their own presence. They talked in low mutters, and their chainmail jangled dully with each step. I counted six pairs of feet go past.

We waited until the evening air was absolutely still again before daring to crawl out. I actually felt relieved to have encountered the enemy, especially after the scare with the hounds. It had been all too easy to imagine Moaradrid's army as some implacable entity contracting around us like a fist. To know they were human, and fallible, was oddly reassuring.

Still, we knew now without doubt that they were hunting us, and that they were close. We travelled in absolute silence after that, taking only the narrowest, most obscure pathways or scrambling through the brush. Our already sluggish progress slowed to a crawl. The night wore on, an endless progression of damp foliage, lashing thorns, and unexpected pitfalls. I didn't dare pause for fear of being left behind. I didn't dare eat, lest even that small sound should bring Moaradrid's hordes down on us.

When Mounteban called a halt at last, it was in a deep recess between two hills, with tangles of bramble and whitethorn closing every direction to all but the most intrepid explorer. We'd spent a miserable ten minutes crawling through the perimeter, and I'd assumed he'd picked the route through stupidity or sadism. Once inside, I realised how well the place was sheltered, from both observers and the elements. It was as safe and comfortable a spot as we could have hoped to find.

Mounteban insisted on posting a watch, however, and declared that he'd take first shift. "Will you join me?" he asked Estrada. "We should discuss our plans for tomorrow."

"Of course," she murmured, and trudged after him into the shadows.

I was glad to see them go. I couldn't have cared less about the tomorrow. I flung myself to the ground, pausing just long enough to drag my cloak around me before my eyes slammed shut. I could hear the others following my example to either side. Saltlick struck the ground like a felled oak. A minute later and their snores were drowning out the faint background hiss of wind through leaves. I lay listening, filled with the strange sensation that my body was still moving even as I lay on the ground.

I began to realise, to my horror, that I wasn't falling asleep. I was beyond exhaustion, yet the dim flicker of my consciousness was refusing to go out. The more I thought about it, the worse it grew. I became suddenly aware of the chill, of the moonlight pressing against my eyelids, of a dozen tiny irritations prodding me towards wakefulness.

I opened my eyes and sat up. I remembered that Mounteban and Estrada were still awake too, talking somewhere off in the blackness. Five minutes of their company would surely lull me to sleep. They might not appreciate my intruding, but tact was the farthest thing from my mind.

There remained the difficulty of finding them. It was impossible to see anything in the shade of the hollow beyond the prone outlines around me and a vague suggestion of deeper dark that must have been bushes. The last thing I wanted was to trip over one of Mounteban's crew and have my sleeplessness cured by a knife in the belly. I settled for crawling forward on hands and knees, using the line of the foliage as a guide. It was a lot of trouble to go to for a little tedious company, but I was so wide awake by then that rest seemed a hopeless impossibility. If conversation stood a chance of curing my insomnia then it was worth damp knees.

I thought after a minute that I could make out hushed voices somewhere nearby. I crept forward and recognised Mounteban's gruff tone, too quiet for me to separate words. I tried to orientate myself by it, and kept moving. There followed a period of quiet. It went on for so long that I began to worry I'd passed them altogether.

Then close by, Estrada spoke. "I never meant that."

"Oh?"

"I didn't. I did what was *needed*."

"What was needed?"

There was an edge to both their voices. I decided

against announcing my presence. I kept still and concentrated on listening instead.

"Castilio, I truly never meant to mislead you."

"All those visits… did everyone in Muena Palaiya receive so much attention? I couldn't understand, at first. Why a woman like you would spend so much time trying to recruit a scoundrel like me."

"We needed your help." Estrada sounded almost tearful. "There's no point discussing this any further. I'm going to sleep. I hope you'll put it out of your mind."

I heard the rustle of her cloak as she stood. Then came another sound, of sudden movement, and she cried out. Her voice was abruptly stifled. There was a loud thump, a body or bodies falling upon the turf, and a series of stifled impacts, with the constant background of Estrada's muted cries.

Mounteban grunted in pain, and she sobbed, "Stop!"

I was on my feet before I knew what I was doing.

"Get off her!"

Silence descended. I realised I had no idea where I was in relation to them. Moments slid by. The dark clotted, the stillness thickened around me.

"*Or what?*"

I turned to where I thought Mounteban's voice had come from.

"What will you do, you little piss-ant pickpocket?"

A good question. The obvious answer was that I'd briefly divert him with the chore of beating my head into a mush before I let him get back to his business.

Why hadn't I kept my nose out? I didn't stand a chance alone against Mounteban.

Except that I wasn't alone.

"What will I do?" I said, with more courage than I felt. "Well, I'll call Saltlick. And I'll tell him what you had planned for his friend. How about that, Mounteban? I doubt he'll take it too well."

"He wouldn't hear you."

"Perhaps you're right. Shall we try?"

I heard the tiniest splash as Mounteban spat into the short grass. "The three of you deserve each other." A moment later, his footsteps were receding into the darkness.

When I was certain he'd left, I said quietly, "Are you all right?"

"No Easie, I'm not all right."

"It's a good job I arrived when I did."

"He wouldn't have done anything." Estrada actually sounded angry with me. Then her voice broke, and she began to cry softly.

I vaguely wanted to say something sensitive, or something that would at least quieten her, but I'd exhausted my supply of sensitivity. Instead, I sat down. With my head that much nearer to the ground, I realised the shock of almost being pummelled had extinguished whatever faint spark had been keeping me conscious. I barely had time to tumble backwards and haul my cloak up over me.

All I could hear as sleep wrapped around me was the lullaby of Estrada's gentle sobbing.

• • • •

I woke to pale sunlight and Estrada furiously shaking my shoulders. I blinked at her, grunted something that was meant to be, "Leave me alone you insane woman," and rolled away.

Then I realised what had been strange about the scene. The sun had been far too high and bright for dawn. I opened my eyes again, reluctantly, to find myself gazing once more into Estrada's panicked face.

"What's going on?"

"They're gone."

"What? Who's gone?"

"Mounteban. His men. They've left us. They're all gone, Damasco."

CHAPTER TWELVE

"This is all your fault."

I couldn't tell whether Estrada looked more hurt or angry.

"I don't mean because of last night," I added hastily. "I'm talking about… well, the whole thing. What were you thinking, asking for help from one of the five most notorious criminals in Muena Palaiya?"

"The other four wouldn't even let me through the door."

That brought me up short.

"Look," she said, "not that I have to explain myself to you, but Castilio has been one of the bravest and most steadfast defenders of the Castoval. I wouldn't be alive if it weren't for him, and neither would you."

"And now we know why."

"Is that how you see it, Damasco? Every good thing the man has done was just a ruse? It couldn't possibly be that what happened last night was the anomaly."

I sat down in the grass, feeling more irritable than I could entirely justify. "How about abandoning us into the hands of our enemies? Is that another 'anomaly'? Because from what I've seen of Mounteban over the years, this is exactly in character."

"'Once a thief, always a thief'... people don't change in your world, do they, Damasco?"

The fact that Mounteban had related our conversation on the mountainside to Estrada only fanned my anger. All the frustration and pain of the last few days was boiling up inside me. I didn't seem able to control it, or particularly want to for that matter. The two of them had dragged me into this mess. Now Mounteban had disappeared in our most desperate hour and Estrada was behaving as though I was the one in the wrong.

I sprang back to my feet. "No, in my world people do what they have to do to survive and they keep doing it for as long as they can get away with it. But at least they don't plot and scheme about it, they don't manipulate people into risking their lives and they don't pretend to value anyone they truthfully couldn't care less for."

I could tell I'd struck a nerve. Once again, I'd forgotten that until recently Estrada had been nothing more than a provincial mayor. Her responsibilities hadn't included matters of life and death, or anything more serious than presiding over the yearly parade. With that in mind, it was impossible to miss the shadows behind her eyes, grim remnants of decisions she'd made over the last few days.

It was too good a weakness not to exploit.

"How many men have to die before you admit you don't know what you're doing? What about me? Or

Saltlick, is he next? You've drawn us deeper and deeper into this mess, without a word of explanation. Now that it's just the three of us, maybe it's time you tried a little honesty. What exactly *are* we doing here, Estrada?"

If I'd hoped for a dramatic reaction, I was disappointed. Her face was inscrutable. Seconds passed. Finally, she said, very softly, "You're bait."

"What?" I couldn't believe I'd heard her right.

This time she shouted it: "You're bait!"

Then, to my astonishment, Estrada burst into tears. I couldn't look at her. I swung away and stormed towards the other end of the clearing, appalled by the use of such an unfair strategy. I sat down again, with my back to her and my face to a line of whitethorn bushes. My anger had frozen into a cold, hard knot in my stomach. *Bait?* I was nothing more to Estrada than a worm wriggling on a hook.

It made sense, of course. What better way to lure Moaradrid than with his insane obsession for capturing Saltlick and me? Rationalising it didn't make me feel any better. A fragment of calm amidst the fury noted how absurd it was that I should feel betrayed when Estrada had never made any pretence of *not* using me. I ignored it. The fact was, promises... well, not promises, but assurances had been... perhaps not made, but implied, definitely implied.

Something heavy tapped my shoulder, so unexpectedly that I almost tumbled into the grass.

"Saltlick?"

The giant hovered over me like some bizarre monolith ejected by the earth.

"What do you want? Can't you see I'm..." I let the sentence trail off, not wanting to say "sulking", and went back to staring at the bushes.

Another tap, this one insistent enough that I felt it in the depths of my collarbone.

"*Sorry.*"

"You want to apologise? Saltlick, for once this is hardly your fault."

He pointed. I followed his outstretched arm. There was Estrada pacing at the far end of the glade. I couldn't tell if she was still crying.

"Sorry."

"You want *me* to apologise? Not a chance. Didn't you hear? All she wants us for is to lure Moaradrid into some trap."

Saltlick sighed violently, and his features contorted with frustration. The hand that had been pointing darted like some fleshy bird of prey and grasped a hold of my cloak. An instant later, I was dangling in the air, a good two paces from the ground.

"What are you doing? Put me down!"

I struggled furiously, and then realised I ran the risk of strangling myself in my own cloak and gave up.

"If you put me down now," I mumbled through the hood now tangled over my head, "we can forget this whole thing."

Evidently, that wasn't the plan. I could hear his trudging footsteps, accompanied by the disconcerting sensation of my entire body swinging at each impact. With a lurch that seemed briefly to transfer my genitals to where my kidneys would normally be, I found myself back on solid ground. I clawed the hood out of eyes, and found myself staring into the face of a confused Estrada.

From behind me, Saltlick repeated, "*Sorry.*"

"All right, damn it. Look, perhaps I was wrong to blame you entirely for all this. Maybe you weren't to know what a despicable cockroach Mounteban is. I mean, I'm sure this absurd quest to free the Castoval is well-intentioned."

A slight smile pushed some of the anger from her mouth. "That's the worst apology I've ever heard."

"Really? Because for me it was pretty good. Care to see if you can do any better?"

Estrada looked puzzled.

"Your apology. I'd like to hear it. I think Saltlick would too."

She glanced up at him imploringly. Either I was right, or he hadn't been following the conversation, because he didn't say anything to contradict me.

"Maybe you're right." She coughed, and stared briefly at her feet. I could swear a tint of red had entered her cheeks. "Maybe I should have trusted you both from the start. It's possible that my faith in Castilio was a little... misjudged... and, well..."

"You shouldn't have used us as bait without so much as telling us?"

"Yes. That too."

"Apology accepted." I spat into my hand, and offered it for her to shake.

This time there was no hesitation in her smile. "Don't push your luck, Damasco."

● ● ● ●

Having assessed the situation with calmer heads, we both realised that a shouted argument hadn't been the best way to keep our presence concealed. We were lucky we hadn't brought Moaradrid's men swarming down on us. With our numbers more than halved and Saltlick's chronic aversion to violence, we'd inevitably be lost in a fight. As much as I hated to admit it, things looked bleak without Mounteban and his thugs to watch out for us.

Estrada, who seemed incapable of giving up, was quick to list the positives. Mounteban had left us more than ample supplies, and yesterday had told her carefully where we were in relation to our next objective, the ferry port at Casta Canto. It was only a couple of hours to the south-west, and should be visible beyond the brow of the next hill. "We'll be safe for a while if we can just find a fast boat."

I nearly asked if by "find" she meant "steal", but decided she'd been taunted on that subject enough by Mounteban. That wasn't our real concern, in any case. More to the point was that any vessel quick enough to afford us an escape would likely be too small to take Saltlick's weight. Would she be prepared to abandon him if the need arose?

For that matter, would I get my chance to leave them both behind?

There seemed no point dwelling on distant dilemmas when we'd be lucky to make it even as far as Casta Canto. Estrada took the lead, pointing towards the brow of one particular hill and declaring, "It should be just over there."

I judged by the position of the sun that she was probably right. Remembering how Mounteban had forced us to crawl through the fence of bramble and whitethorn bushes the night before, I asked, "Saltlick, can you clear a path?"

He glanced at Estrada for confirmation.

"Try not to make too much noise," she said, sounding a little guilty for agreeing with me.

Saltlick plunged a hand into the mass of thorny tendrils. He tore the bush from the ground and tossed it over his shoulder, in one fluid motion. It landed with a rustling crash at the far side of the glade. A moment later, another shared its fate.

We trooped into the gap. A steep climb lay beyond. It soon became clear that it would be too much trouble to have Saltlick deal with every thorn bush or fallen tree-trunk that blocked our path; easier by far to add to the scratches and bruises we'd incurred the day before.

Without Mounteban, we had no idea where to look for paths, if paths there were. The going was slow and difficult. It might have taken a couple of hours by an easier route, but with our approach of meandering through the densest, most inhospitable foliage, it was well past lunchtime before we scaled the hilltop.

By the time we saw the Casto Mara, a distant ribbon of blue-flecked grey far below, even Saltlick was dripping with sweat. There was some small comfort in the fact that straying so far from beaten paths was probably all that had kept us out of Moaradrid's hands.

We sat crouched behind a row of pines, pretending we couldn't be seen when Saltlick was five times wider than the tree supposedly hiding him. Below, a steep wooded slope much like the one we'd just climbed tumbled down to the river, wide and fast-flowing here and laced with fringes of white where it churned over hidden rocks and beds of gravel.

Casta Canto nestled in one crook, a huddle of large wood buildings set amidst great ziggurats of logs: the small town was the main channel through which timber cut in the forests of Paen Acha made its way out into the wider Castoval. A number of flat-bottomed boats were moored around the crude harbour, none of them looking very suited to our purpose. Nearer, the ferry – a fenced rectangular platform strung from chains moored on either bank – was flopping like a dying fish in the middle of the flow.

I'd been through Casta Canto any number of times. As one of the main links between the halves of the Castoval, it was difficult to avoid. A generally quiet town, it was occasionally enlivened by the loggers gathering for wild and random-seeming celebrations, which left everyone else cowering for a couple of days while they drank the town dry. It was a place to pass by for most, not one to stay at – which made the bright hem of tents around its eastern edge all the more suspicious.

I glanced at Estrada, who replied with a nod. Then, her eyes apparently sharper than mine, she pointed out a brown smudge bobbing near the dock. I concentrated, and decided that she was right: it was a single-masted skiff, just what we were after.

"I think we can reach it. If we come in from the north we'll be out of sight of the camp."

We began our descent, heading not so much towards Casta Canto as to a point a half mile above it. A dry streambed took us much of the way down, and made the travelling easier than it had been. Still, it was sluggish work. It seemed at times like some surreal game, as we picked our way from rock to copse and copse to shaded hollow, trying to find a route that kept Saltlick's bulk invisible. Even where the cover allowed Estrada and me to move freely, he mostly had to crawl on hands and knees. By the time we were drawing near the river, he'd fallen far behind, and my patience was wearing thin.

It must have shown. Just as I was about to lose my temper altogether, Estrada whispered, "Do you remember what you said earlier?"

"'Earlier' when? I've been saying things for most of my life."

"You said you don't scheme, or manipulate people, or pretend to value anyone you don't care about."

"I remember."

"That wasn't exactly true, was it?"

I thought about it. "Perhaps not entirely. It's possible I was exaggerating for offence."

Estrada threw a significant glance towards Saltlick, who was currently trying to hide behind a shrub that rose to about a third of his height. "You've manipulated him. You used him, and then tried to abandon him. When that didn't work you lied to him some more, telling him you'd help protect his family."

"I never said that." Then I remembered. I *had* said something along those lines, in the cave after our rescue – and before that as well, in Moaradrid's camp. I cursed beneath my breath. "That's hardly the same thing."

"Oh? Because he's a giant?"

"Because he's an idiot."

Estrada nodded, one of those characteristic half-smiles shaping her mouth. "You've never really tried talking to him, have you?"

"I haven't had a full day free since we met."

"I think he does well, considering that he's self-taught, and that he's only been learning our language for a couple of weeks."

That stopped me in my tracks. It had never crossed my mind that Saltlick was anything but an oversized dolt. What must it have been like to be taken from his home, thrust into a world where everything down to the simplest word was incomprehensible?

Saltlick chose that moment to catch up, and looked at us bemusedly.

Estrada whispered, "I'm not trying to pick another fight, Damasco. I'm just asking you to have a little more patience." Aloud she said, "Not much further."

She was right. We'd practically reached the base of the hill. A labyrinth of pines stretched around us, with Casta Canto just visible to the south, carved into slivers by the trunks. We continued to skirt around the town, keeping our distance. The noise of the river was loud enough to drown our voices by the time it came into view, a torrent of muddy grey and foaming white. We clambered to the narrow strip of gravel beach that ran beside it and then, with the shoreline embankment concealing us from observers above, started towards the town.

As we crept nearer, so did the ferry, skulking spider-like along its chains. It was largely empty of human cargo: two men, presumably merchants, stood at the front, lazing against the barrier and smoking pipes. All the remaining space was taken up with horses, which stared with panic-shot eyes at the water and whickered piteously. There wasn't even need for a pilot, since pulleys and half a dozen hard-working ponies in the shore station propelled the craft. The system was impressive in everything but speed. That tended to provoke amusement more than admiration, or frustration for anyone in the slightest hurry. The idling merchants evidently weren't in that category. Nor, thankfully, were they inclined to look in our direction.

Their presence did highlight a flaw in our plan though. We might be well hidden from Casta Canto and the encampment outside it, but from the river and the far bank, we'd stand out like belly dancers at a funeral. Estrada signalled a halt as the ferry limped the last stretch into port. We were close enough to make out the merchants' voices over the racket of their horses. One had propped up the gate bar while the other struggled to manoeuvre the traumatised animals, which were determined to find a way off that didn't involve going near the river or each other. Though it looked as if it must all end in disaster, the merchants knew their business. Their charges stumbled one by one onto the dock and milled about, grumbling in high-pitched whinnies.

"Here's our chance," I said. "Even if we're seen there's no way past that lot."

Estrada nodded, and we hurried the last distance to the dock. A set of crude steps connected the ramshackle platform to the beach. I went up first, and peered towards Casta Canto. The air was heavy with the tang of sweating horse. A road led up beyond the harbour and a small, timbered plaza, towards the main part of town. There were large drying sheds on both sides, and all the space between was a heaving sea of equine bodies.

The scene was a mass of confusion. There seemed far too many horses to have departed the ferry.

I realised why.

There *were* other horses, almost as many as had just crossed the river, and these with riders, coming towards us from the far side of town. The two parties had met and ground to a halt against each other, with much raising of voices and waving of arms.

It was fortunate for us, because otherwise Moaradrid's men would have been on us in seconds.

"Run!"

I took my own advice, not looking to see if Estrada and Saltlick followed. The boat we'd picked out was the last on the docks. It crossed my mind that we might be better to hide, but I'd no idea whether they'd seen us. Even if they'd missed Estrada and me, could they have failed to notice Saltlick? And there was another worry. The closer I got, the more I doubted the fragile craft could take his weight.

I realised, when we arrived panting at the far end of the pier, that we had an even more immediate problem. Just getting Saltlick into the boat was going to be a tribulation. A glance told me Moaradrid's party had made it through the opposing traffic. There were a dozen of them, and they were too engaged to pay us any attention. They'd dismounted to lead their mounts onto the ferry, and were having as much difficulty as the merchants had had performing the exercise in reverse.

Our luck couldn't hold much longer.

"Saltlick, you go first."

If he was going to capsize our vessel, it was better to find out now. As he made tentative motions toward the craft, it looked as though that was exactly what would happen. It bucked alarmingly when he put the least weight on it. Water sloshed in every direction. He tried one foot then the other, first standing then crouching. I could see his mounting panic. Each attempt sunk our one hope of escape a little further.

Despite my anxiety, I remembered Estrada's lecture. I actually felt a little sorry watching him, for all that his clumsiness was about to cost our lives.

Therefore, to everyone's surprise, it was Estrada who settled the predicament. "Damn it, Saltlick, get in!"

No physical blow could have brought so drastic a reaction. Saltlick fell with a crash into the boat, which lurched up almost end on end, before his mass drove it down with a colossal splash. It seesawed back and forth, each time taking on more water, each time looking as though it must inevitably be sucked under the waves. Saltlick bailed furiously all the while, with cupped hands as big as a bucket. I couldn't tell if he was helping or making things worse.

It was a minute at least before the conflict was played out. Saltlick sat drenched, in a hand's span of water. But the boat was right side up on the river. Estrada and I hurried to clamber in. I was sure we'd be the final straw. Yet somehow, the beleaguered vessel stayed afloat, with a hair's breadth of waterline.

I hazarded a glance behind. Moaradrid's troops had made it aboard the ferry and it was now perhaps a quarter of the way to the far shore, struggling along with its usual lethargy. They had clustered at the front, where there was less risk of being mangled by a stray hoof.

"I don't think they've seen us," I said – just as one pointed in our direction. "Oh shit," I corrected. "We're safe as long as they don't have..."

The first arrow plunked through the surface beside us.

"Saltlick!" cried Estrada, thrusting the oars at him.

He stared at the shafts, as though she'd handed him a pair of live snakes. An arrow rebounded from our stern and shattered, spinning past us in pieces.

"Row!"

Estrada was becoming frantic. Saltlick, though he looked just as distraught, didn't move so much as a finger. A third missile carved splinters from the mast just above our heads. I gazed at Saltlick's hands, clutching the oars like skewered ham hocks.

I remembered what Estrada had told me.

How often did giants row boats?

"Like this," I called, mimicking the motion back and forth. More arrows splashed around us, and he gazed at me, baffled. Then understanding dawned. His first stroke nearly tore both oars from their rowlocks, and we leaped forward almost our own length. The second was a fraction more controlled. By the third, Saltlick was starting to compensate for his own strength.

"They're still too near," moaned Estrada.

She was right. Our sudden motion had thrown off their aim, but it wouldn't take them long to correct. We were too overladen, too low in the water. We'd never get up enough speed, for all Saltlick's strength.

So why was no one shooting?

I dared another glance. I was rewarded by a sight so unexpected that I had to turn around, risk of sinking be damned. The ferry was in chaos. At one end, the horses had kicked the barrier into toothpicks, and a couple were already thrashing in the river. At the front, less than half of Moaradrid's men had managed to stay aboard. The others were swimming with the horses, or clutching the rails to stay afloat.

I couldn't tell what had brought such commotion, until I noticed how the chain was sagging, the raft dragging against it into the flow. I followed its length and saw the smoke, a black column seething from behind the harbour buildings. I remembered the wooden tower that housed the ferry's mechanism. A tremendous crash reached us in the same moment, and the smoke cloud redoubled. The chain drooped drastically, and then flopped into the water. Freed from servitude, the ferry chose the path of least resistance. It lurched away with the river, heading northward, moving ten times faster than it ever had before. Its few remaining passengers, human and equine, decided that swimming for the near shore was by far the safest option.

It was over in a less than a minute. By the time I'd taken it all in, the chain was at the bottom of the river, and the ferry had disappeared around a curve. The only evidence was the smoke still climbing thickly into the still air, and the bewildered figures dog-paddling towards the bank. What had happened? Surely it couldn't have been an accident.

I saw the riders, and understood. They were a half-dozen, streaming in single file up the waterfront towards us, heads down, weapons drawn. They veered into the trees at the point where Casta Canto gave way to the forest, hardly slowing. A moment later, the last had been consumed by the deep arboreal shadows.

They'd been travelling at speed, a good distance away. I wouldn't have recognised them but for one detail. For the briefest instant, their leader had glanced in our direction – and there was no mistaking that florid, eye-patched face.

Castilio Mounteban had saved our lives again.

CHAPTER THIRTEEN

Though the day was still cold, the water was glassy and calm beyond Casta Canto. Willows dredged their leaves from the banks. Waterfowl steered around the leafy curtains and each other in complex, aimless patterns. Sometimes a boat would pass, usually a scow moving cargo to or from distant Altapasaeda. The sight of two people in a nine-tenths-sunk skiff being clumsily rowed by a giant drew questions, jeers or, most often, stares of speechless alarm.

When we had the river to ourselves, there was nothing to hear except the sough of wind in the trees and our oars slapping rhythmically through the surface. No one had much to say after the incident with the ferry, and it made for a strange sort of silence, tense and uncomfortable.

Saltlick appeared to be rapt in his newfound occupation, though perhaps his look of absorption had as much to do with trying not to upset our beleaguered craft. He couldn't have stared more intently into the distance if he'd been powering the boat by sheer force of will. Estrada had been gazing at the forest since Mounteban and his companions had vanished, as though she expected them suddenly to burst forth again. Mounteban had confused the issue of his betrayal by rescuing us, and probably she found the whole matter very puzzling and significant.

It had occupied my own thoughts for all of about two minutes. It was clear that he'd waited near Casto Canto, assuming we'd be too lost and disorganised to deviate from the plan. It was equally obvious that his motive for such a preposterous and melodramatic deed was his obsession with Estrada. The only question in my mind was whether he'd try to follow us further. If he did, he'd have little luck now that the width of the Casto Mara was between us.

With that cleared up, I'd decided I still couldn't give a donkey's arse about the fat old crook. It wasn't me or Saltlick he'd saved. He probably wouldn't piss on me if I was on fire and he had a bladder infection. We would likely have escaped anyway, and without so much carnage or needless spectacle. All told, it was easy for me to put aside the whole shameful incident.

At first, I'd experimented with trying to get comfortable, but I was too cramped to make any headway. Even stretching a foot or twitching a hand sent the boat into dangerous convulsions. I settled for watching the clouds scud by overhead. After a while, I drifted off, half awake. I'd start occasionally, struggle to remember where I was, and look around in alarm at the liquid expanse around me. The sun was lower in the sky each time, there was a little more chill in the air, and Saltlick and Estrada were still gazing at nothing. On the fourth such occasion, I found the sky streaked with melting bands of purple, and the nip in the breeze a distinct coldness. Little else had changed, within or without the boat. Estrada had her eyes closed, Saltlick was still rowing steadfastly, and ducks and moorhens were still bustling about. The river's flow had picked up, however, since my last inspection. The ripples were white-flecked once again, and deep enough that in the failing light the muddy current resembled a furrowed field convulsing under small tremors. We must have travelled quite a distance into Paen Acha. The forest would continue more or less unbroken on the east bank until the tail of the valley choked it off. To the west, it was only a wide stripe across the land, which soon would give way to...

"Saltlick," I cried, failing to keep the alarm out of my voice, "we should stop now."

Estrada's eyes flicked open. "We've an hour's light left," she said, sounding slightly groggy.

"That's nothing to do with it. Saltlick, pull in to the bank."

Estrada, wide-awake now, told him, "Keep going. Leave him alone, Damasco."

"We're getting close to Altapasaeda."

"So?"

"So, there may not be many places where I'm welcome in the Castoval, but there's only one where they'll chop my head off before they even bother to arrest me. The farther I stay from Altapasaeda and their crazy ideas about law enforcement, the less likely they are to find an opportunity."

Estrada looked at me with puzzlement. Then, as though talking to an addled child, she said, "Damasco, where did you think we'd been going to all this time?"

In retrospect, standing up in the boat wasn't the best idea I'd ever had. Alarm at Estrada's revelation seemed like less and less of a good excuse as the night wore on. While it had achieved what I'd wanted, that hadn't proved to be much comfort – not as I tumbled into the river, not while I flailed to keep my head above the surface, not even as I floundered to the bank and lay choking greenish water into the mud.

Nor had it carried much weight with Estrada and Saltlick. Estrada proved a strong swimmer after her initial panic, and Saltlick was able to gain a footing on the riverbed; the sight of his upturned face bobbing shoreward would have been humorous under better circumstances. He'd even managed to salvage our boat, dragging it behind him with one hand.

Once they'd landed, it had provided them a seat from which to ignore me.

Since no real harm had been done, such vindictiveness struck me as uncalled-for. Estrada only broke the wall of silence when – sick of shivering on a fallen tree trunk in my sodden cloak – I decided to build a fire.

"Are you insane?"

I glared at her. "What was that? I couldn't hear for the sound of my teeth chattering. If it was 'Are you cold, drenched and pissed off?' then the answer is yes."

"You know we can't light a fire."

"I know that the troops at Casta Canto were a scout party, and we must be far ahead of them by now. I know we've likely gained the same lead on all of Moaradrid's forces. So I suggest that, when the alternative is freezing to death, we should make the most of it."

"You talk as though none of this is your fault."

"And you talk as if this didn't happen because you've been leading me into the hands of people who want to kill me."

Estrada sighed, ran a hand through mud-clotted hair. "Fine, do what you like. It was stupid of me to think you'd listen to anyone but yourself."

"Whenever I do," I called at her retreating back, "it seems to end badly."

I turned irritably back to my would-be fire. It had been hard to find dry wood, or indeed dry anything, and it was a long time before my carefully constructed heap of grass and sticks produced much besides smoke. I nearly whooped with joy when the first amber tongue licked out from a fissure between two twigs. Conscious of Estrada's eyes on me, I tried to pretend it was exactly what I'd been expecting. After that, it was easy work to pile logs and branches onto the hungry blaze, until it danced waist-high in the twilight.

I'd been wondering if Estrada's stubbornness would win out over her misery. I was pleased when she and Saltlick came to join me, Saltlick still hauling the upturned boat behind him, trailing its broken mast like a tail.

"Are you sure you want to sit here?" I asked, chewing a piece of soggy bread I'd discovered in one of my pockets. "I'm expecting Moaradrid's entire army to arrive at any minute."

"Yes, Damasco. I'd like to share your fire, if that's all right."

"Of course it is, Mayor Estrada."

"And perhaps," Estrada added, with a glance towards Saltlick, "we can save any other matters for a later date."

What she meant was, *Let's not argue in front of the giant.*

Her tone conjured a memory, of my father speaking to my mother when she returned from one of her nights of drunken frivolity. A little, timid man, he would listen to her rant about some inconsequential thing, and then say softly, "Perhaps we can discuss this later, my darling?"

Close on its heels came another vision: Estrada and myself, wearing the joyous expression of proud parents, stood over a gigantic crib in which sat a dribbling, hiccuping Saltlick.

I shuddered.

Still, I'd no desire for any more forced reconciliations; my throat was still smarting from the last one. I managed a smile, and said, "Of course."

Anyway, I had more immediate concerns. The wet bread had only enraged my appetite, and all the rest of my edible supplies had ended up in the river. It didn't make me feel any better to watch Saltlick contentedly tucking into bunches of leaves he'd stripped from a nearby bush.

"Do you have anything we can eat?" I asked Estrada.

"I left my rucksack on the harbour in Casta Canto," she replied, a little guiltily.

"Then I'm going to see what I can find."

Two miserable hours had passed before I returned. The fruit of my labours was a handful of gnarled apples and a rabbit so ancient it would probably have expired that night even if I hadn't clubbed it over the head with a rock. My fire had tormented me all the while as a glimmer of beckoning orange through the trees, and I was depressed to find that Estrada had let it burn down to a heap of flickering embers. I added branches to the neglected blaze, then sat down next to her and set about gutting the geriatric rabbit. Estrada eyed the work with distaste, but said nothing.

I was drooling with hunger by the time I'd rigged a makeshift spit and begun to roast my prize. Yet once it was done and the meat divided, our portions were so meagre that you'd have thought I'd cooked a shrew. With vigorous chewing, it was edible at least, and followed by the apples it dealt with the worst of my stomach cramps. Since Saltlick lay beside the boat heaving out loud snores, I decided the time was right to tell Estrada what I thought of her plot to get me executed.

Perhaps she caught the glint in my eye. "I know what you think about going to Altapasaeda. You made that quite clear when you capsized our boat."

"That was an accident. Not that I wouldn't have done it deliberately if it meant keeping my head on my shoulders."

"I also know how stringently they pursue the law there. Nevertheless, it's crucial that we go to Altapasaeda, and terrible things will happen if we don't. So before we begin arguing again, won't you listen to why? I'll tell you the truth – the whole of it."

Her tone was almost beseeching. This wasn't what I'd expected. "I'll listen, but nothing you say is going to make me value my head any less."

Estrada nodded, gazed thoughtfully into the fire, and said, "I'm not sure where to begin. Anyone else would have worked out most of it already. You've a knack for ignoring the big questions."

"That's untrue. I'm the first to ask what's for dinner, or where the nearest inn is. Perhaps we just disagree about what the big questions are."

"You haven't wondered how Moaradrid recruited the giants, or why?"

I remembered what I'd overheard him say, that night in his encampment. "The 'why' is obvious. Once he's subdued the Castoval, he plans to march north again, against the King. It takes more than a bunch of unwashed plainsmen to pull off something like that."

Estrada looked impressed. "You *have* been paying some attention. But you didn't ask why the giants would follow him when they hate fighting so much? It's not as though they can't stand up for themselves."

"I wondered. Then I got diverted by fleeing for my life."

Her voice dropped to a whisper. "And the stone? You didn't ask yourself what the stone is for?"

Did she mean the jewel I'd left in Reb Panza? No, she could only be talking about that red-striped pebble, which I'd found in Moaradrid's pouch and thought no more about. They'd taken it from me when I was imprisoned in the caves, and I'd hardly noticed the loss. Now that I thought back, though, hadn't Moaradrid referred to a stone as well?

"All right, you've got me there. What is it?"

"It's the answer, Damasco."

I had to lean in close to catch her next words.

"One of our agents found this out, once we discovered what Moaradrid had brought back from the south. Giant society is very simple, you see – what you might call an elective monarchy. They decide on a leader, and that giant has responsibility for the tribe. Since all the giants are more or less equal and they don't tend to argue, or go anywhere, or do anything unusual, it's not the most taxing position – although they take it very seriously.

"Anyway. The giants don't seem to hold much with airs and graces, but their leader does get a staff to mark them out in a crowd. The staff is just a piece of wood; it's probably changed a dozen times over the centuries. What matters is the stone mounted at the top. Simply put, whoever holds that is chief, for as long as they live, absolutely and without dispute."

"That's what it is? That pebble is their chief-stone? And Moaradrid stole it." This struck me as remarkably funny, for reasons I couldn't quite put my finger on.

"Then you stole it from him."

"And he's been chasing me all this time to get it back." The final pieces slipped into place, and then I really couldn't help but laugh. "So that's why you've been using us as bait. Moaradrid will chase up and down the Castoval forever, because if he doesn't then sooner or later he'll have a mob of disgruntled giants to contend with." I shook my head, suddenly bewildered. "All this for a bit of rock. I'd have given it back if he'd only asked."

"It's a good job for the Castoval, for the whole land, that you didn't. He'd probably be sitting in the royal palace by now."

"And I'd be asleep in bed, instead of on a log in the middle of nowhere talking to you. That doesn't sound like such a bad deal." Before Estrada could tell me what she thought of my priorities, I added, "None of this explains why I have to go to Altapasaeda and have my head chopped off."

"That's what I've been trying to tell you. As a mayor, I have diplomatic privileges, and Prince Panchetto wouldn't dare ignore that even now. As long as you're in my entourage, you're safe. I have my own reasons for going there, but as far as the plan is concerned it will give Moaradrid a chance to catch up."

"That's a good thing?"

"It is if we're going to lead him into our ambush. Except, none of that can work if you're not there, because as far as he's concerned you have the stone, or at least are the only one who knows where it is. So you see, Easie, I have to protect you if I'm going to save the Castoval."

"Yes, I see."

What I didn't say was, *"This all assumes you can protect me.* Marina Estrada, mayor of a town that was probably in enemy hands by now, leader of a resistance so petty and muddled that the greater part of the Castoval had no idea it existed. What exactly was the diplomatic status of an ex-mayor, or a failed resistance leader?" Whatever the answer, I doubted her word would carry as much weight in Altapasaeda as she imagined it would.

The question was ultimately irrelevant, because I hadn't the faintest intention of going there. The crucial fact, which Estrada had failed to mention, was that I no longer had the stone. Presumably, she did. If that was the case, there were two possibilities: she'd have to reveal it in order to lure Moaradrid, or her plan would fail, she'd be captured, and it would fall into his possession that way. Whatever happened, I'd only have to stay out of his hands for a week, probably less, and then his interest in me would evaporate. This mad, interminable hunt would be over.

Just to make sure I said, with laboured innocence, "It won't work, though. I lost the stone days ago. I didn't know the thing was important so I didn't think much about it."

Estrada reached up and drew the neck of her undershirt open. For one terrifying moment, I thought she was about to try to seduce me. Then I saw the pouch, worn like a collar over her breastbone.

"We took it from you, while you were asleep in the caves. We genuinely didn't know whose side you were on. Then Castilio suggested sending you to rescue Saltlick, to test you and to put Moaradrid on our trail. It would have been ridiculous to hand it back to you and say 'try not to lose this when you're down there in Moaradrid's camp'. After that there was never an opportunity."

"That's fine. I don't want the damn thing anyway."

"As long as Moaradrid believes you have it, that's all that matters. We could give it to Saltlick and it wouldn't make any difference."

I laughed. "Saltlick, chief of the giants! What would he do? I don't think he's the order-giving type."

Estrada smiled. "I'm glad we talked. I wish I could have been honest with you earlier. You see now why you have to come to Altapasaeda with me?"

"I do."

Which wasn't to say that I planned to. Getting out of her absurd scheme would be another matter – but one that could wait until morning at least.

"We should try and catch some sleep. We've a long day ahead."

"Yes." Estrada slid to the ground, so that her back was propped against the log and her body lay alongside the fire. "Goodnight, Damasco."

● ● ● ●

I woke to shouting. My first thought was that I'd been wrong after all: Moaradrid's men had seen our fire, and I'd be beaten to a pulp at any instant, hog-tied, and dragged off to indescribable torments. Blinking muzzily at a bright morning sky, I felt more irritated at being proved wrong than afraid. How Estrada was going to gloat!

It struck me then that it was her shouting, and only her. Either our assailants were unusually subdued or something else was going on. I stumbled to my feet, knuckled my eyes and glanced around our makeshift campsite. Saltlick was just sitting up, evidently also woken by her cries. I could just make out Estrada through the foliage, standing close to the riverbank, dancing from foot to foot and waving her arms. I couldn't see who she was signalling to, if in fact she was signalling at all and hadn't just gone insane.

Who could it be, out here in the backend of nowhere? *Please not Mounteban*, I thought, *better Moaradrid than that pompous crook*. I clambered over the log that had served as our pillow and jogged towards her. She was veiled by the bank-side willows, so that it was only when I was right behind her that I saw what she was looking at. A riverboat lay moored, close enough that its crew could have leaped ashore without wetting their feet. It was a grubby, unkempt craft, its name invisible beneath anonymous filth that had dripped from above, its cargo hidden beneath sheets of soiled oilcloth. It had a single, tattered sail, currently furled. Two boys lounged on deck and a shovel-bearded man in a long crimson coat – that must have been expensive before decades of disrepair took their toll – leaned over the side towards us.

Estrada, noticing me, said, "Damasco, meet Captain Anterio. I happened to see him passing and thought he might be able to help us. Captain, this is my travelling companion Easie Damasco."

"A pleasure," I said, without conviction.

"The captain was just agreeing to take us up the river."

"Depending on our settling a reasonable fare," Anterio added quickly. Then his eyes widened, and he took a step backward. "What in the hells is that?"

I followed his distraught gaze to see Saltlick ploughing through the trees towards us.

"Ah," said Estrada. "I was about to mention Saltlick."

I never heard the final sum Estrada paid for our passage. I've no doubt it went up considerably when Saltlick entered the equation. Though Anterio eventually agreed to let him on board, he insisted on making him sit at the stern, with his back to us. It seemed a bizarre precaution, but Saltlick didn't appear to mind, and soon we were underway.

Captain Anterio's riverboat stank worse than it looked. Unprompted, he explained irritably that he was carrying a cargo of turnips into the city.

"Why do they smell so bad?" I asked, my voice muffled from trying to speak with my hand around my nose.

"Because they're rotten," he replied, as if it was the most obvious thing in the world.

However malodorous and ramshackle our vessel was, it cut swiftly through the water, propelled by a sharp southerly breeze. I silently cursed both wind and boat. I needed time to think of an escape plan, and it was rapidly running out. We were soon beginning to see signs of civilization, occasional farms and drifts of smoke marking hamlets further inland. What little say I had in my future would be gone if I didn't act soon.

Estrada sat in the prow with Anterio for a long while. I guessed from what snatches I overheard that she was catching up on local news, perhaps even fishing for rumours of Moaradrid or the resistance. It was at least an hour before she stood and walked back to sit with Saltlick. We were passing tracts of pasture, by then, and fields of grain dotted with large farmhouses and barns. I knew we were drawing near to Altapasaeda.

I waited a couple of minutes, then sidled over to Anterio and sat beside him. I tried to judge his age and failed. His face was lined and tanned a ruddy amber-brown, and he could have been anywhere from forty to sixty. I did recognise his jacket, though, as a dress-coat of the Altapasaedan City Guard, and wondered what had led him to be wearing it upon this dingy barge.

He didn't notice me at first. He was concentrating on trimming his beard with a small pair of scissors. It was an occupation he clearly took seriously, though he was dreadful at it. Up close, the wedge of wiry black hair was lopsided and uneven. When he finally looked round, I said softly, "Captain, I have a proposition."

Anterio dropped the scissors into a leather pouch, which he secreted within the folds of his coat. "A good captain is always open to propositions. Some days it's only propositions that pay the bills."

"That's exactly right. In this case," I said, holding out a hand containing five of my remaining onyxes, "it could be very profitable for both of us."

He squinted. "I hope you don't intend any harm to that young lady back there?"

"None whatsoever."

"It might be better for everyone if you drowned the monster," he added vehemently.

"No need for anyone to be drowned. All I ask is this: you drop my companions at Altapasaeda as planned, and then continue upriver until we can find another boat for me, one that's headed away from the city. That's it. Five onyxes for an hour's work."

"That's all?"

"That's all."

Captain Anterio offered me a greasy palm. "Then I accept your proposition."

The rotten vegetable smell had an insidious quality that made it impossible to ignore. I decided, after wrestling with it for a while, to try to live with it instead. I sprawled out on the narrow portion of the deck that was free of mouldy produce and considered a nap.

After our brief conversation, Captain Anterio had devoted his attentions to a series of small jobs about the boat, joined by the two boys, who bore just enough similarity to him that they might conceivably be his sons. Estrada and Saltlick still sat together, speaking in short exchanges. I couldn't guess what it was they found to talk about.

I watched the banks slide by and wondered if my plan could work. Anterio was certainly a man in need of a few extra coins, and it wasn't as though a little additional travel would spoil his cargo. If I could find a boat heading north, I might make it as far as Aspira Nero. Even if Moaradrid came looking for me he'd be hard pressed to catch up. Moreover, since Estrada would have to reveal her possession of the stone or watch her plans go up in smoke, it was unlikely to come to that.

Overall, things looked more promising than they had in days. I found myself almost looking forward to reaching Altapasaeda. The sooner I got there, the sooner I could leave. That nervous excitement and the flavourful stench kept sleep at bay, and I settled for staring into the distance, willing the city to materialise from the haze.

I saw the bridge first. It was the longest and grandest in the Castoval, its arches tall enough for even high-masted boats to pass beneath. They called it the Sabre – for its shape, presumably, and the way it sliced the Casto Mara in two. At that distance, it was a skeletal black outline above the water, and the walls before it just a smudge.

The ground was low and flat. It was possible to see the vast tracts of forest behind us, and even the mountains, a purple border on the edge of vision. We were still travelling through farmland, but the plantations were richer, dedicated to luxury goods for rich city folk. There were vineyards and apiaries, olive trees, and estates devoted solely to supplying the Temple District: with flowers, incense, birds, cloth and statuary. It was a riot of colour, and of heady scents that reached us even in the middle of the river. The road on the west bank was packed with traffic, and we passed more boats than we had the day before.

Soon we were overtaking the suburbs of Altapasaeda – a polite name for the high-class slum that lay like a second shadow beyond the northward walls. I couldn't help looking for signs of Moaradrid's army, but it was impossible to say from a distance whether there were more tents in the chaos of the outskirts than on any other day.

I turned my attention to the city itself. Altapasaeda was unique in the Castoval, an intrusion of northern civilization into our simpler and infinitely calmer existence. Compared with the Castovalian towns, it was like a glamorous but ageing whore: grand and startling, but most of its glamour purely for show and even more simply painted on. High towers jutted above the walls for no purpose but to jut, and hardly a building went unmarked by some architectural eccentricity. It was hard not to be impressed by Altapasaeda, harder still to take it seriously.

It was only when we dipped beneath the rightmost arch of the Sabre that the docks came into view. I squinted against the sudden darkness. There were only

shapes at first, sharp rectangles and triangles glistening
in the sun beyond the bridge. As we broke back into
the light, leaving the dripping grey ceiling behind,
the scene gained depth and perspective. The docks
of Altapasaeda were a far cry from the sagging jetties
of Casta Canto. Here everything was built of stone in
two tiers joined by wide steps and ramps. There were
metal bollards to tie off against, and even a pair of me-
chanically assisted cranes to unload the largest vessels.

It was so busy, both in the water and upon the
dockside, that we wasted ten minutes manoeuvring
for a spot. All the while, the captain and his two boys
shouted incomprehensibly to neighbouring crews, the
harbour hands and each other. I grew impatient, and
a little nervous. There were a handful of guards strut-
ting around. Any one of them might recognise me.
Was all this fuss really necessary for so brief a stop?

Our dilapidated craft sidled into a gap between two
similarly run-down scows, with difficulty and yet
more yelling. I watched Anterio as he hurled a guide
rope to a lad running back and forth on the quay and,
once we were drawn in and tied off, as he swung out
the gangplank.

"Here we are," he called. "Altapasaeda, glorious
lady of the south."

Now was the time for him to put Estrada and
Saltlick to shore. It would be a moment's work to cast
off and withdraw the plank. We'd be gone before
they knew it. But all Anterio did was stand there,
hands on hips. When his two boys scampered ashore,
he made no move to stop them.

Suspicion got the better of me. I sidled up to him and hissed, "What's this? What happened to our arrangement?"

Anterio looked at me with disgust. "What kind of man would try to abandon his pregnant wife and her poor, deformed brother? The lady warned me you'd try something like this." He pressed four coins into my hand, adding, "Less one, to teach you a lesson." Placing a palm on my back, he shoved me roughly down the gangplank.

When I looked back Saltlick was descending, blocking any hope of escape.

I was trapped in Altapasaeda, and there wasn't a thing I could do.

CHAPTER FOURTEEN

We'd been in Altapasaeda all of three minutes before things started to go wrong.

Captain Anterio had said a deferential goodbye to Estrada, glowered at Saltlick and me, and turned his attention to negotiating with a pair of dockhands. All the while, I'd been working out the odds of making a run for it.

It couldn't be too difficult to find a vessel amongst the many moored there that would give me passage in exchange for coin. Performing my escape in plain view of Estrada would lack subtlety, however, and I'd no chance of outdistancing Saltlick if he decided to intervene. The ensuing ruckus would be bound to draw attention.

Just as I'd reached that conclusion, attention found us anyway. Two guards, distinguished from the greys and browns of the dockside by their long scarlet coats and tricorn hats, had been inspecting a heap of crated cargo on the higher level. One pointed towards the far bank, and as his gaze followed his own finger, it swung over us. He elbowed his companion. They both looked in our direction, first at Saltlick and then at me. The one who'd spotted us mouthed something. I was sure it was my name.

"Estrada," I muttered.

"What?"

I tried to point by tilting my head. "Company."

"Oh."

Now they'd started briskly down the steps that joined their level to ours, making a point of looking anywhere but at us.

"We could run."

"And then what?"

"We could jump in the river."

"Damasco…"

I cursed her silently for saying my name loud enough that the nearer guard could hear. He covered the last distance at a jog, and skidded to a graceless halt in front of us. "So… Easie Damasco."

Over his shoulder, I could see his colleague waving other guards over, whilst nervously eyeing Saltlick. Both were keeping their hands very close to their sword hilts.

"You're mistaken. I'm his brother, Santo. People say we look similar, though I fear Easie fared better in the looks department."

Estrada's expression said "shut up" more capably than words could have hoped to. "I'm Marina Estrada, incumbent mayor of Muena Palaiya. These gentlemen are my travelling companions, and we're here to see Prince Panchetto."

As much as she spoke with authority, Estrada's declaration would have carried more weight if she hadn't been filthy with river mud and reeking of rotten turnips. A small crowd of guards was gathering around us. None of them looked very convinced. The one who'd first spoken repeated to his colleagues, "That's Easie Damasco."

"It is," said Estrada, managing to sound only a little exasperated. "If we can see the Prince then I'm sure we can straighten out any questions."

"She says she wants to see the Prince," the guard continued, as though they hadn't all witnessed the entire conversation. Perhaps he was a congenital idiot, or an officer.

Either way, it was his companion who took the initiative. With a furtive glance towards Saltlick, he said, "I think you should probably come with us, madam."

"I hate to say 'I told you so'. Wait, no, I actually quite enjoyed it."

"Everything will be fine."

"For you, maybe. The closest thing I can see to a bright side is that I'll never have to buy another hat."

"It won't come to that."

"Oh really? They might let me off with a bit of light torture and life in the dungeons? Now that I think, I *did* hear something about the Prince having a soft spot for career criminals."

"Shut up," said the nearest guard, clipping me sharply across the head. "Don't you talk about His Highness."

The blow stung enough to keep me from reminding him that we wanted to see the Prince, and that arranging an appointment would be difficult if we couldn't mention him. It was becoming apparent even to Estrada that they had no intention of leading us to the palace.

We'd left behind the grandiose functionality of the harbour, and were trudging in convoy through the Lower Market District which bracketed it to the west. We were making more of an impression than I'd have liked. The cries of hawkers had died away to nothing, and every merchant and shopper turned to watch our passing. It was small comfort that they were all watching the giant striding at our rear and hardly sparing a glance for Estrada or me. I knew how fast gossip travelled through Altapasaeda. Even if Estrada somehow managed to talk our way out of this current predicament, Moaradrid couldn't fail to hear of our arrival.

Our guards seemed just as disconcerted by the attention we were drawing. They'd taken up positions in a loose oval around us, and now were marching at a respectful distance. That distance was considerably more respectful around Saltlick, making the egg shape more of a pear. There wasn't much they could do if he chose to resist, and his compliance – against all the traditional logic of guard-criminal relationships – only seemed to be making them more nervous.

An archway led us abruptly out of the Lower Market District. The stalls were replaced by stucco-fronted shops, decorated with metal balconies and shutters of black wood. Here were perfumeries, delicatessens, florists, vintners, and more than one huge aviary, with cages suspending multitudes of brightly plumed birds over the streets. These streets were less tightly thronged, and their occupants more extravagantly dressed. The men wore long-tailed frock coats, the women wide, bright dresses. More discreet than the market folk, but no less inquisitive, they tried to disguise their gawking with waving of fans and quick turns of heads. That only added to our guards' discomfort. They looked as though they'd cheerfully let us go to avoid more publicity.

I was about to suggest the possibility when our route veered off the main concourse into a narrow backstreet. It ended in a grand plaza that I recognised all too well. Red Carnation Square was picturesquely named for the worn block on a plinth at its centre, and the great quantities of blood that had flowed out from it. Two fears had blighted my brief spell in Altapasaeda. The first was that black-stained wooden oblong, rutted by the presence of countless arms, legs and necks; the second was the building of white stone squatting behind it. It had many windows, but all of them were barred, and few passed through its door that didn't end up on the block outside.

We were ushered to said door, a small panel of dark wood reinforced with bands of tarnished metal. For what was the only way in or out of the most feared prison in the Castoval, it was disappointingly innocuous. The lead guard rapped on the door, and it opened soundlessly. I realised I was holding my breath, and that my knees were suddenly weak.

However, there was nothing beyond except a small office. The gatekeeper – an elderly man wearing pince-nez glasses and the standard guard uniform, though with a skullcap in place of a hat sitting badly skewed on his grey hair – retreated behind a battered desk. He spent five minutes removing and cataloguing our possessions, and then fussily recording our names and brief descriptions. Saltlick seemed to throw his system into chaos, and most of that time was spent with him tutting and chewing morosely at his quill, as though the giant had materialised solely to baffle him.

I was almost relieved when our original captors led us through an archway and down steep stairs into the guts of the prison. Though it was barely noon outside, this lower level was lit by greasy torchlight. As far as I could tell, it consisted of corridors running at right angles to each other, forming a grid with the cells spaced between and around the edges. The place reeked of smoke, though not enough to cover other smells, more human and less pleasant.

Our posse of guards was met by a pair of jailers, their uniforms identical in cut but black instead of crimson. There followed a brief and muddled discussion. I caught our names, the prince's, and laughter. Then the jailers joined our already extensive procession, and together they ushered us towards one of the outer cells.

"In you go," the lead guard said. Saltlick's obedience had done nothing to ease his nervousness, as though he suspected some kind of long-winded trap.

Saltlick tried to ease himself through the low, narrow doorway, and failed. It took him a few seconds of manoeuvring, and in the end of moving sideways in a crouched shuffle, to get inside. All the while, the guard's face melted towards panic, and I struggled not to snigger.

"Right, now you two. Don't try and make any trouble."

"I never try to make trouble. It just seems to happen around me," I replied, stepping through.

I glanced back when Estrada didn't follow. Though she wasn't exactly resisting, there was something in her bearing I'd learned to recognise. It told me our guard's bad day wasn't about to get any better.

He too appeared to sense that he was out of his depth again. "You as well, madam."

"You're not going to tell the prince I'm here, are you?"

He considered. "Not as such, no."

"May I ask why?"

"Because that man there is Easie Damasco, a known and wanted criminal, and your other companion is some sort of monster. This leads me to believe that you aren't the type the prince would associate with." Seeing Estrada's expression, he added quickly, "Also, I'm only a sergeant, and I don't think His Highness would listen to me."

"I appreciate your honesty."

The young guardsman looked relieved. "So if you could step into the cell…"

"Just one more thing, sergeant."

He winced.

"What if you're wrong?"

"Excuse me?"

"I mean, what if I am, as I say I am, the mayor of a nearby town that Prince Panchetto has allied himself with, and what if word was to reach him that you'd thrown me into a prison cell for no apparent crime or good reason?" I could tell she was beginning to enjoy herself. "What I'm asking is, what do you think would happen then?"

The sergeant gulped, opened and closed his mouth, and ended with a shrug that seemed to pass through his whole body. He said, "I don't know, madam. But if you'd be good enough to wait a while in this room behind us then I'll take the matter to the guard-captain and let him decide what's best."

Estrada smiled beatifically, and stepped inside. Behind her, the sergeant shut the door as gently as he could whilst still appearing to slam it.

The show over, I turned my attention to our surroundings. I'd been in worse cells. It was fairly clean, and came with not only a bucket but also a pile of straw in the corner, which Saltlick had promptly begun to devour. We even had natural light from the grill set in the outside wall above our heads.

That, however, soon proved more a curse than a blessing. The window was there not for our comfort but so passers-by could mock and spit at us if the urge took them. We'd been in there hardly five minutes when a mob of youths squatted around the opening, and began catcalling to Estrada and pouring abuse on Saltlick and myself. On a better day I'd have risen to the challenge, but I didn't have it in me right then. I sat in the farthest corner, arms wrapped around my knees, and glared until they got bored and went away.

When we were alone again, I said to Estrada, "You do know who the guard-captain is, don't you?"

"Of course I do."

"And your plan is to have that man come here? He'll probably want to hold the axe himself."

"Everything will be fine, Damasco."

"You said that before."

"I did. Have a little faith. Altapasaeda's the place for it."

I lapsed into silence. I doubted she knew guard-captain Alvantes's reputation half as well as I did, but what was the use of arguing? She'd realise eventually that nobody remembered or cared if she'd once been mayor of some backwater burg. In the meantime, I should try to see the funny side of her stubbornness. A few weeks of being heckled in this dismal box would beat it out of her better than anything I could say.

The shadows of the bars had jutted straight across the room when we'd arrived. Now they were slanting towards the corner where Saltlick sat chewing straw. That made it a little past noon, if my sense of direction hadn't failed me. I was warm enough, and not uncomfortable. Perhaps they'd feed us soon. Maybe they'd forget about us. Maybe the sergeant wouldn't keep his word, or Alvantes would deem the matter beneath him. Maybe...

I'd barely registered the rapid footsteps outside when the door sprang open. I tumbled out of the way. When I looked up, I found myself face to face with the chiselled features of Alvantes, captain of the Altapasaedan City Guard. He looked older than when I'd last seen him. Fine wrinkles had sprung up around his angular jaw; a hint of grey discoloured his close-cropped dark brown hair. His uniform still bulged around wide shoulders, though, and his eyes glittered with their old enthusiasm. Alvantes the Boar, the Hammer of Altapasaeda... of course he would want to deal personally with the infamous Easie Damasco.

Which begged the question: why did he barely glance in my direction? His gaze skimmed over me, took in Saltlick, and settled on Estrada. "Marina."

"Guard-Captain."

"This is... unfortunate. I've spoken with my men."

"They weren't to know."

"Of course. I took that into account. And the fact that you were travelling with..." Now he did look at me, briefly and with disgust. "Well, you can see how misunderstandings might arise."

"Yes. Nevertheless, Easie Damasco is my companion, and under my protection."

"And...?" He nodded towards Saltlick.

"Saltlick too. We wouldn't have made it this far without his assistance."

I couldn't help noticing the smile that curved Saltlick's thick lips.

Alvantes, however, looked less than impressed. "We'll respect that, of course. As long as the thief behaves himself while he's within the city."

There was something going on here that I was missing. The strained formality between Alvantes and Estrada spoke volumes, but about what I couldn't tell. Though turning up as a refugee with an aberration of nature on one arm and a wanted criminal on the other was probably doing little for Estrada's credibility, I sensed it was more than that.

Still, if it got us out of this cell they could start dancing together for all I cared. "My behaviour will be impeccable," I said. "I hope we can put any past misunderstandings behind us."

Alvantes threw me a look of such utter loathing that I actually flinched. "There have been no misunderstandings. If you put one toe astray, no amount of protection will save you." As if nothing had been said, he turned back to Estrada. "Shall we go? His Highness is waiting."

Our second journey through Altapasaeda was more discreet. This time we only had two guards escorting us, for a start. It was more than that though. Somehow, people's eyes slipped away from Alvantes, somehow their feet carried them aside without any indication they'd even noticed he was there. We might have been travelling in a bubble of invisibility for all the attention we were paid. It occurred to me that if Alvantes ever needed a change of career he'd make a fine pickpocket, and the thought almost made me laugh aloud.

Our route this time took us briefly back into the upper-class end of the market district, before spilling us onto the wide boulevard of A Thousand Gods

Way. I knew it as the main thoroughfare of the temple district.

As dubious as the rest of the Castoval found the Northerner religion with its bizarre and endless panoply of deities there was no denying its results were spectacular. Everywhere great arches reared, trailing flowering fronds over our heads; half-human, half-bestial figures gazed down, waved curious weapons, leered madly or smiled secretive smiles. No building lacked columns, minarets, windows of coloured glass, hanging baskets or countless other ornaments, arranged in apparently random combination.

It was somewhat overwhelming, and I was glad when we veered off the concourse. The relief was brief. Ahead was the palace, and as gaudily magnificent as the temples had been, they paled in comparison.

Here was the home of Prince Panchetto, only son of King Panchessa, and his not-inconsiderable court. Word had it that the palace was a means for the king to deflect his vacuous son from the business of politics, to distract him with trivialities better suited to his temperament. If that were true, the diversion was well judged. It was hard to imagine anyone taking anything seriously amidst such preposterous splendour.

Alvantes guided us not through the colossal main gate but through a smaller carriage gate further around. We left our escort behind in favour of two turbaned palace guards, who walked ahead of us through long corridors floored with eggshell white marble, their brilliant azure robes whispering with each stride. Stairs led up to an open courtyard, where four huge, mosaic-engraved fountains spilled water into a central basin. Beyond were further corridors, each so wide that we could have formed a row with Saltlick at the centre and not been cramped.

We drew to a halt in an antechamber where two more guards stood waiting, halberds levelled to block a curtained archway. Alvantes stepped forward and conducted a brief, whispered conversation with the leftmost. Their weapons flicked up, with the most discreet of movements.

Alvantes motioned us onward. "He told me that His Highness currently has another guest, but will still grant you a short audience."

Estrada went first. I heard her gasp, a sharp intake of breath that she stifled immediately. I went after, easing the curtain aside. A chamber the size of a barn lay beyond, dominated by a stepped dais and the ornate, cushion-piled chair upon it. Before the dais was a small, plump figure so extravagantly bejewelled that he could only be the prince.

Another man stood beside him, taller, less gaudily arrayed and infinitely more impressive. Recognition turned my blood ice-cold in my veins.

"Welcome, welcome!" cried the prince. "I believe you already know my great friend and brother Moaradrid?"

CHAPTER FIFTEEN

"How generous of fortune to bring us all together."

The slightest hint of a smile tugged at Moaradrid's thin mouth. Bowing low, he continued, "Mayor Marina Estrada, an honour. I believe we almost met on the plains near Aspira Nero. You left before I could properly make your acquaintance."

Moaradrid looked to me, and I flinched. It was no more than the curl of a lip, but for an instant, the mask of civility slipped. The effect was like standing before an elegant townhouse and realising that a fire was raging behind its windows.

"You must be Easie Damasco, the…" He paused, as though hunting for the right word. "Shall we say 'adventurer'? Didn't I save you from hanging? A little gratitude mightn't have gone amiss."

He turned his attention on Saltlick. "Last, though hardly least, my errant warrior. I can only apologise for any… misunderstandings… while you were my guest."

I'd have never imagined anyone could describe torture as a misunderstanding so convincingly. It was strange to see Saltlick towering above the warlord, yet almost shaking with fear.

"No fight."

It was a plea rather than a statement. If Saltlick believed Moaradrid still had the chief stone, would he follow his orders? Estrada could reveal who really possessed the stone, of course, but with that last secret out, our lives wouldn't be worth a cup of rice.

"Now what's this talk of fighting?"

All four of us turned to Prince Panchetto. He'd been smiling contentedly until then, glancing from face to face as though he really believed this was some gathering of old acquaintances. Saltlick's reply had turned the smile into a nervous rictus.

"My apologies, Prince," said Moaradrid quickly. "The creature is confused."

"The creature," Estrada said, "is our friend and travelling companion."

"Indeed." Moaradrid bowed once more, making no attempt to conceal the irony this time. "And we must choose our friends wisely." He turned back to the prince and added, "Isn't that so, highness?"

"Of course we must. Yes, as the giant so cleverly said, we mustn't fight amongst ourselves. I sense tension amongst my guests, and that won't do at all."

"It could easily be resolved."

"Is that so?"

"A simple matter of…"

"A banquet!" interrupted the prince, with the energy of a philosopher struck by sudden inspiration. "Of course, we must all gather tonight for a banquet.

Nothing dissolves worries like honeyed wine and fine food. And musicians, I think, a few acrobats, perhaps a dancing bear or two..."

"Highness, my suggestion was..."

"Yes! We'll dine, discuss amusing trifles, and your problems will be laid to rest. Won't you all agree? I'd be hurt if you didn't." This last was spoken with such childish entreaty that I had to hide a smirk behind my hand. Moaradrid's expression was like a thunderhead about to burst. He looked as though he could cheerfully have lopped off the prince's head.

Estrada, though, was first to reply. "Prince, it would be our honour and pleasure. You're right. Our disagreements should be settled in a civilised manner." She put the barest emphasis on "civilised".

"Wonderful! Does the lady speak for all of you?"

"She's got my vote," I said, "I've never turned down free drinks in my life."

"A fine and noble philosophy. Giant, what of you?"

"Food good," said Saltlick shyly.

"Indeed it is. Moaradrid, you wouldn't spoil our evening of amusement, would you?"

"My Prince," said Moaradrid, "I wouldn't dream of spoiling your amusement."

The prince rapped a knuckle against a small gong suspended on the pedestal, and four palace guardsmen appeared, two from each of the nearby doorways. With more bowing on our part and nods from the prince, we were ushered into a side chamber, and Moaradrid was led away in a different direction – the only indication I'd seen that Panchetto had even the most basic grasp of the circumstances between us. It said a lot about the Altapasaedan court that an entire war could pass unnoticed. Perhaps it said a lot about the nature of the war as well.

An official in robes almost as lavish as the prince's was waiting beyond the curtain. Bobbing almost to the floor, he said, "It is my honour to act as the voice and hands of Prince Panchetto." He held out an ornate medallion to Estrada. "This indentifies you as a dignitary within the palace grounds. Wherever you go, you will be treated with the utmost deference. If there is anything you desire, simply ask and it will be provided."

"The prince is very generous," said Estrada, accepting the medallion and draping it around her neck.

The official nodded solemnly, as if this was the wisest thing he'd ever heard. He reached into a pocket and drew forth three rings, wide gold bands imprinted with the heron sigil of the Altapasaedan court. "The prince has extended the palace's credit to you for the purchase of certain articles: food, clothing, entertainment, trinkets and other necessities. Show these rings anywhere within the bounds of the city and you will not be charged."

Estrada and I slipped our rings onto whichever digits they fit best. Saltlick, who couldn't have worn his over even his littlest finger, clutched it in his hand instead.

"Rooms have been assigned to you," continued the official. "The prince wishes you a joyous day and anticipates the further delight of your company."

He bowed once more, turned and disappeared through the curtain into the throne room.

Taking this as a signal, our guards led the way through an arch behind us. Five bewildering minutes of wandering the palace's passageways and chambers brought us out at a long corridor with covered porticos spaced along both sides. An intricate mosaic of amber and lapis lazuli crawled up the walls and onto the ceiling, where it burst into bright flowers of pattern. Diamonds of white and grey tiles spread across the floor, and the curtains covering each doorway were a shimmering duck egg blue. We were wordlessly assigned to rooms, and ushered inside with such stark efficiency that we hadn't even time to say our goodbyes.

That was a relief. I had no desire to speak to anyone. I couldn't have felt more raw if every syllable from Moaradrid's mouth had been a physical lash, and I was grateful for the cool silence inside the room. I gazed vaguely around, took in nothing, and collapsed onto the bed.

It was a wonderful bed.

It seemed about as large as Captain Anterio's boat. In every other way, it was the opposite of that miserable craft: soft as moss, smelling faintly of lilac and patchouli, and cut off from the outside world not by reeking river water but by a silken canopy. I decided that if I died right there then my life wouldn't have been wasted. I'd sleep until Moaradrid's assassins came for me, and that would be the end of that.

"Damasco."

Estrada's voice. I ignored it.

"Damasco, we have to talk." She sounded unsteady, even afraid. That was novel, but not interesting enough to drag my head away from those luscious pillows.

"Damasco!"

I opened my eyes, against all my better judgement. "Get out, Estrada. If we're going to die then I'm getting some sleep in first."

She sat with a soft thud at the end of the bed. "It won't come to that."

"It already has. When will you admit you've lost? Why don't you go right now and give Moaradrid that cursed stone? Perhaps then one of us might at least survive the night."

"Damasco, I know things seem bad. You just have to trust me a little longer."

There was something plaintive in her tone that I found infuriating. "Estrada, I've never trusted you. You were just the best of a bad bunch of options. Now you're not even that."

She leaped up as if I'd set fire to the bed sheets. "You… all right. What I came to say – you'll go to the meal tonight, and you'll stay out of trouble. If you don't, I'll revoke my protection quicker than you can blink. After that, Panchetto and Moaradrid can fight over your carcass for all I care."

I was so taken aback that by the time I was ready to tell her what I thought, she'd gone.

I felt numb with anger for a while, and with other sensations too, fear high amongst them. I lay amidst plush cushions and glossy sheets, staring at the wall, bobbing like a coracle on a sea of vague but powerful emotions. All I could think was that I'd been betrayed. Moaradrid had caught up with us and, in this most crucial instant, Estrada had turned on me.

I was on my own now.

The whirlwind of thought settled slowly, leaving a few scattered certainties in its wake. Estrada had led us into a trap, and was too much the fool to admit her mistake. I'd tried to warn her and she'd threatened to abandon me, after everything I'd done for her and her absurd cause. So that was how it was.

No. That was how it had always been.

I tried to consider the positives. I might live another day, at least. It seemed the prince had used "great friend" as little more than an honorific when he'd introduced Moaradrid. After seeing them together, I couldn't imagine two men in the whole of the Castoval less likely to be friends. That said, Panchetto had more in common with the warlord than he had with Saltlick or me. They were bound by northern blood – presumably, what Panchetto had meant by "brother" – and both were rulers of a sort. That would likely tip the scales. If it didn't, if he didn't clap us back into irons and toss us to our enemy as a parting gift, it was perfectly possible that Moaradrid would try to storm the city.

I'd need a way out of Altapasaeda. I'd need funds enough to make sure I could never be found again, not by Moaradrid, Estrada or anyone else. I'd need help too, at least while I was within the city boundaries. Most of all, I'd have to move quickly.

A plan was forming in the deeper depths of my brain, like an itch I didn't dare scratch. I lay back and let it grow.

An hour had passed before I felt sure enough of my course to move. Granted, the delay had as much to do with the glorious paradise that was the bed. While a small part of my brain plotted, the remainder napped. Noises occasionally roused me from the fog of half-sleep – raised voices, and at one point a loud crash from nearby – but I managed to ignore them. Still, the urge to get moving nagged at me, more and more as my plan crystallised. It dragged me steadily away from the surrender of sleep and finally, mercilessly, drove me to my feet.

I explored the room before I left. It was probably simple and homely by the standards of the palace, with no furniture besides the magnificent bed and a marble sink filled with fresh water, but to me it seemed the height of sumptuousness. Near the door was a curtained aperture containing a fresh suit of clothes, grey trousers and a pale green shirt sequined in twin lines down the front and cut in the severe northern style. I decided to steal them, and then realised they'd probably been left for me anyway.

It occurred to me half way through changing that I should probably wash first. Only then did I discover how phenomenally dirty I was. Muck caked every inch of my body, and my hair was like the nest of some filth-loving bird.

With the grime cleaned away, it was as though I'd woken up in a new skin. The clothes turned out to be a perfect fit, and softer than any fabric I'd known. Unsoiled and stylishly dressed, I felt more optimistic. Here stood a new Easie Damasco, one fit to move in the highest strata of Castovalian society and to confound the plans of malevolent dictators and do-gooder ex-mayors alike.

Saltlick's room was at the far end of the corridor, with Estrada's in between. I realised as I tiptoed past that she was speaking to someone. She was talking softly, and the door hanging did a surprisingly good job of muffling her voice. I couldn't separate words when a man replied, but I recognised the speaker.

What was Guard-Captain Alvantes doing in Estrada's room?

Then again, perhaps it wasn't so strange. Alvantes would know about the conflict wracking the Castoval, however oblivious the Prince might be. He'd be equally aware of Estrada's part in it. It would have occurred to him that Moaradrid would move against her if things didn't rapidly go his way. As much as I hated the man, there was no denying that in his blinkered, black-and-white way he understood the Castoval better than most Altapasaedans. Anyway, he was probably doing me a favour. As long as he was bothering Estrada, neither of them was bothering me. If they spent the day arguing then all the better.

Another surprise awaited me when I reached Saltlick's room. Pinned to the curtain was a precisely written note that read: *The giant has been moved to the stables*. A peek through the curtain told me why. As comfortable as the beds might be, they weren't built to take a giant's weight. The grand four-poster was shattered down the middle and the two halves had collapsed in on each other. That explained the crash I'd heard. I couldn't help laughing at the image of Panchetto's servants discovering Saltlick amidst the wreckage. No wonder they'd decided the stables were a safer place for him.

I spent the next five minutes wandering aimlessly through the warren of the palace. I'd just decided that if I ever became a prince my first commandment would be to have maps placed at regular intervals around my home, when I stumbled over a serving girl carrying a basket of linen nearly as large as herself.

"Hey there, can you point me to the stables?"

She stared at me as if I'd asked for directions to the prince's underwear closet. I suddenly remembered the ring I'd been given. I held my hand in front of her face and said, "I'm a guest. Can you tell me how I get to the stables?"

She dropped the basket to point down the passage, and stammered, "Down there, third arch on the right, down the stairs, turn left, turn right and keep going all the way to the end, take the next left through the courtyard and they're right ahead."

I thanked her and followed her outstretched finger, glad of my good memory for directions. The stairs she'd mentioned led down into the nether-regions of the palace, an odorous, noisy dungeon of servants' quarters, kitchens, storerooms and workshops. I felt more at home immediately, and was disconcerted when my new clothes attracted curtsies and bows from the bustling maids and red-faced chefs I passed.

The courtyard the maid had mentioned turned out to be a small walled garden for the growing of herbs, spices, chillies and a few salad vegetables. An ancient gardener tipped his hat to me and mumbled something incomprehensible.

Purely out of awkwardness, I asked, "Are those the stables?" even though I'd have had to be blind, deaf and severely lacking a sense of smell not to recognise them as such.

This was apparently the kind of stupidity expected of passing nobles. He nodded vigorously, grumbled a few more unfathomable syllables, and turned his attentions to a bed of lettuce.

I didn't have to look hard for Saltlick. He was sat between two great mounds of hay, chewing contentedly, surrounded by a mob of fascinated stable boys.

"Hello, Saltlick," I said.

He looked up at me and beamed. He'd also been cleaned up, presumably by the stable staff. His various cuts and scrapes had been bandaged with fresh gauze and linen. He looked as happy as I'd ever seen him, and for the briefest moment I felt a little guilty for what I was about to do.

I pushed the thought aside. It was Estrada who'd landed us in this mess, and nothing I did could possibly make things worse.

"Saltlick," I said, "I've decided we're going to go shopping."

• • • •

It was mid afternoon when we set out, with perhaps a couple of hours left until the shops closed their shutters for the day. Just time enough for what I had in mind. I paced ahead, Saltlick trailing behind like some monstrous puppy. Though I hadn't been in Altapasaeda for a while I could still remember my way around. It was an easy place to navigate, with its clearly demarcated regions and countless landmarks. It only took me a few minutes to get back to the upper-class end of the market district.

Without an entourage of guards to deter attention, we drew more open stares this time. Most of those we passed were well-off Northerners; many drifted southward in the knowledge that their money would go farther in Altapasaeda than in their own lands. The locals treated their odd customs and odder religion with amused indulgence. They were harmless, the prince made no effort to spread his borders outside the walls, and they frequently had far more money than sense.

Not all of those around us, however, would be innocent shoppers. It seemed a safe bet we were being followed.

"I've been thinking, Saltlick," I said loudly. "You can't possibly go for dinner looking the way you do now. Unless you want one of these courtly ladies to die of embarrassment, we need to find you some clothes."

Saltlick looked alarmed, and nodded.

I picked out the clothiers with the widest entrance. Still, it was a chore manoeuvring Saltlick inside, and the proprietor looked less than pleased to see us. I waved my ring in his face and cried, "We are guests of the prince!"

His expression immediately turned solicitous. He stepped forward and bowed at once.

"We need to bring my companion here in line with the standards of civilisation," I said. "Do you think you can help?"

There followed much haggling with the prince's money. Eventually, and despite his claims that such a thing was impossible, I persuaded the clothier to have my order ready for collection at the end of the day. We'd settled on a loose-fitting robe worn under a wide cloak, both adorned with the modifications I'd insisted on when we were out of Saltlick's earshot. He'd come to see things my way once I'd explained that neither price nor quality was an object. The garments would probably cost more than some in the prince's own wardrobe, and would be unlikely to last a week. Neither fact mattered to me in the slightest.

The bargaining had taken longer than I'd have liked, though, and some of the more outrageously priced shops were already closing up. I was lucky to come across my next requirement after only a couple of minutes: a small apothecary nestled in the mouth of an alleyway.

"A moment," I said, and darted inside as though the thought had just occurred.

Saltlick eyed the small flask I came out with curiously.

"For indigestion," I said, displaying the bottle, which had indeed been intended to hold stomach cordial, though its original contents were now in the apothecary's drain. "We've been living on roots and berries these past few days. Mark my words, when we get some rich food inside us the results will be nothing less than interesting."

Though Saltlick looked puzzled – I doubted there was any food so rich that his cast-iron constitution couldn't handle it – he accepted the explanation.

"Just one more stop," I said. "I have a debt to settle with a certain riverboat captain."

Activity at the harbour was starting to wind down as the day drew towards a close. The chaos we'd witnessed that morning had settled to a bustle of loud arguments, dockers staggering beneath bales of cargo, and carts rattling back and forth with no regard for anyone in the way. I breathed a sigh of relief when I saw the vessel we'd arrived on still tied where we'd left it, and its captain sat at the stern with his legs dangling over the water, a pipe clamped between his teeth.

"There he is," I said. "Estrada told me she accidentally underpaid Captain Anterio, and asked if I'd come down to settle the rest. Why don't you wait here? I think the senile old fool is a bit afraid of you."

Saltlick looked hurt by the implication, but stayed where he was, immediately creating a large island amidst the harbour traffic.

Sure enough, when the captain glanced in our direction he jumped nervously to his feet. I doubted it had much to do with Saltlick. I was approaching from the direction of the gangplank, and he had nowhere to go except into the river. He looked as though he might be considering it.

"Captain Anterio," I cried heartily, "no need to be worried."

"Worried? Me? You're a rogue and a scoundrel, and if I thought I'd caused you an iota of inconvenience I'd dance a jig."

"No doubt. But you've been misinformed, Captain." I climbed the gangplank and when I was close enough that he could see, displayed the Prince's ring. "Easie Damasco, officer of the Altapasaedan Palace Guard at your service."

It was a calculated gamble. Anterio's ragged coat told me he'd once served in the City Guard, and it was common knowledge how they worked in dread of the Palace Guard, who were a law only to Panchetto and themselves and wont to interfere in matters of justice on the slightest whim. Anterio stared at me sceptically once his initial shock had worn off, and then pushed his nose very close to the ring to inspect it.

Before he could say anything I continued, "The woman you gave passage to this morning is the owner of a certain notorious establishment in Muena Palaiya, who's been accused of robbing her clientele in their sleep. A friend of the prince's had the matter… brought to his attention, shall we say. Since there isn't any law and order in that mud hole we were bringing her to the city for… ah, questioning."

If Anterio didn't look convinced, I at least had his attention.

"The giant is what you might call a pet of His Highness. He gets restless cooped up in the palace, so occasionally he's allowed out to assist us." I waved to Saltlick. "He's clever enough for simple tasks, so I asked him to escort the woman while I headed back downriver to attend to another matter. We allowed her to pretend she was in charge to preserve some scrap of dignity. Of course, the old harlot found a way to ruin our plans, and now there are enemies of the prince carrying on their business unimpeded because I'm stranded here. Well, you couldn't have known."

"Why didn't you tell me this at the time?"

"Truth be told, I was glad of the break. The matter I have to attend to is rather unsavoury. Still, I'm only a humble servant of His Highness, and I shouldn't prevaricate much longer."

"I can't believe it." Though he spoke flatly, it was easy to detect a note of doubt in Anterio's tone.

"Come now, Captain," I said, "I'm sure you noticed us leading her off this morning, with the assistance of the City Guard. The wench made certain everyone in the market saw us go by, despite our attempts at discretion. Half of Altapasaeda knows she was clapped in irons. The woman has no shame."

Anterio shook his head. "To think. She seemed such a lady…"

"You're not the first to be fooled by that pretty face," I told him, with a sympathetic pat on the shoulder. "So now that you know the truth, perhaps we can reinstate our business deal? Since I'm here I might as well clear up a few loose ends, but I'll need to be off soon."

We made the final arrangements; I gave Anterio back the four onyxes, and turned to leave. I'd been desperately tempted to suggest simply departing there and then, but I knew I wouldn't get far. I was certain now that I was being watched. Half a dozen faces had become familiar since we'd left the palace. Hopefully they'd have overheard the explanation I'd given Saltlick about settling for our morning's passage. At any rate, I couldn't imagine they'd gleaned any clue to my real plans from the afternoon's charade.

Just in case, when I reunited with Saltlick – who was obviously growing tired of being heckled by angry dockworkers – I said loudly, "All done. Captain Anterio has gratefully received his dues from this morning, I have my stomach medicine, and now we'll go and collect your fine new clothes."

It sounded convincing enough. Yet, even as I listened to my own words, a voice of doubt intruded.

Then we'll go for dinner with Moaradrid.

And then – assuming he doesn't climb over the table to cut my heart out right there and then – I'll get to stake my life on the most absurdly dangerous crime of my career.

CHAPTER SIXTEEN

My fears and doubts began to fade as we wandered back from the docks, until I found myself feeling almost cheerful. For the first time in a long while, I was doing something more than being driven by the whims of others. There was a degree of comfort, too, in knowing that the trials of the last few days were, one way or another, about to reach a conclusion. Rationalisations aside, though, it felt good to be simply walking. I'd grown so used to fleeing for my life that just to saunter was a pleasure.

Most of the stalls had disappeared from the market square, leaving a wind-swept space broken up by a few wooden frames stripped of their canvas. Further on, the last shopkeepers were bringing in their produce, collapsing canopies, dropping shutters and bolting doors. The sun was barely halfway down the sky, and it was too early for any kind of nightlife. The streets were nearly deserted, with only a few last-minute shoppers rushing by, too busy to pay us much attention. There were hardly any carts or horses, so we stuck to the middle of the road, picking our way amongst puddles of rotten fruit and vegetables, dung, and other less identifiable refuse.

The respite, like all good things, proved short-lived. I hadn't been unduly worried about being tailed before, when we were safe amongst the crowds and it suited me to have witnesses who'd report my cover story to whoever their paymasters might be. Since we'd started back, though, two men had been staying close to us, making less and less of an attempt to hide their presence. They wore their cloaks loose enough to conceal weapons, walked with a sort of compulsive sneakiness, and in general had the air of gutter criminals. Perhaps I wasn't one to judge on that count, but at least I'd always tried to steer away from violence. Something told me these two didn't suffer from the same compunction.

As the last shop doors slammed shut, as their straggling customers became scarcer, so the pair quickened their pace. My backward glances were met with less than friendly grins. It struck me that they might not be agents of one or other interested party. They might simply be cutthroats who'd spied a well-off tourist and decided to chance their luck. Yet that made little sense. No thief, no matter how desperate, would consider anyone accompanied by Saltlick an easy mark.

Part of me felt that feigned indifference was my best chance. However, it was becoming harder not to hurry. Our pursuers matched every slight increase of speed. They were drawing closer, and any pretence of disinterest had vanished.

If there'd been anyone to see, they'd have wondered why someone with a giant by their side was fleeing two shabby vagabonds. We would probably have looked comical.

I didn't feel it.

I fought the urge to run, and wracked my memory for a route that would take us quickly to some populated area. We were near the edge of the upper market district, heading towards the temple district. That would be equally barren at this hour. The palace was hopelessly far. Surely we'd be safe as long as we stuck to the major thoroughfares, though? Surely they wouldn't dare attack us in the open, where anyone might chance by?

Three figures stepped from the shadows of an alcove ahead. A moment later they'd spread across the road. They looked nonchalant; as though blocking roads was something they did every day. That confidence frightened me more than anything.

An alley threaded off to our right. "Saltlick! This way."

Saltlick, apparently oblivious to the threats now behind and ahead of us, looked puzzled, but followed as I darted into the shadows. The passage was wider than I'd expected, broad enough for him to pass unimpeded. It was longer than I'd hoped it would be. It was also a lot more occupied. These two looked a lot like their friends who'd followed us from the docks, or perhaps a little meaner. If their smiles were anything to go by, they were pleased to see us. I didn't need the sound of footsteps closing behind to tell me we had nowhere to run.

"You look like busy individuals, so I'll save you some time. We don't have any money."

"I think we'd just as soon check for ourselves." That was the one on the left.

"You could try. But would it be worth the bother of having Saltlick here pound you to death with your own spleen?"

His eyes crawled nervously up Saltlick's bulk, and his confidence seemed to flag.

A voice behind us said, "The monster won't hurt anyone, Pedero. Get it done."

"That's what I like to see, people who aren't afraid to gamble with their lives."

The words came out more obviously scared than I'd have liked. The one behind us had sounded too sure. He knew Saltlick wasn't a threat. Bluffing wasn't going to work.

"Saltlick, these men want to hurt us," I said. "Stop you going home, stop us helping Estrada. You're not going to let them are you?"

"No fight." He sounded nervous, but he meant it.

"Told you," said the voice from behind us. "Wouldn't stamp a rat. So get on with it." Then, apparently to us – it was hard to tell without taking my eyes off Pedero – he added, "No one has to get hurt."

"Nobody said we *can't* hurt them."

Pedero planted his palm on my chest and shoved. I tumbled backwards, narrowly missed the pillar of Saltlick's left leg, struck the wall and landed hard. Pedero had a knife out by the time I looked up, one of the jagged blades favoured by local lowlifes. His companion drew his as well. It slid from the oiled leather scabbard with a serpentine hiss.

"Work first, fun later." This from the leader. "Turn out your pockets, and no tricks."

I wondered what trick he imagined would help me out of such a situation. This was no ordinary robbery, that much was obvious. If there was something I could do or say to help myself it lay in that fact, but my panicked brain drew a blank.

I wrenched Panchetto's ring from my finger, dropped it on the pavement in front of me. "That's all I have."

"Sure it is. Keep going."

I realised, as I should have from the start, that they were looking for something in particular. It could only be the stone, which meant these were agents of Moaradrid's. Not his own men, everything about them told me they were local ruffians, but in his pay all right. How else could they have known Saltlick wouldn't resist?

I took out my dagger and the bottle, placed them beside the ring.

"What's that?" Pedero asked, eyeing the bottle distrustfully.

"Medicine," I said. "It's for my stomach."

Pedero ran a thumb along the flat of his knife. "Might take more than medicine," he said.

"Look, I don't have what you're after." I craned my head towards the leader and his troupe. There were five of them blocking the mouth of the alley, effectively screening Pedero and me from passing observers.

"I know what Moaradrid's paid you to find. I don't have it."

If I'd hoped the mention of his employer's name might rattle him, I was disappointed. "It'd be better for you if you did. What kind of thieves would we be if we took your word? We'll just have to keep looking. If it isn't outside, maybe Pedero can turn it up *inside*."

I started to my feet. Pedero stepped forward and I shrank back. The others edged closer too, like fingers of a closing fist. I could barely make out Saltlick through the press. All I could see clearly was the glint of knives. The last vestige of my courage failed. "I don't have it," I sobbed. "But I can tell you where it is!"

Suddenly everything was chaos.

I caught a sense of movement, the semi-circle of bodies crumpled, and instinctively I threw my arms over my face. A blow thrust me sideways. A fraction of an instant later I was dragged upward. I clawed at the cobblestones, as if they'd somehow save me. Seeing the precious ring, I grabbed for it, missed, and caught the bottle instead.

Another lurch threw the ground out of my reach. I stared for a moment into Pedero's face, inexplicably now at eye level. He looked as surprised as I felt. Then he was hurled abruptly backwards. I only realised it was actually me moving when the rest of them jerked into focus.

They were starting to react. One cried, "You told us the giant wouldn't…" and trailed off, as if unsure of exactly what it was the giant was doing.

My addled brain belatedly put the scene together. I could feel Saltlick's fingers, bunched tight in a knot of my cloak. He was holding me stretched out behind him, and moving so fast that by the time I'd worked it out we were almost clear. Our would-be muggers were starting after us half-heartedly. They stood no hope of matching those mammoth strides.

"Go left," I gurgled, and he did, careening out of the alley into the street. The passage had deposited us on the north edge of the market district, a region of small warehouses that met the eastward docks. There was still some traffic there, mostly over-laden carts. Our appearance was met with raucous cries and laughter.

I didn't mind at first – better alive and funny than a serious corpse. I began to reconsider when we were further up the street and it was clear no one was following.

"That's enough, Saltlick."

He stopped so abruptly that my forehead bounced off his thigh.

"Ow! I mean put me down, damn it."

He did, and I promptly collapsed, my sense of balance utterly destroyed. I sat in the filth of the gutter, waiting for the world to stop rotating. When it settled enough that I could wobble to my feet, the first thing I did was punch Saltlick with all my strength. I couldn't reach very high. It still felt good.

He stared at me, obviously more emotionally than physically hurt. "Do wrong?"

"Not wrong. Too late! Why couldn't you have done that in the first place? Before the pushing and the threatening and the point where I nearly got my belly slit?"

He hung his head. "Didn't think."

"And why couldn't you just slap them about a bit? No one's saying you had to tear their heads off, but just standing there like a colossal pudding..."

"No fight."

"You were happy enough to fight when we were escaping Moaradrid's camp!"

It was always hard to read expressions on Saltlick's misshapen features, but the look of guilt that swept over them then was unmistakeable. Of course he'd just been tortured then, and had probably been half out of his mind...

My anger evaporated. I forced a smile. "You did good. Next time just don't wait so long. Well, we'd better get back and start getting ready for the... oh *shit!*"

Saltlick's new clothes! I'd been navigating, without really thinking about it, back to the clothiers before we'd been attacked. Would it still be open? It had damned well better be, given the amount I'd charged to the prince's accounts.

"Come on," I said, leading the way. Then a thought occurred. "If we run into those lowlifes again, you do what you did before. You've got my permission." They might still be scouring the streets, and I could stand a little more indignity if it kept me out of harm's way.

We soon reached a crossroads, where our course intersected one of the main roads connecting the northern gates with the south side of the city. A left turn brought us back within the boundaries of the market district, at the upper-class end. Our appearance was met by strident birdcalls from countless gilded cages suspended beneath a whitewashed arch above. Here there were still a few shoppers, elegant couples challenging the storekeepers to close and so lose their custom. A couple of City Guardsmen loitered on the corner and – thanks perhaps to their presence – there was no trace of our newfound acquaintances.

The clothier was shut, as I'd feared. I hammered on the door. Just as I was about to start shouting, he opened up. He looked alarmed, and the expression only partly left him when he realised who we were.

"Oh," he said. "Well, I told you it was impossible."

"You haven't done the work?"

"No, I have. But the measurements, the cut… you have to understand, I don't get many customers of this gentleman's… ah, stature."

He ducked inside, and returned with a parcel tied with strips of cloth. "They should fit well enough. They might even hold together for a week if he's careful." With a nervous laugh, he added, "Just don't take him to any parties, eh?"

The clear blue sky was streaked with bands of violet and amber by the time we reached the palace. I only realised at the last minute what a state my own clothes were in after my time spent wallowing in the gutter. I couldn't blame the guards for looking cynical when I claimed we were guests of the prince.

They must have heard of Saltlick's presence, though, because he hardly had time to produce his ring before they let us through. I was glad they didn't ask to see mine. One guard led us inside and handed us on to a pair of servants, with directions to take us to our rooms.

"Are you going to be all right with those?" I asked Saltlick, indicating the parcel beneath his arm.

He nodded.

"Well then. I suppose I'll see you at the festivities."

I allowed myself to be led off into the palace. I was starting to form a sense of the layout, and I took care to be attentive this time, noting every turn and adding each new passage into my developing mental map. I got the impression the building was frequently modified – I could imagine the prince demanding a set of kitchens be turned suddenly into a swimming pool, for example – and the design was severely lacking in logic. Still, by the time we arrived at my chamber I felt I'd grasped the basic floor plan.

The first thing I noticed inside was that the room had been searched. It was hardly a ransacking: nothing had been damaged, and it was only a thief's sixth sense that tipped me off. The evidence was there, though, once I started investigating. Most obvious was how the dirty clothes I'd discarded on the floor had subtly moved position. There were other explanations, of course; but servants would have cleaned or made the bed, and no one merely looking for me would have hunted through every nook and cranny. No, after what had happened in the market district I felt certain that this too was Moaradrid's handiwork. He might even have guessed I didn't have the stone on me. Perhaps the mugging had only been meant to ensure I stayed away.

I wondered if Estrada had been similarly molested. Maybe Moaradrid had already secured the stone, and this whole nightmare was over. It seemed too good to be true, and I remembered how I'd heard Alvantes in her room. Had she had the sense to seek out the one person in Altapasaeda who could guarantee her safety?

Given Alvantes's attitude, I doubted the same tactic would work so well for me. I'd have to be watchful for further attacks. I couldn't let paranoia interfere with my plans, though; I had too much left to do, and time was running out.

I spent five minutes cleaning the worst of the dirt from my clothes before I set out again. I'd worked out that the whole north wing was given over to the prince's dependants: the stables, servants' quarters and guest rooms. Our corridor was right upon the edges of the latter two, as befitted unwelcome visitors of lowly stature. I had a rough idea where the other borders were, but there was one crucial question that needed settling.

I followed my recollected map and found a staircase leading to the floor below. Sure enough, here were the more extravagant guest chambers, for visitors the prince valued more than political refugees and their hangers-on. Each room was about twice the size of mine, so far as I could judge. The passage was wider too, and furnished with tapestries and potted palms no doubt imported at huge expense. I spent a minute making sure of my bearings, worrying all the while that a guard would appear. Once I was certain, I selected a doorway, and pushed through the covering drape.

What drew my gaze first was the large sunken pool filling much of the floor space. Steam rose in fragrant curls from its surface, and it looked hugely inviting. Less welcoming was the expression of the small but colossally fat man lying up to his triple chins in the water. He sat up on seeing me, with a splash that sent wavelets flooding into the corners of the room. Our eyes met. His were tiny, round, and a little bloodshot. We stayed like that for a while, my feigned surprise just as exaggerated as his genuine alarm.

"I don't remember having a pool in my room," I said.

The fat man stood up, and – apparently only realising then that he was naked – grabbed a robe from a chair beside the pool and hauled it round himself. "This is my room!"

"Are you sure?"

"Absolutely I am."

I nodded thoughtfully. "Well, I definitely didn't have anything like this." I grinned. "My mistake. I'm Easie Damasco, by the way."

He looked at me blankly.

"I'm with Mayor Estrada."

That sparked a little interest in his beady eyes. "Oh really? But… well, I'd expected you to be… I mean, you're very small for a…"

"For a…?"

"Well, I'd have expected a giant to be a little more *giant*."

"Oh. No, I'm the other one."

"Ah, the… other one."

I'd watched his mouth form around the word "thief". Panchetto hadn't been shy about announcing the presence of his unusual guests.

"Well, I'm sorry for bothering you. Perhaps we'll meet again at the banquet tonight?"

"Oh yes, I always come to the prince's parties. First at the table, last to leave, that's me."

"An excellent attitude. Sorry once more."

I backed out through the curtain. The fat man waved and lost his grip on the towel. The last I saw, he was scrabbling to conceal his very limited assets.

I hurried back down the passage, up the stairs, rushed into the familiar corridor, and barely avoided colliding with Estrada and Saltlick. They were being led by two of the palace guards, the four of them heading away from our rooms.

"Damasco," Estrada said. "Where have you been? We've been waiting for you. The banquet's already started."

CHAPTER SEVENTEEN

Say what you like about Panchetto, the man knew how to throw a party.

We'd been led once more through the labyrinthine passages, to be deposited this time in a hall somewhere deep within the southern wing. It was grand even compared to the rest of the palace: a long space measured by high arches that supported open crescent windows, in turn giving way to an oval cupola set with blood red glass. The tables, following the northern fashion, were set at knee height and bordered not with benches but with heaps of embroidered cushions. Braziers burned at intervals along the arcades, and the ceiling threw back the firelight in shimmering slants.

The entertainers were already in full swing, undeterred by the lack of an audience. A large band played on a stage set in the shadows of the far end; the music was sinuous and complex, so subtle that it hardly registered on the ear. Tumblers and jugglers threaded around each other, performing outrageous stunts with blank-faced composure. There was even the promised dancing bear, though its performance bore little relation to the murmur of pipes and guitars, and was marred by its expression of stolid misery. I decided I'd rather watch the serving girls, who were manoeuvring through the chaos wearing little besides handkerchiefs and smiles.

Panchetto had spared no trouble or expense. Here was a space devoted utterly to the repose of body and mind, and I couldn't help but be impressed by the single-minded lavishness of it all.

It was only a shame that so much effort had been wasted. He could have relaxed us just as well by hurling us into a pit of rabid dogs.

For there, waiting with perfect stillness in an aperture half way along one wall, stood Moaradrid. He was flanked by two bodyguards, neither of them taking any pains to disguise their function. It was clear too that the warlord had picked his position for the vantage point it offered over the chamber. His only concession had been to relinquish his armour for a simple cream robe, belted with a wide bruise-purple sash. I thought for a moment he'd even come unarmed, until I noticed the dagger worn where his scimitar would have been.

Moaradrid's disdain stood out all the more in the absence of other guests. The scattered bunches soon swelled into a crowd, however, as new arrivals appeared by ones and twos. In a few minutes, Moaradrid had been mercifully hidden from view, and I could think about something other than his eyes boring into me. Saltlick, Estrada and I had kept together until then, a gloomy island amidst the throng. I was considering an attempt at conversation when Estrada broke away, and flitted through the shifting mass of bodies towards the entrance. Guard-Captain Alvantes, newly arrived, saw her coming and greeted her with a nod. He was out of uniform, looking uncomfortable in a plain shirt and open waistcoat. A pathetic part of me hoped she'd drag him back to join our group. No such luck. They stayed near the archway and didn't as much as glance in our direction.

I glanced around, hoping to spy someone I could at least say "hello" to. It was galling to realise that, apart from Saltlick and possibly Estrada, everyone I knew there would have cheerfully seen me dead. I had as much in common with the rest as rat droppings to diamonds. My new clothes, which had seemed so elegant in the privacy of my room, were now just barely tailored enough to distinguish me from the servants.

My desperation reached a peak. I began seriously to consider attempting a discussion with Saltlick. I was spared by a gong sounding from the stage, a deep, throbbing note that set the whole room aquiver. The entertainers dissolved away, a pair of handlers manoeuvred the bear out, and the serving girls began to guide us to our allocated places. The pulse of a dozen different conversations fell quiet. All eyes turned expectantly to the head of the table, where Panchetto was the only one left standing.

Arms held high, hands fluttering in the air as though showering invisible delicacies, the prince cried, "A thousand welcomes to my beloved guests! You honour me with your presences. Most of you have attended my little gatherings before, however some are joining us for the first time, and their company is especially delightful. I refer of course to our visiting dignitaries, Moaradrid of Shoan and Mayor Marina Estrada, and to their entourages." Panchetto motioned almost imperceptibly towards Saltlick, and the faintest tremor of laughter ran around the room. "I hope you'll all show them the esteem they deserve."

I hadn't imagined it. Panchetto had just mocked us to his friends. Until then, I'd naively accepted his claim that the get-together was for our benefit. It struck me belatedly that it was a hundred times more likely we'd been shoehorned in as an easy solution to an awkward dilemma – or worse, as titillation for his bored friends. I'd underestimated him. I might almost have been impressed, but for one thing: he in turn was underestimating Moaradrid, and I'd learned myself how catastrophic that could be. For Moaradrid's expression was like a storm shadow; if I was being overly sensitive, I wasn't the only one.

Of course, it might have had as much to do with being seated within spitting distance of myself. We were at the farthest end of the table: me, Saltlick and Estrada on one side, Moaradrid and his grim bodyguards on the other. Captain Alvantes had been placed next to Moaradrid, which could easily be read as a further snub. Was this Panchetto's way of showing the barbarian his true standing in the grander scheme of things?

If so, I could think of easier ways to commit suicide. It was as though someone had carved a line through the table, dividing the two extremes by a fathomless gulf. Around the prince, the hall was a whirlpool of conversation. I noticed the fat man whose room I'd invaded earlier sat close by him, head thrown back in paroxysms of laughter. All of the men were equally overweight and jolly, while their women were dusky and soft-spoken. Their garments were lavish, not quite to the point of extravagance. They wore jewellery, but slyly, so that the nod of a head or wave of a hand revealed some gem that spat back the red-tinged light.

On the other side of the chasm there was us. We looked comically plain in our simple clothes. Estrada had opted for a light linen dress that would have been elegant in other circumstances, but seemed merely rustic in the vicinity of so much wealth. The silence was molten and close, like a burning hot summer's day. I felt sure that at any moment Moaradrid would kick over the table and plunge his knife into someone's chest. The more I imagined it, the more I thought it might be a relief.

When the first serving girl began to bring out food, I nearly leaped to my feet and hugged her. Her appearance didn't so much break the tension as divert it, but at least we could pretend we'd been waiting to start eating rather than for violence to erupt. The procession of bowls and platters reminded me of a bucket chain at a fire, and soon the tables were groaning beneath their weight.

Grateful for a subject that might not provoke bloodshed, I asked Estrada, "Is this really all for tonight?"

She looked surprised. "Damasco, this is only the entree."

Alvantes, seeing my astonishment, said, "What's wrong, Damasco? Confused by the thought of food you don't have to steal?"

"At least I wasn't invited to keep the rabble in order," I muttered, and then – realising I'd just insulted Moaradrid, not to say myself – I bowed my head over my plate and pretended it was absorbing all my attention. It wasn't such a pretence; nor was Alvantes's comment so wide of the mark. After my miserable existence of the last few weeks, it was hard to believe the variety and quantity of food within my reach. Partly to divert attention from my misjudged comment and partly from genuine curiosity, I pointed to one plate and asked Estrada, "What's that?"

"It's spiced fish eggs, Damasco."

"Ugh. How about those?"

"I think they're stuffed dormice."

"Really? And this?"

"Damasco," she said, "if I spend the night giving you a tour of our meal, when do you expect me to actually eat any of it?"

Quietened again, I glanced once more around the table. I wasn't the only one wary of our host's beneficence. Moaradrid was eating sparely, touching no dish that one or other of his bodyguards hadn't tasted first. His paranoia was probably healthy for a man in his circumstances, but I was under no such compunction.

Anyone who wanted me dead would hardly go to the trouble of poisoning me. I settled for sampling a little of everything within reach, until my plate threatened to overflow. I plunged my spoon into the teetering mass, just as a reedy voice from the far end of the table called, "Now that our new guests are settled, perhaps it's time we discussed this nonsense of a war?"

It was fortunate I wasn't eating; I'd certainly have choked. I could hear Estrada spluttering beside me.

"They tell me it's all to do with some stone. Surely that can't be true? Moaradrid, Lady Estrada, my dear friends, please don't tell me you're harbouring animosities over something as silly as a missing pebble?"

I wanted to crawl out of my skin. Since that didn't seem realistic, I settled on scrunching as low into my cushions as I could. I dared a glance at Saltlick to see how he'd reacted to this mention of the giant-stone. The answer was not at all. He either hadn't understood or wasn't listening, because his attention was focused entirely on the heaped bowl of vegetables before him.

Neither Moaradrid nor Estrada had shown any inclination to address the prince's question. He went on, with mock exasperation, "Can't one of you at least tell me how this foolishness started?"

"The details are irrelevant," said Moaradrid. His voice was perfectly toneless. "That thief stole what was mine."

"But really, can it be worth getting so upset about?"

If I hadn't already felt sure that my worst fears were valid, the titters rising from Panchetto's end of the table confirmed it. The prince's regular guests were lapping up this goading of the visiting savage.

I was more surprised that Moaradrid seemed to be just about keeping his cool. "Perhaps not, Highness. Yet there's such a thing as honour. It would be better for everyone if what was stolen is returned."

"You stole it in the first place." I couldn't help myself. As soon as the words were out of my mouth, I wanted nothing but to take them back. Since I couldn't, I kept going. "I'm not saying I have it, but if I did, maybe I'd just be returning it to where it belonged."

"There, the thief is an altruist," cried Panchetto. "What do you think of that, friend Moaradrid?"

"I think that this childishness bores me."

A deep hush fell over the table. Whether the comment was aimed at me or the prince, it was blatant enough to silence even Panchetto.

The servants, misinterpreting the unnatural quiet or the fact no one except Saltlick was eating, began clearing away the tableware. As before, their intervention defused a little of the tension – and as before, I knew it could only be a brief reprieve.

The prince took up another subject, pointedly aiming his remarks at those closest to him. Moaradrid sat very still, with his eyes almost closed and his hands laid flat before him, as if meditating. I could hear his breathing, each exhale sharp as a knife thrust. Glancing aside, I noticed Estrada look anxiously to Alvantes, as if to ask, *"How far will this go?"*

Well, that was easy. Panchetto wouldn't stop baiting

Moaradrid, and Moaradrid wouldn't sit quietly and take it forever.

I couldn't wait any longer.

"They're taking our dinner away," I moaned, as though the serving girl who'd just appeared to remove the bowl in front of me were tearing the food from my very mouth. "Hey, what's that? I didn't get to try any." I grabbed for some strips of meat on the edge of Estrada's plate and my wrist struck her glass, splashing its contents over the table.

"Damn it! Don't worry, I'll get you another."

I snatched up the goblet and chased after the nearest serving girl. Half a dozen semi-clothed beauties were tasked solely with keeping everyone's glasses filled from the amphorae they cradled. I pushed the refilled glass before Estrada, who thanked me with a glare.

The servants worked with brutal efficiency. Hardly a minute had passed before the barely-touched first course had vanished. Close on its heels came the centrepiece of the banquet: a colossal boar, reeking of hot fat, paprika and sweet wine. There followed bowls of rice, some spiced, some mixed with pickled fruit or titbits of seafood; platters laden with every conceivable vegetable prepared in every imaginable manner; and countless pastries, breads and sweetmeats. I wanted to condemn the waste and gluttony – but, sitting in the midst of it, I simply couldn't. I could only be awed, and wonder how I'd ever return to a life of poverty.

Educated by my earlier failure and a growling stomach, I settled for a dripping hunk of meat and some fried rice and tucked in. This was sure to be the grandest meal of my life, and I wanted to try at least a little of it before the prince resumed his unconventional entertainments.

My wolfish eating might normally have drawn comment, but that night I'd have probably had to tip the plate over my head. Everyone not in conversation with the prince was staring at Saltlick, who at that moment was half way through a tureen of vegetables that would have served half a dozen people. He'd been eating steadily since the first dish had been set down, and showed no sign of slowing. There was something awful and fascinating in the way he crammed handfuls into his maw, like watching a forest fire laying bare vast tracts of wilderness. Many of the prince's guests, and especially the ladies for some reason, were so enraptured that they were ignoring their own appetites altogether.

The prince must have considered Saltlick sufficient amusement, because he continued to keep his conversation amongst the chosen few around him. At first I was glad of an interval, but as the quiet wore on the tension grew, until even the effort of chewing ground on my nerves. My stomach began to ache and grumble. I wished the bottle in my pocket really did contain medicine.

I pushed my plate aside and leaned away. Others around the table were making similar motions – reclining, edging back, picking half-heartedly at scraps. I could see the prince's piggy eyes flitting from figure to figure, noting yawns and glazed expressions. I tensed.

"Really," he began, as though the break in conversation had lasted seconds instead of minutes, "the thing I truly can't understand is why you've all come to Altapasaeda. As delightful as your company is, you must know how we detest squabbles."

"We didn't mean to bring our problems to your door, Prince," replied Estrada. It was the first she'd said to him all evening, and the words were very slightly slurred. "Our lives were in danger. We had nowhere else to go."

"In danger? Moaradrid, tell me that isn't true."

"The thief stole from me. This woman is protecting him. She is mistaken in doing so."

"A mistake I'm repeating, eh?" Panchetto's voice held an edge that I'd never have expected. It struck me then that an opportunity to remove Moaradrid without too much show would suit him well, his father even more so. If an excuse arose to arrest Moaradrid then all sorts of fates might befall him in the depths of the palace dungeons, fates that could be kept from his generals until reinforcements arrived.

The same would have occurred to Moaradrid, of course, probably long before he considered setting foot in the city. He was playing a dangerous game, made more risky by his own temper. He managed to control it this time, though barely. "There can be no comparison, Highness. Only you can judge to whom your hospitality extends."

"That's very true. But surely the same can be said of our lovely lady mayor?"

"There's a difference between princely generosity and the harbouring of a fugitive."

"How can he be a fugitive? You don't make the law." This time, Estrada's words came out in one long jumble, and she rested both hands on the table to steady herself.

"I say again: an object was stolen from me. This injustice must be redressed."

"It's like Easie said… you stole it too. You stole it *more*." Estrada pushed back from the table and her entire upper body swayed. "You… it's all your fault." She raised one hand and stared at it, as if unsure where it had come from. "You are a very bad man," she concluded – just in time to keel backwards and roll onto the floor.

I leaped to my feet.

"Marina? What is it? What's wrong?"

I knelt beside her and made a show of checking her breathing.

"She's only fainted," I said, with the assurance of one who'd been studying medicine all his life. I tried to glare equally at Panchetto and Moaradrid. "You should be ashamed of yourselves."

My words brought a sympathetic murmur from around the table. I couldn't have cared less what those pampered lordlings thought, but it was vital no one try to interfere.

Before anyone could, and I could see Alvantes considering it, I turned to Saltlick and said, "We should put her to bed. Will you help me carry her?"

Saltlick nodded and lifted Estrada in his arms. It

was oddly touching to see how gently he held her limp figure, a scene only slightly spoiled by the saliva dribbling from her lower lip.

"Come on," I said, heading towards the entrance. Saltlick fell in dutifully behind me. Panchetto stood at the last moment and – failing to hide his attempt to regain the initiative very well – said, "Won't you wait while I call my personal physician?"

"That won't be necessary. I'm sure she just needs rest and quiet."

"Then I'll send one of my men to escort you." Panchetto motioned to one of the guards.

"We can find our own way," I replied curtly, and was out of the room before he could say anything more.

It was true, I'd taken care to memorise our route, and I made it back to our corridor without difficulty. I led the way into Estrada's room and signalled Saltlick to lay her on the bed. She grunted when he did so, mumbled something incomprehensible, and rolled onto her side. An instant later, the chamber echoed to the sound of snoring.

Saltlick stood close by, gazing down. He turned to me and whispered, "Marina sick?"

"Not really. I drugged her glass when I refilled it, but it'll wear off in an hour or two."

"*Drugged?*" Now his voice was thunderous.

"Keep it down! It was only a little. How else was I supposed to get us away from that insane party?"

That threw him. I could see the confusion and anger battling across his features. Interesting as it was, I had to focus on the task at hand. First, I eased the medallion that Panchetto had given her from around Estrada's neck and draped it round my own. It was harder to untie the pouch at her throat, but eventually I pried loose the knot and it fell into my hands.

I turned to find Saltlick glowering at me. "Stop stealing!"

"I don't think so," I said. "Not when there's a whole palace of wealth up for grabs." I slipped the chief-stone from its pouch and held it up towards his face. "And not when I have my very own giant to help me."

CHAPTER EIGHTEEN

More emotions traipsed over Saltlick's features in the space of that minute than in the entire time I'd known him. The parade began with delight, as though he'd just rediscovered a lost friend. That segued into bafflement, quickly followed by alarm, a brief return of pleasure, something that was possibly shock, and finally, an expression of vague, bewildered horror.

"How..." he asked. Rather than finish the question, he reached towards the stone. I wondered what I'd do if he tried to take it from me – the possibility hadn't entered my mind until then – but he stopped short of even touching it. "How?" he repeated, in the tone someone might use to ask how a loved one had died.

I didn't want to imagine what his reaction would be to finding out I'd stolen the stone with his unwitting help, only to carry it about in ignorance while Moaradrid strove to recover it. And how would he like the news that Estrada had taken it from me, knowing what it was, letting the warlord think I still had it?

"What's important is that I have it, and that makes me your chief. Am I right? You have to do what I say, even if you don't like it?"

Saltlick nodded. I could tell from the way his shoulders sagged that he knew where this was going.

"Excellent. Now listen carefully..."

I gave him his instructions as slowly and precisely as I could, and then repeated them just in case. He looked more crestfallen with each word. I can honestly say I felt a little sorry for him. Moaradrid, Mounteban, Alvantes, that idiot Panchetto and perhaps most of all Estrada, they'd all abused me, tricked me or manipulated me in one way or another. Saltlick had never done anything more offensive than pick his toenails in my presence.

I wasn't about to let sympathy get in my way, though. Not tonight, not when I'd made it this far. "You understand all that? Are you sure? Then get going, and don't foul it up."

Saltlick lumbered out of the room with a last sorrowful glance towards Estrada's prone form. I listened as his footsteps receded down the corridor in the direction of the stables, and then sat on the bed to wait. Estrada made a small, complaining noise and rolled over. The sleeping draught had erased whatever care she'd taken for the party. Her hair was a dishevelled cloud, and a thread of drool still hung down her chin. It had given her face a sort of guileless quality in return. That, together with the moonlight streaming through the window, had smoothed away some of her sharp edges. I could almost see how a man like Mounteban might find her attractive.

I shuddered. Better him than me!

I stood and went out into the corridor. The lamps along the walls were unlit, presumably because the party was supposed to go on until much later. I felt sure I saw I saw a flicker of movement at the end of the passage, which disappeared the moment my eyes passed over it. A spy of Panchetto's? I hoped so. "I'll check in on you later, Marina," I stage-whispered. "Don't worry, I'll only be next door."

I went back into my own room, looking everywhere but where that glimpse of motion had been. Once inside, I checked there were no gaps around the edges of the door-curtain where suspicious eyes could peek inside. Satisfied that I was safe from observation, I moved to the bed. I stripped off the sheets, as quietly as I could manage, and piled them on the floor.

I spent the next few minutes knotting bed sheets end to end, and then testing the knots as well as I could without making undue noise. At the end of that time, I had a rope about the length of the room. I secured one end to the tail of the bed frame, which was of solid wood and easily heavy enough to bear my weight. Then I piled the sheet-rope back onto the mattress. If I was disturbed, it might pass unnoticed in a pinch.

It wasn't the most original scheme I'd ever concocted. Sometimes, though, the old tricks are the best, and it certainly beat trying to smuggle a rope into the palace.

Now came the difficult part. I've never been good at waiting, and those next few minutes passed with all the speed of a mouse through treacle. I'd wracked my brains for a means of surreptitiously manoeuvring Saltlick from the stables to where I needed him. I could have done this with half the dramatics if only I'd had an assistant who was willing and, perhaps more importantly, smaller than an outhouse. In the end, all I could think to do was leave as much time as I dared risk. I hoped Panchetto didn't consider the giant interesting enough to keep a proper guard on and that the presence of a known thief in his palace would focus his attentions.

I nearly jumped out of my skin when I heard the temple gongs ringing midnight. It was the sign I'd given Saltlick. My first impulse was to rush to the window. However, it would take him some time to leave the stables and work his way around. I forced myself to creep over, trailing my improvised rope behind me. I counted to thirty. When there was no sign of him, I did so again, more slowly. Still nothing. I tried to remember the names of every woman I'd slept with and then, realising that might not pass as much time as I'd like, their hair colours and idiosyncrasies.

Nothing. He wasn't coming. He'd betrayed me, his friend and chieftain. Or else he'd been caught, in which case the guards would arrive for me at any moment. Perhaps the oaf had simply fallen asleep, or…

A grotesque shadow jutted into the strip of courtyard below. It was followed an instant later by Saltlick's lumbering form. I'd noted before how ill suited to stealth he was. Watching him creep along, I thought of a tree trying to fall silently.

Still, I couldn't help but feel glad when he saw me and waved. Once he stood beneath my window, I motioned for him to stay where he was.

It was a moonless and pitch-black night, as I'd expected it would be. Everything I'd seen of Panchetto's security led to me to believe he didn't take the threat of burglary very seriously, or rather trusted too much in his unscalable outer walls and well-guarded gatehouse. As far as I'd been able to tell, there were no patrols. If one did happen by then the darkness was deep enough to hide Saltlick from all but a deliberate search.

I tossed the rope down and watched its loops bounce free against the wall. Hopefully the night would hide that too; I was glad the servants had opted for linen of a rich purple shade rather than, say, brilliant white. It reached about halfway to the ground, which was ample for what I had in mind. I clambered onto the ledge and swung down, gasping at the chill night air and momentary vertigo. The rope gave a fraction and held. The bed gave the faintest squeal but stayed in place.

I allowed myself a small sigh of relief and climbed hand over hand down to the next window. I could feel Saltlick's eyes on me. I couldn't guess whether he was thinking of my safety or willing me to plummet to the ground. I swung onto the sill, dropped lightly to the floor, and hauled the remaining rope in after me.

The room beneath mine was just as I remembered it from earlier in the day. Another couple of steps and I'd have fallen into the sunken bath, which had been drained since I'd last seen it. Panchetto's fat guest was evidently still at the party, and likely would be for some time yet.

That didn't mean I wasn't in a hurry.

My eyes had already adjusted to the dark, so I set to it immediately. There wasn't much furniture in the room: an inset wardrobe like the one in my own chamber, a set of drawers with elaborate carved legs and wrought-metal handles, and small cabinets to either side of the bed. I turned up a little loose change, a silver amulet set with carnelian, and a couple of silk scarves. It wasn't much, but it was a start.

I crept to the drape over the door, lifted one edge and peeped out. The passage was unlit like the one above. I flicked a coin against the wall and waited. When two minutes had passed and no one had come to investigate the sound, I felt satisfied the corridor was unguarded. Why would it be? There was no one to defend against but the thief-in-residence, who for all anyone knew was asleep in his own bed.

There were four rooms to either side of the corridor. I searched them all. After a few finds akin to those I'd made in the fat guest's room, and one chamber containing nothing of any value, I was starting to become despondent. Then number six turned up a brimming moneybag and some jewelled earrings that justified the night's work by themselves. I glanced briefly into the last two, conscious of the time, and returned to my starting place. I'd been dropping off my takes as I went along, and the result was a glittering heap beneath the window.

I leaned out and tapped the wall until Saltlick looked up. I held out the first moneybag, gesturing that I planned to drop it. He raised cupped hands over his head, and I let it fall, fully expecting him to miss it and it to explode on the cobbles with a noise loud enough to stir the whole palace. Not so. He snatched it deftly from the air and placed it at his feet, just as I'd instructed. He managed just as well with the next two, and the last few articles I tucked around my person.

I'd intended to tie the fat guest's sheets onto the end of my rope. Reassured by Saltlick's success and anxious for the passing time, I decided instead to climb as far as I could and drop the last distance. Sure enough, Saltlick caught me with hardly a jolt. I glanced at him with new respect. He was proving a capable partner. For a moment, I almost reconsidered leaving him when this was done.

No. It would be better for both of us if we never set eyes on each other again after tonight. Saltlick could return to his tribe and I could go back to the life I'd been wrenched from all those days ago.

I eyed the pile of treasure at our feet. This time there'd be a difference, though. This time I'd be rich.

I spent a minute stuffing moneybags, loose coins, jewellery, scarves, and a fretted silver candlestick that had taken my fancy into the countless pockets secreted in the back of Saltlick's cloak. The formless garment combined with the giant's natural lumpiness hid them from all but careful examination, just as I'd intended. The padding I'd insisted on would muffle any suspicious clinking. Everything was going to plan.

"Time to leave," I whispered, when the distant rap of approaching footsteps froze me to the spot.

I held perfectly still for a moment, and then realised my right leg was jutting half out of the shadows. "Back!" I hissed, louder than I'd intended, and dragged Saltlick with me into the darkness.

I pressed against the wall, pinning him beside me with one arm. Were we visible? I'd miscalculated. Only a blind man could fail to see a giant standing in that strip of gloom.

The footsteps came closer. Perhaps my fear amplified them, because by the time I saw the patrolling guard I'd have sworn it was a carthorse bearing down on us. He was marching with stiff strides, halfway between the palace and the outer wall. He carried no torch, but his armour was so polished that it seemed to glimmer.

He paced nearer, nearer. I could see his fingers closed on the sword hilt at his hip. Was he looking at us? Would Saltlick stop him if I ordered it? Running was out of the question. I could make out trace lines of hard features beneath his helmet. Nearer, still marching, staring into the night, glancing neither left nor right…

Good discipline is a different thing to good guarding. He marched past without as much as a glance towards the walls. His steps were soon just a receding tap, tap, which quickly faded to nothing. All I could hear was Saltlick's hoarse breathing and the pounding of my own heart. When even that had steadied, I said, "All right. Let's go."

I kept well within the shadow of the palace this time, drawing Saltlick with me. It took us a couple of minutes to skirt round the northeast corner to the front. I picked up the pace after that – I'd noticed earlier that the perspective from the gatehouse excluded most of the courtyard – and only slowed again when we drew near the grand main entrance. There was a pool of torchlight there, and I stopped on its edge. There was only one guard visible, and he had his back to us. I hissed a last instruction to Saltlick and stepped into the light.

We were just a couple of guests, now, with every right to be where we were. I changed to a leisurely swagger, but the effort was wasted. The guard was talking with his colleague, who'd been out of view within the far side of the gatehouse. Neither of them looked round until the last moment.

"Hello," I called, too loudly. "We're just, me and my friend here that is, we're just going to…" Most people are hopeless at feigning drunkenness. Those who aren't understand that the trick is to sound as if you're desperately trying to seem sober. "Well, we've had a couple of drinks you see, with His Highness, and we thought we'd head into the city to look for, you know, a *different* sort of entertainment. I mean sort. I didn't mean to say we're looking for midget ladies. Although, if you know of any…" I winked clumsily.

The nearer guard came forward. "At this hour? We have orders to search anyone leaving the palace after dark." He sounded unsure, and I noticed how his eyes were hovering over the medallion around my neck. I suspected the orders had really been *search anyone who looks like they might be Easie Damasco*. That was fine, just as long as they hadn't been told to detain us.

"Certainly, officer," I said, "only too happy to please."

At that, as per my instructions, Saltlick loomed forward. His face was mangled into an expression that suggested rage, toothache, constipation, or some unfortunate combination of all three. It wasn't exactly what I'd asked for – in fact, I struggled to stifle a laugh – but the guards looked suddenly very nervous.

The one who'd spoken spent a few moments searching me, patting his way up from my feet to my collar with practised precision. He turned to Saltlick. If the giant's expression had sagged a little, that made it no less off-putting. Still, the guard was a professional. With a timid, "If you could kneel down, sir," he began his search.

I held my breath.

I needn't have worried. Even with Saltlick kneeling, the hidden pockets would have been out of reach to all except a remarkably tall and determined examiner. The guard was neither. The image that sprang to mind was of a blind man trying to calculate the dimensions of a statue covered in shit. His well-trained hands fairly flew over Saltlick's bulk, and the instant he was done he moved back with a sigh of relief.

"Well, ah… everything seems to be in order. I hope you'll enjoy the rest of your night."

"Thank you, officer," I said, leading the way out through the gates, "I certainly intend to try."

I only let myself relax once we'd turned the street corner and were out of sight. Even then, it proved a mistake. My entire body felt like jelly, jelly someone had pounded with a hammer. I leaned against a window ledge and drew long breaths, until my knees stopped threatening to collapse.

We'd made it!

If the guards on the gate had anything about them they'd notify their superiors of our unusual departure, and odds were someone would eventually come looking for us. However, it was early morning, both prince and guard-captain were indisposed, and the cogs would turn slowly if they turned at all. I should be long gone by the time they'd mustered a response.

"We did it," I told Saltlick, grinning hugely.

He didn't answer.

"You can stop scowling," I said, "it was only supposed to put off the guards."

If anything, his grimace deepened. "Bad."

"What is? Escaping?"

"Stealing bad."

"Appropriating a few trinkets from people more than rich enough to replace them? Where's the harm in that?"

I could tell he didn't agree. I had no time to convince him, and as long as I had the giant-stone, I saw no reason to try. "Your concerns are duly noted, Saltlick, and duly ignored. Let's get going."

I led the way, and though he hesitated for a moment, he followed.

I'd have preferred to avoid the temple district. Its streets were all wide boulevards, humble alleys presumably being an iniquity to the gods. They were lit everywhere by lanterns, and open braziers that burned with strange, chemical blues and greens. Our steps roused the birds in their cages above, stirring countless wings and the elongated scream of a peacock. It was hardly discrete. But it was the quickest route, and haste counted most.

I was more than glad to reach the market district though. I still kept to the main thoroughfares, but here at least they were silent and unlit. We were almost through the more prosperous region, with the market square visible at the end of the road, when I realised Saltlick had stopped again. I glanced round to see him hovering a dozen paces behind me.

"Saltlick, what are you doing? It's this way."

"Not stealing." He looked angrier than I'd ever seen him – but angry like a kicked dog who knows the boot is his master's. "Go back."

"No you won't. I've a skin to save and a living to make, and I need your help." While I could probably have managed without him from there, it was easier by far to have him trailing behind than to try to lug the haul myself. I held the giant-stone up at arm's reach, as close as I could get to his eye level. "Do I have to remind you? I'm your chief. That means you're helping me."

"No more." But he sounded hopelessly unsure. He even took a half step towards me.

Perhaps it was time for a change of tack. "Look… all you have to do is get me as far as Captain Anterio's boat. Then comes the bit you'll like. Once I'm safely onboard, this rock's all yours. You can go home and be lord high muckamuck of the giants, or rescue those friends of yours that Moaradrid's been swindling. How's that for a deal?"

Saltlick looked appalled. "Not good enough!"

"Well it's the best and only offer you're getting." Then my brain caught up, and I realised what he'd meant. "Wait, you're saying *you're* not good enough? Don't be ridiculous. You're strong, you're brave, you're resourceful… you're probably even quite clever by giant standards. What makes you think you wouldn't make just as good a chief as anyone?"

He shook his head. "Not good enough."

"Fine. You can find someone who's worthy and give it to them. How's that? Or if you'd rather, I can throw the damn thing in the river and no one can have it."

That did it. Perhaps Saltlick could stand to see a monster like Moaradrid as chief of the giants, perhaps he could even tolerate me, but to have no leader and no hope of another ever was too much. He lumbered towards me. The anger was gone from his face, leaving behind it an impression of something utterly broken.

I comforted myself with the thought that I'd meant what I'd said. Saltlick would have his precious stone back thanks to me, and maybe even save his people. "Don't worry. A day from now you'll look back on this as the best thing you ever did."

The words sounded hollow even to me. Rather than dwell on that fact, I set off walking again. Saltlick didn't hesitate in following this time. I forced a swift pace through the barren market square, and it wasn't long before we came out on the upper tier above the harbour.

I paused a moment, to lean against the iron railing and make sure everything below was as it should be. It was strange to see the docks so quiet, so dark and empty. There was no activity on the landings, no drunken sailors staggering back to their vessels, and apart from a few large packing crates near the water-side the greater part of the day's detritus had been cleared away. Most of the craft had only a single night-light burning at their sterns. After the hustle and bustle I'd witnessed earlier, there was something dismal about the scene, as though we'd stumbled over a nautical cemetery.

I recognised Anterio's dilapidated tug, moored where I'd left it. I thought I could make out a figure on deck staring back. I waved, and the gesture was returned.

So this was it. In a few minutes, I'd be out of Alta-pasaeda. By dawn, Anterio would have dropped me at some middle-of-nowhere village where I could buy a horse and disappear for good. I took the stairs three at a time, and hurried across the intervening stretch of docks, with Saltlick thudding along behind me. I'd have never imagined a day ago that I could be so glad to see a filthy riverboat or its eccentric captain.

I was almost on the gangplank before I realised it wasn't Anterio.

"I suppose I should thank you for not keeping us waiting, if nothing else."

"Guard-Captain Alvantes… this *is* a surprise." I just about managed not to choke on the words.

"Really? You must hold us in very low esteem. Anterio was a terrible guardsman in his day, but he was never a fool. He contacted me about a suspicious character making outrageous claims about being on some secret mission for the Palace Guard. That tied up with the reports of your movements, of course."

"And you left your dinner to come and meet me? Really, you shouldn't have."

There'd been a playfulness to Alvantes's tone, an uncharacteristic touch of gloating even. Both vanished as he said, "I'd have arrested you hours ago, Damasco. But you had diplomatic immunity and His Highness wanted to make sure you were caught red-handed. Which is exactly what just happened – so now, you're mine. *Guardsmen, to me!*"

That last was shouted past my shoulder, and the words had barely ceased echoing from the harbour wall when I heard the clop of hooves behind me. As I turned, I saw that the packing crates I'd noted now stood open, and that a rider was trotting forth from each dark opening. A moment later, a dozen mounted guards had formed a semicircle around us.

For the briefest instant I felt proud to be the target of so much effort and conniving. That was quickly replaced by terror. My best hope now was to spend the rest of my life in prison, and that was a slim chance at best. More likely, the prince would throw me to Moaradrid as a party favour.

Alvantes waved to one of his riders, and the man wheeled his mount towards the loading ramps at the far end of the harbour. He was back less than a minute later, this time at the head of a small convoy: he'd acquired a coach from somewhere, and another half-dozen horsemen. I thought they were reinforcements, perhaps to subdue Saltlick, until I recognised the figure at their head.

I'd been right, no cosy imprisonment for me. Moaradrid rode behind the guardsman, changed now into his usual attire, and I recognised Panchetto's arms on the door of the coach. Once it had drawn completely to a halt, the prince himself stepped out, wrapped from ankles to ears in a huge fur-lined robe.

"I might possibly have forgiven you for stealing from my guests, Damasco, but to ruin a good dinner party is positively depraved. And giant, you seemed such a sensible sort. Shame on you!"

Saltlick hung his head.

"Now perhaps you'll return your recent acquisitions and we can all go to our nice warm beds?"

Moaradrid drove his mount forward. "Enough games, Panchetto. The thief has shown his true colours. His immunity is insupportable now. Give him to me."

Panchetto looked genuinely shocked. "There's evidently some misunderstanding. I paid you the courtesy of notifying you about tonight's endeavour and allowed you to accompany us. There can be no question of handing an Altapasaedan criminal into your custody. This is a matter for our authorities."

"I won't allow him to escape me again."

"I'm afraid you won't have very much choice."

The Prince's tone was almost as icy as the warlord's was. Yet though there was annoyance on his plump features, it was nothing to Moaradrid's barely-checked fury.

When he spoke, it was in hardly more than a whisper. "You've had every chance and warning. Give me this man."

"I'll do no such thing."

"Very well."

The motion was so quick I could hardly follow it, or register what was happening. Panchetto couldn't have known. Moaradrid's hand moved to his belt, and then drew back. There was the briefest streak of silver, like the tail of a falling star, and a sound as sharp and clear as glass breaking.

Panchetto's body struck the cobbles.

An instant later, his head followed.

CHAPTER NINETEEN

Moaradrid's scimitar hung poised, glistening wetly in the torchlight. Nothing moved except the blood pooling on the cobbles. It seemed to pump unendingly from Panchetto's corpse. His head was an island amidst the crimson lake, scowling at us with the faintest hint of surprise. His lips hung open, as though even in death he had more to say.

It was Alvantes who broke the spell. He leaped from barge to harbour-side and, without pausing, scooped Panchetto's corpse into his arms. His men reacted instantly: the semicircle of riders closed around their leader and their murdered prince.

Yet no one moved against Moaradrid. He was falling back with his own men to a safer distance. I couldn't say I'd liked Panchetto, but to see him struck down with such casual disdain had appalled me. Why didn't Alvantes take this chance to avenge him?

Because unlike the prince, unlike me, he wasn't fool enough to underestimate Moaradrid. A line of dark figures had materialised along the railing of the higher tier. They were likely more hired thugs, and they had the stairs blocked. When an arrow cracked against the cobbles, I realised that was the least of our worries.

Alvantes bundled Panchetto's corpse into the carriage and swung up beside the driver, who was struggling to bring his vehicle round while the riders manoeuvred to cover it. A couple already had arrows jutting from extremities. If they were Alvantes's handpicked men, it would take more than that to slow them.

Only Saltlick and I were doing nothing. On the edge of the docks, we were just out of range of the archers. It was a temporary escape at best. I could see Moaradrid motioning towards me. I still couldn't bring myself to move. Where could I go? Onto Anterio's boat, perhaps, but even if I managed to cast off I wouldn't get far. My only other choice was towards the coach. Alvantes was hardly less likely to kill me than Moaradrid, though. Even if he didn't, the thought of crossing that glistening red pool rooted me in place.

Just as the driver managed to head his coach around, one of the guardsmen gave a gurgling cry and lurched sideways. He struck the cobbles with a nauseating crunch.

"You two – come on!"

It took me a moment to realise Alvantes meant us.

"And bring that."

I saw to my horror that he was pointing at Panchetto's head.

Another guard cried out and wavered, then managed to regain his balance, despite the arrow jutting

from both sides of shoulder. The coach was starting
to resemble a pincushion. It struck me with sudden
clarity that these men, brave and stupid enough to
risk their lives from a sense of duty, would keep dying
until I moved. I might have had trouble living with
that, after what had just happened.

I started running.

I had no intention of picking up Panchetto's head.
Let Alvantes do it himself if he was so damn bothered. Then halfway to the coach, I saw his
expression, the mingled grief and fury. If he couldn't
lay hands on Moaradrid then who was there to blame
but me? It wasn't the time for defiance.

Of all the things I've done to save my skin, that was
the worst. Eyes half shut, I tried to pretend I was
reaching for anything but what really lay there. Any
illusions dissolved in the instant my fingers closed on
blood-slicked hair. I held the thing outstretched behind me, gulped down bile and ran.

The coach door hung open and I leaped inside, drawing it shut behind me. I'd forgotten the carriage was
already occupied. Panchetto's corpse was draped over
the back seats, one arm dangling to the floor, legs levered up to fit the cramped space. The reek of fresh blood
mingled weirdly with smells of leather and wood. Dim
lights in glass sconces cast unpleasant shadows.

I'd have climbed out again, arrows or no. But before I could do more than consider it, the carriage
juddered into motion. I dropped Panchetto's head
and scrambled onto the free seat, trying to press myself as far from my fellow passenger as possible.

We quickly picked up speed. That struck me as strange, since we were on a quayside with nowhere to go. Just as the coach's rattle grew loud enough to drown out the thud of arrows against its roof, the driver threw us hard into a turn. Nearly hurled onto the opposite seats, I hung on until I thought my fingers would snap. The horses screamed, as did our wheels against the cobbles. We tipped. For a moment, we seemed to hang lopsided in thin air.

Then we were round, and on a steep incline. It could only be the loading ramp joining the two levels of dockside. All I could see through the windows, half-veiled by thrashing curtains, was darkness broken into abstract shapes. A rider dashed by. I couldn't tell if he was one of our guards or Moaradrid's thugs. The medley of noise – shouts, cries, the din of steel on steel and rattle of hooves – suggested fighting, but told me no more than that. Were we escaping? Were our guards being slaughtered to a man? In that ruddy light, beset by sounds of violence, I imagined the worst.

And it was all my fault.

I'd had a chance to do the right thing. Instead, I'd turned on my friends, chosen to steal and scheme, in short to do exactly what everyone expected of me. Because of that, Panchetto – ridiculous, childlike Panchetto – and any number of guardsmen who'd done nothing except be in the wrong place at the wrong time had met their deaths. Because of me. Because of the choice I'd made.

Now here I was, hurtling to my doom in this funereal carriage. It seemed both right and fair.

Yet we hadn't stopped – not for all the ringing steel, the shouts and screams, the wild swerves that threatened to overturn us. In fact, the noise of battle was receding. The plunk of arrows was less frequent. Seconds later, it dried up altogether. The shouting faded. We slowed a fraction, to a merely terrifying speed.

I dared a glance out of the nearest quarter light. I could make out the shapes of buildings through the darkness. They were too high for shops; the ghostly white facades made me think we were passing through the poorer residential district south of the market. I gritted my teeth, reached over Panchetto's sprawled remains, and drew the curtain from the slit window in the rear.

I was so relieved to see Saltlick there, thundering along in our wake, that I nearly cried out. His new clothes hung raggedly around the arrow flights protruding through them, he was favouring one leg and his left arm hung limp at his side – but he was alive. Two guards flanked him, one to either side. Both were wounded, hanging on doggedly to their mounts. There was no sign of pursuit.

The fact that we'd survived did nothing to dispel my guilt. I could feel the prince's glazed eyes on me, frozen in annoyed bewilderment. I owed him something, didn't I? Him, Estrada, Saltlick, even that boor Alvantes. Moaradrid had hurt us all. He'd hunted me for the length and breadth of the Castoval, and harmed better people than either of us in the process. I had to try to stop him, if it wasn't already too late.

The many-storeyed buildings of the poor district gave way to the grand houses of the Altapasaedan rich. Our carriage slowed further, so that when we turned into the temple district we hardly tipped at all. The palace loomed ahead. The meagre moonlight reduced its bright towers and minarets to awkward grey shapes. Its elegant stained windows gaped blankly. It looked sad and uninviting, as though the building itself already mourned its fallen prince.

We hurtled through the square surrounding the palace and slowed to turn in. I caught a brief glimpse of astonished guards as we passed through the gates, the same two I'd encountered on the way out. They couldn't fail to recognise the royal carriage. It must be quite a sight, with its bristling coat of arrows and battered, bloody attendants. Rumour spread quickly in Altapasaeda. Panchetto's death would be common knowledge before dawn.

We turned left, the opposite direction to the one Saltlick and I had come from earlier. We trundled around the southeast corner, to a coach yard at the rear. The whole vehicle shuddered and groaned when we pulled up, like a sick man gasping his last breath.

I wanted urgently to get out into the fresh air, away from the stink of death. There was a strong chance, though, that Alvantes had only rescued me out of a warped sense of justice. If he'd let Moaradrid have me, he wouldn't get to see me executed in the proper manner. As long as I stayed where I was, I could delay that possibility at least.

The decision was taken from my hands. The door flew open and Alvantes snarled, "Out."

It seemed a safe bet he was talking to me. I clambered past and stepped quickly back to a safer distance. Two of the household staff were already carrying the coach-driver – who had apparently performed his daredevil escape with an arrow jutting from his stomach – away on a stretcher. Two burly servants disappeared into the carriage, with a second stretcher and a black drape. When they climbed out, their sombre burden rose to an incongruous mound about its middle. Even in death, Panchetto managed to be ridiculous.

Other servants were helping Alvantes's guards inside. The battle had reduced the original dozen to the pair I'd seen from the back window. One of them was clutching a ghastly slash in his chest; he'd be lucky to last the night. Saltlick stood away to one side. As ever, he seemed oblivious to his wounds. None of the staff were making any attempt to aid him. I walked over. When he didn't look up, I said, "Saltlick…"

He ignored me.

"Saltlick, I'm sorry. I shouldn't have made you help me."

I couldn't help noticing how his coat was torn to shreds. The clothier's prediction had proven more than accurate, though I doubted he'd anticipated an armed assault. My treasure was gone, strewn over the streets of Altapasaeda as an unexpected gift for the early-rising citizenry.

Saltlick, as if he sensed my thoughts, reached inside the tattered folds, fumbled around, and drew out a small bag. He dropped it at my feet and turned his back on me.

I wanted to leave it, I truly did. I could feel his contempt radiating like heat from an open oven. My mind told my body to turn away and preserve this one sliver of dignity. But it was habit that won out – that and a voice saying, *you never know when you'll need it*. I didn't have to be poor to be repentant, did I?

My fingers closed around the bag and felt the endlessly comforting heft of coin.

"Damasco."

I crammed the bag into a pocket and span round, trying not to look guilty. Alvantes was glaring at me with unconcealed loathing.

"I'd kill you now and never lose a second's sleep, if it was up to me."

That, of course, implied it wasn't. Which meant… "Estrada?"

"Marina feels some loyalty or pity towards you. Whatever it is, she's asked me to overlook your seemingly endless history of misdeeds. That, of course, was before you poisoned her. Perhaps when she's recovered I can persuade her to change her mind."

"Perhaps."

"In the meantime, Damasco, do what I tell you, when I tell you, without question or argument. Or so help me, not Marina Estrada or anyone else will keep your neck out of the noose."

"I understand."

Alvantes glared at me steadily. "I tried to persuade him to take more guards, to not expose himself. He was a good man at heart. He couldn't understand evil, even when he was face to face with it. So I can't honestly blame you for his death. Yet somehow, I still do."

He turned and marched away.

Part of me wanted to call after him that I did too. The rest of me knew Alvantes wouldn't believe one word of it. Anyway, he might be right but he was still a sanctimonious boor, and I'd be damned before I let him think I agreed with one word that came out of his mouth. If I'd made mistakes, there were some depths to which I'd never stoop.

I turned my attention to the hustle and bustle filling the yard. Coachmen had led away the prince's carriage and brought out another in its place, a coach-and-four of more subdued design. A fresh group of a dozen guards had gathered to replace the wounded.

That was my first thought, anyway. Their livery wasn't that of the royal court; they were dressed instead in dark green, with a serpentine blue emblem on their chests that I recognised as belonging to one of the richer local families. What were they doing here? They were taking orders from Alvantes, odd behaviour for private retainers. I was even more baffled when another mob of guards came out dressed in full cloaks and leading a wagon filled with hay. Moaradrid was still at large, and Alvantes's response was to have his men play dress-up?

Alvantes muttered something to one of the liveried guardsmen, who strode over to me and said, "The captain says get in the coach."

I tried to remember my vow of good behaviour, bit my tongue and marched over, with him close on my heels. I opened the door, and stumbled back. My first thought was that the figure propped in the far corner was Panchetto, and I was doomed to ride for eternity with his pitiful, headless corpse. Gathering my senses, I realised the bundled shape was nothing like the prince's: slim, of medium height and, most significantly, female.

"Captain says you're not to do anything to upset the lady Estrada," the soldier observed from behind me. "She's still groggy, what with you poisoning her. Captain says if you do anything to upset her he'll upset you worse."

"I'll try to remember." I stepped up and took the seat opposite. Only once he'd slammed the door did I add, "Anyway, I only drugged her."

Perhaps I *had* overdone it, though. Estrada was still snoring loud enough to wake the dead. I looked to the windows, which in contrast to the prince's carriage were glassless openings covered with cheap damask. The curtains were half-drawn on both sides. On our left, the majority of the two groups of guards – or hired swords, whatever they were – were mounting up. On the right, two of the cloaked guardsmen were ushering Saltlick towards the cart. Saltlick clambered onto the back, and after some muted discussion back and forth, lay down amidst the hay. The men then spent a minute arranging it over him, until there was no trace that the vehicle contained anything but straw.

Once again, I'd picked the worst possible time to ally myself with the forces of right and justice. They were clearly led by a lunatic.

We jolted into motion, heading back the way we'd come. The household retainers, with their caparisoned mounts and rich tunics, fell in to flank us. I could see the wagon behind once we'd pulled into the streets, similarly escorted by the cloaked guards. They were keeping a discreet distance from us.

This kind of subterfuge was hardly Alvantes's style. Could he really be so afraid to go up against Moaradrid and his band of ruffians?

Only when we passed through the southwestern gate, the one called the Henge, did I understand the sense in Alvantes's elaborate precautions. Perhaps I should have guessed. It wasn't the warlord Alvantes feared, it was the army he'd camped on Altapasaeda's doorstep.

I stared through the gaps in the curtains, trying vainly to gauge the numbers gathered to either side. This force far outnumbered the one I'd encountered outside Muena Palaiya, and probably this was only half of it, since they'd certainly have blocked the northward gates as well.

Though "blocked" was perhaps too strong a word. "Blocked" would have meant an unmistakeable declaration of war, and if Moaradrid had intended that, he wouldn't have wasted time with anything as tiresome as diplomacy. Three separate encampments had formed, one for each gate, but far enough from the road to discourage an impression of blatant hostility.

Still, I could see sentries posted, for all that they were trying not to look like sentries. They would be watching for me, Estrada and Saltlick, and assuming they weren't aware of his murder, for Panchetto, and any attempt to escape to Pasaeda to alert the king.

A throng of peasants travelling together into the farmlands around Altapasaeda, or a wealthy but over-cautious family out on a daytrip, however, were things they might overlook. They'd be suspicious. They might report it back to Moaradrid. They probably wouldn't stop us. Under my breath, I said, "It looks like we'll make it."

"Cretin." The word was slurred but intelligible. I looked round to find Estrada half-sitting, half-lying against the panelled wall. Though she still looked groggy, her eyes were open and fixed on me.

"You're awake."

"No thanks to you." Now even the slurring was gone. Her voice was clear and cold.

"Estrada, I'm sorry. I mean it, I am. I was wrong to drug you, wrong to try and rob Panchetto, definitely wrong to drag Saltlick into that whole sorry mess…"

"Spare me, Damasco."

"What?"

"Spare me. And keep your voice down."

That wasn't what I'd expected. I was repentant, wasn't I? I was even sincere. Weren't good people supposed to respect things like that? Estrada's tone was… well, not quite contemptuous, because that would have implied a degree of interest.

Perhaps I'd really gone too far this time.

I glanced back outside, and saw that we were pulling past the furthest edge of Moaradrid's encamped troops. Though they were paying us more than usual interest, there was no sign they were following, or suggestion of that they would try to stop us.

I remembered what I'd said to provoke Estrada's unkind response. I'd assumed at the time that her critique of my intelligence was just casual abuse. Now I wondered. "Maybe I'm not such an idiot," I said. "Alvantes has led us right through their lines."

Estrada looked at me disdainfully. "No, you definitely are, Damasco. You don't understand at all, do you?"

Her mouth cracked into a faint smirk that never made it as far as her eyes. There was something uncharacteristically cruel in that smile, something that sent fear crawling up my spine. "Alvantes has no intention of escaping. Just the opposite, in fact."

CHAPTER TWENTY

I didn't remember falling asleep, but the next I knew, dreary dawn light was smudging the drapes and we were no longer moving. I was glad to see that Estrada had disappeared. She'd refused to explain her cryptic comments, her tone had remained on the colder side of frosty, and I'd quickly given up any hope of a conversation.

I sat massaging cramp out of my legs and considering my next step. Now more than ever I had good reason to try to escape. Alvantes and Estrada didn't want my help; they'd made that more than clear. I could still repent if I wanted to. The pouch of coin would keep me in comfort for a few weeks, long enough to consider a change of career. I could even go home, see if my parents were still alive. I hated the thought of Moaradrid getting away with his crimes, but what could I do to change it? Men like me didn't stop men like Moaradrid, any more than a rabbit could stop Saltlick. I'd never been anything but a thief. Now that I considered it, I'd never been particularly successful at that.

The door sprang open. I expected Estrada, but it was Alvantes who glared through the entrance. "Good morning, Guard-Captain," I said. "We've stopped."

"Well observed, Damasco."

"Have I got time to stretch my legs?"

"I should think so. We'll be here a while."

I looked at him questioningly, but it was obvious he wasn't going to say any more than Estrada had. I moved to step past him, and felt a hand clamp on my shoulder.

"One moment."

Balanced half in and half out of the carriage, I had little choice.

"You have something that's not yours. It's time you gave it to someone who'll take better care of it."

Well there went any hope of my new life. I pulled out the coin-bag and proffered it to him.

"Not that. Hells, if you survive to spend it you've earned it. No, it's the stone I want."

I drew forth the giant-stone and placed it in his cupped hands. I'd gotten used to its weight. Without it, I felt lighter. "May it bring you as much comfort as it has me, Guard-Captain."

Alvantes gave a barking laugh. "Maybe next time you'll be more careful who you steal from."

I couldn't help smiling. "That's all behind me. I'm a new man."

"Really? We'll see."

He tucked the stone inside his jacket and marched away, back to where his men were waiting. I noticed the mock-farmers had abandoned their disguises,

revealing Altapasaedan City Guard livery beneath.
The others had settled for tearing the misleading em-
blems from their tunics. Though a few of them remained
on horseback, there was little sense of urgency. Some
sat smoking; others were polishing weapons, checking
gear or talking in low voices.

This wasn't just a rest break. We'd stopped altogether.

Were we waiting for the Castovalian irregulars we'd
parted from all those days ago? It was hard to imagine
this nondescript glade as a preordained meeting place.
I tried to remember what Estrada had told me of her
plan, but it had been so absurd that I hadn't paid much
attention, and it all seemed a long time ago.

Perhaps the easiest solution was simply to ask her.
Estrada was sitting with Saltlick in the back of the cart.
He was no longer hidden, and wasn't likely to be
again, since he'd eaten a good proportion of his cam-
ouflage. Estrada was tending to his latest wounds. A
gash in his leg looked particularly raw and unpleasant,
and he was still carrying his left arm gingerly. Still, as
always food seemed to have improved his spirits and
bolstered his constitution. He smiled when he saw me.
Then his mouth turned down belatedly into a frown.

Poor Saltlick, he wasn't meant for holding grudges.

I waved, and called, "Good morning Saltlick,
Estrada."

"What do you want?" Estrada's tone had thawed
slightly, but it was still a long way from friendly.

"I want to know what's happening. Why have we
stopped?"

I climbed onto the back of the cart, Saltlick shifting to accommodate me.

"What difference does it make to you? You'll follow along until you find an opportunity to sneak away, or rob us, or drug us."

"I told you I'm sorry. I want to help. Even if I didn't, I have a right to know what's going on."

"A *right*? You have a nerve, Damasco."

I threw my hands up in an attitude of defeat. "Estrada... Marina... if only to pass the time, could you please let me know what we're doing here?"

She sighed. "We're waiting."

"For the other troops?"

"For Moaradrid."

It took me a moment to digest that. My initial shock was brief, though, for fragments of Estrada's plan were coming back to me. We were bait, she'd said, bait for an ambush. We were drawing close to the southern-most tail of the Castoval, so wherever the meeting place was it had to be close.

Yet if our only purpose was to play hare for Moaradrid's hounds, why had we crept in disguise through his lines?

First things first, though. Estrada was right, I tended not to pay attention to anything beyond my immediate circumstances, and this wasn't the first time it had got me into trouble. I suspected I'd missed plenty of useful details during our time in Altapasaeda, but one gap in my knowledge gaped more widely than the others did. "You knew Alvantes before this week, didn't you?"

"We're old friends."

I'd swear she blushed. Even if she didn't, Estrada was a terrible liar.

"You were more than that."

"All right. We were… lovers, I suppose you'd call it. A long time ago. Then Lunto was promoted…"

"*Lunto*?"

"Lunto Alvantes."

I suppressed a snigger.

"…and I became involved in politics. It got more and more difficult to see each other."

"So that's why he's helping you?"

"He's helping because it's right. Because he doesn't want to see a beast like Moaradrid ruling the Castoval and maybe even be king one day. Panchetto wasn't a bad man, but he could never see farther than the walls of his palace. We never meant for him to be hurt, though," she finished sadly.

It had begun to rain while we'd been talking, weighty drops that shattered on the ground, the cart sides and our clothes like a thousand tiny drums tattooing in unison. Milky light on the horizon gave way to hillocks of grey cloud topped with treacle-black gloom. I noticed then how cold it was. "Why don't we get back inside the coach?" I asked.

"Will you be all right on your own, Saltlick?"

Saltlick had been lolling with his head back, letting raindrops course into his throat. He looked up long enough to nod and grin at Estrada. "Go home," he said.

Estrada glanced towards the mountain peaks that

closed the valley. Hidden somewhere in those heights was giant territory. "Yes. Not long now, Saltlick."

We were in the carriage with the door shut before I asked, "You've told him you'll help him get home?"

"And I will. Once this is over that's my first priority."

Estrada sounded as though she meant it. I made a silent resolution that, whether or not she helped Saltlick return to his family, I would. It was the least I could do after last night, and of all the promises I'd made recently it was the one that most deserved to be honoured.

Of course, from what little Estrada and Alvantes had told me I'd be lucky to help myself, let alone anyone else.

"So you persuaded Alvantes and a few of his men to join up with you. What are they, more bait?"

"Not a few. The entire Altapasaedan City Guard is pledged to us. But hopefully Moaradrid doesn't know that."

"How could he not?"

"They abandoned their barracks during the night, led by Sub-Captain Gueverro. Moaradrid will be led to believe they heard the news of Panchetto's murder, panicked at the thought of a battle and mutinied. Thanks to Panchetto, they've such a terrible reputation for cowardice that he should believe it. Even if he doesn't, it can't make much difference. He'll be in too much of a hurry."

"He doesn't know where we've gone."

"He will soon."

I was beginning to see. If the ambush was set for a particular time then there was no point blundering in half a day early with Moaradrid's army nipping at our heels. All the others would find when they arrived would be our corpses. Alvantes and Estrada must have some way to control when Moaradrid came after us. Deciding that she'd tell me in her own time, I rested my head against the backboard and closed my eyes. The rain was pounding, heavier than before, a rattle that seemed to shake the whole carriage.

When I opened my eyes, Estrada was looking at me.

"Understand, Damasco," she said, "I can't forgive you. You're utterly selfish, you've behaved despicably, and even if this latest repentance is sincere it won't make any difference to how I feel."

"Fine."

"All right. Well, I'd gone to Altapasaeda to ask Lunto for his help, and to buy a little time. I hadn't realised Moaradrid would be able to move so many troops so quickly, or that he'd confront Panchetto so openly when his lines were already weakened. He'd grown desperate. His scheme for the crown was unravelling. He must have realised an attack on Altapasaeda was suicide, but there seemed a real chance he'd try anyway. If he'd won, recovered the stone, and captured Panchetto into the bargain, he might have levered the king off the throne without another drop of blood being shed. Alvantes agreed to pledge the Guard, even though Panchetto would never forgive it. But by then the problem was how we'd get to the rendezvous point at all."

"When we first heard about your deal with Anterio, we thought about confronting you. Then Lunto suggested we use it to our advantage. We'd lead Moaradrid to believe you'd fled upriver with the stone; he'd go hunting after you, and – if the timing was right – run right into our trap. We'd no way to know what would really happen. We had no idea Panchetto would find out what you were plotting, or insist on going along when Alvantes went to arrest you, or take Moaradrid with him."

A thought struck me. "If the Guard have abandoned their barracks and Panchetto's dead then…"

"Yes. Moaradrid's forces are almost certainly in Altapasaeda now."

My jaw dropped. "You've sacrificed an entire city. I can't believe Alvantes let you give up Altapasaeda."

"It's not a sacrifice. It's a gambit."

"Only if it works."

I regretted my insensitivity as soon as I'd said it. Estrada looked, for just an instant, as though she could easily have broken down altogether. I could hardly imagine the strength of will it had taken to conceive this strategy all those days ago, and then to follow it through over every setback and tragedy to this point, where everything hung in the balance and everything was on her head if it failed.

"It *will* work," she said.

"All right," I agreed, trying to sound as though I believed it. "So how can you control when he comes looking for us?"

Estrada's voice dropped lower, as if she had to

drag the words from some internal gulf. "The wounded men from the fight at the harbour are in the palace. Moaradrid will have found them and tortured them. Their instructions were to give us up at dawn."

I shuddered. Alvantes's handpicked guards had been braver and more foolhardy than I'd guessed. I remembered the state Saltlick had been in when I rescued him. I had a fair idea what they would have gone through. Except… "It's long past dawn."

"Yes."

"And we can't be that far from Altapasaeda."

"About three hours."

I realised abruptly that not even the most violent torrent could make the hammering coming from outside. "That isn't just rain, is it?"

Almost in the same moment, a guttural cry arose: "*Move!*"

The carriage leaped into motion, almost hurling me from my seat. Now through the storm I could make out the pulse of countless hooves, far too many to be our small entourage. I darted a glance through the drapes, and wished I hadn't. The road behind was black with mounted men. I only caught a glimpse before the bucking of the carriage dragged me away. It seemed in that instant as though Moaradrid had sent his whole army after us.

The road south from Altapasaeda ran fairly straight. It didn't take us long to achieve the nerve-shattering speed I remembered from our earlier escape. This coach might lack the luxuries of Panchetto's, but –

if there was any sanity to Alvantes's plan – it was sure to be faster. Still, it felt as though it would tear apart at any moment. Through gritted teeth, I called, "How far is it?"

"To the rendezvous? It's set for noon."

"That's two hours away!"

"Alvantes can make it."

"Maybe *he* can. What about us?"

The minutes ground by. I felt as if every spot of my flesh was bruised, and still the bouncing continued, still I was thrown back and forth like a shuttle on a loom. Estrada bore it in silence, and I tried to do the same. They hadn't caught us yet. That was all that mattered.

As far as I could work out, a few small advantages were keeping us alive. Our horses were freshly rested, and likely the fastest Altapasaeda had to offer. Alvantes and his men would know this road far better than our pursuers could hope to. They apparently lacked horse-archers, for no one was shooting. Finally, we had the simple logic of the hunt on our side: the fox is always more motivated than the hounds that are set to tear it apart.

The coach and Saltlick's wagon must have been slowing us, though, despite the hair-raising efforts of their drivers. When a few minutes had passed and we'd preserved our lead, I began to wonder if they were even trying to catch us.

My answer came as a loud crash from the rear of our coach, behind and above Estrada's head. Another followed it, and then a scrabbling sound, as though pebbles were being scattered over the roof.

"We've been boarded," I whispered.

Estrada, nodding, put a finger to her lips. She reached down and drew a wicked-looking stiletto from her boot.

The woman was full of surprises.

There were two of them, I thought, one edging forward over the roof, the other hanging back. Sounds of a scuffle came from the driver's seat. The whole carriage veered sharply, hurling us flat. We left the road, skidded on loose ground. I glimpsed a line of trees, far too close. Then we curved back, with another hard jolt. There was a cry, and a loud impact. The carriage bucked, but held its course this time.

The left side door sprang open. A foot swung into view, followed by a leg. I glimpsed a figure: black leather armour, a short tuft of beard, pin-bright eyes full of fear and rage. He was clutching the rail around the carriage roof. As I watched, he let go with one hand, clasped the inner edge of the doorframe.

Estrada thrust with her stiletto. A lurch of the carriage amplified her strength; the thin blade hammered through flesh and an inch of wood. The scream from outside was appalling. One of the horses added its voice to the racket. We flew into a turn, and straightened with a shudder.

Estrada fought to free her stiletto, without success. She levered it up and down, and every time the Northerner outside yelped pitifully. I could see tears starting in her eyes. He'd managed to lodge one foot inside the door. Now he gripped the frame with his free hand and swung his whole body into the entrance. He was broad enough to fill it. He swiped at Estrada, almost losing his grip as she ducked aside.

The Northerner leaned further in, anchoring himself with a shoulder wedged against the doorframe. His eyes darted between his skewered hand and the sword at his belt, as he struggled to choose between attacking and trying to free himself.

Rather than wait until he decided, I chose to stamp hard on his nearest foot.

He snarled, and went for the sword. Estrada picked that moment to make another grab for her stiletto. This time she managed to wrench it loose, with an awful sound of tearing meat. She swung the thin blade in a raking cut. The man howled, leaned away, and realised he had nowhere to go. He threw out a hand to steady himself. He picked the wrong one, and screamed once more.

I stamped again. He flailed for an instant, and was gone. I heard him pitch into the dirt with a crunch.

I fell back, fighting the urge to vomit. Estrada's chestnut skin was white as snow. She stared at the stiletto clutched in her fingers, its blade dripping red up to the hilt.

"Is he dead?" she asked.

"What?"

"Did we kill him?" The words were almost a sob.

"He would have killed us."

"But he didn't."

The carriage swerved again, though not so sharply. I was certain it was back under the control of the driver, and that the sound we'd heard was him fending off his own assailant. Sure enough, I saw that we were only moving to allow the cart to fall in next to us. I watched it pulling alongside, with Saltlick hunched in the rear.

We were deep into the wilds now, a rocky, tree-flecked region that would soon give way to the foothills of the southern mountains. This road was the less-used route between Altapasaeda and Maedendo, most southerly of the eastern bank towns. It would widen beyond the bridge that capped the southern tip of the Casto Mara, but here it was narrow as any country road. With the cart beside us, we blocked it entirely.

It was absurdly risky. While it kept us safe from further attack, only the skill of the drivers stopped us from spinning into a ditch. The first turn ground the two vehicles together with a crunch of splintering wood. When they tore apart, the cart's near side was crumpled inward.

They couldn't possibly keep this up for long.

Soon, the whole near half of the cart was riven with cracks that spread with each impact. Yet the frame held through the abuse. Estrada and I found positions where we could brace ourselves and hung on for dear life, teeth gritted, oblivious to each other. Concentrating solely on not being thrown from my seat, I grew barely conscious of my bruises, the incessant tramp of hooves, the hammering of rain. I only stirred when a wheel slipped off the road and the whole carriage threatened to tip, or when we skidded and it seemed we'd carry on until a tree or rock obliterated us.

Two things roused me from that stupor. The first was noticing how flattened the shadows were on either side of us. That meant the sun was directly above. Hadn't Estrada said something about noon? Before I could finish the thought, we started forward, with a fresh burst of speed I wouldn't have thought possible.

I didn't see what good it could do. If our horses had that much life left in them, our pursuers' would have too. They'd close the gap in moments. I looked at Estrada, saw that she was staring out the left side window. A flash of recognition lit her eyes. I did my best to follow her line of sight, and realised we were approaching rock formations that encroached on either side, and beyond was a stretch of canyon where the road dipped sharply below the level of the land. Shallow banks of shale and low scrub rose to left and right, topped with knots of dense foliage. It was a perfect ambush point.

Even as I thought it, we slowed, sharply enough to slam me against the carriage wall. Estrada tumbled into the gutter between the seats. Our horses shrieked in protest.

We'd pulled up at an angle to the highway. Back the way we'd come, I could see the mass of Moaradrid's forces bearing towards us. They'd be on us in seconds.

"Is this it?"

"Help me, Damasco."

Estrada was struggling with the door on the opposite side. It was battered and buckled from its
altercations with the cart. The clasp and hinges had
crumpled into shapeless lumps that locked it firmly
in place. I added my efforts to Estrada's. Though it
rattled and shook, it came no closer to opening. A
glance behind showed me riders almost within spitting distance. They were already slowing, drawing
their weapons.

I rolled onto my back, kicked with both legs together. My feet whistled past Estrada's head and struck
the door with a crunch… and nothing else. I tried
again, again. The sound of hooves skidding in the dirt
and of horses whickering filled my ears.

I kicked with all my strength.

The latch sprang loose. The door flew open.

We tumbled out, Estrada first, and fell into the road.
Glancing back, I realised the drivers had used their vehicles to blockade the road. Though it wouldn't stop
our pursuers, it would force them to dismount, or
slow them at least. Why were the horses still in their
harnesses, though? It seemed needlessly cruel with a
battle pending. I looked around for the drivers.

"Oh no."

The words fell from my mouth. It was impossible.

Ahead, a couple of hundred men sat in the dust.
I recognised a few of them from the encampment
above Muena Palaiya. Their hands and feet were
tied. Moaradrid's men stood guard in a circle around
them.

Moaradrid himself waited close by. Beside him, glaring at us from his one good eye, stood Castilio Mounteban.

CHAPTER TWENTY-ONE

"Why are we still alive?"

As usual, it was up to me to say what everyone was thinking. Yet all it got me was glares, from Estrada on my left and Alvantes on my right.

I couldn't tell how long we'd been sitting there. Though it was probably only a few minutes, it seemed far longer. My ankles throbbed where the thick cord bit into them. My wrists itched maddeningly, and every movement seemed to make it worse. The cloud-laden sky was still leaking a cold drizzle and my clothes were sodden. Overall, I was starting to wonder if a quick execution wouldn't have been more merciful than this protracted torment.

Not even Alvantes had tried to put up a fight, though his eyes had blazed with loathing as he handed over the giant-stone to Moaradrid. That done, he'd unstrapped his sword, and at his terse command his men had done the same, piling their blades in the road. There they'd remained, scabbards glinting dully in the grey light, left just out of reach as another small torture.

Moaradrid's troops had searched us then, with far more energy than the guards outside the palace. To my surprise, the brute who patted me down had left my bag of coin alone. Probably he intended to loot it from my corpse later. Now that I'd never get to spend it, the weight against my chest was just another irritation.

Moaradrid's first act upon recovering the giant-stone had been to order Saltlick to sit away from us and keep absolutely still. The soldiers had trussed him anyway, perhaps not sharing their master's faith in the pebble he prized so highly. Yet Saltlick hadn't twitched so much as an eyebrow, either during the ordeal or since. Small wonder Moaradrid was obsessed with having the giants on his side. Size and strength was one thing, but no money could buy such blind obedience.

The rest of us had been placed with the other captives. If they'd looked pitiful from a distance, they seemed doubly so close up. Most were too juvenile or ancient, too starved or sickly to have done much damage to anyone besides themselves. Every last trace of resistance vanished when they realised it was Estrada being shoved down in their midst. They'd had hope before, however slim. Now their defeat was beyond doubt.

If they'd needed further proof, however, the tight circle of Moaradrid's soldiers around us would have sufficed. Assuming he hadn't completely abandoned the siege of Altapasaeda, they could only be a proportion of his full force. Yet in the narrow confines of the valley, it felt as though Estrada's pitiful band of rebels sat huddled at the feet of an army the likes of which the Castoval had never seen. Their rough clothing and scraps of armour might as well have been the silks and silver-filigreed plate of Panchetto's Palace Guard.

Moaradrid and Mounteban stood some distance to our right and a little way up the embankment. They'd been engaged in hushed conversation ever since our capture. Every so often, one of them would glance in our direction. Once, Mounteban waved towards us in some unreadable gesture. Soon after, Moaradrid cursed loudly and distinctly. It was obvious they were discussing us, but I'd no way to follow the debate, except that nothing in their expressions indicated it was good.

I'd been expecting Moaradrid to come and speak to us eventually, to gloat over his victory or to introduce our forthcoming tortures. I was surprised when it was Mounteban who broke away and marched through the intervening crowd, clearing a path with his broad shoulders and barked orders. The soldiers showed him barely more respect than he did them. He stopped, hands on hips, within the perimeter of troops. His gaze swept over all of us, but settled on Estrada.

When he spoke, his tone was oddly subdued. "Understand... you're lucky to be alive. If you want to stay that way you'll listen carefully to what I say."

Estrada's only response was to turn her face away.

"I know what you think. Mounteban, the criminal, has sold his friends for money and power. It isn't true. Yes, I went to Moaradrid, I admit it. I went to talk, as one man of influence to another. Because I'm a traitor to our cause? No. Because this plan was madness and would get us all killed. I tried to tell you, Marina, and you chose not to listen. Well, now you have to. This so-called war has been a farce from the beginning. Moaradrid is not the man you think he is."

Alvantes's voice erupted from behind me. "He's a tyrant and a killer."

"Perhaps. But he's wants only one thing, and that's the crown. All he intended here was to bolster his army with the giants before he marched against Pasaeda and the king. It was we who imagined we were being attacked, we who forced a confrontation. Even then, he'd left without more bloodshed. If it weren't for a gutter thief who should have been hanged years ago, that's exactly what he'd have done."

I'd been trying to keep my mouth shut, but that caught me by surprise. "Wait, this is suddenly my fault?"

Mounteban ignored me. "This can end now. You haven't been harmed; your possessions have been left alone. You can all go home. Marina, you can still be mayor. Alvantes, you can keep your position. Moaradrid hasn't the desire or the resources to hold the Castoval. He'll leave with the giants, and never bother us. All he asks is our cooperation."

Estrada turned back to him. I could never have imagined such violence in those still brown eyes. Her words came in a single long hiss: "What has he promised you?"

For a moment, it looked as though Mounteban would deny the accusation. Then he said, "I'll be mayor of Altapasaeda."

Estrada gave a high laugh. "Of course you will."

Mounteban's expression wavered between shame and anger. He dropped to his knees in front of Estrada. His voice was so low that only the nearest of us could hear as he said, "Will you listen! He's spread his forces too thinly. Moaradrid can't hold the Castoval and he knows it. If he doesn't go after the king now, the king will come for him. I think he was ready to have me killed before he lost his temper and murdered that oaf Panchetto, but since then he's been only too eager to listen.

"There's more... he hasn't said anything, but I'm sure he's run out of money. I doubt he's paid his armies since they came south, he's hardly feeding them, and any fool can see they're restless. He's obsessed with the crown, and every day he's watched it slip further from his grasp. He wants nothing from the Castoval but to leave it far behind."

Mounteban was focused so intently on his speech that only at the end did his realise Estrada was ignoring him. Her eyes had caught on something in the distance beyond his shoulder. Before I could look to see what she was staring at, her gaze snapped back to Mounteban's face. She bent forward, bringing her mouth almost to his ear. I leaned in too, trying to catch her whisper.

"Castilio," she said, "I hope they kill you first."

There was something so hypnotic in Estrada's hatred that I didn't think to wonder who "they" were. Neither, apparently, did Mounteban. He just stared with horror at the face too near his own. Only when the noise from behind us became overwhelmingly loud did he tear his eyes from hers. Then his mouth slid open, though no words came. He leaped to his feet and – with surprising speed for so large a man – bolted towards the eastern bank.

Estrada fell back, as though the effort of so much rage had drained the last of her strength.

Moaradrid's troops were shouting on every side, all at once. Their feet were already churning the road into a quagmire, but no two men were moving in the same direction. The general drift seemed to be away from us, towards the mouth of the ravine. Someone cried out nearby and was abruptly cut off.

My whole body felt taut. I hardly dared to hope.

I recognised the hum of arrows beneath the other, louder sounds. The shots were coming from above; for once, we weren't the ones being fired at. Hooves thundered, but the racket was approaching, not receding. The cries from around us were becoming an overwhelming wave of panic. The thought of being trampled frightened me more than the clamour of violence rising from every direction. I closed my eyes and threw my arms up over my face.

"Keep still!"

I opened my eyes to a blade a hand's breadth from my nose. Just before I started to scream, I realised it was Estrada's stiletto. Her searcher clearly hadn't been as rigorous as mine.

"Put your hands out. It's the Altapasaedan Guard, Damasco."

I thrust my wrists out where she could reach them. "Ow! Be careful."

The stiletto wasn't designed for cutting. Estrada's slip had nearly cost me my thumb. Fortunately, the rope was cheap and rain-sodden. Another slash sent it flapping away in coils.

One of Moaradrid's Northerners chose that moment to stumble backwards into the pile of our weapons, scattering them in every direction. Most clattered beneath the feet of his companions, adding to the chaos, but one short sword skittered within reach. I darted to grab it before it was kicked away. A clumsy slash dealt with the cord around my feet.

"Give me that."

Alvantes had his hands free, presumably thanks to Estrada. He tore the sword from my fingers, severed the binding around his ankles and leaped to his feet. He was just in time to block a blow swung for his neck – a Northerner had noticed our escape attempt. Regaining his balance, Alvantes edged to protect us. The soldier swung for his shoulder and he parried, with more confidence this time, then drove forward. It was a wild blow, easy to defend, but powerful enough to push the Northerner back. He managed three rapid steps before he stumbled over the remains of the weapons pile. Alvantes's second blow killed him before he reached the ground.

Alvantes barely paused. He swung his cloak off and bundled swords into it, then darted back to distribute them. I found myself, seconds later, amidst a ring of armed men. The main fighting had drifted away from us, towards the mouth of the gorge. The Alta-pasaedans must have deliberately struck from that side to draw Moaradrid's troops away. Their initial panic behind them, those troops had formed up near the ruined coach, while the Altapasaedans, seeing their initiative lost, had retreated part way up the western bank.

With even my limited grasp of warfare, I could tell the fight wasn't going their way. With both sides massed together, it was clear how outnumbered they were. There might have been two hundred Altapasaedans; Moaradrid's force boasted five times that number. The only thing that stopped them completely swamping the small band was lack of space. With the carriage, the rock formations at the gully mouth, and their own horses all behind them, the Northerners could hardly manoeuvre.

The Altapasaedans had left a handful of archers on the western brow, who continued to pour down a steady stream of arrows. Yet now that Moaradrid's force had rallied, most of those shots deflected from shields and armour. Even the higher ground wasn't doing them much good. They were fending off sallies from both sides, and only Moaradrid's inability to bring his numbers to bear kept them from being overrun.

The stalemate couldn't last. As I watched, a company of Northerners peeled off from the main body, to retreat through the valley mouth. They'd be hunting for another route to the high ground. Once they found it, they'd have no trouble cutting down those few archers, and the Altapasaedans would be surrounded. All Moaradrid had to do until then was keep them pinned.

As for our Castovalians, they looked only fractionally more intimidating now that they were armed and on their feet. In bare numbers, they more than doubled the Altapasaedans' strength. But numbers were misleading. Most of them had probably never handled anything sharper than a plough. Every third man lacked a weapon. They looked bewildered and scared.

Moaradrid's troops would eat them alive.

If Alvantes saw how hopeless the situation was, he hid it well. Stood at the head of his ragtag brigade, he shouted, "Stay together. Push towards the centre. Stop for nothing!"

Then he turned and ran towards the fighting, before anyone realised this was all the speech they'd get. His entourage of Altapasaedan guardsmen fell in behind him. The Castovalian irregulars were slower on the uptake, and had to sprint to catch up.

I was shocked to see Estrada moving after them.

I caught her arm and cried, "Where are you going?" She jerked to free her arm, but I hung on. "What are you going to do, stab them with your pocket knife? Don't be stupid."

"Let me go!"

"You're no good to anyone dead."

"They're going to get *slaughtered*." All the strength had gone out of her voice, but it was replaced by a cold determination that was almost worse.

I could see she'd rather die than watch the massacre she'd helped orchestrate. Struggling for an argument, any argument, I said, "What about Saltlick? You promised him."

Her eyes flitted to where Saltlick sat, immobile despite the havoc around him.

"Your boyfriend can look after himself. Can Saltlick?"

"He's not my boyfriend." Estrada shrugged her arm free and marched towards Saltlick.

I couldn't help glancing toward the battle as I followed. Moaradrid must have forgotten his captives in the face of the Altapasaedan attack: the Castovalian thrust was wreaking chaos on his flank. I could make out Alvantes within the press of bodies, hacking his way towards the centre of Moaradrid's force just as he'd said he would. The Altapasaedans, exploiting their sudden advantage, had sallied against the Northerners who'd almost hemmed them in. Their archers, too, were making the most of the distraction, finding easier targets now their enemies were defending on two fronts.

Perhaps they hoped the struggle had swung in their favour. I could see the bigger picture, and I knew better. The Northerners would reorganise at any second, and bring their greater strength to bear. Alvantes might be a thorn in their flank, but a thorn could be torn out and pulverised. He'd never struck me as the reckless type. Didn't he understand how hopeless this was?

Then I realised where he was heading.

I hurried to join Estrada, and found her deep in one-sided conversation with Saltlick.

"I know he said you can't move, but what are you going to do, stay here forever? Sit until you starve to death? How is that going help your people or your family or anyone? You're being ridiculous! Moaradrid isn't your chief. He *stole* the stone from you. You don't owe him any loyalty."

"He won't listen," I told her. "That stupid stone, I wish I'd thrown it in the river when I had the chance."

I thought Saltlick's eyes flickered at that.

"What can we do?"

"I don't know. Hope our side wins, I suppose."

I turned back to the drama behind us. I'd been right, surprise had offered only the briefest advantage. All momentum had gone from the Castovalian thrust, and now the Northerners were regaining ground and taking lives with equal ease. Alvantes's farmers were suffering the worst, but even the Altapasaedan guardsmen were taking horrible losses. Only Alvantes and his entourage continued to advance. The Castovalian irregulars were more a distraction than an actual help, but it was a distraction he was making the most of.

Moaradrid, though he'd drawn his scimitar, was concentrated on retreating through the press of his own forces. His troops tripped over themselves to clear a path for him without risking their own lives. He'd already had to abandon the centre. Each step was taking him closer to the western bank, where the fiercest fighting was.

That was Alvantes's plan. It always had been. He couldn't win the battle, but perhaps he could end the war.

Moaradrid realised it in almost the same instant I did – understood that he was being herded towards the Altapasaedans. His reaction was as rapid as it was astounding. He hurled himself with a ferocious cry at Alvantes, who barely had time to throw up his sword. The toll of their blades sung out above the clamour. Moaradrid followed with another strike, another, his blade weaving furiously, each blow ringing like a gong. Alvantes could hardly block, let alone fight back.

A circle was opening around them. Rather than risk getting in the way of their warlord, the Northerners backed frantically away. Alvantes's entourage took the opportunity to stab at anyone who looked as though they'd try to interfere. The pitiful remainder of the Castovalians fell in to shore their line. On the far side, the surviving Altapasaedans seized on the respite to withdraw up the slope.

Suddenly, the entire skirmish had diminished to the two men battling in its midst. Their duel was drawing them further from the northern mouth of the valley, closer to us. Moaradrid was still forcing the attack. If his scything blows had slowed a fraction, they were more than enough to keep Alvantes off balance.

At least Alvantes was beginning to do more than block. Every few steps he'd parry or sidestep, seeking an opening he couldn't find. Moaradrid's style lacked subtlety, but he was strong and fast. His scimitar acted like sword *and* shield, always moving, always outstretched to protect his head and body. Alvantes was the better swordsman, it showed in his every motion. Yet all his skill seemed useless in the face of that onslaught.

Then, for the first time, Alvantes struck back. He stepped deftly around a stab aimed midway up his chest, slid the scimitar aside, and lunged. His blade sliced against Moaradrid's thigh, drew a widening splash of crimson. Moaradrid howled – more with rage than pain, it seemed, as he renewed his attack with even greater fury.

Alvantes was once again forced to lose ground. Yet something had changed. Now he retreated with easy leaps and sideward steps, and an unexpected grace. Now every other block turned into a parry, sapping force from Moaradrid's offensive. The warlord's face was warped with rage. A deep-throated cry accompanied each swing. It did no good. Alvantes anticipated his every motion, was always in the wrong place.

His blade darted again. The blow wasn't so well placed this time; the edge glanced off the sash around Moaradrid's waist. Even from a distance I could see that Alvantes's sword had failed to find flesh.

He'd hit something, though – something that fell free, bounced, rolled to a standstill in the dirt.

It was the giant-stone.

Whether Alvantes had struck there deliberately, he seized the opportunity. He crouched, leaped, grasped the stone and rolled on, avoiding a swipe that passed not a finger's width above his head. He bound to his feet and threw his sword around to ward off the inevitable next blow.

He was almost quick enough.

Moaradrid swung his blade in a wide upward arc, leaving his whole left side exposed. Alvantes saw the opening, moved to exploit it – and screamed. The scimitar flicked back, now trailing a slash of crimson. Something sailed into the air, geysering red. It fell into the mud half way between the fight and us.

I don't know what made me run for it. Suddenly I was on my feet, and though a part of my brain was ordering me to stop, I pounded down the slope with all my strength. Moaradrid twisted to look at me. His lips moved, but no words came that I could hear. Alvantes was staggering away, his face rigid and contorted. He was nursing his left arm in the crook of his right, the sword dangling loose in his fingers.

Moaradrid took a step towards me. He held his scimitar with the tip pointed at my head, and gave an indistinct cry. Then he began to lope towards me, hampered by the slash across his thigh. All his characteristic dignity was gone. He struggled on like a rabid dog, driven by hate and animal desire.

The distance was too great. I reached the spot well ahead of him, and slid to my knees. There, spattered with filth and gore, lying like an overturned crab that would never right itself, was Alvantes's left hand. The giant-stone sat next to it, its surface drizzled with scarlet.

Scooping it up, feeling its coldness against my fingers, I made a silent vow.

This time, it was going back where it belonged.

CHAPTER TWENTY·TWO

Standing in the middle of what minutes ago had been a road and was now a lake of churned filth and freshly spilled blood, an odd thought struck me. If heroism meant making bold and ultimately suicidal gestures, I'd just proved myself every bit Alvantes's match.

I assumed there must be something more to it that I'd missed. Then, as I turned and sprinted towards Estrada and Saltlick, I remembered the sight of Alvantes cradling the bloody stump of his wrist.

Maybe I had the right idea after all.

Estrada had been busy in my absence. She'd freed two of our horses from the stand of trees where Moaradrid's men had tethered them, and stood with the reins knotted around one hand. If they were panicked from the sounds of violence, they were still a better option than an escape attempt on foot.

First things first, though. "Saltlick, get up!" I shouted, holding the giant-stone where he could see it. "You're free. You're going home."

Saltlick leaped to his feet, his face crumpling into the widest grin I'd ever seen. "Go home!" he roared.

Halfway there, I hazarded a glance behind me. Moaradrid was concentrated now on mustering riders from the mouth of the gorge. They in turn were struggling to force their way through the fighting, which had resumed as a series of isolated skirmishes. Alvantes was trying to loop back to where the Altapasaedans were making their last stand. Though his face was frozen with pain and his hauberk drenched with blood, he was still taking time to swipe at any nearby foe with the sword gripped in his remaining hand.

The man was astonishing. He had no idea how to give up and die. But there were Northerners all around him, and I didn't see how he could possibly keep it up for much longer.

I hurried on. Estrada was leading the horses towards me, dragging them as fast as she could without alarming them further. Saltlick trotted behind, still overjoyed, oblivious to the carnage.

I was badly winded by the time we reached each other. As I stopped to gasp for breath, Estrada thrust reins into my free hand.

"Rest later, if we're not dead."

She swung into the saddle. I jammed the giant-stone into a pocket and followed her example. I recognised my steed, a pitch-black stallion with a demented gleam in his eyes, as having belonged to Alvantes. He didn't seem happy with his new circumstances. He whinnied frantically and pawed with his front hooves. I threw my arms around his neck, certain he'd rear. However, Estrada chose that moment to drive her own mount forward, and perhaps mine took the action as a challenge, because before I knew it we were moving too.

But "moving" does that first wild burst of speed no justice. Anyone who'd weathered a typhoon in a coracle might have an idea how I felt. I clung to the fiend, fighting the urge to clamp my eyes shut.

I gave up when we reached the first turn. I opened them again when the sickening sense of being at the wrong angle and too near the ground had passed, to see a long straight stretch ahead. The horse saw it too. To my disbelief, he actually accelerated. My stomach bobbed into my mouth and stayed there.

"Rein him in," cried Estrada from somewhere behind, the words almost torn apart by the wind shrieking in my ears.

"He'll murder me!"

"He'll exhaust himself, and they'll catch us."

I knew she was right. That didn't make the idea more realistic or my horse less crazy. It seemed far more likely he'd throw me off and trample my skull like an eggshell than submit to any sort of control. Yet if I didn't try, he'd be spent in minutes. Without letting go my grip around his neck, I tried to snare the loose-hanging reins. I only dared slacken my grasp a fraction when I had them firmly tangled around my fingers.

He didn't even notice. Whether through fear, excitement or sheer viciousness, he seemed determined to run himself to death. Moaradrid would arrive to find me sat on a dead horse, and perhaps he might even smile for once before he chopped my head off. The thought gave me courage enough for a tentative yank on the reins.

"Wooah, Killer!" I cried, as loud as I dared.

The newly renamed Killer whinnied deep in the back of his throat, tossed his head, and picked up speed. I could feel his flanks shuddering between my legs, jerking in rhythm with his labouring lungs. He was beginning to tire already. All it was doing was making him madder. What was he so angry about, anyway?

Maybe he missed his master.

I jerked back on the reins with all my might and, summoning my best impression of Alvantes, bellowed, "Stop, damn you!"

Though Killer didn't stop, he slowed dramatically. He'd been expecting Alvantes, and nothing could have confused him more than a timid rider. He was used to authority, to knowing his place in the world.

Saltlick picked that moment to trot up beside me and, remembering him sat stock-still at Moaradrid's command, I couldn't help drawing a comparison to the animal labouring beneath me. I knew it was unfair. The giants' system of leadership had probably worked perfectly for centuries when only giants were involved. It wasn't designed to cope with power-hungry warlords, or self-absorbed thieves for that matter.

Saltlick actually looked well. His wounds had knitted faster than a man's would, and his expression remained cheerful. It was as though the morning's carnage had been a mere preamble to his starting homeward. I couldn't find it in me to blame him for that. He'd suffered more than most because of Moaradrid, and with least reason.

Maybe making sure he got back home was the only worthwhile way left to end this. Moaradrid was bound to catch us eventually. I'd been so close to death so many times over the last few days that it was hard to work up much excitement over the idea. Anyway, we had to run somewhere. Perhaps the near-mythical hideaway of the giants was as good a place as any.

Estrada caught up on my left side, and called, "They're close."

I dared a glance over my shoulder. There were riders, sure enough, though Moaradrid wasn't amongst them. They'd just passed the last corner, and would still have been out of sight if this section of road weren't so straight. It was impossible to tell if they were gaining.

"Is this the right way?" I asked Saltlick.

He tried to nod, realised the gesture was futile when his whole body was bobbing with each stride, and pointed ahead. If I remembered the area rightly, we were near the Cancasa Bridge, the southern border of Castovalian civilisation. The road veered outward to avoid an outcrop of the mountainside, just before the point where it met the river. It was there that Saltlick indicated.

Once we'd rounded the next bend, the road dissolved into a series of long curves. It was impossible to see the northern riders after that. The fact made me both glad and nervous. I'd no desire to watch them drawing closer, but knowing they might be and that I couldn't see it was almost worse. If Moaradrid's men were remotely typical of the northern tribes, they'd probably been born in the saddle, whereas my lack of control over Killer was severely slowing us down. He only seemed to understand going too quickly or too slowly, and convincing him to keep a steady pace was a constant struggle. I did the best I could, and willed the outcrop to appear, as though it would offer some miraculous safety.

Inevitably it was a disappointment. Saltlick had taken the lead, his easy strides more than a match for our horses. Where the road jerked aside to avoid a wedge of rocky ground, a rough trail led off to the right. Saltlick turned onto it without slowing, undaunted by the incline. Killer was more nervous, slowing almost to a halt before he got the measure of the looser surface.

It occurred to me Moaradrid's men might miss the turn-off. But there was no real hope of that. Even if there was no one in the party who could follow our trail, it didn't take a genius to guess where we'd be heading. Moaradrid himself had come this way only a month or so ago. I wondered briefly how he'd ever known about the giant-stone. Or had he simply planned to make some deal, or somehow force the giants into service? I didn't dare guess how that wolfish mind of his might work.

I couldn't resist another look back as we began up the hillside, clinging to the absurd hope that for once luck would take our side. The trail curled between slabs of grey rock streaked with chalk, or sometimes banks of hard-packed earth where gaunt thorn trees bent towards us. The main road was hidden from view, and all the perspective we had was the occasional glimpse of river to our left and the ramparts of the mountain rearing ahead. I couldn't tell if Moaradrid's men had taken the turn-off.

As long as I didn't know for sure, I could hope.

The path, which had been steadily worsening, became abruptly steeper. Killer nearly lost his footing, and whinnied irritably. He wasn't bred for this kind of thing. This was literally donkeywork, and torment for an animal born to run on the flat. As distressing as it was to feel him struggling beneath me, my greatest worry was that we'd have to abandon our mounts. After the travails of the last few hours, neither Estrada nor I were in particularly good shape. Having to leave the horses could only work to Moaradrid's advantage.

Of course, I was still clutching to the faint hope that we'd lost our pursuers. It wasn't until the incline took us out from the region of shallow gullies and onto the beginning of the mountainside proper that we had a clear view. There was the river, tumbling from the mountainside to wind into the blue haze of the distance. There was the Cancasa Bridge, looking hopelessly fragile against the backdrop of tumbling white-water, and the road traipsing across it and away in each direction.

Lastly, there was Moaradrid's small band. I was surprised by how far behind they'd fallen. They'd barely made the turn onto the trail. At that distance, they were little more than large specks standing out against the grey of the path.

Nor did they seem to be rushing. I thought about what Mounteban had said – that Moaradrid's unpaid and ill-fed army was close to rebellion. Were they taking their time through half-heartedness, perhaps discussing whether it mightn't be easier just to turn around and forget the whole sorry business? But another detail made me think twice. The party had grown by at least a half-dozen riders, and a couple of what from their outlines must be pack mounts. It was just as likely that they'd waited for support and supplies, perhaps even for Moaradrid himself. Wouldn't he want to see this through?

So maybe they weren't hurrying because they knew we had nowhere left to run.

A thought crossed my mind: If I ordered him to, Saltlick could kill them all. A dozen men – a thrown rock would probably do it. Maybe I should have done it days ago, in Panchetto's palace perhaps. Wouldn't Panchetto be alive now if I had? I glanced at Saltlick. He'd been running, or walking hard, for nearly an hour now, and his skin glistened with sweat. Yet there was no sign of tiredness in his face, only a look of steadfast pleasure.

I couldn't imagine what it would be like for going home to mean that much – enough to eclipse pain and tiredness, to wipe out days of fear and violence. I wouldn't see Saltlick reunited with his people with those bastards' blood still wet on his hands. Damn Moaradrid, let them catch us if they wanted.

Clearly, it was exactly what they wanted. His party were fractionally nearer whenever I looked back. They couldn't do much to narrow the gap with both of us travelling so slowly, but they didn't need to. If they gained a step an hour, it would be enough to overtake us eventually.

I became increasingly aware that I'd have to ignore that contracting gap if I didn't want to die much sooner. The trail was terrible, not really a trail at all. Apart from Moaradrid's force all those weeks ago, I doubted anything bigger than a goat had passed this way in years. There was no way he'd brought an army up here; I could only assume he'd camped them nearby. There was nothing under our horses' hooves but a narrow ribbon of rock, edging a precipice that fell steeply to the boulders below.

We came eventually to a section where the incline levelled out, and the gap between the cliff face to our right and the edge on our left was wide enough for the three of us to travel abreast. Saltlick automatically took the most dangerous position. He moved easily, unperturbed by the altitude or the lethally uneven surface. Estrada rode on the inside, and Killer and I were in the middle.

All fight had gone out of the poor beast. He trod anxiously, giving the occasional worried snort. More and more he expected constant guidance, and made no secret of resenting my over-the-shoulder surveillance of Moaradrid's men. He'd dance a little closer to the edge, as though my reassurance was the only thing keeping us from hurtling over. I realised I'd have to give him my full concentration if he wasn't going to sacrifice us both to prove his point.

That insight proved just a minute too late.

Estrada's mount screamed horribly. He'd completely lost his hoofing, and slid towards me. I reined Killer in, too roughly. Rather than retreat, he stopped dead. Estrada's mount struck his flank and he slipped too. My eyes fell to the cliff, which jerked nearer with nightmarish abruptness.

"Saltlick!"

He looked round to see both horses skittering towards him, hooves dancing out of control. He looked puzzled for an instant. Then he dug his toes in, gripping the very verge of the precipice, and held his palms out, just in time to brace against Killer's flank. That only scared Killer more. He reared, thrashing his forelegs, and I hurled my arms around his neck. Saltlick barely ducked out of the way.

Estrada, to my right, had restored enough control to drag her horse to safer ground. Killer, though, was half-mad with fear. He tried to bolt forward. He might as well have tried to run on ice. The burst only propelled him nearer the edge. He whickered in terror. Beyond the precipice beside us, a landscape in miniature span into view, toy trees and rocks an impossible distance below. Killer tried once more to regain the path, drove himself sideways again. His forelegs kicked against nothing.

We lurched into the void.

I could feel the wind tearing at me. I could hear its screech. I felt myself plummeting.

At least, that was what my brain insisted. My eyes told a different story. They were anchored to the ground far, far below. Seconds passed, and for all that my mind was convinced I should be plunging towards it, it drew no closer.

Even when that eye-watering view swung away, even when the path drifted back into focus, I couldn't believe it. I felt a tug on my right leg. Since when did falling involve having your leg pulled? I looked aside. There was Estrada, one hand still on my knee. There was Saltlick beside her, panting with excerption.

"What happened?" I managed, the words thick on my tongue.

"Saltlick caught you."

"He caught me?"

"Your horse."

"Nobody's that strong."

She managed a thin smile. "Clearly Saltlick is."

We didn't try to ride again after that. Chips of shale littered the trail, and flowed like water under the slightest pressure. That was what had caused Estrada's mount to slip. Leading the horses was only slightly safer, but it calmed them a little at least. Killer had suffered some sort of nervous collapse, and wouldn't do anything without my guidance. I kept a tight grip on the reins bunched in my hand and whispered outrageous lies I thought might keep his spirits up. "Almost at the lake of sugar, Killer," I said, and "don't worry, your barn's just around the next bend."

The accident had occupied less than a minute. Still, it was valuable time lost. If Moaradrid's men fared better, if their horses were more familiar with this sort of terrain, then they'd be on us by nightfall.

Rather than think about that, I concentrated on keeping my footing, and on my one-sided conversation with Killer. Neither went well. I couldn't go ten steps without my feet slipping from under me, and there are only so many absurd promises you can make to a horse. My body, already battered from riding, complained more with each step. My legs felt weak and elastic. I found myself remembering that moment of almost plunging to my death, and my head swam. Added to all those discomforts, the light was beginning to fade. The encroaching night played tricks with my eyes, and brought with it a ferocious cold.

I'd half convinced myself that the razor's edge path across the rock face would never end, so that when it did I halted in confusion. Saltlick, who'd been leading, had disappeared, seemingly into the stone itself. Only when Estrada followed did I see the narrow crevasse they'd entered. It was a sheer split in the mountain, reaching down from high above. It was almost like an open doorway, and the sense of boundary made me nervous.

Weariness had just about worn through the last of my courage. I thought seriously of leaving the giant-stone there on the path in the hope that one of Moaradrid's men would find it – or perhaps trip over it and break his neck.

"Hurry up," called Estrada. "We're out of the wind here."

"Come on, Killer," I muttered, "nearly at the magic castle of hay."

The region beyond the gap was surprisingly spacious, a wide hollow between two slanting planes that tilted together to almost meet far above. It was like a tent of rock, and as Estrada had said, it cut off the worst of the wind. The change in temperature was dramatic.

Saltlick stood in the gloom at the far end. The chasm narrowed beyond him, and curved steeply upward. That must be the next leg of the path, though it looked even less deserving of the term than the route by which we'd arrived. The idea of attempting it made my legs turn to jelly, from my thighs to the tips of my toes. The still-rational part of my brain reminded me that Moaradrid's men must be less than an hour behind us. The remainder, numb with weariness, pointed out how little I cared.

"We'll have to leave the horses here," Estrada said.

Leave Killer? Was she serious? "They can't get down on their own."

"Of course not. But we can't take them any further. If we make it we'll come back for them."

"And if we don't?"

Estrada sighed. "Then it's not going to make any difference, is it?"

It was hard to fault her logic, especially with my brain melting from exhaustion. "Maybe we should take a minute to think about it."

"We don't have a minute. Be reasonable, Damasco."

"Reasonable?" The word came out as a sob. "What's reasonable? We've been on the run all day and I can't keep going! My legs won't work. I'm not made for heroics, Estrada. Please, just let me rest for a little while."

I expected her to shout at me, to accuse me of selfishness and cowardice. I expected an argument. What I didn't expect was for Saltlick to reply before she could. "Saltlick carry." The words rolled out of the shadows, tolled back and forth between the crevasse walls. "Go home."

"What?"

"Saltlick carry." He stepped into the thin streak of light from the fissure far above. Kneeling, he cupped his arms together, hand locked to hand to form a sort of cradle.

"You're joking."

"Carry. Not tired. Go home."

It was as many words as I'd ever heard Saltlick string together. There was a new tone to his voice too; even his monosyllabic grammar couldn't disguise the note of longing. I wanted to tell him it was all right, that I could go on. The truth was, I couldn't. I'd meant what I said. I felt as though the muscles in my calves and thighs were dissolving like ice in a fire.

"All right."

I moved nearer, let him scoop me off the ground. I thought I'd be embarrassed, but all I could feel as my feet left the earth was relief. I let my eyes slide closed, and soft blackness wrapped around me.

"Damasco, you can't... I mean..."

I felt Saltlick straighten up. He held me as carefully as any mother ever had her baby.

"It's okay," I murmured. "Just for a little while. Then it's your turn, promise."

"It isn't that. You'll wear him out."

I let my body go loose when he began to move, let myself bounce along with his steps.

"It's really okay."

"Damasco…"

I woke to a velvet sky splashed with shimmering, fluid stars.

The moon was gibbous, almost full, shining brightly through shreds of cloud. The rock stood out like alabaster beneath its light, glowing faintly, seeming slightly unreal. There was no transition from sleep to wakefulness, and no hint of what had roused me. I had the vague memory of deep, dreamless sleep. My nostrils filled with a musky scent like damp, warm straw, and I breathed in deeply, until I realised it was the smell of unwashed giant.

I remembered where I was.

"Hey, hey… put me down, Saltlick."

Saltlick lurched to a halt, bent his knees, and set me on my feet.

"Better?"

I thought about it. I ached from head to toe, yet it was almost pleasant compared with the numbing weariness of before.

"I am. I can feel my feet again."

"Quiet, Damasco. They're close."

I barely recognised the voice as Estrada's. I stepped around Saltlick, saw her, and gasped. She was skeletal and deathly pale under the moonlight. I fell into step between them and said softly, "Saltlick, can you carry Estrada?"

"Yes. Go home."

"Easie, I don't need carrying."

"Then do it, Saltlick. As your chief, I command you – whatever she says or does."

"Damasco, you..."

Estrada hadn't time to finish her sentence before Saltlick swept her from the ground. She glared down at me and looked as though she'd try to struggle free.

"Listen to sense for once. He can manage."

"Not tired," agreed Saltlick. Though it couldn't possibly be true, he sounded as if he meant it.

"Easie," she murmured.

"Quiet."

And for once, she was. I held a hand near her face and felt gentle, regular sighs of breath. She was fast asleep.

"All right, Saltlick," I whispered, "let's get going."

Estrada and I swapped places twice through that interminable night, one carried while the other clambered up the rock-strewn trail. At least, I assumed there was a trail. I saw no sign of one, but Saltlick seemed to be guided by something. I followed in his footsteps as well as I could. Whenever I diverged even slightly I'd trip over some obstruction or slip on a loose patch of ground.

My first shift on foot ran to around midnight. I remember the moon hanging directly above me like a pendulum, fat and heavy, ready to fall at any moment. Saltlick clambering over a particularly awkward outcrop roused Estrada, and she insisted we change places.

My second shift began a little before sunrise. I woke, saw Estrada labouring beside Saltlick and was overcome with guilt. I'd already regretted my nobility by the time we'd swapped places, but it was too late. Estrada was fast asleep in Saltlick's arms and I was stumbling around boulders beneath the flush of a new day.

It was a glorious dawn, the sky streaked with shades of crimson and orange and bright, brittle pink. It was spoiled only by the crawling black dots far below that represented Moaradrid's men. They were still on our trail. But they were no nearer. Thanks to Saltlick, we'd kept our lead through the night.

If the three of us might not be good for much, we were good at surviving. When Saltlick chose that moment to point with his free hand to a gap in the peaks above and whisper, "Home," I couldn't help but laugh aloud. Against all the odds, through everything Moaradrid and fate had conspired to hurl at us, we'd made it.

That final stretch of mountainside was almost a pleasure. It was as hard as everything that had gone before, and worse for the fact that I could see now how broken the terrain I clambered over was. Yet what did it matter? I'd kept a promise for the first time in my life. It was a good promise and I hadn't broken it. That victory seemed more important to my giddy, sleep-starved brain than the ferocious battle in the valley ever had. I scrambled with gusto, smiling to think of Moaradrid's thugs suffering below. They had no giant to help them, no small triumphs to keep them going.

For the longest while we clambered up wide steps littered with splintered chunks of rock. Then near the summit, those gave way to a wide slope of pebbles and loose shale. If there was the faintest suggestion of a path, it was no less treacherous than the rest of the climb had been. I tripped frequently, only saving myself each time by driving my fingers up to the knuckles into the scree. Even Saltlick, who so far had managed to compensate for the loss of his hands with sheer strength, began to struggle. Estrada gurgled unhappily in his arms whenever he slipped.

The opening was tantalisingly close. Estrada stirred and mumbled something. It seemed a shame for her to sleep through Saltlick's homecoming.

"Wake up," I called. "We're almost there."

She shook her head and wriggled, forcing Saltlick to set her on her feet. She stared around, rubbing her eyes, clearly not quite awake.

"What? Where are we?"

I pointed.

She followed my finger, looked drowsily at Saltlick and back to me. Then her eyes widened, as realisation dawned.

"Oh! Is that it?"

I nodded, grinning hugely.

"Way home," agreed Saltlick.

Estrada gazed back in the direction we'd come from, to the indistinct, dark shapes that represented our pursuers.

She smiled, and the smile widened and ended in a ringing, bright laugh. "We did it. After everything..." The smile flickered, and was gone. "Everything that's happened."

I could practically see the memories parading behind her eyes: that first, hideous battle all those days ago, Panchetto's death, the fight in the canyon and Alvantes's terrible injury. But there was nothing there that could be changed now, and nothing I was about to let spoil my good mood.

I punched Saltlick on the thigh, and said, "Come on. Lead the way."

Saltlick, perhaps following the situation for once, set off hurriedly towards the gap above. I fell in behind, taking more care, and after the slightest hesitation Estrada moved to join me. By the time we'd caught up, he'd come to a halt on the narrow outcrop that topped the incline. Twin crags towered ahead of him like miniature mountain peaks. Between ran the narrow cleft of the opening, and beyond that...

I heard a choking sound, and realised it was me.

"You can't be serious!"

CHAPTER TWENTY-THREE

The gap between the crags ran for perhaps another twenty paces. Beyond that point the trail continued with only empty air to either side. It could optimistically be described as a bridge, albeit one crafted solely by the forces of nature, and then in one of her more capricious moods. Bridges, after all, were traditionally wider, and generally had something to stop a traveller being torn away by screaming winds and hurled into the void.

"You don't really think I'm crossing that?"

Saltlick looked at me questioningly. Then, apparently not seeing any reason for concern, he pointed to the far side.

"Home."

I gulped. I'd never been afraid of heights. I'd never been particularly afraid of bears either, but that didn't mean I'd wrap my head in fresh meat and thrust it into one's mouth. Knowing there was no going back didn't make the prospect any more appealing.

Estrada and I followed Saltlick as far as the end of

the crevasse. He carried on without pause, as if there was no difference to walking between stone walls and terrifying expanses of emptiness. In less than a minute he'd reached the midpoint, where he paused to see if we were following. The bridge was so narrow that he barely had room to turn around, and his feet sent pebbles dancing off the edge.

It was only as I watched them fall that I understood where we'd come out. The span hung over a strip of broiling sea far below, which separated the mountainside we were on from the landmass towering ahead. That was the giant kingdom, hidden on a pinnacle all its own, held apart by this narrow causeway. It rose like the ramparts of some impossible fortress from a froth of white water, and behind, the ocean stretched crystal blue to the horizon.

"Follow?"

Saltlick's cry made the whole span tremble. "Keep your voice down!"

Cowed, he waved instead.

I looked to Estrada, vaguely hoping she would volunteer to go first. She merely stood watching me, arms crossed, a wicked smile playing over her lips.

"Fine. All right."

I closed my eyes, stepped forward.

Then I realised I was standing on a narrow band of rock over a chasm with my eyes closed, and hurriedly opened them again.

The wind wasn't as bad as I'd expected. Its constant push and tug was more unnerving than dangerous. The harder part was knowing where to look. At first,

I focused on Saltlick. That meant I couldn't see where I was putting my feet. I looked down instead, saw how vast the difference between background and foreground was, and felt my legs turn to mush. I dropped to hands and knees, and panted icy air into my lungs.

The fear that an enthusiastic gust would tear me free soon overcame my giddiness. I fixed my gaze once more on Saltlick, who stood waiting now on the far side. I began moving again, this time letting my eyes drift slightly to keep myself on track. My pace would have shamed a baby, and only made the ordeal seem to go on forever. I dared a proper step. When I didn't tumble straight over the edge, I took another.

It was faster going after that. Still, by the time I rushed onto solid ground, Saltlick was staring at me as though I were insane. He'd lived all his life up here, no wonder he didn't grasp the concept of vertigo.

That thought brought another close behind it. "Are we there?"

Saltlick pointed. The opening at this side was wider, and its slight slant meant that only there, on the cusp of the bridge, could I see the gateway at its end. Where the walls ran almost sheer, a palisade of logs filled the gap. The fact that Saltlick seemed surprised by its presence suggested it was a new addition. Security had obviously gone up in priority since Moaradrid's visit.

I looked back and saw Estrada crossing the span. If she was even slightly nervous, she hid it well. She practically skipped across, and finished with a bow as she stepped onto solid ground. Ignoring my scowl, she pointed to the palisade and said, "Should we knock?"

In answer, Saltlick paced into the passage. Half way to the barricade, he cupped his hands around his mouth, and hollered. It sounded like a single word, but I couldn't quite make it out over the cascade of stones and loose dirt he'd shaken free.

"Keep it down, Saltlick!"

He ignored me, and howled again. The second time was even louder and just as incomprehensible. I cradled my head, expecting half the cliff to come tumbling down. Saltlick filled his lungs for another effort. Just in time, a voice called from beyond the palisade: two muffled syllables that sounded something like his name.

The logs swung back and up with a creak of straining timber. Two giants stood beyond, one struggling to knot a length of rope around a post driven into the ground. These two looked subtly different from Saltlick. They were smaller, their features weren't quite so coarse, and though their bodies were equally lumpy, they swelled in noticeably different places.

"Ohhh," I mumbled, as my brain struggled to fit the incompatible concepts of "giants" and "women" together.

"Shol Tchik!"

The giantess who wasn't busy keeping the gate open flung her broad arms around Saltlick, who looked both overjoyed and abashed. Releasing him, she rattled off a long sentence in incomprehensible giantish, clasped his hand in hers, and dragged him inside.

Estrada and I followed at a distance. Having just about come to terms with the shock of female giants, I could finally turn my attention to our surroundings.

One glance and my jaw fell open. Whatever I'd been expecting, this wasn't it.

As far as I could see, we were at one end of a bowl-shaped plateau, ringed on every side by low escarpments to form an immense natural arena. The ground sloped steadily down ahead, before rising to greater heights of mountainside at its distant far end.

None of that was so surprising. But the thick border of grass to either side, the line of trees that swayed ahead? Here the breeze, crisp to the point of chilliness just instants before, felt comfortably warm on my skin, and moist, almost clammy.

The dirt road we were following – which was more of a path by giant standards – descended from the gate, down a short embankment to meet the tree line. To either side I could see that planks had been laid, covering narrow crevices and punctures in the ground. The grass beside was wilted and brown and the air danced with heat-haze. I thought of the medicinal baths near my hometown of Conta Pelia, which drew from a spring heated deep beneath the ground and ran warm through even the harshest winters. Was there something similar beneath this plateau?

We passed through the edge of the woodland. The trees were vastly tall, bare-trunked for most of their height and then exploding into great canopies of fo-

liage at their peaks. They were widely spaced for the
most part, spread like columns in a grand hall. Looking around to see if we were close to the giant
settlement, I made another strange discovery: between many of the trees, huge banners of coarse
fabric had been stretched from bole to bole. It reminded me a little of the streamers of drying cloth
that dyers sometimes hung across the alleys of Muena
Palaiya. Although they were all decorated to some degree, with swirls of symbols in various shades, I didn't
think they were purely for show. Occasionally I saw
one suspended lower than my head height, but most
were so lofty that Saltlick could have easily stepped
beneath them.

As we made our way deeper into the forest,
Estrada and I hurrying to keep pace with Saltlick and
our guide, I noticed more details. I saw how the banners would frequently meet to form a corner, or even
a triangle or square, and how some of these shapes
were topped with canopies of the same fabric hung
taut between the trees. I realised that where crops
were being grown – stands of green cane, a grain that
looked like wheat but grew far taller, bushes laden
with heavy purple and yellow fruits each as big as my
head – the banners separated one from the other.

Then it hit me. They were rooms – giant-sized
rooms. As soon as I realised it, the whole scene
seemed to flip end on end. Gone were trees and
banners and sheets, and in their place a giant-scaled
town, with walled fields and gardens, highways,
vast public areas and enclosed chambers that would

offer privacy from anyone of giant rather than man height.

All the while I'd been waiting to glimpse the giant settlement we'd been wandering through its outskirts.

In the time it had taken me to make sense of our surroundings, a half-dozen more giants had fallen in around us, the news of our arrival having rapidly spread in a receding wave of bellows. Though they all seemed friendly, and overjoyed to see Saltlick, it was intimidating to have so many colossal bodies moving so close together, and Estrada and I hung well back. For that reason, I only realised we'd reached our destination when the wall of stocky legs ahead stopped moving and I nearly bashed my head on a giantess's thigh.

Now I understood the purpose of the tree-banners, I could see that we were in the equivalent of a large circular chamber, with avenues leading off like spokes in a wheel. The space was heaving with giant bodies, perhaps as many as a hundred, all gabbling excitedly together. Though I still wasn't entirely sure about giant anatomy, I thought that most of them were female. The few males were barely taller than I was, and I assumed they must be children. It struck me that Moaradrid had only taken adult males for his army. It was conceivably a sign of mercy, but just as likely forward planning for future campaigns.

The banners there were particularly intricate and brightly coloured, and my first thought was that we'd come to the giant equivalent of a town square. Then, through the throng, I noticed the spike of rock thrust through the turf at its centre, its highest point reaching a little above my head. Near the peak was a smooth, cupped indent, just wide enough that I could have sat up there if I could have climbed it.

Unsurprisingly, however, the giants had chosen not to use the rock as a highchair for passing midgets. Rather, it held a plain wooden rod, almost as long as Saltlick was tall. At one end I could see a simple metal clasp, its prongs wrenched back as if something had been torn from it. I remembered what Estrada had told me that night before we'd reached Altapasaeda. This must be the chief's staff of office, which had housed the giant-stone until Moaradrid's catastrophic arrival.

I was about to point it out to Estrada when the great horde parted, and one particular giantess came hurrying towards us out of the press. She was skinnier than most, her skin puckered and lined, and though she was clearly rushing she was making slow progress. She muttered under her breath all the while, and when she came close enough she hurled herself onto Saltlick, ringed her arms around his chest, and sobbed, "Shol Tchik! Shol Tchik!"

It could only be his mother. I realised belatedly that those words the giantesses kept saying must be Saltlick's true name, which Moaradrid's men had mispronounced. Saltlick didn't hesitate this time to return the show of affection. He clung to her as if his life depended on it, and both their faces were soon streaked and grubby with tears.

This was what he'd struggled for: his place, his people and his family. A sudden sadness knotted my throat. I had none of those things. Still, in that moment, I understood perfectly.

With that insight, a new thought occurred to me. I drew out the giant-stone and held it up.

"Saltlick," I called. "You need to take this now."

Saltlick looked at me, with surprise at first and then with horror.

"I know, I know, you're not good enough. Well, I'm not an expert on giant politics, but you seem popular at least. So maybe you can just be the stand-in chief until someone better comes along." I pointed. "Either way, that staff isn't going to mend itself."

I could see he was about to protest again; but the nearby giants had seen the stone by then, and suddenly the air was filled with deafening, delighted cries.

"Saltlick... take it." I had to shout to make myself heard. "Mend the staff. Make things right."

Saltlick gave the barest nod. He reached down and plucked the giant stone from my hands.

Abruptly, a cry went up from every corner of the square: "Shol Tchik! Shol Tchik!"

He walked with slow steps to the centre of the clearing. He lifted the staff with one hand, holding it as gently as if it were a sleeping baby, and with the other pressed the stone into the clasp. Then he closed his fist around both stone and clasp and squeezed. When he took his hand away, the staff was whole again.

The resultant cheer was so thunderous that I thought my eardrums would explode. When Saltlick reached out to put the staff back on its perch, the wail of protest was if anything louder. He hesitated. Then he drew it back, planted its base in the ground before him, and bowed his head. Every giant fell silent, so suddenly that it seemed all sound had been sucked from the world. As one, they dipped their heads, just as Saltlick had done.

If there was more to the inauguration ceremony, I never saw it, because at that moment, a shout rang from the edge of the clearing behind us. I couldn't be sure, but I thought I recognised the giantess who'd opened the gate for us. She beckoned to Saltlick, cried his name, and rattled off a sentence in giantish. Then she turned and pointed back the way we'd come.

Saltlick hesitated for just an instant, his eyes flickering over those gathered around him. Then he began to run, still clutching the staff.

"What? What is it?" I cried as he bolted past.

When he didn't answer, I fell in behind him, and Estrada followed us both. We charged out of the clearing, Saltlick gaining distance with each stride. I had no idea what the giantess had said, but the sinking sensation in my stomach gave me a fair idea of her meaning. I ran with all my strength, until my muscles shrieked with pain. I ran on and on, past the blur of endless trees, past the banner-walls, out through the suburbs of the giant settlement.

By the time I caught Saltlick, we were in sight of the gate. He'd stopped at the base of the embankment and stood with his head cocked to one side. I came to a stumbling halt and hunched over with my hands on my thighs, gasping for breath. Estrada, arriving next to me, just barely managed to keep to her feet.

At first, I couldn't make out anything over the sound of my own heartbeat pummelling my ears. Then, as the drumming subsided, I heard it. The shout was faint, distorted by distance. For all that, my blood turned to frost in my veins.

"Giant! Thief!"

It crossed my mind simply to ignore him. He was outside and we were safe inside, so why shouldn't things stay that way indefinitely? But if Moaradrid had come here, it stood to reason he had the means to make us listen to whatever he had to say.

"We're here," I cried, as loudly as I could bear.

"I have someone here who needs your help. A certain guard-captain of your acquaintance."

Estrada put a hand to her mouth and made a small, choked sound.

"This bridge clearly wasn't intended for cripples, so you may wish to hurry."

"Oh no." Her eyes met mine. "Damasco..."

I thought about pointing out how much Alvantes hated me, and how I didn't feel much more warmly toward him. I thought about pointing out that we'd won, that I'd done what I came to do, and couldn't we just leave it at that? I thought about a lot of things, but none of them did anything to change the look in her eyes – the desperation, the pleading, and behind all that, the faint glimmer of hope.

"He's going to want the stone," I said to Saltlick.

"He'll try and trade Alvantes's life for it. Maybe I could bluff him, or keep him talking while…"

Saltlick reached up and tore the giant-stone free of its clasp.

"Oh. That would work, too."

He took a stride towards the gate.

I darted in front of him. "Wait, wait! Let me. He'll *want* it to be me. And let's face it; you're not exactly built for rescue missions on narrow rock bridges. It has to be me, Saltlick."

Saltlick considered for a moment. Then he reached down and handed me the stone.

"We'll get it back."

I knew it wasn't true. I could see in his eyes that he knew too: that he'd brought hope to his people only to snatch it away again. My witless attempts to help had only made things worse. I decided that overall it might be easier to have my head lopped off by Moaradrid – easier at least than having to see the results of more of my mistakes. I turned and hurried up the bank.

Saltlick bounded ahead, caught hold of the rope and began to hoist the gate open. As soon as there was a gap, I ducked and slithered through. I sprinted through the crevasse and came out on the other side, to the narrow outcrop that met the rock span. I saw Moaradrid. I saw his men. I saw Alvantes, and my heart sank.

He waited just in front of the warlord at the dead centre of the bridge. A half-hearted attempt had been made to bind and strap his mutilated arm, but it was largely defeated by the coils of rope that bound him shoulder to wrist.

He was barely recognisable as the man I'd once found so formidable. His skin was sickly-pale, he was dishevelled and dirty, and only the way he held himself upright despite obvious pain and exhaustion hinted at his former strength.

Moaradrid too appeared tired, and though his leg wound was better bandaged, the linens were pink-stained, and he stood uncomfortably. Even his men, waiting on the far mountainside, looked worn out.

Moaradrid acknowledged me with a curt inclination of the head. "There you are."

I stepped onto the beginning of the bridge.

"Here I am."

"Are you prepared to get this over with?"

I took a couple more steps. I heard Saltlick arrive on the outcrop behind me, and felt an urge to say something, anything, to delay the moment when I dashed his hopes for good.

"You won't win, Moaradrid."

He was smiling, but the smile seemed frozen in place. There was no trace of it in his voice as he said, "Stupid little thief. No understanding of anything bigger than yourself. Of course I'll win. What's more, I'll be a good king. Far better than that oaf in Pasaeda."

I took another step. "Let him go."

Moaradrid gave Alvantes a nudge that made him stumble towards the edge. "Please. Choose your words with a little care."

"I mean… it's me you want. Me and the stone."

"My stone. Yes, I'd like that back. You I care little for. Though maybe if you were dead you'd finally learn to keep out of my business."

"I'll bring it to you."

"And quickly, please. I think you're friend is getting dizzy."

I gulped, tried to keep my voice steady. "I can see that. So once he's safe on our side, you can have it."

Moaradrid's smile dissolved. "What do you think is happening here, you ridiculous mooncalf? Have I come all this way to haggle like a market trader?" Abruptly, he caught hold of the rope behind Alvantes's shoulders and shoved him to the very brink, so that only Moaradrid's grip kept him from tumbling into the ether. "Be careful, thief. Irritation makes me careless."

I took out the giant-stone, held it out over the edge. "I have a similar problem. Only in my case, it's blind terror and vertigo."

There was that smile again. Then, with cat-like fluidity, Moaradrid drew Alvantes back to the centre of the span and gave him a light push, as of encouragement, towards our side. "You've been paying attention after all. Have your guard-captain then. He's a fair trade for a crown."

Alvantes started towards me, and with each shambling step I feared he'd topple over the edge. I doubted very much that they'd fed him or given him water since the battle, and that combined with blood loss had left him on the very point of collapse. Alvantes might be a pompous ass, but I knew in my heart he was a decent man, and it appalled me to see how he'd been treated.

It struck me that I truly wanted to hurt Moaradrid, as he'd hurt Alvantes, Panchetto, Saltlick, Estrada and so many others.

Yet what hope was there of that?

I began walking.

There was barely room for Alvantes and me to pass each other. He looked round at the last moment. Though his face was knotted with pain, his voice was perfectly calm when he spoke. "Don't let him win, Damasco."

"I don't think I can stop him."

Alvantes gave me one last glance and stumbled on, towards where Saltlick and Estrada waited. Saltlick would look after them, far better than I could. Stone or no, he'd protect them – I had to believe that. I didn't dare look at them, for fear my resolve would evaporate entirely.

Instead, I kept walking.

I'd half-expected Moaradrid to scythe my head from my shoulders the moment I came close enough. I was a little surprised when he simply held out an upturned hand. His sword hung at his side.

I could fight...

I could wrestle him, force him over the edge...

I placed the stone in his palm.

In that split second, I felt nothing but relief. All I'd done since I first set eyes on it was run, and I was tired out with running. Moaradrid allowed himself a shuddering sigh, as if he too was briefly overcome.

Then he drew himself together, held his head high to glare down at me.

"So our business is done."

I had to ask, for all I knew I shouldn't. "Isn't this the part where you kill me?"

He laughed. "I thought you were starting to understand. No, thief, I'm not going to kill you. That's not how power works."

I nodded, as though I had the faintest idea what he meant. "Well, then."

I turned away. Of course I didn't believe him. Of course I expected a scimitar between my shoulder blades. But what could I do? Though I wanted to run, I didn't. There'd been a sense of sympathy between us, almost an understanding. Even if it only existed in Moaradrid's insane mind, it might still last, if only I kept calm. If I ran, I knew he'd change his mind.

So I placed one foot ahead of the other.

I walked across that sliver of rock, hardly daring to breathe.

And I stepped onto solid ground.

Alvantes was sat on a shelf of rock, while Estrada tried hopelessly to unpick the ropes that bound him with only her fingers. Alvantes, for his part, was struggling not to wince every time the slightest impact jolted his mutilated arm. I guessed he'd live, so long as the wound wasn't infected. Saltlick stood a little to one side, still holding the disfigured staff, and though he must have been devastated by the loss of the chief-stone, he didn't show it.

Our fight for the Castoval, for the safety of the giants, was over. We'd lost, and Moaradrid had won. But at least we were all alive, and that was a better outcome than I'd expected.

Of course, the day wasn't over yet.

"Giant."

The word rang out clearly behind me.

"Giant, pick up your friend there and choke him to death."

Saltlick jerked to attention. He gazed over my head to where Moaradrid still stood, stone held high in one hand, the other pointing towards me. Saltlick's eyes grew wide, his mouth hung slightly open, as though someone had slapped him.

"I know you heard me. Obey your chieftain."

Saltlick took a laboured step towards me.

"*Obey your chieftain.*"

I wanted to back away. I knew there was nothing behind me except a very long fall.

"Saltlick…"

One moment his hand hung at his side, the next it was around my throat. I hadn't even time for a last breath. My lungs heaved in my chest. Pinpricks of light exploded, a waterfall of sound cascaded through my ears. Through it, dimly, I heard Estrada's voice. "Saltlick, oh no, you don't have to, you don't have to listen to him, not after everything…"

The words continued. It was too much trouble separating them from the sluice of noise. Why listen when Saltlick wasn't? He'd been told to kill me. Killing me was what he was doing.

Only he wasn't. Not quite.

He was strong enough to crush my throat like a bundle of dry twigs. Yet I was alive. It hurt beyond imagination, but I was alive. Maybe Saltlick was having trouble after all – just as when he'd resisted me in Altapasaeda.

Except that in Altapasaeda, he'd given in.

Moaradrid's voice pushed through Estrada's pleading and the roaring surf. "Once that's done, you can round up your women and children."

The pressure relaxed, just fractionally.

"I was merciful before."

I sucked air into scorched lungs.

"Maybe your friends will be more committed with them in tow."

And suddenly, I was free. I lay still, panting like a sick dog. Saltlick was staring past me once again. There was an expression on his face I'd never seen before. It was like the look of someone waking from a deep sleep, but with something terrible behind it, something fierce and sad.

"Bad chief."

Moaradrid looked taken aback for the first time. "What does that matter?"

Saltlick's first stride carried him onto the rock bridge. "Bad order." He moved with the slow inevitability of an avalanche.

"It doesn't matter. I have your stupid stone!"

"Bad chief."

"*It doesn't matter!*"

But it did.

I couldn't guess at what was going through Moaradrid's mind. He looked more stunned than afraid. Saltlick reached out with one huge hand. Moaradrid stepped back, raising his arms to shield himself.

I wanted to cry out, *"He just wants the stone!"* The words fell in a gurgle from my crushed throat. Moaradrid drew back. Saltlick moved forward. It seemed very slow and precise, like a dance: Moaradrid back, Saltlick forward, Moaradrid back.

Until there was nothing left beneath him.

I saw him realise. I watched the knowledge light his face like a beacon fire. Saltlick saw too. He reached out. Moaradrid, even in the moment of falling, pulled away.

There was nowhere to go but down.

He didn't scream, exactly. But he did cry out. It was a guttural, animal noise, something wrenched from the darkness inside him.

It seemed to last for a very long time.

CHAPTER TWENTY-FOUR

"It wasn't your fault."

Saltlick didn't seem to hear me.

"You wanted to save him. In the end… well, I don't think a man like Moaradrid could understand that."

"Stone gone."

So that was what was bothering him? Not Moaradrid's plunge into the abyss but the loss of the chief-stone he'd taken with him. No, I'd heard how Saltlick had bellowed when he realised the warlord wouldn't let himself be saved. I recognised that tortured glint in his eye.

But now there was something else there as well, something I hadn't seen before. It was present too in the way he moved, and in a new set to his features. I couldn't begin to guess what was going through his mind.

I glanced nervously to the far side of the chasm, where a minute ago Moaradrid's men had been waiting, poised to intervene. They were gone. Apparently, avenging their master's death wasn't a higher priority than saving their own skins.

Would the rest of his army flee too, back into the distant North? We could only hope.

I turned my attention to Estrada and Alvantes. Alvantes's face was ashen and waxy, and his eyelids flickered constantly, as though even staying conscious was a struggle.

"We should get him inside," I said, "and see if we can tend that wound."

That brought Saltlick out of his stupor. "Help Alvantes," he rumbled.

He stomped over, and went to lift Alvantes from where he sat.

"Careful!" I squatted in front of them and asked Estrada, "Do you think he can walk?"

Alvantes glared at me. "I can walk."

He stumbled to his feet, and would have fallen as quickly if Estrada hadn't slipped her shoulder beneath his outstretched arm. Alvantes grunted with pain and resignation, and sagged against her. I moved quickly to support him on the other side.

In that manner we reeled along behind Saltlick, who'd gone ahead to call for the gate to be reopened. Fortunately, a number of the giantesses had followed behind us, and had been waiting in a crowd on the far side of the palisade. There followed a brief discussion, with Saltlick translating and much gesturing on all parts, as to the best way of getting Alvantes somewhere where his injuries could be treated. In the end, Estrada and I donated our cloaks to form a makeshift stretcher, which four giantesses took up. All together, we trudged down the bank and through the tree line.

A minute later, the giantesses indicated that we should separate, pointing Estrada and I to one of the banner-walled "rooms" while the rest trudged on with Alvantes.

"Hey," I cried, suddenly alarmed. Did they know what they were doing? What if giant anatomy was radically different from ours?

They only clucked at me and kept going.

"Heal well." Saltlick spoke with such certainty that I couldn't doubt him. Without Alvantes to worry about, my thoughts turned to myself. I couldn't quite persuade my mind or body to believe it was all over. My legs ached with the need to keep moving, as though they'd forgotten how to be still. My mind was in turmoil, images and sensations popping like sparks behind my eyes. I felt violently tired and fiercely awake. I flopped onto the grass and lay back, propped with my arms behind me.

"We won."

The words sounded hollow. Moaradrid was dead, a sorry and stupid death. His armies still squatted throughout the land. The giant-stone was lost, the giants split over the length of the Castoval.

Still. We *had* won. I tried hard to feel glad of the fact.

Saltlick sat beside me. One glance told me he was going through much the same internal struggles as I was. That change I'd noticed before remained, though, and I thought I recognised it now. If he was distraught, he nevertheless seemed stronger than before, more sure of himself. Perhaps his ever-so-brief spell as chieftain had given him a little self-insight; perhaps he approved of what he'd discovered.

Saltlick's mother had stayed behind with a couple of the other giantesses. They busied about, bringing first buckets of water and then fresh fruit and vegetables from the wilderness nearby. I was glad of the water, but the thought of food turned my stomach – until I tried some.

Everything was delicious beyond my wildest imagining. I knew I hadn't eaten in well over a day, and that probably accounted for why it was so good now, but all I really cared about was the pleasure of cramming food into my gullet. I ate until I couldn't manage any more. Then I lay back and closed my eyes. A giantess draped a blanket over me, and raised my head to tuck beneath it something soft and yielding.

I smiled, too drained to express my gratitude in any other way, and hoped they'd understand.

It was still light when I woke. I looked around, to discover that Estrada was kneeling beside me. Behind her, the giantesses had lowered the banners almost to the ground, creating a little privacy more suited to our scale.

"Good afternoon," I said.

"Actually it's early morning. You slept all day and night."

"Did I? I feel like I could do with a few more hours."

"Well, the giants say you can stay as long as you like. But Alvantes and I are starting back in a few minutes. I came to ask if you wanted to join us, or to say goodbye if you didn't."

"What about Saltlick?"

"He's said he wants to talk to us all."

I threw off my blanket. "If Saltlick has a speech planned I want to be there for it. At the very least it should be a masterpiece of brevity."

Estrada smiled. "He's been acting strangely. Well, not strange exactly…"

"Determined?"

"Yes. That's it."

"I noticed that." I climbed to my feet, and stretched until I felt as though my joints would pop. "He would have been a good chief, wouldn't he? I was so convinced he was just an oversized dolt."

"You know what I liked most about being mayor?" asked Estrada, drawing a flap in the wall-banner aside. "The way that when it came to it – when what needed doing seemed too hard, when I thought I was asking far too much of them – people always surprised me."

I nodded. "I can see how that might appeal."

Estrada motioned through the gap. "Shall we see what he has to say?"

She led the way, and a minute later we were once more within view of the gate. There were giants everywhere, in a loose crowd up the embankment. At the base of the slope, keeping well apart from the press, stood Alvantes. His foreshortened arm was strapped with bandages of coarse, green-tinged fabric, and he was supporting himself against a crutch tucked beneath the other shoulder. His face had been carefully cleaned, revealing countless small abrasions over a background of blackening bruises. For all that, he looked far better than when I'd seen him last.

He tilted his head in acknowledgement as we drew close. "They're arguing about something," he said, "but I'll be damned if I can tell what."

Saltlick was standing at the cusp of the bank with a dozen giantesses close around him, amongst them his mother. They were all speaking together, though it was clear that Saltlick was directing the conversation. That was new in itself. As Alvantes had pointed out, there was a definite sense of discord in the air, and Saltlick's mother seemed particularly agitated.

"Is everything all right?" Estrada asked.

Saltlick nodded. "Told them, tell you. Go find brothers. Bring home. No more fight."

His mother moved nearer and clutched his arm imploringly.

Not looking quite at her or away, he added, "Mother sad. Son come, son go. But must do."

"What about the chief-stone? Do you think they'll follow you back here without it?"

Saltlick's expression told me she'd struck a nerve. "Have to," he said flatly. "Only way."

Poor Saltlick. He'd come home only to leave again almost straight away. Well, at least he *had* come home. Anyway, I'd made up my own mind. "I'm coming with you. I mean, maybe not to rescue your friends, but some of the way anyway."

And so we said our goodbyes. What for Estrada, Alvantes and I was merely awkward, given the lack of any shared language, was clearly heartrending for

Saltlick. I only really understood then that the giant-esses had thought their kidnapped men-folk dead, and what a miracle it had been when he returned. His mother wept floods of tears, as did many of the others. There was much embracing and reassurances back and forth. Saltlick stood like a monolith amidst all that wild and giant-sized emotion: I knew he was trying to reassure them, though I couldn't under-stand the words. In the end, he gave his mother a last hug and walked to join us where we were waiting just outside the gate.

"Ready?" Estrada asked.

"Ready," he agreed.

It was much easier going down than it had been com-ing up.

We took our time though, however much Saltlick must have wanted to hurry, and took frequent breaks for Alvantes to rest. Late in the afternoon we reached the crevasse that marked a rough halfway point to the valley floor. I whooped with joy to see our horses still there – I'd had dreadful visions of them plunging off the cliff side.

I was hurt, though, that Killer seemed more pleased to see Alvantes than me. He whinnied dementedly until Saltlick produced a small bale of dry grass from one of the parcels he'd carried with him and split it between the two of them. At that, all thoughts of re-union were forgotten. Once they'd eaten, we watered them from our flasks and brushed them down as well as we could.

It was almost dark by then, and we had no choice but to make camp. I lay awake for a long time, despite my tiredness, staring up between the lips of rock at the sliver of sky above and at the myriad stars that glimmered there. I felt smaller than I ever had in my life, and the world seemed bewilderingly huge – larger than just the Castoval, or even the kingdom.

I thought about what I'd told Estrada in the caves behind Muena Palaiya: "I'm a large part of a picture only slightly bigger than I am." Had it really only been a few days ago? It seemed as though a lifetime separated me from the Easie Damasco who'd so casually said those words. I listened to Saltlick and Killer battling to out-snore each other. I drifted to sleep with the mingled scent of giant and horse in my nostrils, and didn't resent it one bit.

We woke before dawn, cold and stiff, and were glad to make an early start. We travelled in convoy, Saltlick first, then Alvantes, myself, and Estrada. Alvantes bore his injury stoically, though more than once I noticed him try to do something that required two hands and flinch with realisation.

Since he had to rely on his crutch on the loose ground, he grudgingly allowed me to lead Killer. I tried to reassure the horse with more realistic promises this time: "If your master there lets me, I'm going to take you to an inn and dine you like a king, you mad old mule."

He seemed to appreciate my candour.

With a bright sun above and no one pursuing behind, it was actually quite pleasant to trudge down the uneven path. I felt almost wistful when the end of the cliff trail loomed into view. I tried not to think about the carnage we'd have to pass on the road: the familiar faces frozen and lifeless, the reek of two-day-old death. I focused on that inn I'd promised Killer, on wine, good food, a night in a proper bed.

Whatever I was looking forward to, it wasn't an ambush.

One moment we were trudging down the last stretch of broken path. The next armed men surrounded us on all sides. The two ahead held swords outstretched. The dozen on the rocks to either side aimed taut-strung bows. There was no time to react, nowhere to run. They had us at their mercy.

"Gueverro?"

Alvantes hobbled forward, and seeing him, the leftmost swordsman lowered his blade. I recognised him as the leader of the Altapasaedan guardsmen whose intervention had saved us from Moaradrid.

"Guard-Captain?"

Alvantes's face cracked, just for a moment. All of the cold arrogance, the world-weariness, the stubborn nobility slewed away, leaving nothing but joy. "I thought you'd be dead to a man."

Gueverro grinned crookedly. "Moaradrid's troops gave up and ran. They'd have beaten us eventually, but we'd shown them what it would cost. With Moaradrid gone, their hearts weren't in it."

"Then why are you still here?"

"We waited to see if you'd come back. A party of riders came down in the night and managed to

fight their way through. We thought Moaradrid
must have been with them, but there was still a
chance..."

"Moaradrid's dead."

Gueverro nodded wearily. "Well, that's good news.
The man was poison. It isn't done, though, is it? His
army's still spread through the Castoval."

"Tomorrow we'll worry about Moaradrid's army,"
said Alvantes. "Just for tonight, it's done."

Barely a hundred men had survived that battle
three long days ago. Perhaps half were Altapasaedan
guardsmen, the remainder from the bedraggled force
Estrada had brought together. They'd built a crude
camp near the river, sheltered by stands of silver
birch, and besides waiting to see if anyone came
down from the mountain they'd mainly passed their
time recuperating.

There was good hunting in the woods on the other
bank, so at least no one had gone hungry. We dined
that night on freshly shot venison bolstered with fresh
fruit and the remainder of our own supplies. We
talked about nothing of consequence. True to Alvantes's word, no one so much as considered out loud
the tomorrow.

We lay out once more beneath an open sky, and
again I found that I had little desire for sleep. A hundred questions darted through my mind, and seemed
to dance in time with the shimmering lights above. I
felt as if I'd come to the end of something. Now the
future lay before me, enormous and vague.

In the morning, Alvantes gave a brief speech to his ragtag army. He thanked them for their courage, their steadfastness in the face of hopeless odds. Those that wanted to go home could, without question. Those who had no families to go back to or wanted to serve the Castoval yet further were welcome to stay with him. He was heading back to Altapasaeda to see how things stood.

A couple of men took him at his word, and left – but only a couple.

Alvantes joined Estrada, Saltlick and I.

"What then?" Estrada asked.

"I'll see. If the dregs of Moaradrid's army are in Altapasaeda then perhaps we can persuade them to move on. I have a few resources left in the city, enough to deal with a handful of stragglers. Either way, it can only be a passing visit. Someone has to officially tell the king his son is dead."

"How will he take the news?"

"I have no idea. Still… it's the right thing to do. After that, I can start looking for that traitorous wretch Mounteban. He's got plenty of good men's blood on his hands." Alvantes sighed. "What about you, Marina? Where will you go?"

"Home, of course. Muena Palaiya still needs a mayor."

"Things may not be how you left them."

"Then I'll deal with that when I get there. Anyway, Saltlick will need a travelling companion."

Saltlick nodded, and grinned from ear to ear.

Estrada turned to me and said, "Will you be travelling with us, Easie?" Seeing Alvantes's expression, she added, "We'd never have made it if not for him. He's learned his lesson, Lunto."

I'd learned plenty of lessons over the last few days. I chose not to guess which one she was referring to.

"I don't think you'll be returning to your old ways, will you?"

Ah, *that* lesson. Well, I'd given the question some thought last night, and she was right in a way. Stealing from the poor was never going to be profitable. Stealing from fat merchants was better, but before you knew it people were chasing you out of town and you had a price on your head, which tended to mitigate your already hard-earned profit.

"So will you join us?"

Thieving from invading warlords, on the other hand...

Oh, it might bring its share of problems. Perhaps I'd worn my shoes out quicker than I'd otherwise have done, accumulated some cuts and bruises, even narrowly avoided death on a few occasions. Hadn't it been worth it though, in the end? I'd helped fend off an invasion that would have left the Castoval in shackles. I'd rescued a giant, and made sure he saw his home again. I'd made a little money, and even managed to hang on to some of it.

"We'd be glad to have you along. I think Saltlick would miss you after everything you two have been through."

Maybe I'd even made a friend or two.

If purloining one unremarkable stone and one hopeless, homeless giant could bring about so much, what else might I be capable of?

The fact was, I'd been stealing from the wrong sorts of people. I'd been failing to fulfil my potential, picking easy targets. I'd been lazy, maybe even a little cowardly.

In short, I'd been aiming too small.

I grinned – at Estrada, at Saltlick, even at Alvantes.

"I'd be honoured to travel with you. Now, did I hear something about visiting the king?"

ABOUT THE AUTHOR

David Tallerman was born and raised in the north-east of England. A long and confused period of education ended with a Masters dissertation on the literary history of seventeenth century witchcraft that somehow incorporated references to both Kate Bush and HP Lovecraft.

David currently roams the UK as an itinerant IT Technician-for-hire, applying theories of animism and sympathetic magic to computer repair and taking devoted care of his bonsai tree familiar.

Over the last few years, David has been steadily building a reputation for his genre short fiction and increasingly his writing has tended to push and merge genres, and to incorporate influences from his other great loves, comic books and cinema. He's now hard at work on a new Easie Damasco adventure, *Crown Thief*.

DavidTallerman.net

THANKS...

First, always and above all to my mum. For endless support and faith. For reading every word before anyone else had to.

Giant Thief would never have gotten started without Rafe, let alone finished – let alone been any good. Meanwhile, Tom gave me the right ending, along with countless other improvements, and Grant encouraged me tirelessly through the long months of rewrite, when this point seemed impossibly far away. Likewise Loz, who gave me a kick up the butt when I most needed it. Without a particular pep talk on a rainy day in London, I might never have been in the right place at the right time to make *Giant Thief* a reality.

That place turned out to be Fantasycon 2010. Thanks to the British Fantasy Society and the Fantasycon committee for making it possible, and to Al for nudging me in the right direction.

Seriously. Thank you all.

This couldn't have happened without you.

Imaginary Prisons

First published in Theaker's Quarterly Fiction

His sword arced up from the body of the second Goblin, ending its trajectory in a glancing blow upon the third. There was hardly any strength behind it, but somehow the blade found flesh, slipping beneath the nape of the creature's helmet, slicing neatly through its throat.

Corin nearly dropped the weapon, fatigue compounded by surprise. It had been an improbably lucky blow; he should be dead now. Then, as his breath began to return and his sides to stop heaving, he thought, *no, not luck*. For how could he die, here and now?

Having checked the bodies of the three Goblins, Corin started again up the rough trail that diagonally traversed the foothills. It wasn't long before the way became more difficult: by mid-afternoon the pines and wild foliage of the low ground were thinning into brush and tangled grasses and by evening the path

served only to join one mound of boulders to another. By the time night fell there was no path at all.

He had been travelling for fifteen days, he was exhausted, and it was disheartening when he finally had
to fall on hands and knees. Before him Torbeth reared
up, inconceivably high, and as the last light faded and
the way became ever harder he considered making
camp. Then he remembered – *he shall journey for fifteen
days and fifteen nights* – and he knew that he couldn't
stop, that it was impossible. Steadfastly he crawled
from ledge to ledge, finding his way by touch alone,
trying to drive the fatigue from his mind.

Corin had lost any track of time when, drawing his
aching body over a jut of rock, he glanced up to see
light glittering far off in the darkness. Then the fog
shifted and the light became indistinct, only to be obscured altogether an instant later. It had seemed to
be the flicker of a campfire, though he couldn't be
sure. Crouching on the projection, shoulders
hunched against the bitter-cold winds sweeping from
above, he found that he wanted nothing more than
to seek the distant fire out. But such a moment of
weakness was nowhere to be found in the predictions
that had guided him here.

Finally, as the stupefying weariness let go a little,
it occurred to him that it was a cave he sought, and
that high on a gale-torn mountainside, where else
could a fire burn? This logic was so convincing that
he immediately stumbled to his feet, and set out
again in the direction he thought the light to have
come from.

Sure enough, as the mist lifted for an instant he saw it again, nearer now. A little strength returned to his aching muscles and he clambered with new vigour, keeping his eyes upon the spark of shivering fire. It was a hard ascent, and obstructions frequently blocked his view and made him doubt his course. But the thought of warmth and comfort, and even the slight hope of having found his object, drove him on.

Eventually, after a tortuous climb up a particularly steep crevasse, he collapsed onto the overhang above. And there it was, the hectic dance of firelight reflected from the wall of a cave-mouth ahead. Corin leaped to his feet, and in something between a run and a stagger made his way there and all but fell through the wide opening.

Inside he came to an abrupt halt. Sure enough there was a fire burning, uncannily bright in the darkness, and hot enough that he could feel its luxuriant warmth the moment he entered. But, as he turned a corner into the heart of the grotto, he was alarmed to find something other than the blazing pile of brands that had brought him here.

Beside the fire there stood an old man.

Corin could only stare. He wore a long robe of deep crimson, which covered all but his hands and feet, was of fine silken cloth, and glimmered with reflected luminance. His face was skeletally thin, with the brittle skin stretched taut around the skull, and his expression showed no surprise whatsoever; in fact, it was closer to impatience.

"Prince Corin, I presume?" he asked, as though it were the most natural thing in the world that they should be meeting here in this hidden cave, high upon the face of Torbeth. His voice was fragile with age, but there was a resonance in it that suggested authority. Corin nodded hesitantly, while fighting the urge to bow.

"You took your time, boy. It's nearly morning you know. Do you always have such a lackadaisical approach to your destiny?"

A little of Corin's self-possession was beginning to return. "Who are you? And how do you know my name?"

"I am the sage Calaphile, of the Grand Ziggurat."

"That means nothing to me, and you've only answered my first question. Have you been sent here to try me? Are you a servant of the Goblins?"

Calaphile gave a wheezing laugh, which sounded to Corin like two plates of rusted armour grating against each other. Eventually the self-proclaimed sage composed himself enough to reply, "You may be certain that I'm not a servant to anyone. As to whether I'm here to try you – well when you reach my age, should you be careful and fortunate enough to do so, you'll find that most things in life are a trial of one sort or another. But I ask for only a little of your time. I choose to view it as a lesson, and if you think of it likewise it may pass quite amicably."

"I've no time for lessons, old man!" exploded Corin, who was beginning to find the whole situation unbearably irritating.

"Then you'd prefer to consider it as a test?"

"I've overcome enough tests!"

"There's always another test, my boy; that's something else you learn at my age. But really, all I wish is to read you a few passages from the book I have here." Saying this, he drew a tome from within the folds of his cloak, bound in red leather that matched the garment. "Perhaps you could humour one who has seen more than his share of life? You might even learn something, and that's always worthwhile, is it not?"

His anger beginning to give way to tiredness and the lure of the fire, Corin leaned against the rough cave wall. As one final protest, he exclaimed, "I have a destiny to complete, old man. There's a prophecy that must be fulfilled!"

At this, his companion began to leaf through the book. "Ah yes, I have it here."

"What do you have?"

"Prince Corin, the twenty-first to bear that name... da da da... it shall fall upon him to defeat, once and for all time, the Goblinish foe... da da... fifteen days and fifteen nights... da da... shall seek out the sword Cymerion, left by his ancestors upon the mountainside of Torbeth, that he may unite the people before it... yes, that's the one."

Corin stood aghast. He had heard these phrases three times before, read on each occasion by the most venerable priest of the temple of Corinil, in utmost secrecy. "How do you–"

"Rather prosaic, isn't it? The Goblin version is far more entertaining."

"The Goblin–?"

"It's only short, I can read it all if you'd like. Only a rough translation of course, they have such an erratic approach to grammar... ah, here we are:

"'Thinking he can beat wise and mighty Goblins, foolish boy-man goes looking for rusty trinket-sword lost by grandfather after much ale. Fifteen suns and moons he goes, getting lost and falling over often, until he is lucky and finds cave where useless sword is. Greatly I've done, he thinks, but just as he is picking up blunted pig-sticker, stupid man-child stumbles over own feet, falling on arse and smashing puny head into many pieces.'

"Not the most literary people, are they? But it's always nice to see a sense of humour exhibited in these things."

Bewildered, Corin sat down on the rough stone floor. He had been prepared for many trials, had trained long and hard so that he might best any man or beast in combat. But he'd never expected anything like this. He felt sure that his best course would be simply to seek out his prize and be gone. But a seed of doubt had been sown, and he couldn't bring himself to do anything except sit and listen.

Seeing he had a rapt audience, the old man continued cheerfully, "Now, the account told by the high priests of Zor-Tola is quite similar to your own. You succeed in recovering the sword and make it home in one piece. The only difference is that you still lose the war, Corinil is put to fire and the sword, and your people are wiped out. But other than that the details are largely identical."

Corin had never heard of the high priests of Zor-Tola and had no idea why they might have seen fit to prophesise upon his fate. However there seemed no point in asking, and in any case the old man had only paused for breath.

"A tale kept in the Grand Library of Forpoth is basically the same, until the point where you return to find that in your absence the Goblins have invaded your home and all your friends and family are dead. Understandably, you're driven mad by grief. It dwells at great length upon this part, to a rather depressing degree."

Finding he could keep silent no longer, Corin cried, "What's your point, old man? That the prophesy of Corinil is a lie? That I'm doomed to failure or madness? Do you seek to dissuade me with your stories?"

Calaphile appeared a little hurt by this outburst. "Nothing of the sort, my boy. Why, in the manuscript held by the king of Far Brinth you actually succeed in repelling the Goblin invasion, and single-handedly end the war. You do then become rather crazed with power, only to be assassinated by your own most trusted advisor and recorded by posterity as Corin the Cruel. But if I've given the impression that all versions purport an unsuccessful end to your venture–"

"How many are there," Corin interrupted, "how many versions?"

"Well, no more than a dozen."

Corin sighed deeply. For as long as he could remember his destiny had been the sole certainty in his life; the prophecy had guided and moulded his every thought and action. That it should be nothing more than a tale amongst a dozen others, a possibility not a certainty – the thought filled him with despair. Finally, he looked up wearily, and said, "It's clear that you know more about my fate than I ever will. So tell me, what do I do now?"

"Well you might as well take the prize you've come all this way for. You'll find it over in the back of the cave."

Corin looked past the ancient scholar. Sure enough, sunk into a recess in the rock face was a long, ornate box of dark wood. He could just make out his family crest glittering above the latch. He stood hesitantly. "Will any good come of it?"

"My boy, don't be so pessimistic. You may be surprised. It may even be that you'll surprise yourself."

"Perhaps," said Corin, "and perhaps I have no choice in the matter. Either way, I've dallied here long enough."

He walked over to the alcove. The box was handsomely carved, an elegant piece of craftsmanship hardly diminished by age or weathering. If the container is so impressive, he thought, what must its contents be like? And a shiver of hope returned to his heart.

There was no sign of lock or keyhole so he placed a hand on the clasp and drew it up, and with his other hand tried to raise the lid. Sure enough, it opened freely. Using both hands now, he strained to draw it wider. Finally it fell back with a dull thud against the stone, and he gazed with awe into the shadows inside.

The box was completely empty.

Corin didn't even have time to be taken aback before something struck the back of his head, at the exposed point where his helmet met the hem of his chain-mail. He found himself collapsing forward helplessly. His last dazed thought, before he lost consciousness completely, was that perhaps the Goblin prophesy had been right after all.

When Corin awoke, daylight was filtering into the mouth of the cave and the fire had burned down to ash and glowing brands. As his head began to clear he struggled to a kneeling position and strained to look around. He wasn't surprised to find that his antiquated assailant had vanished. What did startle him was that where he'd stood and proselytized there was now a scroll of old paper, bound with a strip of red cloth that must have been torn from his robe. Not feeling ready to stand quite yet, Corin crawled over to the parchment, curious despite himself. He was groggy, his fingers felt numb and bloated, and it took a few minutes to unravel the scroll. But by the time he'd done so the agony in his head had faded to a steady throb. Feeling capable of standing, he walked to the cave-mouth where the light was better. He saw then that the paper was actually a torn page, presumably ripped from the same tome that the old man had carried with him. There was a title followed by three short paragraphs:

The Prophecy of Calaphile of the Grand Ziggurat

In his hundredth year, it shall fall to the sage Calaphile that he shall seek out a sword named Cymerion, hidden treasure of Corinil, which he shall find upon the mountainside of great Torbeth.

Another will also hunt this prize; Prince Corin shall come seeking his inheritance, that he may end the war between his people and the Goblin hordes. But he shall be easily overcome, for he is a slave of his destiny and cannot see beyond it. Then Calaphile shall secure Cymerion, and it shall serve as the capstone to his Grand Ziggurat. He shall die in peace, and his spirit shall pass safely beyond the bounds of this world.

As for the Prince Corin, in his undoing will be found his greatest victory, for on his return he shall craft a peace between the races that will benefit both peoples for a hundred generations.

Corin found that he was laughing, despite himself. He wasn't sure exactly what he found so funny. Nevertheless he continued to laugh, long and loud, until his sides ached to match his head. When he finally calmed himself he read through the scroll again, with a broad smile on his face.

It struck him that he held no resentment towards the old sage, who had toyed with him and beaten him and had given him a new future as recompense. And suddenly it occurred to him that he had little grudge against his Goblin enemies, either. In retrospect it had been his own father who'd sparked off this latest fracas between the two races, when he'd encroached upon Goblin lands. It had never occurred to Corin that they were anything more than dumb brutes; certainly he'd never imagined they might be reasoned with except by the blade. But then nor had it crossed his mind that they might write prophesies, indeed that they could write at all, or that they were astute enough to use satire as a weapon. In any case, the war had been at a stalemate almost since it began. Perhaps an attempt at peace wouldn't be such a bad alternative to rallying his people behind some antique sword.

Corin hoisted his pack onto his shoulder. In the daylight he could see now that there was a trail down the mountainside; a rough one, certainly, but far preferable to the climb of last night.

He began towards it – his eyes set on the far silver towers of Corinil, his thoughts upon the terrifying wonder of an uncertain future.

Wake eat read sleep repeat.

Twitter @angryrobotbooks

A TREASURE BEYOND RICHES
Collect the whole Angry Robot list

DAN ABNETT
- [ ] Embedded
- [ ] Triumff: Her Majesty's Hero

GUY ADAMS
- [ ] The World House
- [ ] Restoration

JO ANDERTON
- [ ] Debris

LAUREN BEUKES
- [ ] Moxyland
- [ ] Zoo City

THOMAS BLACKTHORNE
(aka John Meaney)
- [ ] Edge
- [ ] Point

MAURICE BROADDUS
- [ ] King Maker
- [ ] King's Justice
- [ ] King's War

ADAM CHRISTOPHER
- [ ] Empire State

PETER CROWTHER
- [ ] Darkness Falling

ALIETTE DE BODARD
- [ ] Servant of the Underworld
- [ ] Harbinger of the Storm
- [ ] Master of the House of Darts

MATT FORBECK
- [ ] Amortals
- [ ] Vegas Knights

JUSTIN GUSTAINIS
- [ ] Hard Spell

GUY HALEY
- [ ] Reality 36

COLIN HARVEY
- [ ] Damage Time
- [ ] Winter Song

MATTHEW HUGHES
- [ ] The Damned Busters

TRENT JAMIESON
- [ ] Roil

K W JETER
- [ ] Infernal Devices
- [ ] Morlock Night

J ROBERT KING
- [ ] Angel of Death
- [ ] Death's Disciples

GARY McMAHON
- [ ] Pretty Little Dead Things
- [ ] Dead Bad Things

ANDY REMIC
- [ ] Kell's Legend
- [ ] Soul Stealers
- [ ] Vampire Warlords

CHRIS ROBERSON
- [ ] Book of Secrets

MIKE SHEVDON
- [ ] Sixty-One Nails
- [ ] The Road to Bedlam

GAV THORPE
- [ ] The Crown of the Blood
- [ ] The Crown of the Conqueror

LAVIE TIDHAR
- [ ] The Bookman
- [ ] Camera Obscura
- [ ] The Great Game

TIM WAGGONER
- [ ] Nekropolis
- [ ] Dead Streets
- [ ] Dark War

KAARON WARREN
- [ ] Mistification
- [ ] Slights
- [ ] Walking the Tree

IAN WHATES
- [ ] City of Dreams & Nightmare
- [ ] City of Hope & Despair
- [ ] City of Light & Shadow